Helen Warner is a former Head of Daytime at both ITV & Channel 4, where she was responsible for a variety of TV shows including *Come Dine With Me*, *Loose Women*, *Good Morning Britain* and *Judge Rinder*. Helen writes her novels on the train to work in London from her home in Essex, which she shares with her husband and their two children.

D0112056

SHE

HC WARNER

ONE PLACE. MANY STORIES

HQ
An imprint of HarperCollins*Publishers* Ltd
1 London Bridge Street
London SE1 9GF

This edition 2020

5
First published in Great Britain by
HQ, an imprint of HarperCollins*Publishers* Ltd 2020

Copyright © Helen Warner 2020

Helen Warner asserts the moral right to be
identified as the author of this work.
A catalogue record for this book is
available from the British Library.

ISBN: 9780008216986

MIX
Paper from
responsible sources
FSC™ C007454

This book is produced from independently certified FSC™ paper
to ensure responsible forest management.

For more information visit: www.harpercollins.co.uk/green

This book is set in 10.7/15.5 pt. Sabon

Printed and bound in Great Britain by
CPI Group (UK) Ltd, Croydon, CR0 4YY

In memory of Claire Warner,
who really was the perfect girl.

To my dear daughter,

You will never read this letter but I needed to write it all the same.

I am so sorry for everything. If I could turn back time and change the past, I would. But the one thing I would never want to change is you. I'm sure your mother will have told you things about me and I will admit that some of them, to my shame, are true.

But, whatever she may have told you, I promise that from the moment you were born, I loved you. I know that you will grow up into a lovely young woman. I'm certain you will be as beautiful as your mother – maybe even more so. I hope you will be a good person and that one day you will be able to find it in your heart to forgive me and understand that every single one of us is flawed and anything I did, I did out of a father's love for his child.

Love always,
Dad

'She seems perfect.' Jo waved one last time, as her son drove his new girlfriend away from the house, the wheels of his black, open-top Mercedes spitting up the gravel on the driveway behind them as they departed, before she swung the heavy front door shut and looked up at Peter. 'Don't you agree? Don't you think she seems like the perfect girl for him?'

Peter exhaled loudly and his eyes crinkled with tiredness. She could sense his irritability and there was a slight sheen of sweat on his tanned, lined forehead. 'You said that about the last one.' His words came out in one long sigh.

'Well, Charlotte was perfect at the time.' Jo couldn't keep the defensive tone out of her voice, even though she knew he was right.

'Hmmm . . .' Peter pursed his lips disapprovingly, before turning and walking with a laboured stride along the cool, dark, flag-stoned hallway towards the sprawling, open-plan kitchen, which was suffused in a pale pink glow from the setting sun. 'Except for the small matter that she dumped Ben and broke his heart.'

Jo hesitated, thinking, before following her husband. 'You

know, now that things have worked out the way they have, maybe it was for the best. Maybe she did him a favour?'

Peter picked up his half-finished glass of red wine from the pale granite worktop, and took it out onto the vast, sandstone terrace, which was now pleasantly warm after the searing heat of the late July day. He sat at the large glass table and looked out over the velvety green lawn, sweeping down towards the azure swimming pool, which looked like it was twinkling with a thousand dancing diamonds in the early evening sun.

Jo watched him for a few moments, letting him walk ahead, before picking up her own glass and heading out to join him. He seemed jittery and upset, which was out of character. She sat down at the table beside him. 'Are you OK, darling? You seem a bit . . . uptight.'

Peter didn't answer but gave a slight shrug.

'You're not sure about her, are you?' Jo watched him closely, as she took a sip of her wine, which tasted slightly metallic after drinking several glasses of it.

'No.'

The speed of his answer took her by surprise. 'Why? She was perfectly charming.'

Peter pursed his lips again. It was as if he was trying to stop the words escaping. 'Yes. Very.' His tone was dry. Sardonic.

'What then?'

Peter turned his sleepy gaze towards her. She loved his dark brown eyes, still framed by long lashes. He didn't look younger than his 63 years, thanks to his cropped grey hair and tanned, lined skin, but he was certainly still a very handsome man. 'I'm not sure.' He hesitated and it was obvious that he was holding back. He tilted his head upwards, as if seeking inspiration from the sky. 'She's like a ghost that just appeared out of nowhere. And it's all happened a bit too quickly. He's on the rebound.'

Jo considered his words before replying: 'You're just being over-protective of your son.'

Peter sighed and looked back at her, his eyes clouded with worry. Jo frowned, as she fixed him with an intense stare, willing him to open up a bit more about his feelings. Seeing her expression, he tried to rearrange his features into a smile, before his face became serious again. 'Maybe. But . . .' He shook his head slightly, swatting away the thought. 'Oh, I don't know. Ignore me.'

Jo reached across the table and took his hand in hers. 'I'm sure you're worrying unnecessarily. Relax, she seems like the perfect girl for him.'

PART ONE

PART ONE

CHAPTER ONE

'Pull over here!'

'What?' Ben turned towards her in surprise. 'Are you OK?'

'Pull over!' she repeated.

Ben frowned to himself but immediately indicated and pulled into a small layby overlooking the patchwork of green and gold fields that criss-crossed the Suffolk landscape, undulating down towards the river. His heart hammered with sudden trepidation, as he turned off the engine and looked over at her expectantly. He cleared his throat. 'What's up?'

Bella turned her huge, dark eyes towards him, causing his stomach to flip. Despite being in his open-top Mercedes, he could still detect notes of her scent on the light summer evening breeze. 'I'm pregnant.'

There was a rushing sound in Ben's ears, as if a giant wave was thundering into shore behind him and he gripped the steering wheel to steady himself against its onslaught. 'Pregnant?'

Bella looked away, her exquisite face still and expressionless.

Ben swallowed hard. 'Are you sure?'

At his words, she closed her eyes for a moment, as a shadow

of temper briefly swept over her smooth brow. 'Yes.' The word came out as a hiss.

Ben's mouth formed a silent 'oh'. He didn't know how he was supposed to react. Didn't know what he was supposed to say. And it was so *soon*. They had only been together for a couple of months.

He tried to grab onto the thoughts careering through his head. 'How long?' he said, snatching at the only one he could keep hold of.

Bella bit her plump bottom lip, which was quivering slightly. He couldn't tell if it was nerves or tears. 'I think about eight weeks. But I won't know for sure until the scan.' Her voice had taken on a robotic edge and she continued to stare straight ahead, with a slightly glassy expression that unnerved him.

Ben nodded, his mind whirring back to eight weeks previously. She must have conceived on their very first night together if that was the case. He leaned heavily against his seat to anchor himself. To steady his thoughts. His mouth was suddenly dry and his hands clammy. How was that possible? he wondered distractedly. That one part of your body dried up while another produced moisture. Shock, he supposed.

He became aware that Bella was watching him and allowed his gaze to shift back towards her. She gave him an uncertain smile. 'Are you happy about it?'

'Of course.' The words came out automatically. What else could he say? It didn't really matter what his feelings were, there was only one answer he could give. He tilted his head so that he could look at her properly. 'How about you?'

Bella's heart-shaped face melted into a demure smile. 'I'm happy. Just . . . it's a bit of a surprise, that's all.'

Yes, Ben thought, she could say that again. His mind drifted to the day he had first met her, back in May. He was having a drink after work with Matt, his oldest and closest friend. Bella had been sitting at a table near to theirs, clearly waiting for someone who hadn't shown up. Ben had been vaguely aware of her presence but was too engrossed in his conversation with Matt to really notice her.

Eventually, Matt nodded towards her, with an amused expression on his face. 'I think you've got an admirer, mate.'

Ben frowned, before following Matt's gaze. He didn't believe in love at first sight and had always scoffed at the idea of a 'lightning bolt' moment, but that was exactly what happened when their eyes met. His mouth shifted into the shape of a smile without him telling it to. She smiled back and it was like a door opening to allow sunlight to flood in. Long, glossy dark hair, deep brown eyes, razor-sharp cheekbones and straight white teeth that looked even whiter in the darkness of the bar. She wasn't just pretty. She was breathtakingly, head-turningly perfect.

As if on auto-pilot, Ben picked up his drink and walked over to her table. He thought he heard Matt mutter something along the lines of 'Don't mind me, will you?' but he was oblivious to everything else around him, except her.

'Hello.' He put his drink on her table and sat down. For some reason, it didn't occur to him to even ask if she minded him joining her. He just knew with absolute certainty that she didn't.

She blinked slowly, her long black lashes almost sweeping the tip of those incredible cheekbones as she did so. 'Hello.'

There was a long pause, as Ben looked at her, drinking her in, before he realized that he needed to say something. 'I'm Ben.'

Her full lips parted into a smile, revealing those startlingly white, even teeth again. 'Nice to meet you, Ben. I'm Bella.'

Ben nodded, unable to tear his eyes away from her. 'Bella,' he repeated, trying it out for size. He liked it. It was certainly the right name for someone who looked like her. 'Can I buy you a drink, Bella?'

'Thank you, yes.' Her expression was a mixture of amusement and curiosity.

'Champagne?' he guessed.

She shook her head. 'Sparkling water.'

Ben raised his eyebrows in surprise. 'OK . . .'

He stood up and as he did so, he suddenly remembered Matt sitting alone at a nearby table.

'Oh! Matt . . . I'm just getting some more drinks in. You're welcome to join us?' He desperately hoped Matt would decline.

Matt responded with a knowing smirk and a shake of the head. 'Thanks, but I'm going to call it a night.' He drained the rest of his beer and stood up. 'Have fun,' he added, patting Ben on the back as he left the bar with a purposeful stride.

Ben was as quick as he could be getting their drinks, not wanting to leave Bella unattended for long, just in case someone else took his place. He breathed a sigh of relief when he returned to a still-empty chair.

'Thank you.' Bella picked up her glass and took a long sip. Ben did the same, watching her over the top of his beer bottle, mesmerized. Everything about her was perfect, even her hands.

'So, Ben,' she began, her huge, exotic eyes drawing him in like a magnet. 'Are you single?'

Ben spluttered on his beer. 'Um, yes. I am. Definitely. Single.'

Bella smiled. 'Good.'

'Are you?' he countered, suddenly nervous.

Bella dropped her gaze. 'I am.'

'Good. And do you get hit on by lots of men who aren't single?' Ben could feel his hackles rising on her behalf.

Bella looked back up at him with a half-smile. 'All the time. That's why it was my first question.'

'Ah. Well, it looks like you got lucky with me then!' Ben tried to keep his tone jokey but found he was uncharacteristically nervous and he didn't quite manage to pull it off.

Bella seemed not to notice. She flashed him a wide, dazzling smile. 'It looks like I did.'

They chatted easily for a while, before Ben motioned to Bella's glass. 'Another drink?'

She tilted her head, causing the sheet of shiny black hair to slide over her shoulder in a sleek wave. 'I'd prefer dinner,' she said, with a mischievous glint in her eye.

Ben grinned. 'So would I.' Simultaneously, they pushed back their chairs and stood up. Standing, she was even more of a vision. Tall and slim, dressed in a dark green silky wrap dress and high-heeled strappy nude sandals, she walked confidently in front of him towards the door, as if she knew that the eyes of every man in the room were turning towards her as she passed. Already, Ben could feel a swell of pride that it was him she was with.

As they stepped out into the cool night air, she reached over to take his arm, as if it was the most natural thing in the world. 'Where are we going?' she asked, as they fell into step with each other.

Ben wondered for a moment if he was dreaming this whole episode, it seemed so surreal. He wasn't used to picking up women in bars. In fact, he had never picked up a complete stranger before. And yet, it seemed so right, as if he already knew her from somewhere. There was no awkwardness or hesitation. It all had a strange inevitability about it. His mind raced, as he tried to give off an impression of cool insouciance. 'I know a great place.' He gave her what he hoped was a knowing smile and steered her in the direction of his favourite restaurant, praying that Nigel, the maître d' would have a table.

Nigel greeted them like old friends and, after pocketing the £50 Ben had surreptitiously slipped him, led them to a table by the window, with a spectacular view of London lit up and twinkling in the inky night sky as far as the eye could see.

'Wow,' Bella gazed out, her eyes shining with delight. 'What an incredible view. And what an incredible place.'

Ben smiled to himself, hardly able to believe his luck. Out of the blue, he was sitting opposite the most stunning girl he had ever met, about to eat in one of London's swankiest restaurants. Already he could feel the malaise that had been suffocating him for the previous few months, ever since Charlotte told him she needed some time apart to work out what she wanted, lifting. He swallowed and pushed all thoughts of Charlotte to the back of his mind. He wanted to clear his head to concentrate on this vision in front of him.

Sometimes, Ben reflected, sitting beside Bella in his car two months later, as he tried to digest her news, life just took you by the hand and led you in a certain direction. He wondered if he would have been able to stop the course of events, even if he had wanted to. Unlikely, he decided.

Just a year ago, he was flying high in his work as an advertising executive, still living with Charlotte, planning to propose and thinking that he knew exactly how his life was going to play out. But then Charlotte had dropped her bombshell as they returned to their flat in London, after spending Christmas with his parents in Suffolk. He remembered her words with an aching clarity: 'I think we need to have some time apart.'

He had actually laughed. He had thought she was joking. When he became aware that she wasn't laughing with him, he glanced over at her and saw a tear sliding down her cheek. 'What? But why?' His throat dried around the words and he felt his stomach contract. She was deadly serious.

Charlotte swiped at the tears with the back of her hand. 'I need to be sure that this . . .' She motioned from him to her. 'That this is right for us. Both of us.'

Ben frowned and tried to focus on the road, although his mind was racing and he could feel his own tears threatening.

'It's right for me, Charlie. I'm not having any doubts. What's brought this on?'

Charlotte had shaken her head. 'I just . . . I just feel like I need some time, Ben. Ever since Dad died, I've been feeling so confused. And a bit rudderless. Wondering if this is it. I'm sorry.'

Ben had frowned to himself. He knew her dad's death the year before had hit her hard but he didn't realize how hard. Now that he thought about it, the signs were there: the faraway look she got in her eye more and more often. The sense that she wasn't listening when he spoke. But there was something else too: the name she had started mentioning whenever she talked about work; the way her eyes danced as she regaled him with stories. He somehow felt it was connected.

They had driven the rest of the way home enveloped in

a thick, dark silence, both of them immersed deep in their own thoughts. Charlotte leaped out of the car as soon as he had parked and disappeared into the flat, while Ben stayed put, still unable to digest her words. He tried to convince himself that she was just having a moment. That he would walk inside and find her waiting on the bed, laughing at how she had 'got him'.

But as he finally let himself into the flat, he already knew that although he would find her in their bedroom, she wouldn't be waiting for him on the bed, she would be packing.

'Where will you go?' He stood in the doorway, watching as she threw her clothes into two large suitcases. Not just an overnight bag. This was serious. She wasn't planning to come back.

Charlotte ran her hand through her long, fair hair and bit her lip. 'Lucy's.'

Ben nodded. 'Does she know you're coming?'

Charlotte blinked quickly, as a flush spread up her pale, slender neck. Finally, she looked up and met Ben's eye. 'Yes.'

Ben felt his legs weaken. He took a deep breath and grasped the doorframe to support himself. 'So you told her before you told me?'

Charlotte's eyes filled with tears. 'I just told her I was confused, Ben. She said if I ever needed some time out, she had a spare room.'

'God.' The feeling of betrayal seemed to squeeze the air out of Ben's lungs. He had always thought Lucy was his biggest ally, often taking Ben's side over her own sister's.

'Don't look like that, Ben. Lucy adores you. For what it's worth, she said that you're one in a million and I'd be an idiot to let you go.'

Ben smiled sadly. It was a small crumb of comfort. 'Then don't let me go.' It seemed so simple, so straightforward.

Charlotte hesitated, as different waves of emotion crossed her pretty, unlined face. After a moment, she seemed to make up her mind. She closed the cases and zipped them up carefully. The sound of the zips seemed to have a certain finality to it. Like a full stop at the end of a sentence. 'I have to,' she said. 'I'm sorry.'

It had been six months since she left. How much his life had changed in that time. Here he was, living with someone new – Bella had gone home with him that first night and never really left – someone he would previously have thought was way out of his league, now expecting their first child. It made him feel dizzy to think about it. He wondered how Charlotte would react when she heard. Would she feel pleased that he had moved on with his life? Or would she feel regret that he seemed to have got over her so easily?

'Ben?' said Bella, as she laid her head on his chest that night.

'Hmmm?'

'I'd like to get married. Before the baby comes.'

Ben felt his whole body instinctively tense. He knew that having a baby was a much bigger commitment than getting married but somehow this seemed to loom so much larger. Less than a year ago, he had been planning to propose to Charlotte. Had envisaged her reaction as he asked her at sunset on their favourite beach in Portugal, her blue eyes glinting as she tearfully accepted.

Instead, he was unable to see Bella's face in the darkness as she issued her declaration. It wasn't a question. It was a statement. She had made her mind up and he would have no influence at all. It was going to happen. 'Right,' he managed.

There was a long, heavy silence and soon Bella's breathing became regular in the way it always did when she dropped off to sleep. Ben couldn't sleep. His mind was too preoccupied. He loved her, of that he was certain. She was sexy, clever and utterly captivating. She made his head swim and his heart dance. But for the first time, Ben thought, there was something else about her. He stared into the darkness, trying to put his finger on what it was. Eventually, just as his eyelids were beginning to droop, the words came to him. Sometimes . . . she scared him.

CHAPTER TWO

'How's Ben?' Charlotte deliberately kept her eyes on her cappuccino, stirring it rhythmically, as she waited for the answer.

She had been surprised by the call from Ben's sister, Emma, asking her to meet, sensing that there was an ulterior motive. Around them, the cramped coffee shop in Soho was beginning to fill with lunchtime customers and the noise levels were rising with them. Someone bumped the back of Charlotte's chair, causing some of the milky coffee to spill into the saucer.

'He's good. Really good, actually.'

Emma's emphasis on the word 'really' made Charlotte look up. 'Great. And he's still with . . .?'

'Bella,' Emma cut in. 'Yes. Very much so.'

Charlotte nodded, knowing she had no right to feel anything other than pleased for him.

'Actually,' Emma continued. 'I've got some news. He asked me to tell you.'

Charlotte felt her stomach clench in anticipation. So she had been right. There was an ulterior motive and it sounded ominous. 'OK.'

Emma took a careful sip of her coffee, which was black and

decaf. No fattening cappuccinos for her. Then she took a deep breath, before blurting out her words. 'They're getting married. She's pregnant.'

Charlotte's vision blurred momentarily and she reeled backwards slightly, grateful for the steadying resistance of the leather cushion behind her. 'Pregnant?' she stuttered. 'But . . . it's so quick!'

'I know.' Emma put her coffee cup down on the saucer slightly too hard so that some of the dark liquid sloshed over the rim. 'We're all a bit in shock but Ben is doing a good impression of being delighted.'

Charlotte tried to take stock of how she was feeling. She had no right to be upset. She had broken Ben's heart and left him feeling wrung-out and confused. But the truth was, she *was* upset. She felt, bizarrely, like he had betrayed her. She took a sip of her cappuccino, aware that her hand shook slightly as she lifted her cup. 'Do you not believe him then, that he's happy about it?'

Emma raised a prettily arched eyebrow. 'Who knows? I'm only his sister and we're not as close as we were . . .' She paused, her eyes momentarily drifting. 'But he isn't saying anything other than that he's delighted. At the very least, he must be pretty shocked.'

'Unless they planned it?' Charlotte ventured. 'He never made any secret of the fact that he wanted children . . .' She tailed off, as she thought about the number of times she and Ben had discussed it. Maybe it was that that had spooked her enough to leave. It seemed so huge. And although she knew that she wanted kids one day, she still felt too young.

'I don't think they planned it.' Emma shook her head

vehemently. 'Definitely not. They would only have been together for a week or so when she conceived – if that! – and although it's true that Ben has always wanted children, he's not the reckless type. He would have wanted to make sure they were ready before taking such a big step.'

Charlotte nodded. Emma was right. Ben wasn't the reckless type. But he did seem to have fallen madly in love very quickly. Maybe it had clouded his judgement. 'What's she like?'

'Bella?' Emma raised her large blue eyes as she considered. 'She's sort of perfect.'

Charlotte felt a little spike of jealousy shoot through her.

'She's so good-looking, it makes me sick,' Emma continued, seemingly unaware of the turmoil she was creating in Charlotte's head. 'And she's certainly lifted him out of himself. He seems genuinely happy again. I was a bit worried about him for a while there . . .'

Charlotte shifted uncomfortably in her chair. 'Well, that's good. He deserves to be happy.'

Emma nodded fondly. 'He does. He's a good boy.' Even though Ben was 30, she still referred to her younger brother as a boy. She fixed her wide blue eyes on Charlotte. 'And how about you, Charlotte? How are you getting on?'

Charlotte smiled. 'I'm OK. I'm starting to get myself together again – at last!'

'Still living with Lucy?'

Charlotte nodded. 'But I think I might have outstayed my welcome. Need to think about finding somewhere of my own.'

There was a pause, before Emma gave her a sly look. 'And what about your love life?'

Charlotte felt her cheeks flush. 'What love life?' She tried to make the remark light-hearted but her voice cracked slightly as she spoke.

'Oh.' Emma looked down. 'I thought you had met someone else. Ben certainly seemed to think so . . .'

'He was wrong about that,' Charlotte interrupted her. She paused, unsure how to articulate what she wanted to say. 'I know he thought that maybe I had something with a guy from work but we're just friends. I think it made it easier for him to think that . . . rather than that I just wanted some time on my own to work things out.'

Emma nodded. 'Do you think . . .' She hesitated, as if she sensed that she might be stepping over a line. 'Do you think you would have gone back to Ben, once you'd had some time to yourself?'

Charlotte swallowed hard. It was the question she had been asking herself every day since she left Ben. 'It's irrelevant, isn't it? By the time I had worked things out in my head, he was all loved up with Bella. It wouldn't have been fair to get back in touch.'

Emma frowned. 'Wouldn't that have been for him to decide? He was so heartbroken when you left, Charlie. It might at least have helped restore his confidence.'

Charlotte shrugged again, trying to feign a nonchalance she didn't feel. 'Well, I didn't, so like I say, it's irrelevant now.' She didn't want to say that she felt huge regret that she hadn't gone back to Ben sooner. Being without him had shown her that he really was the only one for her.

She had been with him for twelve years, ever since they met at university and it was once they started talking seriously about marriage and children that, for some reason, she got cold feet.

She still didn't understand why. But a short time apart was all it took to make her realize how much she loved and needed him.

'It's never too late you know . . .' Emma said, almost to herself, as she drained her coffee.

Charlotte gave a wry laugh. 'I think you'll find that in this case, it is very definitely too late.'

CHAPTER THREE

Matt glanced out of the window of their ground-floor Victorian conversion flat. 'They're here!' he called out, as he headed towards the door.

His wife, Freya, emerged from the kitchen, smoothing down her navy bodycon dress, which showed off her slim figure and surprisingly ample bust. 'I'm a bit nervous!'

Matt smiled at her appreciatively, thinking how effortlessly lovely she looked. 'Don't be. Ben wouldn't be with her if she was horrible.'

'I know. It's just . . . well, it was so easy with Charlie, wasn't it? I can't imagine how he'll be with someone new.'

'Well, we're about to find out.' The buzzer rang and Matt picked up the intercom to let them in through the main front door, before opening the door to their flat. 'Hello! Come on in!' he called, poking his head out into the scruffy, brightly lit hallway, keen to get them into the considerably more glamorous surroundings of the flat.

Bella and Ben stepped inside, armed with flowers and wine. Matt gave Ben his customary bear-hug and stepped back, unsure how to greet Bella. A kiss felt too forward for their first meeting.

A handshake too formal. In the end Bella gave a small but friendly wave and a nervous giggle. 'Hi, Matt, lovely to meet you. I've heard so much about you.'

'Ha! All good I hope . . .?' Matt tried to pull his eyes away from her but found that he couldn't. She was definitely the most strikingly attractive girl he had ever set eyes on. No wonder Ben had fallen for her so quickly and so deeply. Behind him, Freya cleared her throat pointedly. 'Oh! Bella, this is my wife, Freya.'

'Hi, Freya,' Bella said, giving Freya a warm smile. 'These are for you.' She handed her the flowers.

'Thank you.' Freya's cheeks had flushed slightly red and she looked uncharacteristically shy as she took the expensive-looking bouquet of lilies.

'You have a lovely home,' Bella added, gesturing around the open-plan living/dining space that Freya had lovingly decorated with chalky, muted colours on the walls, offset by splashes of bold colour in her choice of cushions and rugs. She had a talent and a passion for interior design and Matt knew that Bella would have scored an immediate bulls-eye with her appreciation of it. He wondered if Ben had armed her with the information in advance or if she genuinely loved it.

There was an awkward pause as they all stood around, shuffling from foot to foot. Finally, Ben broke the silence. 'Well, I'm starving! I hope you've made my favourite, Matt.'

Matt grinned back at him, pleased to see how happy and well he looked. ''Course I have, mate. Make yourselves at home and I'll just go and put the finishing touches to it.'

'I'll get the drinks,' Freya chipped in, already turning towards the kitchen. 'Red or white?' she threw back over her shoulder.

Bella and Ben exchanged glances. 'Red for me, just water for

Bella. She doesn't drink.' Ben nodded encouragingly at Matt as he spoke.

'Result!' Matt replied, thinking how fabulous it must be to have a designated driver all the time. He motioned to them to take a seat on the sofa, before following Freya into the kitchen. 'What do you think?' he hissed, as he stirred the huge pan of paella he was preparing.

Freya's head was bowed, as she concentrated on pouring three glasses of wine and a glass of water, so he couldn't read her expression. 'She's stunning-looking.'

'I hadn't noticed,' Matt lied. 'But she seems very nice, too, doesn't she?'

'Hmmm.' Freya looked up, her large grey-blue eyes clouding slightly. 'I wish she wasn't tee-total.'

'Why?'

Freya grinned sheepishly. 'It makes me nervous. She'll be able to remember every second of every drunken evening.'

Matt laughed. 'Well, she can fill in the blanks for us then!'

Freya pulled a face. 'That's what I'm afraid of.'

The evening went better than Matt had dared hope. Any concerns he might have had that Bella wouldn't be as much fun as Charlotte disappeared almost instantly. She was charming and funny, but more importantly, she was happy to let Ben shine. Ben had always been the life and soul of the party and she had sat back, listening intently and laughing loudly, as he regaled them with hilarious stories.

She asked Matt and Freya lots of questions about themselves and seemed genuinely interested in their answers. At the end of the meal, as they were drinking their coffee, Ben tapped his spoon against his cup in a jokingly self-important way. 'Bella and I have an announcement!' he said, slurring slightly.

Matt looked at Freya, who seemed to have sat up a bit straighter, as if steeling herself for a blow.

'Bella is pregnant!' Ben reached out and took Bella's hand in his, as they gazed at each other adoringly.

There was a beat of silence, before Matt spoke. 'Wha—what?' he spluttered. 'Oh my God. That must have been a bit of a shock?'

Ben began to nod but Bella's voice cut through firmly. 'No, not at all. We're delighted, aren't we, darling?'

'Of course!' Ben agreed quickly but Matt could see in his eyes that delight wasn't the only emotion he was feeling.

'Congratulations!' Freya's voice sounded much higher than usual. 'That's lovely news. When are you due?' Freya was a midwife, so knew all there was to know about pregnancy.

Matt glanced at Freya, curious at her tone, before turning back towards Bella and Ben expectantly.

'The beginning of January.' Bella gave a strange little smile. 'There's a possibility we might be spending New Year's Eve in a maternity ward. Maybe it'll be your ward, Freya!'

Matt watched Ben carefully, noticing that he blanched slightly at Bella's words and wondered how he must really be feeling. If it was him, he knew he would have very mixed emotions. Yes, Bella was gorgeous and she certainly seemed like a funny, pleasant, intelligent woman. But to have a baby together after such a short period of time felt like an enormous leap of faith.

He and Freya had only recently started discussing whether they should think about starting a family, now that they had celebrated their second wedding anniversary. But they had been together for nine years, so it felt like a natural progression. It would have been the same if Ben had announced that Charlotte was pregnant. But this news was like a sledgehammer, coming out of nowhere.

As Bella looked at her watch and yawned, Ben took the hint and stood up. 'I suppose we'd better be making a move.'

Matt nodded. 'Fancy a quick stroll to clear your head first? To the end of the road and back?' It was traditional with Matt and Ben that after every dinner party, they would take a quick walk to have a furtive smoke and a chat while Charlotte and Freya pretended not to know what they were up to.

Ben nodded enthusiastically. 'Definitely!' He looked at Bella. 'I'll just be five minutes, darling.'

Bella smiled pleasantly and stood up. 'Sure. I'll get my jacket.'

Ben and Matt exchanged confused glances. 'Um, no need for you to come, too, darling.' Ben nodded at her reassuringly. 'We'll only be a few minutes.'

Bella fixed Ben with a determined stare. 'I'd like some air, too. Don't worry, you won't even know I'm there.'

There was an embarrassed pause, before Ben shrugged apologetically at Matt. The three of them let themselves out of the house and turned into the street. 'You go on ahead,' Bella said, hanging back.

'OK.' Ben and Matt walked briskly ahead, both of them painfully aware that they were being watched.

Matt took a packet of cigarettes out of his pocket and offered them to Ben. He looked back over his shoulder at Bella, who was walking about twenty paces behind them. 'Nah, I'd better not,' he muttered, gesturing backwards.

Matt frowned. 'She won't mind you having one, surely?'

Ben pursed his lips. 'She might.'

Matt put a cigarette between his lips and lit it, earning him a longing glance from Ben. 'So, what do you reckon then? About the baby?'

'I'm really happy about it,' Ben fired back instantly, a note of defiance in his voice.

'That's good.' Matt deliberately left a pause, knowing Ben wouldn't be able to help filling it.

'I must admit it was a bit of a shock, though.'

'I bet.' Again, Matt left a pause.

Ben glanced back at Bella nervously. 'I keep thinking about Charlotte and me.'

'And?' Matt exhaled a long trail of smoke, which floated up into the still, dark air, before dissipating.

Ben sighed. 'I think it just wasn't meant to be. All that time and we never had an accident. First night with Bella and . . .'

'Bingo!' Matt finished the sentence for him.

Ben gave a dry laugh. 'Yeah. Bingo.'

'Well, as long as you're happy about it, I'm pleased for you, mate.' Matt blew out another long trail of smoke, before stubbing out his cigarette on the pavement.

Together, they turned towards Matt and Freya's flat. Now in front of them, Bella turned, too, and began to walk slowly back the way they had come.

'Does she always do that?'

Ben looked at Matt curiously. 'Do what?'

Matt gestured towards Bella. 'Follow you everywhere you go.'

Ben laughed. 'No! 'Course not. I think she did just want some air.'

Matt grinned, feeling slightly stupid. 'She's an absolute stunner, mate. You certainly seem to have struck gold there.'

Ben looked up at Bella, who was now waiting for them at the gate to the flat, with shining eyes and a wide smile. 'Yup,' he said matching her smile. 'I certainly did.'

'So . . . What did you think?' Freya pulled on one of Matt's T-shirts and climbed into bed beside him, wrapping herself around him as she did every night, using his body as a human hot-water bottle.

Matt pulled her towards him so that she was resting her head on his bare chest. He kissed the top of her head, enjoying the smell of her. Not quite perfume. Not quite natural. A heady mix of the two. 'I like her. She lets him be himself and he seems happy. Let's face it, it's been a while since we've seen him smile that much.'

Freya nodded but didn't reply.

'What about you?' he prompted, after the silence had stretched just a beat too long. 'What did you think of her?'

'Hmmm. Well, she's lovely-looking and she was friendly enough.'

'But?'

Freya sighed. 'But nothing, really. I can't put my finger on it but there was just something about her that I found a bit unnerving.'

Matt stroked her silky blonde hair. 'Sure you're not feeling a teensy bit jealous?' he teased.

Freya tensed immediately. 'No!' she snapped. 'Why would I be jealous?'

Matt rolled his eyes in the darkness. Talk about putting his foot in it. 'I'm just teasing. Relax, honey.'

Freya tutted. 'Well, don't! No, I'm not jealous of her. She might be beautiful but I think she's also a bit weird. A bit intense.'

'It was odd the way she insisted on following us on our walk,' Matt agreed.

'Exactly. What did Ben say about her?'

'He seems happy.'

'Did he mention Charlotte?'

Matt shifted uncomfortably. He always told Freya everything but wasn't sure if he was betraying Ben's confidence in this case. 'Um, he just said it obviously wasn't meant to be. That's all.'

'Why not? They were together for years. He was going to ask her to marry him.'

'I know, but . . .' Matt paused, trying to find the right words. 'He thinks it's a sign that Bella got pregnant almost immediately, whereas he and Charlotte never even had so much as a scare.'

'Well, we've never had so much as a scare either.' Freya's voice suddenly sounded very small. 'I hope you don't think that means we're not meant to be?'

'Don't be daft!' Matt gave her shoulder a squeeze. 'I don't really share his view that the pregnancy is some kind of miracle . . .'

'What, you think she may have deliberately trapped him?' There was a sudden note of excitement in Freya's voice.

'No!' Matt said quickly, although that was indeed what he thought. 'But it does seem a bit odd that he would have been taken so much by surprise. He clearly thought she was taking precautions . . .'

'Hmmm. It does,' Freya agreed. 'I miss Charlotte.'

'You still see her.'

Freya laughed. 'I know, but it's not the same. I miss her being part of our foursome. It was so easy. I never had to check myself with her. I knew she loved me whatever.'

'You'll get used to Bella. I'm sure she'll grow to love you just as much as Charlotte did.'

'You sound like you've got used to her already.' Freya adopted a sulky tone. 'That didn't take long.'

Matt sighed and kissed Freya's head again. 'Shut up and go to sleep.'

CHAPTER FOUR

Jo twirled in front of Peter. 'Will I do?'

Peter gazed down at her, his eyes swimming with love. 'You'll do very nicely. You look stunning.'

Jo smiled and smoothed down her taupe, fitted dress as she stepped into her high-heeled, nude Louboutins. She had left it until the last possible moment to put them on, as she would be wearing them all day and knew that her feet would be protesting loudly by the time she took them off again tonight.

'I wish it wasn't . . .' Peter began, before stopping for a second, thinking. 'It's not how I imagined Ben's wedding would be.'

Jo looked up at Peter, handsome in his bespoke dark grey suit. He had been uncharacteristically quiet all morning. Actually, the truth was that he had been quieter in general ever since Ben first brought Bella home. 'I know you're not keen on her, but it's not up to us. She's Ben's chosen partner, so we have to just accept her. And he seems happy, doesn't he?'

'Does he?' Peter shot back far too quickly, before checking himself. 'Yes, I suppose you're right. He does seem happy enough.'

Jo sighed heavily. 'Look, Peter . . . Whatever either of us

thinks of her, she's pregnant, with his child . . . and they're getting married. Whatever doubts any of us might have, we need to put them to one side and support them, for Ben's sake.'

'Hmmm.' Again Peter hesitated, his eyes clouding with worry. 'I know you're right. I suppose I just wish . . .'

Jo tilted her head to look at him properly. 'Wish what?'

'That it wasn't her. There, I've said it.' He shrugged apologetically.

Jo wrapped her arms around Peter's waist and reached up to kiss him. 'I know. But it is her. I'm sure it'll all be fine, don't worry. Now, come on or we'll be late.'

Downstairs, Ben was sitting in the kitchen with Matt, drinking coffee. Jo gave Matt a hug. 'Hello, darling, lovely to see you.'

Matt grinned back. Although he was now a fully grown, 30-year-old man, Jo could still see in his face the cheeky little 7-year-old boy she had first met all those years ago, when he and Ben had become friends at primary school. 'You look lovely, Jo.'

Jo flushed with pride. Matt had spent so much time at their house over the years that he had become like a second son and Jo adored him. 'Thank you, Matt. And so do you. How is Freya?'

Matt beamed. 'She's really well. She's going to meet us at the registry office.'

Jo had no idea what to expect from today at all. She had always known that when Ben got married, it would be his bride who decided everything. But she felt sure that Charlotte would have at least involved her and Peter in the planning and preparations. Aside from telling them where and when, Bella and Ben had excluded them from any discussions, insisting they wanted to do everything themselves.

'OK, well, I guess we'd better get going then.' Jo walked over to Ben and adjusted his tie fractionally. She looked up at him, marvelling at how the years had galloped by – her baby boy, who had struggled to take his first breath, was now this tall, handsome young man about to get married.

The tears pricked at the back of her eyes and she smiled in an exaggerated way to try to quell them. Sometimes she felt as if Ben was at the end of a string connected directly to her heart. He pulled at her in a way that, although she and Emma were incredibly close, Emma had never done. 'You look so handsome, sweetheart,' she told him now. 'Bella is a very lucky girl.'

Ben flashed her a smile that was a mirror image of his father's but she could see from his dark brown eyes that he was nervous. 'Thanks, Mum.'

Peter drove the four of them in his Range Rover into the centre of town, where he parked in the car park of the rather ugly Seventies building that housed the registry office.

As she walked into the foyer, Jo spotted Emma, engrossed in an intense conversation with Freya. 'Hello, girls!' she called, just slightly too loudly as she approached, in the hope that they wouldn't think she had been ear-wigging.

Emma and Freya both jumped and looked up at her guiltily. It wasn't difficult to guess what they had been talking about. Emma stood up and kissed her mother on both cheeks. 'Hi, Mum, you look fantastic. Love that dress.'

Jo smiled appreciatively. 'So do you, darling.' It was true. Emma was a yoga obsessive who rarely ate anything containing sugar, caffeine or wheat. As a result, she had perfect, glowing skin, a toned, flat stomach and blonde hair that gleamed like a sheet of gold to her narrow shoulders. She was wearing a grey fitted dress that showed off her slim figure and long, shapely legs. People often commented that Emma was a Mini-Me of Jo but Jo would always reply that she had never looked anywhere near as good as her pretty daughter.

'And you look as fabulous as ever, Freya.' Jo turned towards Matt's wife and gave her a hug. The thought flitted through her mind that she wished Freya was going to be her new daughter-in-law rather than Bella, but she mentally swatted it away and inwardly chided herself.

'Where are the boys?' Emma looked over Jo's shoulder expectantly.

'Parking the car.' As she spoke, Peter, Ben and Matt walked through the door and were immediately enveloped in hugs and kisses by the two girls.

'Nervous?' Emma smiled up at her brother.

Ben shook his head firmly. 'Nope. Just looking forward to it.'

Jo caught Matt and Freya exchanging a look she couldn't quite read. 'Well, I think maybe we should go in then?'

Inside the room where the ceremony was taking place, there were already around twenty people, all of them seemingly on Ben's side of the aisle, seated on the silver chairs that were laid out in rows. There was a small spray of white roses at the end of each row, with a more elaborate floral display at the front and a string quartet playing in one corner. Despite the adornments, Jo couldn't help feeling a sag of disappointment at the unexciting surroundings. As Peter had said earlier, it wasn't what she had envisioned for Ben's wedding.

Jo made her way to the front, looking nervously towards Bella's side of the room, which was empty, except for one woman, who Jo could see instantly was Bella's mother. She had suggested to Bella that maybe they should have a pre-wedding dinner, so that they could meet each other before the big day but Bella had curtly rebuffed the idea, saying they were not sociable people and would be quite happy to meet on the day. Now that she knew that only Bella's mother would be attending, Jo could understand why Bella had been so reticent.

Bella's mother looked up as Jo approached. She looked a little careworn and nervous but she still had enough of her beauty to confirm where Bella had inherited it from. She had shoulder-length, very dark brown hair, smattered with grey, and large brown, slightly hooded eyes. She shot Jo an uneasy smile and stood up. 'Hello. You must be Ben's mother . . .?'

'Jo,' Jo replied, reaching back to take Peter's arm. 'And this is my husband, Peter.'

Bella's mother nodded knowingly. 'Of course. I can see the resemblance! I'm Lynda.'

Peter shook her hand, before they shuffled into their seats beside Ben and Matt.

'Who's giving her away?' Peter hissed as they sat down.

'No one, apparently. Bella insisted that she didn't belong to anyone and therefore she was perfectly capable of giving herself away.'

Peter raised an eyebrow. 'That bodes well. Still, I suppose if the father's not on the scene, then it makes some sort of sense.' Bella had always shut down any conversation relating to her father and Ben had told them simply that he hadn't been around since she was small.

Jo glanced again over to Bella's side of the room and she felt a stab of guilt. Ben's side was almost full. 'Should we ask some of ours to move over?' she whispered.

But before Peter could reply, the string quartet struck up with the wedding march and it was too late.

All eyes turned expectantly towards the back of the room, as Bella appeared, walking serenely and confidently down the centre of the aisle, clutching a simple bouquet of velvety white roses with both hands. Jo's breath caught. She had never seen anyone look quite so exquisitely perfect, as Bella made her way up the aisle towards Ben. Her dress was a cleverly cut style, that clung to her slim figure, yet concealed any sign of a bump. Her long, dark hair shone in loose waves over her shoulders and her subtle make-up only emphasized the dramatic loveliness of her features.

Jo glanced at Ben, who was gazing at Bella adoringly. Their eyes were locked onto each other with such intensity that it felt almost intrusive to be watching. As she drew level with Ben, Bella reached out and took Ben's hand, still holding his gaze.

Jo nodded to herself. Whatever she felt about Bella, there was no doubting the connection between her and Ben. They all needed to accept now that they were together and support them, instead of dwelling on 'what ifs' and unanswered questions.

After the short wedding service, they drove to the smart country restaurant where they were having the reception. It was an embarrassingly one-sided affair, with Bella's mother the only representative of her family. Jo made a bee-line for Lynda and tried to engage her in conversation, to see if she could find out anything more about her new daughter-in-law, but Lynda was just as evasive on the subject of her background as Bella. 'Is Bella's father still alive?' she ventured, hoping that she would learn something a bit more illuminating than the 'he's not on the scene' that she got from Ben.

Lynda's face remained impassive. 'I believe so. We haven't seen him since Bella was very young.'

Intrigued, Jo nodded encouragingly. 'Oh, so you're divorced?'

Lynda's eyes slid away and she pointed to Ben and Bella, who were mingling with the guests as they waited for dinner to be served. 'Don't they make a lovely couple? Ben is a wonderful man.'

Jo acknowledged the pointed change of subject, before following Lynda's gaze, feeling suffused with pride at hearing her son described in such glowing terms. 'Thank you. And yes, they do make a lovely couple. Bella is certainly the most beautiful bride I think I've ever seen.'

Lynda smiled but Jo noticed that the smile didn't reach her eyes. She had the same invisible barrier that Bella had, when discussing anything personal, and she sensed that they weren't at all close.

After chatting for a while longer and getting nothing more than vague platitudes out of Lynda, Jo excused herself and headed over to Emma. 'Hi, darling, I've just been speaking to Bella's mum. I wanted to see if I could get any more out of her about Bella's background but she's even more of a closed book than Bella.'

Emma nodded. 'I know. I tried to speak to her, too, but I got the impression Bella's got her well-trained and she didn't dare give anything away.'

Jo felt a niggle of discomfort and foreboding. Again, she wished that Ben had gone for someone who was a bit more open and a lot more friendly. *Like Charlotte*, she thought, before mentally scolding herself for such a treacherous wish.

'It's all a bit odd, isn't it?' Emma was saying, her eyes scanning the room. 'I mean, she doesn't seem to have any friends. Don't you think that's a bit . . . well, strange? For your mum to be the only guest from your side at your wedding? And even they don't seem that close. Bella's hardly spoken to her.'

Jo pursed her lips, watching as Bella and Ben mingled with all the guests from Ben's side of the family, laughing and chatting easily, Bella clearly charming everyone she met. 'You know, you could argue that there might be advantages to her not being close to her own family.'

Emma raised a sceptical eyebrow. 'Really? How?'

Jo shrugged. 'You know the old expression: "A son is a son 'til he marries a wife . . . a daughter's a daughter for life"?'

Emma nodded.

'Well,' Jo continued, 'that's because the son usually gravitates towards his wife's side of the family. As Bella doesn't seem to have much of a family, she won't be interested in taking him away from us, and we get the best of both worlds. So,' she concluded, feeling more optimistic than she had all day, 'there's every possibility that we may have struck gold with Bella.'

CHAPTER FIVE

Ben felt uncharacteristically nervous, as he carefully navigated the icy country lanes. It was Christmas Day and they were heading out to Suffolk for their annual gathering at his mum and dad's house. The weather was clear and crisp, with the sun reflecting on the patchwork fields, making them look like they were wearing a twinkling coat of frost.

This time last year, he mused, as he steered to avoid the patches of black ice that greeted him at every turn, it was Charlotte sitting beside him and he was still expecting to propose to her in the New Year. Now it was Bella in the passenger seat, her hands carefully resting on her neat, football-shaped bump.

Ben almost laughed to himself as the thought left his head. She may not have been actually driving the car, but there was no way anyone could describe Bella as being in the passenger seat. She was the one steering their lives in whatever direction she wanted them to go, of that he was quite clear. Sometimes, very occasionally, he wanted to object. To say that he didn't want to do this or that. That he would prefer to stay in on a Saturday night and watch TV, rather than going to the theatre, but he had very quickly learned that it wasn't worth the grief it caused.

He thought back to the time, not long after their wedding, when he had invited Matt and Freya round for an impromptu meal one Friday night. He had casually mentioned it to Bella as they'd eaten breakfast in the kitchen of their flat that morning. 'Oh, by the way, Matt and Freya are coming round tonight. I thought we could get a takeaway.'

He was scrolling on his iPad at the time and wasn't looking up at Bella but he sensed, rather than saw, the furious expression on her face. Looking up, he almost recoiled. Her beautiful dark eyes were blazing and her mouth was set in a grimace. 'No, they're not. It's not convenient.' It wasn't the opening to a discussion of any kind. It was a statement that was intended to shut down any further debate.

Ben frowned. 'But . . . I've already invited them. And they've accepted.'

Bella's face took on an amused expression. 'Well, you shouldn't have. Not without clearing it with me first.'

Ben took a deep breath and drew himself up to his full height. 'I'm sorry, darling. You're right. But I've asked them now so they're coming. I'll know better next time.'

Bella looked at him for a long moment, before standing up and throwing her paper napkin on the table. She pulled her short satin robe around her and strode out of the kitchen. Ben watched her go, feeling a mixture of annoyance and worry. It was such a strange over-reaction to something that was no big deal.

Matt and Freya were always popping round for hastily arranged dinners when he was with Charlotte. He didn't remember her ever objecting, even the time he'd forgotten to tell her altogether and she was in the shower when they arrived.

She had just pulled on some sweat pants and a T-shirt and joined them at the table with her wet hair hastily scraped into a bun on top of her head.

He shrugged to himself and tried to shake off the feeling of unease. He certainly wasn't going to cancel. It would be rude and embarrassing. And it wasn't as if Bella had any friends she wanted to invite instead. No, he decided, she would have come round by the time they arrived. Even so, he made a mental note to make sure that he gave her a bit more notice in future.

By the time Matt and Freya arrived that evening, Bella still wasn't home. Ben had been calling her frantically for several hours but her phone appeared to be switched off. Her job as an executive PA to the boss of a large investment company in the City meant her hours were very regular. There was no reason why she would have been delayed at work, especially on a Friday night, when the whole company tended to head off home an hour or two early.

'Hi, mate!' Matt held up in front of him a carrier bag stuffed with wine and beer. 'I've brought the usual!'

Ben smiled as convincingly as he could. 'Fantastic! Come on in. I'll order the food. What do you fancy tonight – Chinese or Indian?'

Matt and Freya dumped their coats in the hall and followed Ben into the kitchen, almost as familiar with his flat as with their own. 'Ummm . . . Indian, I think.' Freya opened the kitchen drawer and took out the bottle opener. Then she took four glasses out of the cupboard and poured three of them. 'What's Bella drinking?' She turned towards Ben expectantly.

'Um, she'll probably just have water.'

Freya's face fell slightly. 'Of course. Where is she?' She looked over Ben's shoulder, as if expecting Bella to materialize.

Ben swallowed. 'Um, yeah, she sends her apologies but she's been held up at work. Hopefully she'll be here soon. Let's just order the food and I'll save her some.' He saw a look pass between Matt and Freya and felt himself redden slightly. He hated lying to them but he especially hated lying to them when they knew it.

They ordered the food and ate it at the round, modern table in Ben's kitchen, as they always had. The gap where Bella should have been sitting and where Charlotte always used to sit, seemed to loom large and the conversation didn't flow quite the way it usually did. Ben tried to ignore the undercurrent of tension but there was a knot in his stomach and despite drinking a fair bit, his throat seemed dry, making it difficult to eat. He couldn't remember the taste of anything.

Finally, earlier than they ever had before, Matt and Freya started looking at their watches. 'Listen, we'd better be off.' Matt threw Ben a sympathetic look that caused his stomach to knot even more. 'I'm playing football in the morning.'

'And I'm on night shifts from tomorrow night, so . . .' Freya added, pushing back her chair.

Ben nodded and stood up. 'No worries. It was good to see you guys.'

Freya gave him a hug. 'Give our love to Bella.' Her words were heavy with unspoken meaning.

Ben could feel himself reddening again and cursed himself for it. 'I will.'

After he shut the door behind them, he stood in the kitchen with his hands on his hips, wondering what to do. Should he be worried? Somehow he didn't think so. He knew instinctively that she was punishing him. He began to clear up the plates and glasses and put the remains of the Indian takeaway in the bin outside the back door. Bella hated the smell of food in the flat.

When everything had been cleared away, he went into the lounge and sat on the sofa, waiting, his heart thudding. The ticking sound of the clock over the fireplace seemed to echo loudly around the room and Ben wondered why he had never noticed it before. Finally, as the hands of the clock clicked round to one o'clock, he heard the key in the front door and stiffened as a wave of anger surged through him. How dare she show him up in front of his oldest friends? And what was wrong with having them round on a Friday night? It was his bloody flat, after all!

He listened as Bella dropped her bag in the hallway and made her way straight through to the bedroom. With his anger growing, he leaped up and marched into the bedroom behind her. 'Where the bloody hell have you been?' he hissed, through gritted teeth.

Bella, who was sitting on the edge of the bed with her back to him, shook her head.

Ben rolled his eyes. 'Well?' he demanded, a deep torrent of rage soaring up inside his chest. 'Answer me! Do you have any idea how embarrassing that was?'

Bella turned her face towards him and he immediately recoiled in shame. Her make-up had run and the tracks of her tears were still visible. Her large, brown eyes were ringed with dark circles and she was deathly pale. 'I've been at the hospital,' she whispered. 'I thought I was losing the baby.' As she finished speaking, she dissolved into tears and put her head in her hands.

'Oh my God! Why didn't you call me?' Ben dashed to her side and put his arms around her slim, shaking shoulders. All his anger had evaporated in an instant and he now felt like the lousiest husband in the world.

'There wasn't time . . . I just wanted to get there. Marcus took me.'

Ben bristled. Marcus was Bella's boss and a very successful banker, with whom he knew she had had an affair in the past. 'Right,' he managed.

'He was so lovely,' she continued, her sobs beginning to abate. 'He waited while they checked me over and then insisted on bringing me home.'

'That was very nice of him,' Ben agreed, stroking her silky hair. 'But of course, if you'd rung me, or not had your phone switched off, I would have come straight away.'

Bella nodded and wiped her eyes, further smudging her mascara. 'I know, I'm sorry – but I didn't want to spoil your evening with Matt and Freya . . .' She let her words hang in the air. Without her having to say it, the unspoken suggestion that he had prioritized a night of drinking with his mates over looking after his pregnant wife was loud and clear.

Ben swallowed the lump in his throat. 'So what happened? What made you think you were losing the baby . . . and is it OK?'

Bella shook her head and made a swatting motion with her hand. 'I don't want to talk about it. But the main thing is that everything is OK and the baby's fine.'

'Oh, thank God!' Relief made Ben feel momentarily light-headed. He was glad he was sitting down. 'I'm so sorry I wasn't there for you, darling.' He kissed the top of her head and squeezed her towards him.

Bella gave him a watery smile. 'It's OK. Luckily Marcus was there, so he took care of me. Don't feel bad.'

OK, Ben thought, so she was definitely punishing him. But then again, he reasoned, he probably deserved it. 'Well, let me look after you now,' he said, bending down to take off her shoes. 'From now on, I'm not leaving your side.'

Bella allowed herself to be gently laid down on the bed and smiled up at him. 'Thank you,' she whispered, as Ben tried to ignore the slightly triumphant gleam in her eyes. It occurred to him that she had just won a battle that he wasn't even aware he had been fighting.

CHAPTER SIX

Ben and Bella pulled onto the gravel driveway, Ben's Mercedes sighing to a halt, as if it had run out of breath. They didn't get out of the car immediately, but seemed to be having a terse conversation, both their faces set rigid as they stared straight ahead.

Jo felt a prickle of unease, as she watched them from the doorway. She had had a strange feeling of foreboding since she woke up this morning and couldn't put her finger on why.

She hoped she was imagining it, but Ben's body language seemed different, as he finally got out of the car and opened Bella's door, before helping her out.

Jo plastered a smile on her face as she swung open the door and waved. 'Hello, you two! Happy Christmas!'

Ben grinned as they reached her and he bent down to kiss her on the cheek. 'Hi, Mum, happy Christmas.'

'And look at you!' Jo beamed, motioning to Bella's rounded stomach. 'You're cooking nicely.'

Bella's face hardened as she offered her cold cheek to accept a kiss from Jo. 'You make me sound like a bloody turkey!'

Jo looked at her in surprise. 'Oh! Well you're certainly the most glamorous turkey I've ever seen.'

There was an awkward pause as both Jo and Ben watched Bella to see if she would accept the compliment. 'Right,' she said eventually. 'Are we standing out here all day or are we allowed to come in?'

Jo's unease deepened. Why was Bella being so bloody prickly? She decided to blame the pregnancy hormones and gave what she knew was a fake laugh. 'Of course! Come on through. Peter's in the kitchen.'

Ben took off his jacket and hung it on the coat rack in the hallway, before turning towards Bella and reaching out to take her coat. 'Leave it!' she snapped, slapping his hand away. 'I'm cold.' Jo caught Ben's eye for a split second. There was a look of resignation there that she didn't like one bit.

'Look who's here!' she said brightly, as they reached the kitchen, where Peter was busy stirring his mulled wine on the Aga. He made it every year at Christmas and every year they all pretended to like it. The time had long since passed when they could tell him they all thought it was disgusting. At least the home-made mince pies went some way towards taking the taste away.

Peter wiped his hands on a tea towel and turned towards Ben and Bella. 'Hello, you two. Happy Christmas!'

Jo watched with interest to see if Bella gave Peter the same prickly response but to her surprise, and annoyance, she moved into Peter's arms and gazed up at him with a radiant smile. 'Happy Christmas, Peter! That mulled wine smells divine . . . almost makes me wish I could drink it.'

Peter flushed and flicked Jo a panicked look, before clearing his throat. 'Well, you'll be pleased to hear that you can . . . I made it non-alcoholic this year, knowing that you didn't drink.'

'Did you? You didn't say.' Jo felt a sudden spike of anger towards Peter that took her by surprise.

But either Peter didn't hear her or chose to ignore her, as he reached for one of the pewter goblets he had lined up on the pale granite work surface and poured Bella a generous serving. Bella took it with her eyes shining, as if he had handed her a goblet of solid gold. 'How wonderful,' she murmured, sipping it, gazing at Peter over the top of her glass. Jo watched her carefully, noting the slight blanch as she swallowed each mouthful, clearly detesting it but valiantly hiding her dislike from Peter.

'Well,' Jo clapped her hands a little too over-enthusiastically, 'let's go through and make ourselves comfortable, shall we? Bella, are you sure you won't take off your coat?'

'No.' Bella didn't look at Jo as she spoke. 'I'd rather keep it on as I'm feeling a bit chilled.' She glanced up at Peter with an apologetic smile.

'Oh dear, I do hope you're not sickening for something?' Peter said, causing another ripple of annoyance to quiver through Jo's chest. Peter was notoriously unsympathetic to anyone who was ill. Then she wondered if he was being sarcastic. She couldn't tell.

'Pregnancy's not an illness, is it, Bella?' Jo was aiming for a jokey tone, but her voice sounded sharp.

Bella raised her large eyes towards Jo with a hurt expression. 'Um, no, I guess not.'

Ben looked at Jo with an accusing stare and she could feel a flush spreading up her neck. Why did she feel as if she was in the wrong when it was Bella who was being so offhand?

After an awkward silence, the four of them made their way

through into the sitting room. Jo had spent days decorating the freshly cut Norwegian Spruce Christmas tree and trailing pretty lights and baubles around the large marble fireplace and along the picture rail, but no one seemed to notice or made any comment. With the fire lit and roaring, the room was cosy to the point of being too warm and Jo wondered if Bella might actually take her coat off at last, but instead, she pulled it around her tightly, wincing with an exaggerated grimace as she sat down gingerly on the plump grey sofa.

Ben's forehead creased with concern. 'Are you OK, darling?'

Bella threw him a brave smile. 'Yes, I'm sure I'll be fine.'

Jo took a couple of deep breaths, trying to dampen down the irritation that was still quivering through her chest. She wondered why she was the only one who could see that Bella's behaviour was simply attention-seeking, rather than due to any kind of genuine discomfort.

'What time is Emma getting here?' Ben addressed the question to Peter.

Peter looked at his watch. 'Any time now, I should imagine. I told her she should have hitched a lift with you two. Seems a bit crazy to bring two cars to do the same journey, especially as the roads are so icy.'

A look passed between Bella and Ben and Jo knew, without them saying so, that Emma would not have been offered a lift. She thought back to last Christmas, which suddenly seemed like a lifetime ago, and how much things had changed since then.

Emma and Ben had always been so close. Even when Ben was with Charlotte, his relationship with his older sister had remained strong. But since meeting Bella, there seemed to be a distance between them. Emma was as perplexed as Jo and the two of them had spent many hours discussing whether she might have done something to upset him.

Jo had never voiced it, but she knew instinctively that it was Bella who had a problem with Emma and that Ben was just going along with it for an easy life. She looked at Bella now, so beautiful and so charming when she chose to be. So cold and brittle when she didn't. She wished she could shake off the heavy feeling of anxiety that had dogged her ever since they announced that she was pregnant and they were getting married.

Looking back, it was then that Ben had started to change towards them. Well, that wasn't quite right. He had started to change towards Jo and Emma. He had become more distant and a little more formal. He seemed fine with Peter, which was ironic, considering it was Peter who had voiced his reservations about Bella and the speed of their relationship in the first place. But he had also changed in himself. He was becoming quieter and less confident, as if he was slowly but surely having the stuffing pulled out of him.

As if she sensed her watching, Bella suddenly turned her gaze towards Jo. Jo quickly rearranged her features into a smile but Bella's large brown eyes narrowed and there was a glint of something that Jo couldn't read, except that she knew it wasn't pleasant.

She sighed and stood up, fed up with being excluded from the conversation.

No one seemed to notice as she left the room. Walking back into the kitchen, she caught sight of the pan of mulled wine gently bubbling on the Aga. Feeling a sudden spike of annoyance, she picked it up and tipped it down the sink. She watched the dark red, gloopy liquid congeal around the plughole, with its crimson tendrils clinging to the stark white walls of the sink like blood. She turned on the tap and swished water over the incriminating evidence until it was all gone.

She stared at the empty pan guiltily. But, she reassured herself, it was about time someone told Peter the truth about what they all thought of his horrible yearly concoction. She wished Emma would get here. She needed an ally, someone to tell her whether she was imagining Bella's offhand behaviour.

As if on cue, her mobile rang. She snatched it up as she saw Emma's name flashing on the screen. 'Hi, darling, where are you?'

'Mum!' Emma sobbed. 'I've had an accident. I hit a patch of ice on a bend and I've spun off the road.' Her voice was audibly shaking.

'Oh my God! Are you OK? Are you hurt?' Jo's legs suddenly felt weak.

'Bit of a bump on the head. And my neck is killing me. But I think I'm OK.' Jo could hear her holding the phone away from her body as she examined herself.

Jo swallowed down the tide of panic that was rising up inside her and tried to keep her voice steady and calm. 'Right. Daddy and I are coming to get you. Where are you?'

Emma began to cry, causing Jo's heart to constrict. Emma rarely cried. She was so composed and she always seemed to be in control of her emotions. Hearing her lose it completely told Jo that they needed to get to her as quickly as possible. 'I'm at the corner of Bramble Lane and Mill Road, near the pub,' Emma managed, through giant, gulping sobs.

'We'll be with you in ten minutes. Just stay where you are.'

Jo dashed into the sitting room, where Peter, Ben and Bella were still chatting, seemingly unaware of her absence. They all looked up at her in surprise as she entered. 'Emma's had an accident. We need to go and get her.'

Peter and Ben both leaped out of their seats. 'Shit! Is she OK?' Ben's face creased with concern and Jo could see that he was genuinely worried for his sister. It gave her a small crumb of comfort to see a glimpse of the old Ben.

'She's very shaken and upset and I think she's bumped her head but she was talking coherently, so hopefully she's fine. Come on, Peter, we need to hurry.' She gestured towards the door expectantly.

Peter nodded quickly and strode past her, already scooping his car keys from the glass bowl on the console table in the hallway.

'I'll come!' Ben followed Peter towards the door.

'No, Ben!' Bella shouted suddenly, causing all of them to stop in their tracks. 'You can't go.'

Ben scowled irritably. 'What? I need to go with them in case Dad and I have to pull the car out of a ditch or something.'

Bella's face darkened. 'You can't leave me here on my own!'

Jo felt a sudden urge to slap her daughter-in-law's pretty face. 'Come. Don't come,' she snapped at Ben. 'But make your bloody mind up because we need to get to Emma.'

Ben hesitated and Jo could see the dilemma he faced. If he came with them, Bella would be furious with him. If he didn't come, he would be furious with himself. 'Sorry,' he said to Bella, seemingly having made up his mind. 'I'll only be a few minutes. You'll be fine.'

There was a short, awkward pause, before the three of them

raced out of the door, leaving Bella looking so angry that Jo imagined she could almost see the steam coming out of her ears.

As they rounded the corner of the road where Emma had told them she was, Jo gasped, clamping her hand over her mouth. Emma was sitting on the still-frosty grass verge with her head in her hands. Even at a distance, Jo could see that she was very distressed. Her mint green Fiat 500 was neatly nestled up against a tree, almost as if it was giving it a hug. Flimsy plumes of smoke rose lazily from beneath the bonnet. Peter pulled the car over and they all leaped out. Jo knelt down and put an arm around Emma's shaking shoulders. 'It's OK, sweetheart, we're here now. You're going to be fine.'

Emma let out a sound that was a cross between a groan and a sob and nodded. Ben moved round behind her and put his hands under her armpits, before lifting her gently to her feet. She took a deep breath to steady herself and gave him a watery smile. 'Cheers, Ben.'

Ben smiled back, his face still full of concern. 'No worries. That's quite an impressive bump on your head.'

Jo followed his gaze. A huge egg-shaped lump was forming on Emma's forehead. It reminded her of the time when she was three and she had fallen down the stone steps in the garden, resulting in a similar-shaped bump.

'Come on, piglet, let's get you home.' Peter pulled Emma into his arms and steered her towards the Range Rover, where he carefully helped her into the back seat.

Jo could see that Emma was violently shaking and climbed in beside her, wrapping one arm around her and taking her hand in the other.

'I'll drive Em's car home,' Ben said, heading towards the Fiat.

'Is it OK to drive?' Jo looked dubiously at the little car, which was looking very sorry for itself. 'I don't want you having an accident, too.'

'I think it'll be fine. Let's just get it home and we can get someone to take a look later.' Peter was already starting up the Range Rover and putting it into gear.

A few minutes later, they arrived home and helped a still-trembling Emma out of the car and into the house. Peter steered her towards the kitchen and settled her on a chair at the huge granite island in the middle of the room. 'I know what you need – a glass of mulled wine.' He turned expectantly towards the hob and stopped in puzzlement. 'What's happened to the mulled wine?'

Jo could feel her cheeks reddening. 'I tipped it away.'

'What did you do that for?' Peter frowned and looked at Jo in astonishment.

'Because . . . oh, because it was horrible!' Jo waved her hand dismissively. 'And I think Emma needs something a bit stronger than a non-alcoholic mulled wine anyway. Go and get her some whisky!' She knew she was blustering because she was embarrassed. She had tipped the mulled wine away in a fit of pique because Peter had prepared it especially for Bella.

Peter tutted and continued to frown but, after a moment's hesitation, he found the whisky and poured Emma a generous slug.

'Thanks.' Emma picked up the glass and drained it.

'Would you like to go and have a lie-down?' Peter had poured himself a whisky and raised his eyebrows questioningly at Jo, who nodded, suddenly desperate for a drink.

'No.' Emma held out her glass. 'But I'll have a refill.'

Ben joined them in the kitchen looking sheepish. 'Um, Bella's not feeling too good. I'm sorry but I think we'd better go home.'

Jo's shoulders sagged with disappointment. 'What? But what about lunch, your presents . . . you were supposed to be staying the night?'

Ben's eyes slid away from Jo's, as he glanced towards the door nervously. 'I'm sorry, Mum.'

Jo watched him go, feeling weak with disappointment, as well as the shock of Emma's accident catching up with her. She looked at Peter beseechingly. 'Peter, can't you speak to her? See if you can persuade her to stay? She seems to like you more than me . . .' Her words hung in the air between them.

Peter hesitated, looking uncomfortable. 'I'd rather not. I'm not sure it'll do much good anyway and if she's genuinely not feeling well . . .'

'Please, Peter. It'll spoil everything if they leave and I can tell Ben doesn't want to. It's her. She can't bear the attention wandering from her for a second. She's such a little bloody madam! Honestly, Emma, you should have seen her earlier, refusing to even take her coat off!'

As she finished speaking, she became aware that both Peter and Emma were looking over her shoulder with horrified expressions and she sensed, rather than heard, that both Ben and Bella were standing in the doorway. She swallowed hard and closed her eyes momentarily to steady herself, before spinning around to face them. Ben was staring at her in shock but Bella looked triumphant, a tiny smirk on her lips. 'Wow, thanks for that, Jo. It's a good job we're leaving – I certainly know where I'm not wanted.'

'Bella, I . . .' Jo fumbled for words as she reached out to take Bella's arm.

Bella shook her off roughly. 'Let go of me! Come on, Ben. We're going.'

Ben looked like he might cry. 'I'm really sorry but we have to go. Em, I hope you're OK?'

Emma nodded and raised her glass. 'Thanks, I'll be fine,' she slurred. 'Happy Christmas.'

Ben hesitated and for a moment, Jo thought he might hug her but another yell from Bella sent him scurrying after her.

Jo slumped down beside Emma at the island and burst into tears. She had had such a lovely day planned and now it was all ruined. But as she drained her glass of whisky, she somehow knew that it was more than just Christmas Day that was ruined.

CHAPTER SEVEN

Charlotte scanned the busy, dimly lit bar, her eyes hunting out Matt and Freya. Finally, she spotted them at a table in the corner, deep in conversation. 'Hey, guys!' she said, dumping her huge grey leather tote bag down on the floor and slumping into the seat they were zealously guarding for her. 'Matt, be a love and get me an enormous glass of white wine, will you?'

Matt beamed at her fondly and stood up. 'Your wish is my command, Lady Charlotte!' He planted a kiss on top of her head as he squeezed past her and disappeared into the crowd towards the bar.

Charlotte smiled at Freya, holding her gaze as she acknowledged the familiar tug of longing that she felt every time she saw her old friends. She missed them so much. Missed the closeness and the laughter they used to share as a foursome, before she made the biggest mistake of her life by breaking up with Ben and blowing it all apart. 'So . . . how are you, my love?'

Freya stood slightly and reached across the small wooden table to hug her, holding on for just slightly longer than normal. 'I miss you.' There was a slight tremble in her voice as she spoke.

Charlotte tilted her head and examined Freya's face. She

looked strained and tired. 'What's wrong? Is it work?' Her job at St Thomas' hospital was enormously stressful.

Freya shook her head and pushed back her blonde hair nervously. 'No, work's OK. It's . . . well, it's Ben, actually.'

Charlotte's stomach plummeted with fear. 'Ben? Why, what's happened? Is he all right?'

Freya's grey-blue eyes locked onto Charlotte's. 'Yes, as far as we know, he's fine. It's just that Bella's had the baby. A girl.'

Charlotte's mouth dried instantly. She nodded, trying to digest the news, wondering why it was such a shock when she had known it was coming for months. 'Well, that's good, isn't it?' she managed.

'Yes, I suppose it is.' Freya shrugged.

'What have they called her?'

'Elodie.'

Charlotte nodded again and attempted a smile. 'Elodie. That's a pretty name. And is everything OK? How are they managing?'

Freya made a 'pfff' sound and rolled her eyes. 'That's the thing . . .' She picked up her glass and took a large sip of wine. 'We don't know. We haven't seen them.'

At that moment, Matt arrived back at their table and put a large glass of chilled white wine down in front of Charlotte. She gave him a quick smile, before turning her attention back to Freya. 'Thanks, Matt. Why haven't you seen them?'

Matt looked at Freya and threw his hands up helplessly. 'We've got no idea. She just doesn't seem that keen on us.'

'Have you spoken to Ben?'

'Yup, briefly, when he called to tell me about the baby being born.' Matt looked slightly crestfallen as he spoke. 'But I think she might screen his calls. I rang once and obviously my number was displayed, so they didn't answer. But when I blocked my number and rang back, she picked up.'

'Well, call his mobile then?'

Matt scratched his cheek. 'Nope. Tried that. He must have changed his number.'

Charlotte frowned. 'How weird. Why would he change his number and not let his friends know?'

'Because his fucking bitch of a wife told him to?' Freya cut in, shaking her head in disgust.

Charlotte's stomach churned with a dozen different emotions. Knowing that she no longer had Ben's mobile number unnerved her hugely. Made her feel as though she had been cut adrift from her anchor. And hearing Bella described as his wife was like a punch to her kidneys. It was ridiculous, of course, but she couldn't stop the feelings that were coursing unstoppably through her. She gave herself a shake. She needed to get a grip.

'And how was she? Bella, I mean, when you spoke to her on the phone?'

Again, Matt glanced at Freya and gave a resigned sigh. 'Frosty, I suppose, is the best way to describe it. Very offhand. Made it clear she didn't want me calling.'

'I hate her,' Freya said suddenly.

'Freya!' Matt shot her an appalled look. 'That's a bit strong. We don't even really know her.'

Freya shrugged apologetically. 'I know, I know . . .' She turned towards Charlotte. 'But it feels a bit like a bereavement, except that he's still alive and well and living just a mile or so away.' She bit her lip and glanced at Matt. 'And he wouldn't say so but I know how hurt Matt is. Ben is his oldest, closest friend and yet he doesn't even hear from him anymore.'

Matt's eyes clouded slightly and he picked up his bottle of beer. 'That's not strictly true. He calls sometimes when she's out.'

Charlotte tutted, infuriated and unnerved by what she was hearing. 'But why would she not want him to speak to you guys?'

Matt and Freya both shook their heads. 'No idea. Control, maybe?' Freya said at last. 'She does seem very possessive and domineering.'

Charlotte nodded, feeling guilty. This was all her fault. If she hadn't broken up with Ben, he would never have met Bella and maybe it would be the two of them celebrating the birth of their first child. There was no way she'd have allowed Ben to shut out his oldest friends. They would have been with them every step of the way. 'What would happen if you ignored the way she's been behaving and just acted the way you always did? Why don't you just go round with some flowers and a present for the baby? You used to pop by all the time, so it wouldn't be anything out of the ordinary.'

Matt recoiled in horror. 'It would now! Honestly, Charlie, you have no idea how different things are to when you two were together. She's so cold towards us. She would make it clear we weren't welcome.'

'So what?' Charlotte looked from Matt to Freya defiantly. 'You aren't there to see her, you're there to see your friend and his new baby daughter. If she doesn't want to see you, she can always go out.' She could feel the anger bubbling up inside her and knew it was borne out of guilt. But on the other hand, they couldn't just accept that a lifelong friendship was over because Bella wanted him all to herself. 'And I'm sure she's not that bad?'

'She is!' Freya shot back. 'Matt's not exaggerating when he says she's really off with us. She just has this way of making you feel so unwelcome, even when we're not at their flat.'

Charlotte tried not to feel hurt at the description of the flat as 'theirs'. Yes, Ben's parents had bought it for him but it was she who had helped him choose it and furnish it, back in the days when she and Ben were so happy and excited about the future. But it was also she who had walked away from it, leaving Ben battered and broken, and vulnerable to the attentions of someone like Bella. 'Well,' she said at last. 'I think you should just turn up and act like nothing's wrong. Buy something lovely for the baby and behave as you normally would. You owe it to Ben . . .'

Matt stood up suddenly. 'Just going to the loo,' he said, by way of explanation as he strode off.

Charlotte and Freya watched him go. 'He's taken it quite badly,' Freya began. 'I think he's just so unbelievably hurt. He and Ben have been inseparable since primary school. It just seems so unfair that this . . . this bitch, can have got her claws into him so quickly and so bloody effectively.'

Charlotte shifted in her seat uncomfortably. 'It does,' she agreed. 'What if you were to speak to him? Alone.'

'How?' Freya looked gloomy. 'She never leaves him on his own for a minute.'

'She's not with him at work. You could go and wait for him outside his office.'

Freya smiled slightly, as she digested the idea. 'What? Ambush him, you mean?'

Charlotte picked up her glass and took a large slug of her wine. 'Well, yes, I suppose that is what I mean. But at least Bella wouldn't be there and you could ask him outright why he's shutting you and Matt out all of a sudden.'

Freya squirmed in her seat and worry lines creased her brow. 'I don't know . . . what if he gets cross with me?'

'Why would he? You haven't done anything wrong. And you know Ben – he absolutely adores you.'

'Do you think so?'

'Yes, absolutely!' Charlotte could feel herself warming to her theme. 'And you never know, he might have a perfectly rational explanation that will put your mind at rest and then you can reassure Matt that it's just a temporary blip and things will be back to normal soon.'

Freya reached across the table and took Charlotte's hand in hers. 'Oh God, I miss you so much, Charlie. We both do.'

'I miss you guys, too.' Charlotte swallowed hard, afraid she might cry.

'Is there anyone on the scene at all?' Freya dropped her hand and changed the subject, as if sensing that Charlotte might be wobbling.

Charlotte wrinkled her nose and shook her head. 'No, not really. I don't think I'm in the right frame of mind to have a relationship at the moment, anyway, so it's probably no bad thing.'

'No, maybe not.' Freya looked suddenly wistful and smiled. 'Although it would be great if you could find someone nice and we could have a whole new foursome.'

Charlotte tried to smile, but found that the corners of her mouth refused to turn upwards. 'The trouble is that I found someone nice and dumped him, like the complete bloody idiot I am. Now all I can think is that there'll never be anyone as good as him again. '

Freya shook her head. 'I'm not going to say that I always thought there was something lacking in your relationship with Ben because I didn't. But for you to have broken up with him when you did, when he was on the verge of proposing . . .'

Charlotte spluttered on her wine and her eyes widened. 'What?'

Freya's cheeks flushed slightly and she nodded. 'Yes . . . I thought you knew? He didn't exactly make a secret of it.'

Charlotte looked away, thinking. Yes, she probably *did* know, and maybe that's what had made her get cold feet so suddenly. It was the enormity of it all.

'So, what I'm saying,' Freya continued, 'is that you obviously did think there was something not quite right. Don't be too hard on yourself, Charlie, because maybe, just maybe, you did the right thing for you.'

Charlotte so wanted to believe her. To think that she had been unhappy and that the relationship had run its course. But she knew deep down that it hadn't and that she had just had a panic about the future and wanted to clear her head. Now it was too late and whatever she did, she couldn't turn back time and make everything right again.

CHAPTER EIGHT

Freya pulled her fitted leather jacket a little tighter around her body. It was a surprisingly chilly day for early March and she stamped her feet to try to warm up her feet inside her ankle boots, as she scanned the lunchtime crowds for Ben's familiar dark head. As he was usually a few inches taller than everyone else around him, she had thought that he'd be easier to spot, but she hadn't caught sight of him yet and was beginning to worry that maybe she'd missed him.

She was just contemplating giving up, when he appeared, head down and his hands stuffed deep in to the pockets of his coat, which looked considerably warmer than hers.

'Ben!' Freya stepped into his path and gave a nervous wave.

Ben's eyes widened in surprise and he pulled up sharply. 'Hey, Freya! What a lovely surprise!' He held his arms out widely and pulled her into a hug.

Freya allowed herself to be drawn into his embrace and held on to him for what she knew was a fraction too long. She could feel the tears pricking her eyes as she felt a wave of longing. The aching familiarity of him was so strong that, for the first time, she realized how painfully she had borne his absence and truly understood how Matt must have been feeling.

'What are you doing here?' Ben gently extricated himself from her arms and shoved his hands back into the pockets of his overcoat, shuffling from foot to foot.

Freya took a deep breath. 'I wanted to see you. You haven't been returning our calls and our texts aren't getting through . . .' She hesitated. 'I just wanted to make sure you were OK.'

Ben frowned. 'Yeah, everything's fine. Look, I was just about to grab a sandwich, do you want to join me?'

Freya beamed. 'I'd love to.'

They headed for a café near Ben's office and found a table. 'What can I get you?' he asked, gesturing towards the counter.

'Oh, thanks, Ben. A cheese and ham toastie would be lovely.'

Ben smiled. 'Of course. I should have remembered. I'll have the same.'

Freya watched him ordering and paying for their food, trying to analyse whether there was anything different about him. He looked a bit more tired and there were shadows under his eyes but that was understandable with a new baby. Other than that, he looked pretty much the same as he ever had.

He carried a tray over to their small, round, marble table. 'Dinner is served!'

Freya laughed. 'And very nice it looks, too. Thank you.'

Ben took a seat opposite her and picked up his toastie, taking a huge bite. 'Mmmm, I haven't had one of these for ages. Bloody lovely!'

'Yep,' Freya agreed, as they chewed in comfortable silence. 'So, how is Elodie?'

Ben smiled, as crumbs spilled out of his mouth and he wiped them with a napkin. 'She's adorable. Really gorgeous.'

'Got any photos?'

'Hang on.' Ben finished his toastie with one final huge bite and wiped his hands on his napkin before fumbling for his phone. He frowned slightly as he scrolled through his pictures, until he found one he liked and handed it to Freya.

On the screen was a picture of Bella looking serenely at the camera, clutching a beautiful baby girl with a shock of black hair to her chest. 'Oh my, Ben, she is so, so lovely. They both are.' As she looked back at the screen, a message notification flashed up, blocking the photo.

Bella: *Where the fuck are you?*

'Oh! You've got a message,' she said, feeling embarrassed for him as she handed back the phone.

Ben raised his eyebrows in surprise and took the phone from her. He read the message and flushed slightly.

'Is everything OK, Ben?' Freya asked gently, knowing that she needed to seize the opportunity.

'Of course. Why wouldn't it be?' Ben was immediately on the defensive, his eyes flickering from side to side.

'It's just that . . . well, we haven't seen you. Matt's called you several times and you haven't called him back. We haven't even met Elodie yet. I just wondered if there's something going on?'

Ben's face darkened. 'Is that why you ambushed me?'

Freya sighed. 'Well, yes. How the hell else are we supposed to see you if you won't return our calls? If you change your mobile number and don't let us have the new one?'

Ben's eyes held hers for a moment, before sliding away. 'I didn't even know you'd called . . .'

'Didn't Bella mention it?'

'No.' Ben's chewed the inside of his lip. 'But she's been a bit busy lately . . . it probably just slipped her mind.'

Freya's chest quivered with irritation. 'Really? Only Matt's called quite a few times. He's so hurt, Ben.'

'For fuck's sake, he's not five years old!' Ben's cheek pulsed and he tutted to himself.

'OK.' Freya stood up, her metal chair scraping on the tiled floor as she pushed it backwards. 'I don't know what's going on with you, Ben, but you're behaving like a dick. Frankly, I don't give a damn if you don't want to see me but the least you can do is give Matt a call back.'

Ben looked up at her in surprise. 'I will!' he snapped. He ran his hand through his hair and sighed. 'It's just a bit hectic right now.' He reached out to take her arm. 'Don't go like this, Frey, I'm sorry. Stay and finish your toastie.'

Freya hesitated, before sitting back down. 'Lots of sleepless nights, is it?'

Ben nodded. 'Yeah. She's a good baby but they're bloody hard work, you know?' He gave a small, apologetic laugh. 'I love being a dad but I hadn't expected it to be so . . . *draining*. Honestly, it's just relentless and the lack of sleep does get to you.'

'I can only imagine.' Freya could feel herself softening towards him again, glad that he was opening up a bit.

'Bella's coping brilliantly. But it gets lonely for her, at home on her own all day. She's desperate for some adult company and for someone else to take over by the time I walk through the door. No matter how busy I've been at work, it's nothing compared to the drudgery of looking after a baby all day.'

Freya smiled sympathetically. 'I'm sure. But I bet your mum

and Bella's mum have been a permanent fixture. That must be a big help.'

'Hmmm.' Ben looked away, clearly embarrassed. 'Bella's mum is around a bit but my mum's keeping her distance. I think she's worried about being seen as the archetypal interfering mother-in-law.'

'Jo would never be that!'

Ben pulled a wry face. 'Not sure Bella would agree with you there.'

A tiny alarm bell rang somewhere in a distant corner of Freya's mind. 'Do they not get on then?' she ventured tentatively, wary of setting him off again.

'No.' Ben shook his head slightly. 'There was . . . there was a bit of an argument at Christmas. Bella overheard Mum describing her as an attention-seeking little madam.'

Freya tried to keep a straight face. It sounded like a perfect description of Bella to her. 'Ouch.'

Ben laughed. 'Yeah, you could say that. It didn't make for a very happy family Christmas, put it that way. We headed back to London there and then and we haven't seen her since.'

Freya gasped. 'So she still hasn't seen the baby?'

Ben suddenly looked desperately sad. 'No.'

Freya was so shocked it took her a few moments to find her voice. 'But . . . that must have been devastating for her. When is she going to see her?'

'I'm not entirely sure. Bella's insistent she won't let her visit but she won't let me take Elodie to see her alone either. Don't think she trusts me to look after her by myself!' He tried to laugh again but it seemed to dry in his throat.

After another stunned silence, as she tried to digest his words,

Freya shook her head and spoke: 'Well, you obviously can't carry on like this. Why doesn't Jo just apologize?'

Ben shrugged. 'She's tried. She's phoned, sent a card, sent a text, but I think Bella was so hurt that she refuses to accept it.'

Freya frowned. 'Poor Jo.'

'Poor Bella, you mean?'

'No, actually, I don't.' Freya paused. 'It's really unlike Jo to have said something like that. What was the reason?'

Ben shrugged. 'She doesn't seem to need a reason. She's never liked Bella.'

Freya shook her head fiercely. 'No! That's not true, Ben. Your mum is one of the nicest people I've ever met and she's never said anything to suggest that she doesn't like Bella. Something must have caused her to snap like that. Was she under a lot of stress at the time?'

Ben pursed his lips, as if he was considering whether to say what he was about to say. 'I suppose so. Emma had had a car crash and . . .'

'Oh my God!' Freya interrupted him, clamping her hand over her mouth. 'Is she OK?'

'Yeah, she's fine.' Ben batted her concern away with a wave of his hand. 'Bit of a bump on her head and she was pretty shaken up.'

'Well then!' Freya cried. 'Of course that's the reason. It's so out of character for Jo. Surely Bella can understand that? Especially now she's got a little girl of her own! She must understand how upsetting it is for your child to be injured, however old they are . . .?'

'I don't know.' Ben sounded weary. 'She doesn't seem to be in the mood for reconciliation anyway, so there's not much I can do, is there?'

'Oh come on, Ben! Are you honestly going to let one little comment come between you and your lovely mum? I just don't understand it – you've always been so close.' Freya could feel the tears threatening on Jo's behalf. She just knew how devastated Jo would be feeling, especially to have been kept away from her first grandchild. It seemed so cruel.

'Oh God, I know, it's just that I feel a bit torn. Obviously, my loyalty has to be with Bella and Elodie right now.'

Freya tried not to let her irritation show. 'Of course it does. But you shouldn't be put in a position where you have to choose between your mum and your wife. There's room for both of them, surely?'

Ben exhaled loudly. 'To be honest, it's not worth the grief I'll get.'

Freya could feel her eyes narrowing, despite trying to keep her expression neutral. 'That's why you've cut us off, too, isn't it? Because Bella doesn't like us?'

'No!' The defiance flashed back into Ben's eyes.

Freya shook her head sadly. 'I should have known, after the last time we came round and she didn't turn up.'

'There was a very good reason for that and it had nothing to do with you coming round.'

'Really?' Freya couldn't hide her scepticism.

'Yes!' Ben shot back crossly.

'OK, if you say so.'

There was a long, awkward pause. Around them, the café was filling up with lunchtime customers and the sound of clattering plates ricocheted from wall to wall with a jarring, discordant beat.

'Look, Ben,' Freya began, wondering how far she could push

it. 'All I'm saying is, it seems a real shame that you've suddenly stopped seeing your family and friends, when we were always so close. It was never like this when you were with Charlotte . . .' She paused, knowing she was stepping onto dangerous territory.

'Oh yeah, and look what all those years of being with Charlotte did for me!' Ben snapped. '*She* dumped *me*, remember!'

'I know. Believe me, she regrets that now.'

Ben bit his lip, and looked out of the window onto the pavement beyond, where dozens of pedestrians danced balletically around one another, hurrying on their way. 'Does she?'

'Yes, of course she does. Her dad dying affected her really badly and she just had a bit of a panic. By the time she realized what she'd done, it was too late.'

'How is she?' Ben continued to stare out of the window as he spoke, trying to feign indifference.

'She's OK.'

'Is she . . . is she still single?'

Freya smiled. 'Yes. Believe it or not, you're quite a hard act to follow, Ben Gordon.'

Ben gave a hollow laugh. 'I thought she would end up with that guy, Luke, the one she worked with. She certainly talked about him a lot, just before we broke up.'

Freya shook her head. 'No, they were just friends. Still are. He's with someone else.'

Ben nodded and looked back at Freya. 'It doesn't matter now anyway.'

'No,' Freya agreed. 'And she's happy for you that you've moved on and that you and Bella have had a baby. She knows how much you wanted kids.'

'Yeah, I think that was part of the problem. I did, she didn't.'

'It's not quite that simple. It wasn't that she didn't want kids, I think she just wanted to be absolutely sure that you were the right one to have them with.'

'Yeah, I get that. Oh well, it obviously wasn't meant to be or it wouldn't have gone wrong, would it?' He stood up. 'Anyway, I really need to be getting back to work.'

Freya stood up too and they walked out of the café together. 'It's lovely to see you, Ben, I've missed you.'

Ben reached down to hug her. 'You too.'

'And I know things are busy but will you give Matt a call when you get a chance?'

Ben nodded. 'Sure. 'Bye, Freya.'

''Bye,' she called after him, realizing as he was swallowed up by the crowd that she should have asked for his new number. As she watched him go, already on his phone, presumably to explain his whereabouts to a furious Bella, she had a horrible feeling she wouldn't be seeing him again for a very long time.

CHAPTER NINE

'So, what were you doing today that was so important you ignored my calls?' Bella's dark eyes blazed with a barely concealed fury.

'I didn't ignore your calls.' Ben tried to eat his risotto but his mouth felt dry and it tasted a lot like cardboard. The atmosphere since he had walked through the door an hour ago had become increasingly icy. He knew if he told Bella the truth about his whereabouts when she was trying to get hold of him at lunchtime, it would only make things worse. 'I was at work, Bella. I can't just drop everything and take a personal call every time my phone rings. It's unprofessional and it will get me into trouble. We can't afford for me to lose this job.'

Bella threw down her own fork with a clatter that made them both jump. 'But what if it's urgent? What if it's something to do with Elodie?'

'Well, then of course I will drop everything and come running. But it wasn't about Elodie, was it?'

Bella's bottom lip started to tremble and Ben could feel himself physically having to squash down the impatience that was rising in his chest. Every time he even slightly challenged her, she either threw a tantrum or cried. It was becoming increasingly wearing.

But, he reminded himself sternly, she was a new mother and her emotions and hormones were running amok. He had to be patient with her. 'Come on, sweetheart. Don't get upset. You are doing a fantastic job with our gorgeous baby. I'm so proud of you.'

Bella gave him a watery smile and wiped her eyes. 'Thank you. I'm sorry for calling so often, it's just that I get so bloody lonely sometimes. It's really, really hard.'

Ben reached out and took her hand in his. 'Of course it is. I completely understand, darling. But . . . You don't *have* to be lonely.'

Bella took her hand away and sat up a bit straighter, as if anticipating what he was about to say.

'I'm sure Mum is desperate to see Elodie and she'd be so happy to help out. To give you a bit of a break.'

Bella pursed her lips and looked away.

Ben took a deep breath. 'Why don't we invite her round? Come on, Bella, otherwise it's a bit like cutting off your nose to spite your face.'

Ben tried to read her expression. The fact that she hadn't immediately jumped down his throat gave him a tiny scintilla of hope.

'Maybe,' she began, blinking slowly. 'But you have to be here, too. I don't want to see her on my own, just in case . . .' She left her words hanging in the air.

Ben nodded furiously, not caring what Bella was insinuating. 'Of course I'll be here. How about this weekend? Shall I ask them to come here then?'

'Them? Invite your dad, too?'

Ben frowned. 'Well, yes. I'm sure he's as desperate to meet his first grandchild as Mum is.'

Bella looked away again, her expression unreadable. Finally, she shrugged nonchalantly. 'I suppose so.'

Ben felt giddy with elation. It hadn't struck him until now how much the strain of being estranged from his family was affecting him. He missed them desperately and seeing Freya had reminded him that they weren't monsters and that his mum had been under huge stress the day she snapped at Bella. And a tiny part of him also felt that maybe his mum had had a point. Bella had behaved like a spoilt child at Christmas with her strange behaviour.

He finished his dinner, trying to eat as slowly as possible so as not to look too eager to get to his phone. 'Why don't you go and have a relaxing bath while I clear up?' he suggested, not wanting her to overhear his conversation. 'I'll listen out for Elodie.'

She hesitated, before nodding. 'OK, that would be nice. Thanks.'

Ben busied himself tidying up until he heard her turning off the taps and climbing into the bath.

'Mum, it's me,' he said, as soon as Jo answered.

'Oh, Ben!' Ben could hear the tears in Jo's voice. There was a long pause before she spoke again, having composed herself slightly. 'Sweetheart, it is so lovely to hear from you. How are you, my darling?'

Ben suddenly thought he might cry. He took a second to compose himself before he spoke. 'Good, Mum. I'm really good.'

'And Elodie? How is she?' There was a nervousness in Jo's voice that made Ben feel instantly ashamed. This was Jo's first grandchild and she was clearly scared to even ask about her.

'Well, that's why I'm calling, actually. We wondered if you and Dad would like to come and visit this weekend? Say, Saturday.'

There was a short pause before Jo answered. 'We'd love to, of course we would. But is it OK with Bella? I don't want to upset her.'

'Of course! She'd love to see you too.' Ben almost choked on the lie but there was no other answer he could give.

'Oh, well, in that case we'd be delighted to come. Thank you. What sort of time?'

Ben tried to remember the details of the routine Bella had got Elodie into but he couldn't recall the exact times. 'Um, about midday? We'll do lunch.'

'Oh how lovely!' Jo sounded thrilled, causing Ben to feel even more guilty. 'We'll see you then.'

Ben hung up, wishing he had suggested it to Bella much sooner. His parents were good people and it wasn't fair to have punished them for a slip of the tongue when they were very stressed.

'Midday?' Bella's voice cut through Ben's thoughts and he spun around to find her watching him with a deep frown creasing her smooth forehead.

'Yes. What's wrong with that?' Ben's heart immediately sank again. He should have known it wouldn't be straightforward.

Bella rolled her eyes theatrically. 'Oh, nothing, except that Elodie will be asleep. I thought they were coming to see her?'

Ben sighed. 'They *are* coming to see her. Surely it won't do any harm to keep her up a little bit longer for once?'

'Oh for God's sake, Ben!' Bella spat. 'That's typical of you. You aren't the one who's worked your backside off to get her into her routine. I'm not wrecking all my hard work just to suit you.'

'Fine!' Ben snapped. 'Then we'll have lunch first and they can see her when she wakes up.'

Bella tipped her head to one side and put her hands on her hips. 'Well, you needn't think I'm cooking lunch. I've got enough to do, thank you very much, without having to entertain your parents.'

Ben could feel his temper starting to rise. She was so bloody unreasonable sometimes. And having broken the deadlock with his parents, he was suddenly desperate to see them. He couldn't let her ruin it. 'I'll do the cooking,' he cajoled, his jaw tight with tension. 'You can sit and chat to them.'

'Oh yes, that's a good idea, because we get on so well.' Bella gave a haughty toss of her head.

Ben walked over to her and pulled her into an embrace. Her body was stiff and unyielding. 'Please, Bella, don't turn this into a feud. They're my parents and they're Elodie's grandparents. I don't want them to become strangers.'

He felt Bella soften slightly as he spoke and she lifted her face to look at him, reminding him just how truly beautiful she was. 'I'm sorry, Ben. I just . . . feel that your mum doesn't like me and it's really hurtful.'

'She does like you.' Ben tried to quell the urge to tell her that her own behaviour had been far more hurtful towards his mum, especially keeping her away from her first grandchild. 'So don't go looking for insults and slights. Just be yourself and they will love you as much as I do.'

Bella smiled, immediately lighting up her delicate, heart-shaped face. 'I love you, too. I'm just so tired all the time. How about we get an early night?'

Ben grinned, all irritation instantly forgotten and feeling a surge of love for his gorgeous wife. 'There was a time when that would have meant something else entirely. And do you know what? Even though I know you're only talking about going to sleep, I can't think of anything I'd love more.'

'Who says I'm only talking about going to sleep?' Bella gave him a seductive look over her shoulder as she took his hand and pulled him towards the bedroom.

CHAPTER TEN

'Gosh, I'm so nervous that my hands are sweating!' Jo shook her head and tried to laugh but found that she couldn't. 'It's ridiculous, isn't it?'

Peter glanced in the rear-view mirror, before pulling out and overtaking an ancient campervan that was dawdling along the dual carriageway in front of them. 'I'd say it's perfectly understandable, given the way she's behaved.'

Jo shot him a grateful look. She should never have doubted it, but she was pathetically relieved that he hadn't blamed her for the rift.

After Bella and Ben had stormed out, she had spent the whole of Christmas Day crying. Emma had more or less passed out on the sofa, having drunk half a bottle of whisky to alleviate the shock of her accident, while Peter had finished preparing a lunch that none of them wanted, leaving Jo to sob into her wine glass.

'It'll be OK,' Peter had reassured her, although the tiny muscle pulsating in his cheek had given the lie to his words.

'It won't!' Jo wailed. 'She's won, Peter. She wanted him all to herself and now she's got him. I can't believe I thought we'd struck lucky with her because she wouldn't want to take Ben away from us – how wrong could I have been! If only I hadn't opened my big bloody mouth.'

Peter's own mouth had set in a hard, straight line. 'It wouldn't have made any difference. If it wasn't that, it would have been something else. She was just waiting for her moment.'

Jo burst into tears again. 'But why? What have we done to her to make her hate us?'

Peter shook his head. He had a look of cold fury in his eyes. 'Who knows?'

Jo blew her nose. 'And you were being so extra nice to her, too.'

'I was being nice to her because I knew she was waiting for us to make a wrong move. I was determined not to give her the ammunition.'

It all made sense now, the non-alcoholic mulled wine and the over-enthusiastic welcome. 'But then you didn't need to give her the ammunition – I did it for you.'

Jo covered her face with her tissue, letting it absorb the tears that refused to stop falling.

Peter put his heavy, reassuring hands on her heaving shoulders. 'It was bad luck, darling. She caught you at a particularly bad moment.'

'You don't blame me then?' Jo looked up at him through her swimming eyes.

Peter gave her a tired, worried smile. 'Of course I don't. I could never blame you for anything.'

'What the hell are we going to do though, Peter? I can't bear the thought of losing Ben.'

Peter shook his head. 'We won't lose him. We just have to

wait. She'll come round, eventually. Mark my words, once the baby arrives everything else will be forgotten.'

But it had taken so much longer than any of them had ever imagined. Jo had sent a card apologizing for what she said, as well as texts and calls but they all went unacknowledged. When Elodie was born, all they received from Ben was a short text telling them her name and weight and confirming that everything was OK.

Both Peter and Jo had called his mobile number, which seemed to be no longer in use. Emma had also tried repeatedly without success, which hurt Jo far more than their refusal to have anything to do with her and Peter. Emma was as bewildered and perplexed as her parents but as she was travelling a lot for work, she didn't have as much time to dwell on it as Jo did.

Day after day, Jo clung to her phone, praying for it to ring. She felt as though someone had taken her heart and wrenched it out of her chest. The cold fingers of fear that she really might never see her darling boy again tightened their grip with every passing week.

She thought about calling Matt, reasoning that any information, even second-hand, would be preferable to the deafening silence they were currently enduring. But as she began to dial his number, she was overwhelmed with shame and embarrassment. What if Matt knew about the row she'd had with Bella and had taken her side? She felt so fragile that she didn't think she could take another barrage of criticism.

So she waited, trying to distract herself with her voluntary work at the local hospice and consoling herself that while her life was something of a struggle right now, at least she had a life.

These poor people were nearing the end of theirs and it did at least help to put her own problems into perspective.

If anything, Peter took the estrangement even harder than she did. He and Ben had always been extremely close and he seemed to be finding it almost impossible to process why his only son would cut them off so abruptly. He wasn't sleeping, he had lost weight and his blood pressure had shot up. Jo knew it was all stress-related and yet she was utterly helpless to do anything about it. Only a call from Ben would put things right.

By the time the invitation to visit came, she had almost given up hope. She was at home one evening, staring unseeingly at a drama on the television that she was only vaguely follow-ing, when her mobile rang. She glanced at the screen and did a double-take as his home number flashed up. Once upon a time it was a mundane, sometimes even unwelcome sight. Now, it was as if she had won the lottery. Almost not daring to believe it, she answered the call. Hearing his voice after so long brought instant tears to her eyes, especially as he sounded so normal, as if everything was just as it ever was.

And now here they were, on their way to visit them for the very first time since Elodie was born. Jo ran her hands over her jeans, hoping they wouldn't still be sweating when she held her. It was so daft, to worry about how to hold a baby when she had managed to bring up two children of her own quite happily. But she knew her every move would be under scrutiny and she couldn't afford to make any more slip-ups.

They pulled up outside the red brick Victorian block that housed Ben's flat. Peter turned off the ignition and turned towards Jo. 'Well, here goes . . .'

Jo nodded, not trusting herself to speak, reassured that Peter was obviously as nervous as she was. She gathered the flowers and presents from the boot before making their way to the front door. Just as Peter was about to ring the bell, the door swung open and Ben was in front of them.

'Hi, Mum, hi, Dad.' He hesitated before reaching out to give Peter a hug. 'You've lost weight, Dad, are you OK?'

Peter smiled, although it didn't reach his eyes, and nodded. 'I am now.'

It always made Jo feel emotional when she saw her husband and son embrace and today even more so, as it seemed to hold so much more meaning. 'Hello, darling, these are for Bella – and Elodie.' Jo thrust the bag of presents and flowers towards Ben, feeling awkward and shy.

Ben grinned. 'Thanks, Mum, come on in!'

They followed him into the flat, nervously looking around for Bella. 'Bella's just put Elodie down for her lunchtime nap,' Ben said, pre-empting the question. 'She'll be out in a minute.'

Jo exhaled as she sat down gingerly on the soft taupe sofa. Peter joined her. 'So . . . cup of tea?' Ben offered. They both nodded gratefully.

As he retreated to the kitchen, Jo looked up at Peter questioningly. He threw his hands in the air with a 'don't ask me' expression. She didn't dare speak, in case Bella overheard her. Eventually, Ben returned with two mugs of tea and placed them on the coffee table, before sitting down in the armchair. 'So . . . how have you been?' His voice was slightly higher than usual.

'Fine . . .' Jo began, but Peter interrupted her.

'Not great – we've been wondering when we'd finally get to meet Elodie.' His words came out in a torrent, as if he had been waiting a long time for them to spill out.

'Peter . . .' Jo reached out and touched his leg but he silenced her with his hand.

'No, Jo.' He fixed Ben with his steely gaze. 'I want to know why you haven't been in touch. Have you any idea how upset your mother's been? How upset I've been, for that matter?' His voice caught as he finished speaking and for a horrible moment, Jo thought he might actually cry. She had never seen him like this before, almost shaking with pent-up emotion.

Ben's face reddened and he swallowed hard. 'I'm sorry.' He looked down as he composed himself. 'We've been so busy with the baby. Time ran away from me.'

'Rubbish!' Peter spat. 'You forget that we've had two children ourselves and yes, it's hard work, but it's also possible to find time to make a bloody phone-call! How could you have left it for so long? Do you have any idea how hurtful that was?'

His face by now almost puce, Ben opened his mouth to reply.

'It was because of me,' said Bella, who had appeared silently at the door.

Jo and Peter both swung around to look at her in surprise. Over the distance of the past few months, Jo had re-imagined her daughter-in-law as some kind of monster, with evil eyes and a snarling mouth. Yet here she was, looking serene and pretty, her slim figure showing no sign of a recent pregnancy in her skinny jeans and fitted shirt.

Bella stepped into the room and faced them. 'I didn't want Ben to contact you. I'm sorry. I was just so hurt by what happened at Christmas and . . .'

'Of course you were!' Relief made Jo gush as she leaped to her feet. She reached out to hug Bella but thought better of it when Bella wrapped her arms defensively around her body.

'I am so sorry for what I said, Bella, it was in the heat of the moment and I was feeling very stressed after Emma's accident . . .' Jo tailed off, unsure how to continue.

Bella nodded and adopted a stoic expression. 'It's fine. Let's forget about it.'

Jo nodded. 'Thank you. How are you, Bella? You look truly amazing! I can't believe how quickly you got your figure back.'

Bella smiled. 'Apparently my mum was the same with me. Lucky genes, I guess. She says Elodie's identical to me as a baby, so hopefully she's inherited them, too.'

Jo tried not to think about Elodie's other grandmother having already spent lots of time with her, presumably bonding with her before Jo had even clapped eyes on her. 'And what's she like? Elodie, I mean? I can't wait to see her.'

Bella beamed, lighting up her lovely face. 'She's perfect. She'll be up in a little while but you can have a peep at her if you like?'

Bella may as well have told Jo that she had just deposited a million pounds into her bank account, she felt so elated. 'I'd love to!'

She tiptoed behind Bella, taking care not to make any noise as she followed her into the baby's bedroom. Jo's eyes took a few moments to adjust to the gloomy light as she made her way over to the white wooden cot in the corner. Elodie was lying on her back, her tiny hands clasped into fists either side of her head, as if she was cheering in her sleep. She had a shock of soft, downy dark hair and a perfect rosebud mouth that was slightly open as she breathed in and out, causing her chest to rise and fall in her snow-white babygro. Jo could feel the tears welling but she fought them back. 'She's so lovely,' she told Bella. 'And she looks so much like you.'

Bella followed her gaze and smiled. 'Thank you. And yes, I think she's lovely too but I'm a bit biased.'

'You're allowed to be. You're her mum,' Jo whispered, greedily drinking in one last look before leaving the room.

After the awkwardness of the first few minutes, the mood of tension soon lifted. Ben prepared lunch while they sat at the table in the kitchen, chatting and laughing. In complete contrast to what Jo had been expecting, Bella's demeanour could not have been more welcoming or friendly. Unlike at Christmas, she chatted easily and laughed readily.

'And how has Ben been looking after you?' Jo asked Bella, beaming with pride as he dished up a delicious-looking lasagne.

Bella seemed to think about it for a few seconds before she answered. 'He's been amazing. But he works such long hours. I think we might need to rethink.'

Ben frowned as he scooped up a forkful of lasagne. 'Rethink what?'

Bella smiled. 'Your job. It's not even as if you love it that much. A fresh start somewhere out of London might be good for all of us.'

'You never mentioned it before.' Ben had flushed slightly but his tone was still light-hearted. 'What's brought this on?'

Jo stole a glance at Peter, whose eyes had narrowed.

'Oh, I don't know. Maybe hearing your mum and dad's stories about you growing up in Suffolk. It sounds idyllic. I'd like Elodie to have that sort of upbringing.'

'What was your childhood like, Bella?' Jo put down her fork and took a sip of wine. 'I'm not sure I've ever heard you talk about it.'

'That's because I don't want to bore everyone rigid. It was as dull as ditchwater.' Bella rolled her eyes and exhaled. 'There's honestly nothing to tell.'

'I'm sure that's not true,' Jo persisted. 'Where did you live again?'

Bella put a hand to her ear and grinned. 'I think I can hear a certain little someone stirring!' She stood up and left the room, leaving Jo straining to listen. She was pretty sure she hadn't heard anything. But her stomach started to turn butterflies, as she waited to meet her grandchild for the first time.

Moments later, Bella padded into the room, carrying a sleepy-looking bundle. 'Here she is!'

Peter and Jo stood up and automatically moved to stand either side of Bella so that they could take a proper look. 'Oh my word, she's just perfect!' Jo cooed. 'Isn't she, Peter?'

She looked across at Peter, who was gazing at Elodie with nothing short of awe. 'She certainly is,' he breathed. 'Can I hold her?'

'Of course.' Bella gently lowered Elodie into Peter's arms, where she lay peering up at him with a surprised look on her face.

'What do you think then, Dad? Do you think she looks like me?' Ben came over and tickled Elodie's stomach, causing her to squirm and smile at the same time, eliciting delighted 'oohs' and 'ahhs' from Jo.

'Not really, son.' Peter pulled his eyes away from Elodie and looked up at Ben. 'She's far more beautiful than you!'

They all laughed and Jo sighed happily. It had been a long wait but now that it was over and everything was back to normal, she could tell herself that it had all been worth it.

'Well, that couldn't have gone better,' she told Peter, as they drove away from Bella and Ben's flat a couple of hours later. All the misery and angst she had bottled up over the past months was completely gone. Bella had been a different person to the one who visited them at Christmas and Jo concluded that it must have been her hormones affecting her personality back then. Some women just hated being pregnant and it dramatically changed the way they behaved. Bella must be one of those women, she decided, because her demeanour and friendliness towards them today could not have been lovelier or more welcoming.

'No,' Peter agreed. Already, she could see that some of the tension had drained away from his face, leaving him looking a lot more like his old self.

'What did you make of Bella? I thought she was lovely.'

Peter paused for a minute before speaking. 'She was friendly enough.'

'But?'

Peter sighed. 'Nothing. Ignore me.'

'You've never been sure about her.'

'No.'

'Why do you think that is? We know she can be tricky at times after what happened at Christmas, obviously, but you didn't take to her from the start. What made you dislike her?'

Peter shrugged. 'It's not that I dislike her, exactly. We don't know anything about her. She always seems to deflect the conversation if you ask her any questions. Like when you asked her where she grew up and she pretended that the baby had woken up. I didn't believe that for a second. I think she just wanted to change the subject.'

Jo thought about it for a moment. 'Maybe she's ashamed or embarrassed. Maybe they didn't have any money and she doesn't want to admit it to us in case we think less of her. We're not short of money and Ben was privately educated. Perhaps she just feels a little bit inferior and doesn't want to be reminded of her past.'

'Hmm. Maybe.' Peter stole a glance at Jo. 'Do you think Ben seems happy?'

Jo could tell that it was a loaded question. Clearly Peter didn't. 'He seems a bit tentative. Like he's walking on eggshells. But then, she is a new mother and her moods are probably a bit unpredictable. I'm sure I was the same when I had Emma.'

Peter reached across and put his hand on Jo's thigh. 'Actually, you weren't. You took motherhood completely in your stride. And you didn't have anyone to help you. It made me love you even more.'

Jo smiled. 'Thank you. Oh, but it was so wonderful to see Elodie, wasn't it? She's the image of Bella.'

'She certainly is,' Peter said with a sigh.

'She's absolutely beautiful. I'm just relieved that we got to see her. There was a time there when I wondered if we ever would.'

'Me too. It was a huge overreaction.'

Jo shrugged. She didn't really care why Bella had finally decided to stop treating them like pariahs. She was just glad that she had.

CHAPTER ELEVEN

The profile of her face was so achingly familiar and yet so strangely out of context that it caused Ben's stomach to flip. She was sitting at a table across the restaurant, having lunch with another woman who Ben recognized as a TV presenter.

As if she could feel him watching her, Charlotte turned and met his gaze. She frowned very slightly, as he'd seen her do so many times in the past when she was concentrating on something, before her face broke into a wide smile of recognition. She said something to the woman she was with, before standing up and walking over to Ben's table.

She hesitated as she reached him and he stood, the table between them acting as a barricade to any kind of embrace. In the end, he reached out and touched her arm. 'Hello, Charlotte.'

He thought the smile she gave him in return contained more than a hint of sadness about it. 'Hello, Ben. This is a nice surprise. What brings you to this neck of the woods?'

'Change of direction, in lots of different ways.' Ben motioned for her to sit down. 'Take a seat, my guest has been held up.'

Charlotte hesitated, glancing back towards her own lunch companion, who was chatting happily on her mobile phone.

'OK, but I'd better not be long.' She sat down and smiled at him again. 'You look well.'

'So do you.' Ben thought she had lost too much weight and that it had given her a gaunt appearance but decided against saying so. 'How are you?

Charlotte nodded. 'Good. Really good. I've just moved, actually. Lucy got so fed up with me kipping in her spare room, she was very helpful in finding me somewhere!'

Ben laughed. 'And are you living alone?' He faltered slightly before adding, 'Or are you sharing?'

Charlotte's eyes flickered with uncertainty. 'I'm, er . . . sharing. We've found a nice house that's a bit further out on the Surrey border but it's worth the extra travel to get more space.'

'Oh yes? And who are you sharing with?'

She sighed. 'With a guy called Luke. I work with him.'

Ben nodded slowly, wondering why he felt so shaken by her words. He had always wondered about Luke, but hearing her actually admit that they had moved in together still gave him a pang of longing. 'And work's going well?'

'Yes, it is. I've been, well, since you and I, er, well, since I've been single, I've kind of thrown myself into it and it's paid off. I've been promoted and I'm looking after lots of different shows now. '

Ben smiled. 'That's great, Charlie, I'm pleased for you.'

'Thanks. And what about you? How are you finding married life and being a dad? Congratulations, by the way!' There was a forced jollity to Charlotte's words that made Ben cringe inwardly.

'It's great. Actually, it's a good job I ran into you, as I was going to get in touch, anyway. We're on the move too. We'll be selling the flat, so obviously I'll be making sure you get what's rightfully yours from the proceeds.'

The flat had soared in value since his mum and dad had bought it for him ten years previously and Bella was adamant that they would be able to afford something amazing if they moved out of London. She also seemed certain that his mum and dad would make up any shortfall, which he really didn't want. They had already been incredibly generous in buying him the flat in the first place and he wanted to show them that he could stand on his own two feet now that he was a husband and father. But Bella was also agitating for him to give up work to look after Elodie, as she wanted to throw herself into her career on her return from maternity leave, so maybe they would need some more help from his parents.

He hadn't yet dared broach the idea with Bella that Charlotte would be entitled to half of the money from the flat, having lived with him for ten years and contributed to the upkeep and decoration.

Charlotte looked aghast. 'I don't want anything, Ben. It's your flat, not mine.'

Ben tried not to compare Bella's attitude that she was fully entitled to everything and more, when they had only lived together for a short time, to Charlotte's. 'It's only fair. You contributed plenty over the years.'

Charlotte's face softened. 'But I also walked away from it. That was my own stupid choice.'

Ben looked up sharply, his heart flipping at her words. 'Stupid?'

Charlotte nodded and sighed. 'Yep, stupid. I panicked, Ben. I needed some space and by the time I realized what a fool I was being, it was too late.'

Ben fleetingly allowed himself a moment imagining how different things would have been, if Charlotte had come back to him before he met Bella. But then, he thought, swatting the idea away, he would never have fallen in love with Bella. Would never have had Elodie, would never have been about to embark on a new adventure. No, the way things had turned out was obviously the way it was meant to be.

'I think everything happens for a reason, Charlie. You weren't happy with me . . .' He let his words hang in the air for a few seconds. 'Or you would never have left in the first place. And now you've moved on with Luke.'

'No!' Charlotte shook her head vehemently. 'No, it's not like that with me and Luke at all! We're just friends. He's got a girlfriend.'

Ben raised one eyebrow sceptically. 'Well, whatever. It doesn't matter anymore. It's got nothing to do with me.'

Charlotte's eyes filled with tears and Ben looked away, not wanting to be drawn into any kind of an emotional connection with her. He'd spent plenty of nights crying over her but she had still been adamant that she'd needed to leave. She hadn't seemed to give too much thought to the distress he was experiencing.

Charlotte wiped her eyes cursorily with the back of her hand and stood up. 'I'd better be getting back to my table . . .'

'Yes,' Ben stood up and faced her. 'Well, 'bye then, Charlie.'

Charlotte gazed at him for a split second too long. ''Bye Ben. Good luck with everything.'

Ben watched her walk back to her table, wondering what would happen if he ran after her and told her to run away with him. He had no doubt she would do it and it gave him a small sense of victory. But just then, his guest arrived and all thoughts of Charlie were firmly consigned to history.

CHAPTER TWELVE

Matt rang the familiar doorbell and looked down at Freya nervously. 'Ridiculous to be this nervous with one of my oldest mates.'

Freya nodded and bit her lip. 'I feel the same. Not sure what sort of welcome we're going to get, that's why.'

Eventually, the door swung open and Ben stood in front of them, looking harassed.

'Hey, mate!' Matt tried to ignore Ben's flustered demeanour and held up a carrier bag full of beer, wine and crisps. 'Good to see you. I've brought the usual supplies!

Ben smiled but the smile didn't reach his eyes. 'Uh, yeah. Look I'm really sorry, guys, it's not a great time . . .'

Matt and Freya exchanged glances. 'Oh! Sorry, mate, I must have got the date wrong.' Matt frowned. 'I thought we'd arranged today.'

'We did,' Freya cut in, fixing Ben with what Matt called her 'uh-oh' stare. He always knew he was in trouble when he saw it. 'What's the problem, Ben?' There was a steely edge to her voice that made Matt shudder inwardly.

Ben glanced over his shoulder nervously, before closing the

door a fraction more. 'Bella's not feeling too good.' His eyes flickered away from them as he spoke and he pursed his lips slightly.

'What's the matter with her?' Freya's tone suggested she didn't believe for a second that Bella was ill.

'Um,' Ben swallowed hard and looked up, as if hoping for inspiration from the sky. 'She's . . . er, she's just . . .'

'She's refusing to see us, isn't she?' Freya sounded furious.

'Freya!' Matt shuffled from foot to foot, feeling a mixture of embarrassment for his friend and sadness that he was allowing Bella to remove them from his life so effectively. A sudden wave of emotion passed over him. He loved Ben like a brother and it felt like a bereavement to lose him like this. In some ways it was worse than a bereavement because the person he'd lost was alive and well and standing in front of him, apparently happy to cut Matt out of his life for ever.

'I'm right, aren't I, Ben?' Freya's voice pierced Matt's thoughts.

Ben sighed and ran his hand through his hair. 'No, Freya, you're not right,' he said, in a weary, sing-song voice. 'She's just not very well.'

'How very convenient!'

Matt put a warning hand on Freya's arm but she shook him off crossly. 'Ever since you met her, Ben, she's been trying to cut you off from us. And your family . . .'

'She's fine with my family, actually,' Ben interrupted.

'Is she?' Freya stormed. 'Because that's not what you told me when we had lunch.'

Suddenly, Bella stepped into view behind Ben, glaring at the back of his head. 'Ben! Can you close the door, please, you're letting in a draught.'

'Hi, Bella, you look well?' Freya snapped, her voice sharp with sarcasm.

There was a tense silence, during which it seemed as if time stood still. Matt thought he could actually hear his own heart thumping, as he watched Bella's fine, delicate features harden. Her eyes narrowed and her chin jutted out slightly further as she moved from behind Ben. 'Actually, I'm not well,' she said defiantly, her expression challenging them to dispute her. 'Ben, close the door, please.'

Ben hesitated, before throwing a pleading glance in Matt and Freya's direction. 'I'm really sorry, guys. Let's rearrange for another time, eh?'

Matt nodded unhappily and began to turn away but Freya wasn't giving up without a fight. 'There won't be another time, Ben! Don't you see what she's doing? For Christ's sake, why don't you grow a pair? Matt is your oldest friend and you're treating him like shit! Shame on you!' She reached for Matt's hand and together they walked away, leaving Ben watching their retreating backs. As they reached the end of the path, the front door slammed with what sounded to Matt like a sickening finality.

They didn't speak as they walked towards the tube station, the leaden grey sky and the indecisive drizzle that fell half-heartedly, matching their gloomy mood. They gripped each other's hands for support, both in shock at what had just happened. Matt could feel Freya's concerned eyes watching him and he felt a sudden surge of love for her. She was so loyal, so easy-going, so *reasonable*, compared to the prickliness of Bella. With Ben apparently gone from his life, he would need her more than ever. He pulled her into an embrace as they stood on the station platform. 'I love you,' he whispered in her ear. 'Thank you for always being there for me.'

He could feel her nodding, before she pulled away from him. Her eyes were glassy with tears as she gazed up at him. 'I feel so sad for you, Matt. I know how hurt you must be.'

Matt swallowed down the lump in his throat and nodded. 'Part of me feels sorry for him. At least I've got you. He's only got her and she's just so . . . horrible.'

'And the baby,' Freya added. 'He's got Elodie, too, we need to remember that. Maybe having a child changes things and you just want to retreat into your own little family unit.'

'Would we be like that, though? I don't think so. We would want to share it all with our families, with our friends. She just seems to want to have him all to herself.'

Freya smiled. 'I don't think we'd be like that, either. But I suppose there's only one way to find out?'

Matt frowned. 'What do you mean?'

Freya swatted him playfully. 'Don't be so dim, Matt! I mean, why don't we have a baby?'

Matt grinned as realization dawned. He hadn't felt ready before. He'd been too preoccupied with his career, making money, enjoying himself. But looking down into Freya's open, trusting face, he suddenly wanted nothing more than to see himself reflected back in their child's eyes. 'OK,' he said. 'Let's get home and get started, shall we?'

CHAPTER THIRTEEN

Ben closed the door as Matt and Freya reached the end of the path. He paused for a split second, trying to collect his thoughts before turning around to face Bella, who he knew would be glowering at him. He could almost feel the steam coming off her in waves as her big, dark eyes blazed with fury.

'So you had lunch with Freya, did you?' She folded her arms. 'You obviously forgot to mention it.'

'I didn't forget to mention it, Bella. It was just that I knew how you'd react, so I deliberately didn't tell you. Anyway, it wasn't arranged. I just bumped into her and we had a sandwich, that's all. No big deal.'

Bella almost stamped her foot. 'No bloody big deal? You having lunch with another woman behind my back and moaning about me?'

Ben closed his eyes momentarily, suddenly so weary of everything and still reeling from the look on Matt's face as he sent him away. 'For a start, Freya is not "another woman". I have known her for so long that she's more like a sister. And I wasn't moaning about you.'

Bella stuck her bottom lip out. 'Then what did she mean about your family and me not being fine with them?'

Ben hesitated. 'It was just that she was a bit shocked that Mum and Dad hadn't seen the baby at that point.'

Bella's defiant expression faltered slightly. 'Why did you tell her?'

Ben sighed. 'Because she asked. Honestly, Bella, you're making a mountain out of a molehill here.'

'Well, I just don't like the thought of you talking about me behind my back. Anyway,' she continued, clearly keen to change the subject. 'I was obviously right about Freya and Matt not liking me. You heard the way she spoke to me.' The defiant expression was replaced by a triumphant one.

Ben thought, but didn't say, that Freya had been remarkably restrained by her standards. He wanted to go after them both, to apologize and to explain that seeing them just wasn't worth the hassle, nagging and upset that would result.

Before they arrived, Bella had thrown an enormous tantrum, screaming and crying that she was feeling ill and as usual, he was putting his mates before her and Elodie. No amount of reassurance and cajoling on his part could calm her down, as he kept one eye on the clock, knowing that they would be arriving any second and one eye on his hysterical wife. In the end he was left with no choice but to promise her that he would send them away, even though it had felt like a dagger through his heart to do it. He loved Matt. And he loved Freya, too. But Bella was determined that there wasn't room in his life for both them and her.

He ran his hand over his face. 'Well, they've gone now, so you can go back to bed and sleep off whatever lurgy you've picked up.'

Bella brightened instantly, all signs of her earlier tears and trauma now evaporated. 'No, it's fine,' she beamed. 'I feel much better now.'

The landline phone was ringing as Ben walked into the kitchen. Bella was sitting at the table, tapping on her mobile phone, while Elodie lay on the wooden floor in her baby gym, gurgling happily and grabbing at the various rattles and mirrors dangling above her.

'Why are you ignoring the phone, darling?' he said, as he snatched up the handset. He could see from the caller display that it was his mother calling. Bella gave a tiny smile but didn't reply. Ben sighed and pressed the 'answer' key. 'Hi, Mum, how are you?'

Jo's voice sounded muffled. 'Hi, sweetheart, I'm sorry to call you . . .'

'Don't be daft,' Ben frowned, sensing something bad was coming. 'Is everything all right?'

'No . . .' There was a pause as Jo gulped back a sob. 'Ben, I'm at the hospital. Your dad's had a heart attack.'

Ben's legs went weak and buckled under him. Sitting down abruptly on a kitchen chair, he tried to compute what Jo was saying. 'A heart attack?'

'Yes.' He heard Jo blow her nose on the other end of the line.

'Oh my God. How serious?' Ben stole a glance at Bella, who was watching him with an intense frown.

Jo burst into another bout of tears. 'I don't know but I think it might be really bad! Oh Ben, what the hell am I going to do?'

Ben swallowed back his own tears and sat up a bit straighter. This was not the time for him to crumple. He needed to be there for his mum. 'Right, don't worry, I will be there as soon as I can. Which hospital?'

'Ipswich.'

'OK. Get yourself a coffee and I'll be there in a couple of hours. Does Emma know?'

'No, not yet. I need to call her.'

'I'll do it,' Ben cut in, feeling a sense of pride and relief that his mum had turned to him first. 'And I'll pick her up and bring her with me.'

'Thank you, darling. Drive safely . . . but please hurry.'

Ben felt an ache of longing to get to his mum and protect her. 'I will. Love you,' he added, as he hung up.

'What's happened? Is it your dad?' Bella stood up, her eyes huge in her suddenly pale face.

Ben nodded, biting his lip to fight back the tears that still threatened. Bella came over and wrapped her arms around him. He could feel her shaking and even in his panicked state, it touched him that she was so affected.

Ben took a deep breath. 'I need to call Emma and go now.'

Bella nodded. 'Of course you do.'

Ben gazed at her in surprise. He had grown so used to her prickliness where his family was concerned, that he was almost expecting her to tell him he wasn't allowed.

'Let me know the second you have any news,' she added.

Ben nodded. 'Of course. Just keep an eye on our baby girl while I'm gone.' He knelt on the floor and kissed Elodie, who beamed up at him with a gummy smile, oblivious to the turmoil going on around her.

'I will,' Bella said, her face a mask of worry. 'And we'll be waiting for you when you get back.'

***

When Ben walked into the hospital with Emma almost three hours later, he knew instantly that they were too late. Jo's face was ashen and her eyes were sunken with shock. She gave a small shake of her head and reached out her arms towards them.

Ben's hand flew to his mouth and he thought he might be sick. Emma fell into her mother's arms with a shriek of 'No!' before dissolving into tears. Jo clung to Emma, stroking her silky blonde hair and soothing her like a child.

Ben slumped onto a chair and put his head between his knees as his vision blurred. It wasn't possible. Surely his tall, strong, handsome father hadn't *died*? 'There must be some mistake,' he told himself firmly, shaking away the dizziness.

Jo sat down beside him and put her arm around him. After a few minutes, he sat up slowly. He looked at her and took a deep breath. 'There must be some mistake,' he repeated. He felt as though he was underwater with everything blurred and muffled.

Jo opened her mouth to speak but he could see that she was too shocked to make any coherent sounds. Instead, she just shook her head helplessly. She suddenly looked so small and vulnerable.

In front of them, Emma was slumped against a wall, crying piteously. 'Emma,' Ben said, almost surprised at how normal his voice sounded.

Emma shook her head and put her hand up, warning him off.

'Emma,' Ben repeated. 'Come and sit down.' He thought maybe he should go to her but knew that his legs were too weak to hold him up.

Emma hesitated, before coming over to sit in the chair the other side of Ben. He put one arm around her and the other around his mum, pulling them into him. They sat locked in a cocoon of shock, each lost in their own stunned silence, while drawing comfort from each other for several minutes before Ben finally spoke: 'What happens now?'

Jo turned towards him. He had never seen anyone look so scared. 'I have no idea.'

'OK.' Ben took a deep breath and disentangled himself from them both before standing up. 'Don't worry about anything. You two go home and I will sort everything out.'

Jo immediately dissolved into tears. 'We can't leave him!' she cried desperately.

A sob rose in Ben's throat, catching him by surprise. He put his hand to his mouth, trying to compose himself. He had to be strong now for his mum and his sister. It was a horrible, terrifying sensation to realize that he was the man of the family now. The only one left. He crouched down in front of Jo and took her hand. 'We're not leaving him, Mum. He's not here anymore. He's gone.' The words tasted bitter as they left his mouth.

He steeled himself for Jo to shout, or scream or cry. But instead she became suddenly still, as if he had injected her with some kind of sedative. 'Mum?' he prompted.

Jo lifted her head to meet his gaze. There was such a look of utter despair in her eyes that for a moment he almost crumpled. 'He's gone,' she whispered, as if trying to compute the words.

Ben nodded and took her hand. 'You and Emma go home. I will come as soon as I can.' He gave her hand what he hoped was a reassuring squeeze.

Jo gave him a bleak half-smile. 'Thank you.'

Ben watched as his mum and Emma shuffled out of the hospital, clinging to each other for support. Jo looked like she had aged years in just a few short hours and he wondered if it was the same for him. It certainly felt like it.

He fished around in his pocket for his phone and dialled Bella's mobile. It went straight to voicemail. He tried the landline but that too was picked up by the Ansaphone. He started to leave a message but stopped short, unable to say such horribly unspeakable words into a machine. He would tell her later.

He slumped down onto the chair his mum had just vacated, overwhelmed by the enormity of the responsibility. He knew he needed to speak to the nursing staff, to sort out the practicalities, but all he felt capable of was curling into a ball and hoping it would all disappear. He stared at his phone again. Before he knew what he was doing, he was dialling Charlotte's number.

She picked up immediately. 'Hello?'

'Charlie, it's me. Ben,' he managed before he burst out into a torrent of sobbing.

'Ben!' she cried. 'What on earth has happened? What's wrong?'

Ben tried to speak but found the words just wouldn't form.

'Take your time,' she soothed. 'It's OK. Just take a few deep breaths and try and tell me what's happened.'

Ben followed her instructions. Eventually, he found his voice. 'Charlie, it's Dad . . .'

There was a beat of silence. 'Oh my God . . .' she whispered. 'What about him?'

'He's dead, Charlie. He died.' Ben could hear the disbelief in his own voice.

'No! Oh my God, that's not possible.' Charlotte paused to compose herself. 'Oh darling, I am so very sorry. What can I do? Where are you? Do you want me to come to you?'

Ben closed his eyes. *Yes*, he wanted to say, *I do want you to come*. But then he remembered that they weren't together anymore. It wouldn't be right for her to come. 'No,' he managed. 'I just needed to talk to someone. To tell someone.'

'Of course you did.' Charlotte's tone was gentle and reassuring, despite the tremor of shock.

'I've sent Mum and Emma home. I said I'd take care of the practicalities but the trouble is, I don't know what to do. I thought you might know . . . after your dad.'

There was a short pause before she replied. 'I can't really remember, to be honest, Ben. It's all a bit of a blur. Why don't you call Matt and Freya? Freya will know what to do.'

Fresh tears sprang into Ben's eyes. 'I'm not sure they'll want to hear from me.'

'Of course they will! You're Matt's best friend. Why wouldn't they want to hear from you?'

Ben sighed and shook his head, too ashamed to tell her how and why they had parted on such bad terms the last time he saw them. 'Oh, it's a long story. I'm sorry, I shouldn't have called you. It's not fair.'

'Don't be silly.' Charlotte's tone was brusque. 'Look, would you like me to call them for you?'

'Would you?' Ben felt a surge of gratitude for Charlotte's practical, no-nonsense attitude.

'Of course. Which hospital are you at?'

'Ipswich.' A very small part of him hoped that she would just get in the car and come, even though he had told her not to. He was suddenly so desperate to see her and if she turned up without him asking, well, Bella couldn't blame him for that, could she?

'OK. Sit tight. I'll call you back shortly. Or they will.'

'Thanks, Charlie.'

'And Ben?' Charlotte cut in before he could hang up.

'Yes?'

'I am so very sorry. He was a wonderful man. I know how much you loved him. We all did.'

Ben nodded, too choked to reply. He managed a sort of half-grunt, before hanging up. Yes, they had all loved his father. *Except Bella*, said a little voice inside his head. Bella, who had caused his father so much stress over the last few months of his life. It was ever since he first brought Bella home that his father's health had begun to deteriorate. And he knew Bella would have been happy for Ben never to see him again.

A bubble of anger seemed to pop inside him. Why had he let her come between him and his dad? What had his parents really done that was so bad? He swallowed hard, trying to quell the bitter taste of fury. It wasn't her fault, he admonished himself. She had no idea that this was around the corner, lying in wait for them like a silent landmine.

After what seemed like hours but was only a few minutes, his phone rang. Freya's number flashed up on his screen. He reddened with shame instantly, before picking up. 'Hello, Freya.'

'Oh my God, Ben. Charlotte's just rung. I can't believe the news about Peter! I am so, so sorry.'

Ben shook his head. 'I can't believe it either, Frey.'

'What can we do to help?'

'You can tell me what to do now because I don't have a clue. I sent Mum and Emma home, saying I would take care of everything but I realized that I don't actually know.'

'OK, I'll talk you through it all . . . Here's what you need to do.'

By the time Ben drove back to his mum and dad's house a couple of hours later, he was exhausted. He drove on auto-pilot, barely aware of his surroundings, still too numb to feel anything other than disbelief. As he pulled up in their driveway, he remembered that he still hadn't told Bella. Steeling himself, he called her number. 'Ben?' she said, sounding uncharacteristically nervous.

'Yes,' Ben felt his eyes fill with tears at the sound of her voice.

'How is he?'

Ben swallowed, knowing he would have to learn to say the words many times over the coming weeks and months. 'He's dead. He died, Bella.'

Bella gasped. 'What? No! That's just not possible!' There was genuine shock in her voice. There was a pause as she digested the news. 'My God, I can't believe it.'

'I know. I've just arrived back at Mum and Dad's—' Ben stopped speaking, unable to continue. It wasn't his mum and dad's anymore. It was just his mum's. His dad was gone. The realization washed over him like a giant wave and he put his hand over his face, which was wet with tears.

There was a long silence at the end of the line. Finally, Bella spoke.

'Are you coming home?'

'Not tonight. I need to stay here with Mum and Emma, to make sure they're OK. Just look after Elodie and I'll call you in the morning.'

'OK.' Bella's voice was barely a whisper and Ben could hear how devastated and upset she was. Somewhere at the back of his mind, it touched him.

The house was deathly quiet as Ben let himself in. He walked from room to room, looking for his mum and Emma, before deciding that they must be upstairs. He found them in his parents' bedroom. Jo was under the duvet, propped up on a pile of white pillows, while Emma sat on the edge of the bed, holding her mum's hand. Both were pale with shock.

'Hey.' Ben sat down beside Emma, giving her a quick hug as he did so.

Emma gave him a wan half-smile. 'Thanks for sorting everything out.'

Jo nodded her agreement. 'Yes, thank you, darling.'

Ben tried to smile, thinking how tiny and frail Jo suddenly looked. She was a small woman anyway but she seemed to have shrunk into herself and aged a decade in just a few short hours.

'Charlotte phoned,' Emma said, breaking into his thoughts.
'Did she?'

Emma nodded. 'She spoke to Mum, too. It was nice of her.'

'She loved Dad.' Ben thought back over the various holidays, family meals and nights out that he and Charlotte had enjoyed with his parents. Charlotte had truly felt like part of the family, even more so after her own dad died. She and Peter had a warm, easy relationship and he knew that she would be deeply affected by his death.

There were no such happy memories of Peter and Bella and Ben felt a sudden, physical squeeze of pain that Elodie would never know her grandfather.

The weight of grief was already beginning to settle on his

shoulders, the physical heaviness almost unbearable. 'What do we do now?' he said aloud, not really asking the question, just voicing his thoughts.

Emma reached out and took his hand in hers. 'We carry on. That's what we do.'

CHAPTER FOURTEEN

The day of the funeral dawned bright and sunny, with just the odd cloud scudding across a clear cobalt sky. Jo gazed up resentfully, thinking that it felt wrong, somehow. She wanted it to pour with rain and a thunderstorm to rent the heavens apart, with a viciousness to match her mood.

Two weeks on and she still felt hollowed-out with shock and grief. She had met Peter when she was 25 years old and she could no longer really remember her life before him. He was three years older than her and she had met him at a party in London, being thrown by her best friend's brother.

She thought back to the tall, handsome man who had confidently introduced himself, looking at her with his smiling brown eyes and remembered that she had had an immediate, unshakable premonition that she would marry him.

But she had made him work hard to get her. She wasn't going to fall into bed with him straight away and forced him to woo her for several weeks before she agreed to sleep with him. He sent flowers, took her for dinner and even rowed her around the Serpentine one particularly lovely, sunny afternoon, which was when she finally succumbed.

They married at a sweet little country church near her family home in Surrey and moved to their first house just outside Guildford. It wasn't a big house but it was a beautiful, chocolate-box-style cottage with roses around the door and a garden big enough to accommodate a swing for Emma, once she came along. Peter commuted to his job in the city and they were deliriously happy.

Jo often thought she would have been happy to stay at Rose Cottage for ever, but Peter's career was flying, so they bought the much larger house in Suffolk, where he could commute into the city more easily and they could add to their little family. The pressure of Peter's career meant he had to spend a couple of nights every week in London but the huge improvement in their circumstances made it worthwhile.

The biggest blip in their relationship came when the children were 8 and 11 and she discovered that he had been having an affair with a work colleague. She had been stunned and devastated and had immediately told him to leave. But he seemed genuinely sorry for what he'd done and had begged and begged her to give him another chance. Although it took time for the hurt and anger to recede, she was glad that she had forgiven him. They had been very happy together ever since, even though she knew that he had had other dalliances over the years. But she had made a decision to turn a blind eye in future, reasoning that, as long as she and the children remained unaware, what they didn't know, wouldn't hurt them.

As she pulled on the black dress she had chosen to wear for the funeral, Jo reached around to do up the zip and realized that she couldn't fasten it all the way up. She opened her mouth to call for Peter, before remembering that he was no longer here.

A wall of grief hurtled towards her, hitting her with such force that she slumped down onto the pale grey carpet. She couldn't even cry. There were no more tears left. She knew that this was how it would be from now on, the little things having the power to floor her on a daily basis.

'Mum?' Emma was in the doorway, looking pale and weary. 'Are you OK?'

Jo shook her head. 'I can't do up my zip.' Her voice sounded childlike to her own ears.

Emma's eyes filled and she nodded her understanding. 'I'll do it.' She came into the room and reached out a hand to Jo, helping her to her feet. She finished doing up the zip and gently turned Jo around to face her. 'You'll feel better when today's over.'

Jo tried to smile but found her mouth simply wouldn't cooperate. 'I hope you're right but I'm not so sure, Em. I don't think I'll ever feel better again.'

Emma gave her a quick hug.

'I just feel sick to my stomach all the time,' Jo continued. 'And I'm dreading today.'

Emma sighed and nodded. 'I know. We all are.'

'Is Ben here yet?'

Emma shook her head. 'No, but he'll be here very soon.'

As she spoke, Jo heard the crunch of wheels on the gravel driveway. She walked over to the window and looked down in time to see Ben's new SUV pulling up. He got out and lifted Elodie from the back seat. Jo's heart leaped at the sight of the little girl, so much like her mother and already so changed in the short time since she last saw her.

Her throat constricted at the realization that that visit was the final time Peter had seen her. Elodie would never see him again; would never know him as she grew up, except through photos and stories. The physical pain was almost too much to bear. 'But that's the circle of life, isn't it?' she murmured to herself. 'As one life ends, another is just beginning.'

Emma came to stand beside her and put an arm around her shoulders. She followed Jo's gaze and they both smiled as Bella scooped Elodie out of Ben's arms and lifted her above her head, blowing raspberries on her belly and eliciting squeals of delight from her.

Emma steered Jo out of the bedroom and down the stairs. She opened the front door and her spirits were lifted again by the sight of Ben, looking tall and handsome in his slim black suit. He pulled Jo into a huge bear hug and held her in his embrace for several seconds. As the tears threatened, Jo blinked hard and tried to smile at Bella. 'Hello, Bella.'

Bella looked slightly uncomfortable and distracted herself by rocking Elodie gently from side to side. 'Hello, Jo. I'm sorry about Peter.' Her words sounded clipped and forced.

'Thank you.' Jo tried to give a weak smile but found she couldn't speak and turned away abruptly, not wanting Elodie to see her cry.

They all made their way down the wide flag-stoned hallway into the kitchen, where they sat on stools around the large, granite-topped island. Emma bustled about briskly, making tea and coffee and running through the order of the funeral. Jo knew that for Emma, in particular, being busy was the only way she could cope, whereas Jo found it almost impossible to concentrate, her brain too muddled and full to take it in. She decided she would just let Ben and Emma take the lead and try to get through the day as best she could.

Finally, after what seemed like an eternity, they heard the

cars arriving. With a struggle, Jo got to her feet, her whole body shaking with fear and adrenaline. Unsure whether she would actually be able to make it to the door, she instinctively reached for Ben's arm.

Ben looked down at her in concern. 'Are you OK, Mum?'

Jo took a deep breath. No, she wasn't OK, she wanted to scream. She would never be OK again but there was absolutely nothing anyone could do about it. 'Yes,' she lied. 'My legs are just a bit shaky, that's all.'

Ben nodded sympathetically and tightened his grip on her. Behind them, Elodie started to cry. Ben turned back towards Bella, who was following them down the hallway with the baby in her arms. 'Shhhh, don't cry, sweetie,' he soothed.

'She's a baby, Ben,' Bella snapped. 'That's what babies do!'

Ben frowned slightly but didn't reply. Instead, he led Jo out to the driveway where the hearse and the family car were waiting. The two of them pulled up sharply at the sight of the coffin and Ben let out a guttural moan, before putting his hand over his mouth. Jo knew she should offer him some words of comfort but she was too numb. Too exhausted by grief. It all felt so surreal, as if she was watching someone else going through the worst day of their life.

Emma came to hold Jo's other hand, while the undertaker opened the car door for them. Jo looked at her gratefully. She was being so strong and so capable but Jo knew that the enormity of losing her father hadn't hit her yet. She distractedly hoped that the stress of it wouldn't trigger the anorexia that had first become apparent in her late teens and had dogged her at difficult times ever since.

Emma and Peter had been so close and he had been

unbelievably proud of the young woman she had grown into. She was kind and funny and hugely successful, having graduated from Oxford with a double first before seamlessly carving out a career for herself as an international lawyer.

Being such a high achiever, she had concentrated first on her studies and then on her career, to the detriment of any kind of meaningful relationship, although she got lots of offers. Peter had often told her that it was all very well working hard but she needed to make sure she played hard, too. But Emma seemed happy to remain single and would breezily assure them that she didn't have time for men, anyway.

Once she hit her thirties, Jo noticed a subtle change and Emma would say that she was open to settling down but that all the suitable men were married now and that she'd missed the boat. Jo hoped she was wrong about that but at 34, time no longer seemed to be on her side.

They climbed into the car, which had enough seats for the three of them. 'What about Bella?' Jo asked Ben, suddenly aware that there wasn't room for her and Elodie.

'She's driving our car so that she can put Elodie in the carseat.'

'Ah, OK.' Jo could see that Bella looked far from happy about the plan but she simply didn't have the energy to think about it any further.

The journey to the church passed in virtual silence. Jo sat between Ben and Emma, tightly holding each of their hands, wishing she could find the strength to comfort them. As they pulled up, the surprisingly large crowd of mourners stepped back to let them through. Jo stared unseeingly at the familiar faces, their presence only dimly registering, as she nodded her hellos.

Ben led the way towards the church doorway and stopped abruptly as Matt stepped forward from the crowd to hug him. For a moment Jo thought he might lose his composure but as he pulled away and murmured his thanks, he took a deep breath and nodded, as if giving himself a pep-talk. Charlotte and Freya came over to Jo and Emma, embracing them both. 'I'm so sorry,' Charlotte said, taking Jo's hand in hers. 'You must feel so lost without him. I know how much you loved him.'

Finally, the wall of numbness that Jo had felt around her all day began to crack and she squeezed Charlotte's hand. 'Thank you, Charlie. I don't even know where to begin.' She shook her head helplessly. 'I already miss him so, so much. I feel so alone.' Her voice broke as she finished speaking.

Charlotte's eyes filled with tears. 'I know. But you have Ben and Emma and they will be there for you. You aren't alone, I promise you.'

Jo swallowed away the lump in her throat. 'Thank you for coming, Charlie, it means a lot.'

Charlotte shook her head. 'We all loved Peter. There is no way we wouldn't have been here today.'

Jo smiled gratefully. 'Please make sure you sit with us at the front. We'd all appreciate it.'

Charlotte's eyes flickered uncertainly. 'Are you sure? We wouldn't want to take anyone else's seat . . .'

'No, Mum's right,' said Ben, appearing at their side. 'You should sit with us. It would really help, especially Emma,' he added, his eyes sliding towards Emma, who was now crying piteously, as one of her aunts comforted her.

'OK.' Charlotte gave Jo's hand another squeeze before stepping back. 'We'll see you in there.'

It was a small country church and by the time they took their seats, it was already packed, with many people standing in the side aisles and along the back. Jo looked at Ben, who was staring straight ahead, apparently stoical, but the pulsating muscle in his cheek gave away how stressed he was. Bella sat to his right, holding Elodie, who was gazing around her in puzzlement. Bella's expression was outwardly blank but Jo could tell she was simmering about something beneath the surface.

To Jo's left, Emma was weeping openly, while Charlotte rubbed her back rhythmically. Matt and Freya sat in the pew directly behind them and Matt also placed a comforting hand on Emma's shoulder. Matt had known Peter since he was a young boy, so she was glad of his presence today, knowing he was one of the few people who would really understand how Ben and Emma were feeling. She hoped it would bring them closer together again, as she got the sense that they seemed to have become slightly estranged recently.

She sighed and looked again at Bella, who was now gently rocking Elodie to sleep in her arms. She was the picture of contented motherhood, with a look of deep and genuine love in her eyes, as she gazed down at her baby girl. But when she looked up and caught Jo's eye, her expression changed subtly but noticeably to one of dislike. For the millionth time, Jo wondered what she had done to provoke such a reaction in her daughter-in-law.

As the church was filled with the first few bars of Peter's favourite hymn, 'I Watch the Sunrise', everyone stood and Jo turned to the front, her thoughts now focused on just him.

As the vicar invited Ben to give the eulogy, he stood up shakily and made his way to the lectern. After swallowing several times, he started to speak. 'My dad was my best friend,' he began in a trembling voice. 'He never, ever let me down and was always there when I needed him.' He paused, trying to recover his composure. 'And I honestly don't know how any of us are going to cope with losing him.' Tears rolled down his cheeks and when he opened his mouth to speak again, he emitted a loud sob, before breaking down completely.

Matt stood up and walked purposefully towards the altar. He reached Ben in a couple of strides and put one arm around his heaving shoulders, while taking his speech from him with the other. 'Would you like me to continue for you?' he asked gently.

Ben nodded, so Matt began to read the words on the page in a calm, clear voice, which somehow made them sound all the more poignant. As he finished, he looked at Ben, who gave him a grateful smile and a nod. 'Thank you,' Ben mouthed, as the two of them made their way back to the pews.

'I'm sorry, Mum,' Ben whispered, as he sat back down. 'I just couldn't do it.'

Jo took his hand, her heart breaking for him. 'I know, darling, we all understand.'

As they filed out of the church at the end, Jo reached out to hug Matt. 'Thank you so much for helping Ben, Matt. It means the world to us.'

Matt hugged her back. 'We'll always be here for him, Jo. And for you and Emma, too. Don't ever forget that.'

Jo nodded, aware that there was more meaning in his words than she was hearing but she was quickly swept away to greet the procession of mourners who were now leaving the church and she didn't have time to dwell on it.

CHAPTER FIFTEEN

The sun was a ball of orange fire, hanging low over the Suffolk fields, the few clouds creating purple shadows on the landscape, like bruises. Ben drove in silence, exhausted by the stress of the day. Beside him, Bella also sat in silence, while Elodie slept soundly in her car-seat in the back.

He hadn't wanted to leave Jo. She looked so small and vulnerable standing at the door to the home that she had shared with his dad for more than two decades. He had hesitated as he started the car and looked at Bella. 'Should we stay? I feel bad leaving her.'

Bella's expression hardened. 'No. She'll be fine. We need to get Elodie home.'

So Ben had driven away, feeling like the lousiest son in the world abandoning his mum. Bella had spent the entire day in a surly, dark mood, standing apart from everyone and giving cursory, barely polite answers to anyone who approached. Ben wanted to talk to her about it but he knew it would result in a row and he felt too drained and upset to get into one right now.

Bella sighed loudly and he could feel her eyes boring into him, demanding a reaction.

'OK,' he said, glancing at her wearily, knowing that he had no choice but to deal with it now, regardless of the emotions coursing through his brain. 'What's the matter?'

Bella sighed again, this time in a more exaggerated fashion. 'I can't believe you didn't notice the way your mum treated me today. She made me feel like a piece of dirt! And she barely even looked at Elodie . . .'

Ben frowned. 'That's not fair, Bella. It was her husband's funeral – she's in shock.'

'She wasn't in so much shock that she couldn't fawn over Matt and Freya, not to mention how she acted like your bitch of an ex-girlfriend was her daughter-in-law instead of me! Honestly, Ben, you have no idea how hard today was for me.'

Ben took his hand off the wheel and rubbed his forehead. He wanted to point out that today had been hard for him, too, but knew that wasn't what she wanted to hear.

'I don't think Mum would have done anything to upset you deliberately.'

Bella pulled a face and emitted a 'pah' sound. 'She was off with me from the minute we arrived. She barely said "hello" then turned her back on me and stomped into the kitchen without even attempting to take Elodie. You'd think she'd have been desperate to see her.'

'As I said, I think she had other things on her mind. Come on, Bella, give her a break.'

'She didn't worry about how I was feeling when she insisted that your bloody ex come and sit with us and went out of her way to make me feel left out.'

Bella's voice broke slightly as she finished speaking and Ben knew that tears would follow. He gripped the steering wheel hard, in an attempt to quell the sudden urge he had to slap her. 'You didn't exactly try to integrate, though, did you?'

'I did!' Bella protested furiously, wiping away the tears that were now coursing down her cheeks. 'But you were too busy ignoring me to notice!'

Ben gritted his teeth, not trusting himself to reply. He hated it when Bella got like this. There was simply no reasoning with her and he knew he would have to go through a massive scene before she would calm down, only when he apologized.

'You can't even deny it,' Bella said, with more than a note of triumph.

'Oh, for Christ's sake!' Ben slammed the steering wheel with the flat of his hand. 'It was my dad's funeral, Bella! Why are you being like this?'

Bella visibly jumped and cowered slightly in her seat. 'Ben! Stop being so aggressive! You're scaring me and you're scaring Elodie.'

As if on cue, Elodie, who had been sleeping soundly in her car-seat, started to cry. Bella made a huge point of shushing her, while shooting accusing glares in Ben's direction.

Ben wanted to cry himself and could feel the tears welling up in his own eyes. He just wanted a little bit of sympathy and some understanding but he had known all along that Bella would turn today into an excuse to have a go at his family and make it all about *her*.

It had been such a difficult day and he was struggling to process his feelings. It still didn't feel real that Peter was gone for ever and Ben knew that it hadn't sunk in yet.

He could feel Bella's eyes on him. 'So you're sulking now, then?'

Ben sighed. 'No, Bella, I'm not sulking. I'm just trying to get my head around today. It's been a horrible day.'

'Yes, it has.' Bella's voice was a little quieter. 'I'm glad it's over.'

Ben didn't reply.

'And at least we've got the move to focus on now.'

'Yes.' Ben had been putting the house move to the back of his mind. He didn't have enough room in his brain to think about it with everything else that had been going on. But there was no reason to delay it any longer and there was nothing to keep them in London, now that he no longer saw Matt and Freya. The plan was for him to give up his job and stay at home to look after Elodie, while Bella returned to work. It was a plan that he hadn't had much say in and he knew that Peter would have strongly counselled against it. But Bella had decreed that that was what they were doing, so he had gone along with it to keep her happy. And in truth, he loved the idea of spending more time with Elodie and knew that he would be good at it, whereas Bella was clearly going stir-crazy being at home. He hoped that going back to work would make her less possessive and a bit more relaxed about him seeing his family and friends.

'You know, maybe we shouldn't move to Suffolk, after all?' she said now, interrupting his thoughts. 'Maybe Surrey would be better.'

Ben's senses tingled with alarm at Bella's tone, which he had heard many times before. It meant she wasn't consulting him; she was telling him.

'No, Bella. You were super-keen on Suffolk and being near my parents, so I don't know why you'd suddenly change your mind. Anyway, it's too late.'

Bella gave a dismissive wave of her hand. 'Not necessarily. We can still pull out of the Suffolk house.'

'No. You insisted on Suffolk, so that's where we're going. And I like the house. Plus, it'll be good being so close to Mum, now that she's on her own . . .'

Ben could sense Bella's body stiffening beside him. He rarely stood up to her and almost always ended up backing down but he was determined that this was too important to just roll over the way he usually did.

'It has to be a joint decision,' she snapped.

'It is a joint decision. We chose it together, remember?' As he spoke, Ben realized that although he had been present for the viewings, he had had absolutely no say in the house she eventually picked. 'Although, to be honest, you didn't really give me much say in the choice, did you?'

Bella's face clouded and her eyes narrowed dangerously. 'Don't play that card with me, Ben. While you've been dashing off to be at your mother's beck and call, I've had to sort everything out by myself. So now I've decided that Surrey would be better instead.'

'And remind me how far it is from your mum's house?'

Bella tutted and rolled her eyes. 'Oh, for Christ's sake! We'll need my mum's help with Elodie so it's a good thing that she'll be so close.'

Ben thought about letting it drop and just doing what he always did, which was to let her have her own way. But after such a stressful, upsetting day, he didn't want to. 'My mum would be just as much help, especially now that she's on her own. It would give her a focus.'

'She's not as good with Elodie as my mum. I wouldn't feel

happy leaving her. Your mum seemed completely disinterested in her today . . .'

'Well, I expect burying her husband might have meant her mind wasn't fully on Elodie.'

'There's no need to be sarcastic, Ben.'

Ben gritted his teeth. 'Of course my mum isn't as good with Elodie as yours, because she hasn't had a chance. If she'd spent as much time with her as your mum, she would be just as capable. It's not her fault that she was banned from seeing her for the first months of Elodie's life.'

As he finished speaking, Ben thought about how hurt his dad had been by being prevented from seeing his first grandchild. Had the stress of that contributed to his death? He swatted the thought away, unable to bear the thought that he and Bella might have been somehow responsible.

'That was her own fault for the way she attacked me at Christmas. And she hasn't exactly tried to make it up to me since. No, considering how strained our relationship is now, I definitely think Surrey is the best option.'

Bella's words were clipped and precise, as they always were when she was refusing to budge. Not for the first time, Ben felt hemmed in and trapped. Yes, Bella was stunning and could be utterly charming and funny when she wanted. He loved her and when she was in a good mood, he enjoyed being with her. But more and more often, she scared him with the darker side of her personality.

As they arrived home at the flat in London, Bella put Elodie straight to bed, then returned to the kitchen where Ben was sitting at the kitchen table, nursing a glass of red wine. He had been desperate for a drink all day but Bella had insisted that he should drive home, so he had had to stay sober, while she decided to have a glass of wine for the first time since he'd met her. She was smiling broadly as she took a glass out of the cupboard and helped herself to some iced water from the fridge. 'Well, cheers!' she said, tapping her glass against Ben's and taking a long drink.

Ben did the same, feeling lonelier than he had ever felt before.

'Oh come on, Ben. Please stop sulking.' A deep frown of annoyance crumpled Bella's forehead.

'I'm not,' he protested wearily. 'I'm just upset. I still can't believe that Dad has really gone. That I'll never, ever see him again. That Elodie won't know him growing up. It all just makes me feel unbearably sad.'

Bella rolled her eyes. 'Well, she won't know mine either, so we're sort of even, aren't we?'

'Good God, Bella, it's not a competition!'

Bella fixed him with a steely glare. 'I never said it was. Stop putting words into my mouth.'

Ben tutted and shook his head.

'Don't you dare tut at me!' Bella hissed, her eyes suddenly blazing. 'I've had just about enough of this!'

'Well, that makes two of us!' The words were out before Ben could stop them and they seemed to hang, suspended in the air between them for a long moment, before they landed. Bella's grip on her glass tightened momentarily, causing her knuckles to turn white, before she raised her arm and threw it towards him. Instinctively, Ben ducked and it smashed against the wall behind him with a strangely musical tinkling sound. 'Bella!' he yelled in shock, turning to look at the wall, which was dripping with water. 'What did you do that for?'

But before he knew what was happening. Bella was on him, pulling his hair and pummelling him with her fists. As he was sitting down, she had the advantage of both surprise and height and he was all but helpless to fend off her blows, which were landing with painful accuracy. 'Stop it, Bella!' he shouted, as loudly as he could, trying to get through to her. But she was like a wild animal, clawing and slapping him with such ferocity that she was almost grunting with the effort.

Finally, panting with exhaustion, she stopped as suddenly as she had started. Throwing Ben one last cold stare, she turned on her heel and walked out of the kitchen to the bathroom. She slammed the door and locked it behind her. Moments later he heard the water running as she filled the bath.

Numb with shock, Ben was unable to move from his chair. He swallowed back the tears that threatened to erupt, like a dam about to burst. His head hurt where she had pulled his hair and he knew that there would be livid scratches and bruises all over his arms and back. He just couldn't make sense of it and the shame and humiliation of it was already enveloping him like a blanket.

After a while, he felt able to get to his feet, his heart still pounding and his legs still shaking. He heard the sound of the plug being pulled out of the bath and fear crawled at his insides. Too scared to move, he stood rooted to the spot, his ears straining to hear where she was.

Finally, the lock turned with what sounded to him like a sickening crack, causing him to jump, even though he knew it was coming. Bella emerged, her hair wrapped, turban-like, in a white towel, with another tied around her body. She was about to walk into the bedroom, when her head spun around and she locked eyes with him. 'What are you doing standing there like that?' she said, with a half-laugh. 'You look like you've seen a ghost!'

Ben frowned. 'Bella, we really need to talk about what just happened,' he began, mustering his courage. He was aware that his voice was trembling, giving him away.

Bella looked perplexed. 'What are you on about? Nothing happened.'

'You attacked me!' Ben shook his head, unable to believe what he was hearing.

'No, I didn't. Don't be so ridiculous! As if someone the size of me could attack anyone, let alone a six-foot-two hulk like you. You must be having some kind of hallucination. Listen,' she said, adopting a softer, more sympathetic tone of voice. 'It's been a long, stressful day – for both of us.'

Ben was aware that his mouth had dropped open slightly, as he listened in disbelief.

'So . . .' She came over to him and put her hand on his arm, causing him to wince slightly. He wasn't wrong about the number of bruises there would be when he finally looked. 'Why don't we get an early night and try to put everything else to the back of our minds? Let's remind ourselves why it's just you and me that matters. We don't need anyone else. It's better when it's just us.'

Ben gazed into her deep, dark eyes, now swimming with love and serenity. And that's when he got really scared.

PART TWO

PART TWO

CHAPTER SIXTEEN

I had prepared my answer, ready for a question that, surprisingly, never came. I had also done my research. I knew that this particular bar was the perfect place to find him. I clocked the two of them almost immediately and took up my position at a nearby table, pretending to wait for someone. There was no one, of course.

He was handsome, in a preppy sort of way and he was tall, which was always a plus. But there was also a sense of vulnerability about him that I liked. He had a sadness in his eyes that told me he was in need of someone like me to lift him out of himself.

I had never struggled to attract men. I know it sounds arrogant but it's also true. Usually, all it took was a certain look from under my eyelashes and a flick of the hair and they appeared at my side as if by magic, offering champagne, dinner and, in one case, an immediate proposal of marriage.

But this one took his time. I liked that. His friend had noticed me almost immediately. But he was obviously happily married because it was with amusement, rather than interest, that he observed me staring over at their table.

The other one was more engrossed in both his conversation and his drink. It was clear that they were more than just work colleagues meeting for an after-hours beer, as there was a closeness and familiarity about them. I wondered briefly if they might be brothers but then I remembered that he didn't have a brother.

Eventually, the fairer-haired one said something to him and he finally looked up in my direction. I prepared myself, ready for the moment when our eyes met and I knew the second they did that it was a bulls-eye. Without saying a word to his friend, he picked up his drink and moved over to join me at my table, with a slightly goofy grin and a glimmer of excitement in his eyes. He was better looking close up, with dark, soulful brown eyes, of course. He needed to have those brown eyes.

'Hello.' He put his drink on the table and sat down.

I adopted my most sensual pout. 'Hello.'

There was a long pause, as he looked at me, drinking me in, before he seemed to realize that he needed to say something. 'I'm Ben.'

'Bella.' I made sure I held his gaze, hoping for a hypnotic effect.

'Bella,' he repeated, with a slightly dazed expression. 'Can I buy you a drink, Bella?'

'Thank you, yes.' I hoped he'd say something original, but he didn't.

'Champagne?' he guessed, predictably.

'Sparkling water.'

Ben raised his eyebrows. It worked every time. It immediately reassured them that I wasn't a gold-digger.

He stood up and as he did so, he seemed to suddenly remember his friend sitting alone nearby.

'Oh! Matt . . . I'm just getting some more drinks in. You're welcome to join us?'

I felt a momentary wave of panic. That wasn't part of the plan. It might even ruin it altogether.

Thankfully, his friend responded with a knowing smirk and a shake of the head. 'Nah, I'm going to call it a night.' He finished his beer and got to his feet. 'Have fun,' he said, patting Ben on the back as he left the bar.

'So, Ben,' I asked, as he returned with our drinks. 'Are you single?'

Ben coughed through his mouthful of beer. 'Um, yes. I am. Definitely. Single.'

I could feel myself smiling. 'Good.'

'Are you?' he countered nervously.

I dropped my gaze, feigning shyness. 'I am.'

'Good. And do you get hit on by lots of men who aren't single?'

I looked back up at him with a knowing smile. 'All the time. That's why it was my first question.'

'Ah. Well, it looks like you got lucky with me then!' He seemed to relax and leaned back slightly, a cute grin spreading across his face.

'It looks like I did.' I couldn't believe quite how easy it had been.

'Another drink?' he asked eagerly, after we had chatted for a while.

'I'd prefer dinner.' It was bold but there was no time to waste.

Ben smiled. 'So would I.'

Bingo.

CHAPTER SEVENTEEN

'I'd like you to meet my parents.'

My heart gave a little leap. We were lying in bed together at his flat a month or so after that first meeting. I had gone home with him that night and never left, knowing it was the only way for my plan to work within my timeframe. Things had progressed faster than I had dared imagine. He was well and truly hooked. Yes, he was obviously a little damaged by his ex dumping him but he seemed to have got over her surprisingly quickly.

'Really?' I pushed myself up onto one elbow bunching the white cotton duvet under my stomach and looked down at him. 'And what do you think they'll make of me?'

Ben grinned up at me with his slightly lopsided smile, his brown eyes dancing with excitement. Since meeting me, he had visibly blossomed, like a plant bursting into bloom at the onset of summer. The downbeat, hesitant manner that he had shown that first night had been replaced by a relaxed confidence. He reached up and ran his hands through my hair. 'They will absolutely love you. Just like I do.'

I allowed my eyes to widen in surprise. 'Wow. That's the first time anyone's said that to me.' The lie tripped off my tongue with a practised ease and I dropped my gaze demurely.

A shadow of concern passed over his face, causing a deep, vertical line between his eyebrows. 'Well, I'm saying it now. And I'll keep saying it until you believe it. I love you, Bella.'

I smiled uncertainly. 'I . . . I think I love you, too.'

His look of unbridled joy at my words tugged at my insides. I didn't love him but it was impossible not to be moved by his reaction. He wasn't a bad person and actually I was even quite fond of him. I could tell myself that I was doing him a great service by helping him to recover from the heartbreak of his bitch of an ex-girlfriend dumping him. I had seen a few photos of her and he had definitely traded up with me – she was so average-looking. 'I would love to meet your parents,' I prompted, keen to return the conversation to his invitation.

Again, Ben's face softened with tender adoration. 'I'll call them tomorrow to sort it. I can't wait for them to meet you.'

I smiled to myself as I settled down to sleep. This was proving so much easier than I ever expected.

We went the following weekend. I had worked hard on my appearance. I was aiming for wife material, rather than stunning girlfriend, so I pulled my hair back into a pretty but unthreatening ponytail, toned down my make-up and opted for tight-fitting Capri pants with strappy nude sandals and a simple white T-shirt that clung in all the right places and was slightly transparent. Ben whistled as I emerged from the bedroom. 'Oh my God, how do you manage to look so sexy without even trying?'

I almost laughed. If only he knew.

Nevertheless, my heart was pounding as we pulled up on the gravel driveway of his parents' house in Suffolk. The house was pretty much as I expected – a handsome, Georgian sandstone, standing in vast, manicured grounds, with lakes and trees surrounding it. Ben looked at me shyly as we walked towards the front door, clearly trying to gauge my reaction. 'Wow!' I breathed dutifully. 'It's beautiful.' Ben nodded, apparently satisfied with my level of awe.

His mum pulled open the heavy, grey painted front door. I was slightly taken aback by how attractive she was. Slim yet curvy, with shoulder-length blonde hair, expensively highlighted with caramel tones and her skin was tanned yet surprisingly unlined. Probably thanks to Botox, I thought meanly. Immediately, my eye was drawn to her bare feet, which were tiny with perfectly manicured toenails. My large, slightly mis-shapen feet were my Achilles heel and I felt a spike of jealousy at her good fortune. 'Hello!' she beamed, revealing straight, white teeth.

She was so much better looking than I had imagined that it threw me momentarily. 'Hi!' I managed, proffering the lilies I had bought, not from a supermarket as I would normally, but from a small independent florist near Ben's flat. 'I'm Bella.'

Jo took them delightedly and I knew instantly I'd made the right call. 'Lovely to meet you, Bella, and thank you for these. They're absolutely beautiful!'

There was a short pause while Jo admired the flowers, before seemingly remembering that we were there. 'Come in! Come in!' she trilled, making a sweeping gesture with her arm. We squeezed past her into the wide, flag-stoned hallway, with Ben leading the way through to the back of the house. Jo gabbled on, although I was oblivious to what she was saying, as we made our way towards the kitchen, my heart pounding furiously.

Peter appeared in the doorway, momentarily blocking out the light, so his face was in silhouette, but even so, I could picture his stunned expression. Ben embraced Peter with a hug, before turning towards me with shining eyes. 'Dad, I'd like you to meet Bella.'

I stepped forward, giving Peter the benefit of my most dazzling yet coy smile. 'Hello, Peter, lovely to meet you.'

Peter turned slightly, so that his face was in the light. He blinked quickly, as if to snap himself out of his trance, before reaching out to shake my hand. 'Lovely to meet you, too, Bella.' His voice trembled slightly and his hand felt clammy to the touch. I smiled to myself, pleased that I was clearly having such an effect on him. It wasn't surprising. It was just satisfying.

'Well, let's go through into the garden!' Jo's voice was high and ever so slightly annoying. I resisted the temptation to roll my eyes and nodded instead, following Ben and Peter through the French doors and out onto a terrace that overlooked sprawling pea-green lawns, with a grass tennis court and a pristine swimming pool, glinting in the sunshine.

On the terrace was a large table that had been set for lunch and was already laden with exquisite-looking platters of antipasti. It looked so much like a magazine shoot that I half expected the food to be fake when touched.

Ben pulled out a chair and I sat down, gazing surreptitiously around me at the sumptuous surroundings. They had undeniably good taste, with every feature finished to perfection. But it was also a bit of a cliché and, I thought, not very creative to have everything just so. It was almost as if they had a long list of items that had to be ticked off in the home of a stereotypical rich person.

Peter reached into a giant silver ice bucket and retrieved a bottle of vintage champagne. Without asking, he filled my glass.

'Oh! Thank you, Peter, but I don't drink.' I accompanied my words with a smile, to avoid any perceived slight.

Peter looked at me for a long moment, his eyes narrowing very slightly. 'Really?'

I nodded apologetically at Jo. 'Sorry, I should have said sooner.'

Jo batted away my apology and shook her head furiously. 'No, no! Not at all! Peter, swap Bella's glass with mine and pour her some sparkling water.'

God, she was bossy. But to my amazement, Peter didn't seem to notice and did as she told him without complaint. 'Thank you,' I breathed gratefully, smiling at Jo until I felt like my jaw might lock.

'I'm not drinking either – I'm driving.' Ben told his dad, as Peter went to fill his glass too.

Peter frowned, his irritation obvious. 'Right,' he said curtly, before turning to Jo. 'Looks like it's just you and me drinking this then, darling.'

Jo giggled girlishly. 'You say that like it's a bad thing!' She held up her glass and took a huge slug of champagne. Once again, I had to resist the urge to roll my eyes. Or slap her.

The afternoon slipped by pleasantly enough. I had to hand it to Jo, she was an excellent cook and a very generous host. 'Gosh, not more food!' I groaned, as she brought out a huge cheese board and placed it on the table.

Ben helped himself to some biscuits and cut several large pieces of cheese. 'That's Mum all over, never knowingly under-catered!' He grinned, before stuffing a whole biscuit into his mouth. 'Aren't you having any?' he added, spraying crumbs as he did so.

I rubbed my flat stomach. 'No, thank you. I'm stuffed! I don't know where you put it all, Ben.'

'He's always been able to eat what he likes and never put on weight, just like his dad,' Jo chipped in.

I turned towards Peter, who met my eye almost defiantly. 'That's right. He's got good genes.'

'He certainly has,' I replied, eliciting another look from Peter.

I decided I needed to work a bit harder at charming everyone. So for the next hour, I asked lots of questions, listened to the rather long-winded answers and gazed dutifully and adoringly at Ben as much as possible.

'So what about you, then, Bella?' Jo asked, when there was a lull in the conversation. 'What do you do?'

I shrugged nonchalantly. 'Oh, nothing too exciting. I'm a PA for an executive at Norton Banking.'

Jo wagged her finger. 'Now don't go putting yourself down, Bella, there's absolutely nothing wrong with being a PA.'

I could feel my hackles rising. I hadn't said there was. But I gave what I hoped passed for a grateful smile.

Jo frowned. 'I'm surprised that you've never met Peter before. You sometimes deal with Norton, don't you, darling?'

Peter shot me a look before shrugging. 'Sometimes, yes.'

I decided to have some fun. 'Actually,' I began, deliberately stringing out the word. 'I think that maybe we *have* met before . . .'

Everyone turned towards Peter, who pursed his lips, as if in contemplation. 'No,' he said firmly. 'Pretty sure we've never met . . .'

'You *do* look familiar, though.' I shook my head as if unable to figure it all out.

Jo gazed from me to Peter, perplexed. 'Well, I suppose Ben does look like Peter, so maybe that's why you think he seems familiar?'

'Maybe,' I agreed, although I maintained my frown.

Peter drained his glass and helped himself and Jo to a refill. 'Anyway, you were saying about your job?' He was pointedly changing the subject back to me.

'Oh, it's fine,' I said, giving a dismissive wave of my hand. 'It's just that it's not quite as exciting as Ben's job.'

Jo smiled at Ben fondly. 'He's done very well,' she agreed. 'And it's to his credit that he seems to have kept doing well, even when things were a bit . . .' She reddened, suddenly aware that she was about to put her foot in it. 'Tricky,' she finished lamely.

'I am here, you know!' Ben waved theatrically. 'Hello!'

Jo laughed shrilly, clearly glad of the diversion from her faux pas. 'Sorry, darling. But you know what I'm like, I can't help bragging about how brilliant you are.'

'Fair enough,' Ben gave a resigned shrug, and we all laughed, loudly.

After a while I needed to use the bathroom. Jo saw me starting to get up and leaped to her feet. 'I'll show you where it is,' she offered eagerly.

'No,' Peter said, in a voice that brooked no argument. 'I'll show her.'

'Oh, OK then . . .' Jo sat back down, looking a little non-plussed.

I followed Peter out of the blazing sun into the coolness

of the house, watching his straight back as he strode ahead. I could tell just by his upright posture what the expression on his face would be. He didn't turn around until we were in the hallway, at the door to the downstairs cloakroom. Although I was expecting it, the look he gave me still made me recoil. He gripped my arm tightly and hissed through gritted teeth. 'What the hell are you playing at?'

I blinked deliberately slowly, buying myself some time. 'I have no idea what you're talking about.' I pulled my arm from his grasp and rubbed it pointedly, whilst throwing him my most innocent gaze.

'You might think it's funny but it's not. This is not a game and you have no right to involve my family.' A sheen of sweat had broken out on his forehead and his skin was flushed.

I looked up at him, so pompous in his outrage and felt a wave of fury sweep through me. 'And you have no right to cast me aside like a piece of rubbish that's served its purpose and act as if I never existed.'

A look of genuine fear glimmered in Peter's eyes. 'Look,' he began, running his hand through his hair distractedly. 'Don't do this. Don't hurt the people I love most in the world.'

'I think you'll find it's not me that did the dirty on them. Seems like a funny way to treat the people you purport to love.'

Peter's face creased with pain, and for a moment I thought he might cry. It was a satisfying sight. 'I'm not proud of it. Of what happened. But don't take it out on Ben. He's had a really hard time of it and you can have your pick of men – find someone else.'

'No.' I felt a sudden urge to hit him. How dare he tell me what to do. 'I don't want anyone else. I want him.'

Peter shook his head. 'No, Bella, you don't. You want me.' He paused to swallow. 'But that's not going to happen. It's over.' A pulse throbbed in his cheek and he fixed me with his gaze imploringly. 'Tell Ben it's over and leave us alone.'

I could feel a smile tugging at the corners of my mouth but managed to clamp my lips together to stop it. 'Well, you see, that's not going to be possible, I'm afraid.'

The look of fear reappeared. 'What do you mean?' he hissed. Aggression had been replaced by a tentative whisper.

'I'm pregnant.' I didn't even try to hide the triumphant note in my voice. Let him squirm for once.

He visibly reeled. 'You . . . you can't be.' I could see his mind whirring back through the weeks, trying to calculate. Again, the irony of someone who was so gifted at maths being unable to count a few short weeks made me want to laugh.

'Yes. I can be. And I am.'

Peter exhaled loudly and put his hands on his hips. 'Well, it's not mine.'

'Actually, it is.'

It was almost funny, the way the colour drained instantly from his handsome, smug, tanned face. He stumbled slightly and I wondered if he might faint but he seemed to recover his composure quickly. 'No,' he said, his voice reedy at first. He cleared his throat. 'No,' he repeated, more clearly this time. 'I don't even believe that you're pregnant. But *if* you are, then it is someone else's.'

I flashed him my widest smile, enjoying his discomfort. 'I think you'll find that it's most definitely yours. I'll do a DNA test to prove it.'

Peter looked away and rubbed his hand over his face. 'How much?' he said at last.

I raised my eyebrows theatrically. 'Peter! I'm shocked. I hope you're not suggesting that I get rid of . . .'

'Of course I'm fucking suggesting that!' he spat, and this time the tears of panic were brimming in his dark brown eyes that had gazed at me with undisguised lust so many times in the past. 'Look . . .' He took a deep breath to try to calm himself down. 'I will pay whatever you need to, uh, deal with it. And then I will pay you whatever it takes to make you go away and leave us alone. Just tell me how much you want.'

I shook my head sadly. How could he have got me so wrong? 'Oh no, Peter, I'm afraid I'm not some little problem that you can make disappear by throwing cash at it. But I am going to make you pay for dumping me the way you did. And the fact is, no matter how much money you have, you will never be able to afford what it's going to cost you.'

Peter's face creased with anguish. He made as if to reach out towards me but seemed to think better of it and withdrew his hand. 'Please, Bella, don't do this. Don't hurt Ben.'

I locked eyes with him and held his gaze for a couple of seconds. 'I'm not hurting him. He's very happy with me. And let's face it, he would never have got anyone in my league normally, so he wins, too.'

Peter hesitated. 'But, when he finds out that you're pregnant with my child, he'll . . .'

'He won't find out,' I cut him off. 'I'm going to let him think the baby is his.'

'You're not going to tell him the truth?' Peter narrowed his eyes slightly.

'No. I'm not going to tell anyone.'

Peter's mouth dropped open and he exhaled with relief. 'But,

I don't understand . . .' he began. 'I thought you said you were going to make me pay?'

'I am. I'll be a part of your family from now on and every time you look at your baby you'll know that you and I will be linked for ever. So rather than casting me aside like you wanted to, you will have to be so nice to me that it will make you choke. You will have to coo over this baby and pretend to be thrilled for me and Ben. Because if you don't, I'll tell Jo and Ben the truth.'

I watched each word land like a knockout punch, as the gravity and awfulness of his situation dawned. 'You're blackmailing me,' he said at last, with a weary resignation.

I nodded. 'Yes, Peter. I am. But I'm not after money. I just want revenge. So you play nicely and I'll play nicely too. There's absolutely no reason why there should be any unpleasantness.'

Peter gave a dry laugh. 'No unpleasantness? The very sight of you is as much unpleasantness as anyone can take in a lifetime.'

The words stung but I just shook my head calmly. 'No, Peter. That's not the way to behave. You need to learn to fuss and fawn over me as much as you do that bloody perfect daughter of yours. Don't worry, you'll get used to it soon enough.'

Pure hate shone from Peter's eyes but he nodded slowly. 'Right. Well, I'd better go back outside before they wonder what's going on.'

I laughed. 'Yes, God forbid they think there's something "going on"! You run along now like a good boy.'

He fixed me with one last look before turning on his heel and making his way back out onto the terrace.

All the way home I kept smiling to myself at Peter's shocked reaction. He was always so sure of himself and cocky that it was a truly delicious sensation to see him so wrong-footed and upset. I could actually feel him shaking as he kissed me goodbye.

So now that I had put my plan into action, I needed to tell Ben the good news.

'Pull over here!'

'What?' Ben turned towards me with a look of surprise. 'Are you OK?'

'Pull over!' I repeated.

Ben frowned but immediately indicated and pulled into a small layby overlooking the rolling patchwork fields of the Suffolk countryside and the sparkling river beyond. He turned off the engine and looked over at me expectantly. 'What's up?'

I adopted my most nervous and wide-eyed expression, before taking a deep, calming breath. 'I'm pregnant.' I was pleased with the slight break in my voice as I spoke.

Ben gripped the steering wheel so tightly that his knuckles turned white. 'Pregnant?'

Irritation quivered in my chest and I turned away quickly, not wanting him to see it.

Ben gulped slightly. 'Are you sure?'

I closed my eyes briefly, trying to control the surge of temper I could feel growing within me. He wasn't a bad person, but he was so irritatingly stupid sometimes. 'Yes.' The word came out in a sigh.

There was a long silence before Ben exhaled loudly. 'How long?'

I was suddenly a bit concerned that he might not be quite as easy to dupe as I had expected. So I bit my lip, which was quivering slightly and gazed up at him with what I hoped was a scared expression. 'I think about eight weeks. But I won't know for sure until the scan.' I needed to keep things vague in case he started to question the dates.

But he just nodded. 'Wow.'

I reached out to put my hand on his thigh and gave him an uncertain smile. 'Are you happy about it?'

'Of course.' His answer came satisfyingly quickly. He tilted his head so that he could see my face, his expression one of love and concern. 'What about you?'

I smiled again. 'I'm happy. Just . . . It's a bit of a shock, that's all.'

Ben nodded his understanding but there was a faint clouding in his eyes and I could see that he was wrestling with his emotions. After a long, long silence, he started the car again and pulled back onto the road.

We didn't talk much on the journey home to London but every now and again I could feel Ben looking at me sideways. A tiny part of me felt sorry for him. But at the same time, there was no way he would ever have pulled someone in my league if he had just been any old Joe Bloggs, so I was doing him a favour really. And he would love being a dad. I was fairly sure that it wouldn't make any difference that he wasn't the biological father. What he didn't know wouldn't hurt him.

Later, as we lay in bed together, me with my head resting on his chest, it occurred to me that everything would be a lot more plausible if we were married. I formulated a plan to get him to propose, before deciding that we didn't have time for that. He'd been with Charlotte for twelve years and still hadn't got around to it. I would have to take the initiative myself.

'Ben?' I said, into the darkness.

'Hmmm?'

'I'd like to get married. Before the baby comes.'

I felt his body tense and wondered if I should have been a little more tentative. But I couldn't be doing with any more hanging around.

'Right,' he said.

It wasn't a great response but it would have to do. I sighed happily, as I felt sleep start to envelop me. It had been an altogether very satisfying day.

CHAPTER EIGHTEEN

The next couple of months passed in what I could even describe as a fairly pleasurable way. Ben was much more pliable than his dad and I quickly realized that I could be as demanding as I wanted and he wouldn't resist. Yes, he had a lot less charisma than Peter, but he actually wasn't bad company. And he had fallen for me so completely that it was hard not to enjoy being the centre of someone's world.

Until now, I had always been 'the other woman' and it was a strangely enjoyable experience to be the number one priority for once. Ben couldn't do enough for me and he didn't try to conceal how much he loved me. It made me like him more than I expected to. I had thought I would have to tolerate him just long enough to make Peter's life a complete misery, before dumping him and living off the money I would make both Peter and Ben pay to support the same child.

But on our wedding day, seeing the look of complete and utter devotion in Ben's eyes, as I walked down the aisle towards him, made me think that maybe I could tolerate him a little longer than I thought. I certainly didn't love him the way I had loved his father, but I did like him.

I was glad to get the wedding out of the way. The whole day was a strain, as I could feel Peter's eyes watching me nervously, scared of what I might do. The worst part came when the registrar asked if anyone knew of any lawful impediment to the marriage and I heard Peter loudly clearing his throat. For a moment, fear gripped me that he might be about to blurt out the whole story to the assembled congregation but when I glanced back at him, he gave me an almost imperceptible nod and I nearly fainted with relief.

I wished that Peter didn't have so much influence over me but the truth was that I was only behaving the way I was because I was so hurt. I had really loved him and he had just used me and cast me aside, as if I was nothing more than a cheap fling.

From the first moment I met him, I thought he was different from all the others. I had enough experience of married men to know that they never, ever left their wives but we had such a connection that I always felt with Peter that maybe he would.

My boss, Marcus, with whom I had also had a relationship, had a meeting with Peter and asked me to keep him entertained while he finished up a phone-call that was over-running.

I walked out into the lobby and saw a man standing with his back to me, as he gazed out of the floor-to-ceiling windows at the London skyline. Even from behind, I could tell that he was attractive by his height, his lean physique and his confident posture. But as he turned and our eyes locked, there was a moment when my knees actually went weak with lust. His cropped, grey hair showed off his velvety brown eyes and square jawline. His dark grey suit was bespoke and his hand-made white shirt was just fitted enough to see his tanned, taut stomach beneath.

He smiled, causing another tremor of excitement to render

me temporarily speechless. No man had ever had such a powerful physical effect on me. 'Hi,' I managed at last. 'You must be Mr Gordon?' I extended a hand, aware that it was trembling.

Peter's eyes danced with amusement. He took my outstretched hand, but held my gaze. 'Peter,' he said, in a slightly husky voice that perfectly matched the sexiness of his appearance. 'Call me Peter.'

I never got flustered with men. I always maintained an air of slight aloofness that seemed to attract them all the more. But I was definitely flustered with Peter. I could feel an unfamiliar heat in my cheeks and my voice quivered as I replied, 'Nice to meet you, Peter. I'm Bella. Marcus will only be a few minutes. Is there anything I can get you?'

Peter smiled again and raised his eyebrows. 'Now there's an offer . . .'

I rolled my eyes, trying to regain some semblance of control over the butterflies in my stomach. He was clearly as attracted to me as I was to him and I knew without any doubt that he would be asking me out. 'OK, well let me know if you change your mind,' I told him, before returning to my office, knowing he was watching and thanking my lucky stars that I had worn the tight black pencil skirt and five-inch stilettos that showed off my bum and legs to perfection.

When his meeting with Marcus ended, I walked him to the lift, again making sure to walk slightly in front of him so that he could admire me from behind. By now, my heart rate had calmed slightly and I felt more in command of my emotions. I pressed the call button and turned back towards him with a knowing smile.

He returned the gesture. 'So, Bella . . . would you like to have dinner with me tonight?'

I raised an eyebrow and shook my head slowly. 'I can't. I have plans.'

He smiled and raised an eyebrow back at me, already enjoying the sport. 'Cancel them.'

Part of me wanted to tell him to get lost for his arrogance but already the attraction between us was too strong, too magnetic to resist and we both knew it. 'I'll see what I can do.'

The lift arrived and Peter stepped in but held his hand over the door to stop it closing. He reached into his pocket with his other hand and pulled out a card with a number written on it. He fixed me with his sexiest stare. 'Here's my number. Call me.'

I took the card and turned as the lift doors swished shut. As I made my way back to my office, I was unable to stop smiling.

Marcus came out of his office and walked over to mine. 'Well, you seem to have an admirer . . .'

My smile widened as I looked up at him. 'Do you think so?'

'I know so.' Marcus came and perched on the edge of my desk, looking at me contemplatively.

'Are you jealous?' I teased, leaning back in my chair and pretending to examine a nail.

He grinned. 'Of course. I'm ragingly, furiously jealous!'

I laughed. 'Good.'

'You know,' he began, making tiny circles on the desk with his fingernail. 'If things had been different . . .'

'Shhhh!' I interrupted him sharply. 'Don't even go there.' We both knew that he and I were about sex and nothing more. He would never have left his wife and I would never have wanted him to. I liked him but not *that* much. He was a bit of fun. Nothing more.

'So did he ask you out?'

'He did.'

'And when are you seeing him?' Marcus's tone was back to playful and I was grateful that he wasn't being possessive.

'Tonight,' I replied, mentally running through a checklist of preparations I needed to make.

'Well,' he said, standing up. 'All I can say is, "lucky him"!'

Peter suggested we meet for dinner at a beautiful hotel restaurant not far from my office. He was waiting at a discreet table in the corner and stood up as I reached him, taking my hand and kissing me on both cheeks, so that I caught the scent of his beautiful cologne. I wasn't the only one who had been busy making preparations.

'Wow – great view,' I said, gesturing towards the cityscape of London, laid out hundreds of metres below us.

Peter kept his eyes firmly fixed on me. 'It certainly is.'

The waiter appeared with two glasses of champagne and placed them before us. I looked up and met Peter's eye. 'How do you know I drink?'

He tilted his head to one side in surprise. 'Don't you?'

I thought about lying, just to show that I was different from the others. But I was desperate for a drink. 'Yes,' I said, picking up my flute and reaching across to clink it with his. 'I do. I'm just teasing you.'

Over dinner, we chatted non-stop, with almost every line of conversation loaded with hidden meaning and sexual inuendo. After coffee, Peter sat back in his chair and fixed me with what I would soon learn was his 'come to bed' expression. 'So, beautiful Bella . . . how would you like this evening to end?'

I mirrored his actions and leaned back in my chair, too. 'Have you booked a room?'

A flicker of uncertainty passed over Peter's face and he hesitated before replying. 'Should I have done?'

'It's not really a question of whether you should have done or not . . . it's more a question of whether you did?' I smiled to soften any sting from my words.

Again, Peter hesitated, before apparently reaching a decision. 'Yes,' he said, putting his napkin on the table and standing up. 'Of course I did.'

I stood up, too, excitement rendering me momentarily weak-legged. 'Of course you did.'

He reached out to take my hand as if it was the most natural thing in the world and we walked towards the lifts as if we were a proper couple. He didn't seem at all concerned about being spotted with me, which was such an unusual experience that I felt nervous about sex for the first time ever. This man was already so different from anyone else I had had a relationship with that I wanted it to be special.

He led me in to the sumptuously furnished, modern suite, which had a glass wall with a view over the whole of London that was so magnificent it was dizzying. I walked towards it and gazed out at the glittering spectacle laid out before me. 'This is beautiful,' I sighed.

Peter came and stood behind me, putting his hands on the tops of my bare arms. It was a simple gesture but it was also deliciously erotic. 'So are you,' he whispered. I continued to look out at the London skyline as his hands moved from my arms to my hips and slowly moved lower. He stopped when he reached the hem of my top and slid it smoothly and deliberately up over my head. Then he unzipped my skirt and let it fall to the floor.

I heard him inhale sharply when he realized that I was completely naked underneath. I hadn't had time to go out and buy new underwear so I decided to let my body do all the talking. It had never failed me yet and judging by Peter's reaction, it wouldn't fail me now.

He pushed me gently towards the glass, so that my body was pressed up against it, as he planted delicate, butterfly kisses all over my skin. My nipples hardened against the cold glass and I let out a small moan. Peter unzipped his trousers and slid inside me in one fluid movement, causing me to gasp with shock. The element of surprise, the sensation of the glass, the view and the rhythm of his thrusts was too much and I orgasmed instantly, my body shuddering with the sensation.

Peter leaned forward and kissed my neck as he continued to thrust, this time more sensuously, sending crackles of electricity surging through me. He increased momentum so that his breath was coming in short pants until he finally came with a long groan.

We stood locked together for a few moments, both breathing hard, Peter's hands pressed with mine against the glass. 'Wow,' he said, leaning his head against the back of my neck. 'That was amazing.'

I smiled and turned so that I was facing him. He looked down at me and stroked my face tenderly. 'You are the most beautiful woman I have ever set eyes on,' he said, shaking his head slightly. 'I can't believe you just walked into my life when I was least expecting it.'

I wrapped my arms around his neck and pulled him into

a kiss. 'Strictly speaking,' I said, as I pulled away. '*You* walked into *mine*.'

Peter grinned. 'Shut up and kiss me again.'

The rest of the night was gloriously sleepless. In my dreams, I was happy and smiling in a way I hadn't felt in the real world for as long as I could remember. I would half-awaken to find Peter's strong hands stroking my back, my legs or my breasts, his seemingly insatiable sexual appetite only temporarily sated, as time and again we would writhe together before collapsing; our glistening bodies entwined. During those moments, I realized I was both fully relaxed and smiling broadly. It was as if I'd finally found what I'd been searching for and I didn't think I had ever felt so happy.

Our affair gathered pace more quickly than I think either of us was expecting. He rented an apartment in the city and stayed up at least two nights every week, which meant that we could spend a lot of time together. Usually, I would go to the apartment after work and be waiting by the time he arrived at around 6 p.m. His appetite for sex was voracious and he never seemed to be able to get enough of me.

Sex was a huge part of our relationship, but over the weeks and months, we grew closer and closer, until I was deeply, hopelessly, in love with him. The age difference didn't seem to bother either of us and although any amateur psychologist would probably have suggested that I was trying to fill the gap left by my father, I knew it was more than that. It was a meeting of minds, as well as bodies and everything about him made me happy.

I had never been in love before and felt almost scared by

the way it unbalanced me. I was normally so in control of my emotions that it was unsettling and even slightly worrying that I couldn't control the way I felt about him. I had never let myself go in the past because I wanted to protect myself from being hurt. But with Peter, I was powerless to stop myself from falling for him.

It had never bothered me with other lovers when they talked about their wives and families but whenever Peter mentioned Jo and his children, I began to bristle. I wished he would either be horrible about them or never bring the subject up. But he seemed unaware of the effect his words were having on me and would talk with pride about how Emma was going to take on the world with her incredible career, or that Ben and his girlfriend had spent the weekend with him and Jo and that Jo was such an incredible cook.

Eventually, I snapped. 'Well, if your life is so bloody perfect, what the hell are you doing here, in bed, with me?'

There was a shocked pause, as Peter digested my words, before easing himself up into a sitting position. He looked down at me and sighed deeply. 'I don't know how to answer that one. Because I like you very much. Because you're beautiful, funny and interesting, I suppose.'

I propped myself up on one elbow. 'Hmmm . . .'

Peter stroked my hair contemplatively. 'I know it doesn't justify what I'm doing. I know that it's wrong . . . But I just don't want to give you up.'

'Good!' I didn't want to scare him off by getting too heavy. I gazed up at him, feeling dissatisfied. I wanted him to tell me that I was his grand passion; that he felt the same way about me as I felt about him but I knew deep down that it wouldn't happen. I needed to think of a way to make him realize that he couldn't live without me. A way to make him commit to me properly.

I had been on the pill for years and decided that maybe now was the time to give my body a rest. After all, it wasn't supposed to be good for you to be on it for too long, was it? I didn't need to mention it to Peter, who had always clearly just assumed that I was taking precautions – because he certainly wasn't.

So for the next couple of months I stopped taking it. Because of the number of years I had been on it, I assumed that it would take a while for me to become fertile again. But I couldn't have been more wrong. When my period didn't arrive, I put it down to my body taking time to regulate itself. But when my breasts also began to feel tender and grow at an alarming rate, I realized there may be another explanation.

I bought a two-pack pregnancy testing kit in my lunch hour and sat on the loo shaking, as I waited for the result to arrive. When the positive sign appeared in the window of the first one, I looked at it in disbelief, before ripping open the second test and repeating the process. Again, the positive result sign appeared, a little faint, presumably because it was so early but still clear enough to be sure. I stared at it for several minutes, trying to process how I felt. I was shocked and scared, but also excited and thrilled.

I was going to be a mother. The words kept going round and round in my brain. And not only that, I was going to be the mother of Peter's baby. It was as if the love I felt for him was already suffusing the little life just beginning to take shape inside me and tears of pure joy began to roll down my cheeks. I had never really had anyone who loved me unconditionally. Maybe my dad, but he was long gone. My mum probably did love me, too, but she was more scared of me than anything. This baby would be the first time I had known that pure, unbreakable love that I had always craved.

I returned to my desk just as Marcus was coming back from his lunch. He stopped short when he saw me. 'Hey, you OK?'

I nodded, not daring myself to speak in case I either burst into tears again or blurted out my precious, wonderful secret.

'You look . . . different,' he said, watching me with a frown.

'Different how?' I managed, trying to look busy, as I scrolled through my emails.

'Not sure. Just different.'

I laughed. 'OK. Well, I'm going to take that as a compliment, even though I'm not sure it is.'

Marcus laughed back, before walking into his office. 'Oh, it's definitely a compliment.'

I smiled to myself. I couldn't wait to see Peter that night, to tell him the news. He would be shocked, of course. But once he got used to the idea, he would see that we worked as a couple and we could work as a family.

The text came at around 4 p.m.

Bella. I know this is the coward's way out but I also know that it is the only way I can do it. I have loved our time together and you are a very special lady but I have to end our relationship. I am so sorry and I want to thank you for the incredible memories. I will never forget you. Be happy. Peter.

It was the second shock I had had in one day but I reacted very differently to this one. I didn't cry. I didn't shake. I didn't even feel angry. I was just serenely numb. It didn't seem possible that it could be true. I hadn't seen him for about ten days, which was slightly unusual but the last time we had been together, he had seemed, if anything, more intense than ever. He had looked deep into my eyes as we made love, as if he was trying to see into my soul and had held me afterwards as if he never wanted to let me go. So, with a surprisingly calm, steady hand, I replied: *Let's discuss tonight. Love, Bella x*

I finished work and made my way to the apartment as I usually did, still feeling absolutely certain that there was nothing to worry about. I knew Peter too well. He would take one look at me and we would pick up right where we'd left off. He was obviously having a crisis of guilt, probably after a holiday with Jo, but it would be forgotten the moment he set eyes on me, of that I felt sure.

But when I arrived at the apartment block, something that I can only describe as a sixth sense meant my certainty began to waver. I took the lift to the fifth floor and took out my key. Even before I tried to put it in the lock, I knew it wouldn't work. But I also couldn't accept what was happening either, so I tried to force it, with greater and greater ferocity.

Suddenly, the door flew open and a be-suited man, roughly the same age as me, with a handsome, haughty expression and blond curly hair, stood in front of me, looking furious. 'What the bloody hell are you doing?' he shouted, in a cut-glass accent that screamed public school wealth.

I was rooted to the spot with shock, only now beginning to feel the creeping horror of realization that Peter might have actually gone. 'My, er, my boyfriend lives here,' I managed to stutter, even though my throat had dried completely.

The look of anger melted away from the man's face, to be replaced by something much, much worse – sympathy. 'Right.'

He hesitated and ran his hand distractedly through his mane of blond curls. 'Well, I'm sorry to be the one to tell you this, but the guy who rented this flat before has moved out and now I live here . . .' He grimaced, looking embarrassed. 'I'm sorry.'

All at once, every ounce of adrenaline left my body and I could feel my legs start to give way.

'Whoa, hey . . . take it easy now.' The man stepped over the threshold and caught me under my arms, easily supporting my weight. 'Take some deep breaths,' he said, as my knees buckled. I did as I was told. 'Look, do you want to come in for a minute?' he offered, his tone gentle. 'I can get you a glass of water.'

I really, really didn't want to go inside, but at the same time I didn't feel that I had the strength to stand up properly and walk away either, so I nodded mutely and allowed him to escort me into the flat. He deposited me on a bar stool and opened one of the cupboards to take out a glass. I looked around me in a stunned silence, my brain still unable to take in what I was seeing. All Peter's furniture and belongings had gone, to be replaced by a whole new interior.

I took the glass of water the man offered with a shaking hand and sipped it gratefully. 'How long?' I whispered between gulps. 'How long ago did you move in?'

The man leaned back against the worktop and eyed me with concern. 'At the weekend. I think, um, the other guy, moved out the week before.'

I nodded. So when I was last here, Peter already knew that he would be moving out. That he would never be seeing me again. The intensity that I had mistakenly thought was love, was actually him saying goodbye. How could he have been so treacherous? The betrayal felt like being stabbed in the stomach repeatedly. I swallowed the last of the water and took a deep breath. 'Thank you. I'm sorry if I gave you a shock but . . .'

The guy shook his head and waved his hand dismissively. 'Not at all. It sounds like you're the one who's had a shock. Don't worry about it, honestly.'

I could feel my eyes filling with tears, so I slid off the bar stool and picked up my handbag. 'Thank you for being so kind. I'll go now.'

The guy nodded. 'Are you sure you're going to be OK? You still look a bit pale . . .'

'I'm fine.' I walked to the door, now just desperate to get out and away from this place.

The man followed and opened the door for me. 'OK, well . . . goodbye. And, sorry.'

'Goodbye. Thanks again.' I walked out with my back straight, trying to muster as much dignity as I could.

As the door closed behind me, a huge sob escaped as if it had been trapped inside me for ever and a torrent of tears began to fall. I stepped into the lift and crouched into a ball in the corner, rocking back and forward to try to ease the pain. I couldn't believe that this man who I had loved so much, who I had imagined building a future with, whose baby I was carrying, had excised me from his life with such clinical precision that he may as well have killed me using a scalpel.

I walked back towards my own small, scruffy rented flat on the south side of the river, fighting my way through the throngs of commuters hurrying home to enjoy the early spring sunshine that seemed to taunt me. I stood on Tower Bridge and looked down into the murky brown depths of the Thames. It would be so easy to vault over the barrier and be swallowed up for ever by its muddy, swirling waters.

Who would miss me if I did jump? My mum, I supposed. But she was pathetic herself. She had made a bloody mess of her own life and screwed mine up in the process when she had my dad put away, accusing him of crimes too heinous to ever be spoken about. I didn't have any friends who would care. Yes, there were colleagues who would whisper in shocked tones that they couldn't believe someone as beautiful as me would have had reason to kill herself. 'Just shows that you never really know what's going on in someone's life,' I imagined them saying. But I had never made any real friends, as other women were always jealous of me and saw me as a threat. Marcus would be upset. But he would get over it and he would probably quickly employ a new PA that he could have some fun with.

I pulled out my phone and stared at it. A tiny part of me had hoped that Peter might have messaged, saying he had made a terrible mistake and begging me to forgive him. But my message inbox remained stubbornly empty. I swallowed down another sob and began to type.

Peter, please don't do this to me. I am pregnant with your baby. I am standing on Tower Bridge and if I don't hear from you within the next fifteen minutes, I plan to jump. The pain is unbearable. I can't go on without you.

I pressed 'send' and waited. Almost immediately, the text bounced back. *Message failed to send.* I tried again. And again, stabbing at the screen in fury. He had changed his phone after his message ending things with me earlier. He had planned everything down to the minutest detail. I leaned over the rail and stared again at the water, willing myself to jump. To put an end to it all. But from deep inside me, a well of white-hot anger began to bubble up.

I didn't want to die. I wanted to live and I wanted to have this baby. How dare Peter drive me to the point where I would consider suicide, meaning that our baby would die with me. Even though I had only known of the baby's existence for a matter of hours, I already knew that I loved it like I had never loved anything before.

I put my hand to my stomach. 'Fuck you, Peter. You are not getting rid of me that easily,' I said aloud.

'Good for you, girl,' said a young woman striding past in a suit and trainers.

I watched her walking away, thinking. How many times had I heard the expression, 'Don't get mad, get even'? Well, now, instead of thinking it, I was going to do it. Peter had no idea what hell he had unleashed for himself but he was going to pay for what he had done. Right at that moment, I wasn't quite sure how, but I knew I was going to exact a revenge so terrible that he would be begging me for a reprieve.

Over the next few days, a plan began to form. I needed to get to Peter via a different route. I thought about causing problems for him at work, about concocting some kind of sexual assault or rape allegations that would have him shamed and fired from his oh-so-bloody-successful career. But there was the small matter of Marcus and probably quite a few other people at my company knowing that we had been openly having a relationship for months and I wasn't sure I could convince anyone that I had been an unwilling participant.

No, it had to be something else. Something personal to do with his family, that would hurt him as much as he'd hurt me.

I wracked my brains to remember the stories he had told me about them, cursing myself now for my huffy disinterest. Then, one night, as I was cleaning my teeth, a genius thought popped into my head, as I stared at my reflection in the bathroom mirror. I suddenly remembered that after Christmas, he told me that his son, Ben, had been dumped by his long-term girlfriend and had taken it very badly.

I remembered thinking that with any luck, Jo would do the same to Peter and then he'd be all mine. I opened my laptop and began to search. It took less than five minutes to find him through LinkedIn. He worked in advertising and his profile picture showed a handsome man who was a little older than me. He looked a bit like his father, which was a plus. But he also looked less arrogant than Peter, with a kinder face, probably because his jawline wasn't quite so square and chiselled.

I found out that he worked near Covent Garden and waited for him to leave a couple of evenings, to see where he went. He seemed to favour a certain bar, which I checked out after he had gone and it was perfect.

On the night I decided to put my plan into practice, I took the afternoon off work, so that I had time to go home and get ready first. I knew I had one chance to get this right and I didn't want anything to go wrong. I noticed him and his friend as soon as I walked in and waited at the bar until the table near them became free. The only problem was the number of men who approached, offering to buy me a drink. I adopted my steeliest expression and coldly rebuffed them, staring pointedly at Ben until finally, finally, his friend noticed me.

He was so happy to have secured a table at the restaurant

he took me to, blissfully unaware that it was exactly the same location as my very first date with Peter. Oh, the irony.

I went home with him that night and made sure he had the best sex of his life, ensuring that he got so caught up in the moment that he didn't stop to think about protection. By the morning I knew I had snared him and that I wouldn't be going back to my own dingy little flat anytime soon.

CHAPTER NINETEEN

As long as it was just the two of us, when Ben seemed happy to be bossed around by me, things were fine. The only problems arose when other people entered our bubble. He always changed slightly in the company of others and quite often, we would have an almighty row about it afterwards.

To begin with, he seemed to want us to spend lots of time with his sister, or his friends, or worse, his mum and dad. I had no desire for Peter to see me while I was pregnant, as I felt fat and unattractive; although I knew that Ben's ex, Charlotte, wasn't in my league looks-wise, she was quite slim and I didn't want any unfavourable comparisons made about our figures.

So I made it clear I preferred it when it was just the two of us and, although it took a while, he seemed to get the hint, at least where his annoying, little-miss-perfect sister was concerned. The crunch point came when he said he wanted to call in and see her on her birthday, as we drove home from a restaurant one evening.

I was tired and fed up and she was the last person I wanted to see. She was so bloody boring and I had heard plenty of gushing about her from Peter, who had always seemed to idolize her. He must have told me twenty times that she went to Oxford and was hugely intelligent and successful. I always took it as a slight on me, who never quite made it to university and pretty much flunked my A Levels. Not that I told him that. I would make vague references to 'uni' and always changed the subject if he asked too many questions about my background. Luckily, he was quite self-obsessed which meant he never really enquired.

So when, despite me telling him that I didn't want to visit her, Ben carried on driving towards Emma's little terraced house in Fulham and insisted we would only be there 'about five minutes', I lost my temper. 'No!' I screamed, making him jump visibly in the confines of the car. 'I don't feel well and I want to go home!'

Ben sighed heavily.

'And don't damn well sigh like that either! How dare you make me feel like *I'm* in the wrong because I'm pregnant and I just need to get to bed.'

'Sweetheart . . .' he began, reaching over to put his hand on my knee.

I swiped it away furiously. 'Don't you "sweetheart" me! You obviously couldn't care less how I'm feeling!'

Ben frowned. 'That's just not true. You know I put you first all the time and look after you incredibly well. But it's Emma's birthday and I've always arranged to see her at some point on the day, even if it was just to drop off her card on the way home.'

'Oh yes, I'm sure bloody Saint Charlotte spent half her life cosying up to your perfect sister. Well, I'm not Charlotte and I find Emma snobby and boring. She doesn't even try to hide what she thinks of me.'

Ben pulled up in the street outside Emma's house and turned

off the ignition. 'You've only seen her once or twice and she was perfectly nice to you. I don't know why you have this thing about her.'

Little did he know that my hatred of Emma was born long before I ever clapped eyes on her and stemmed from Peter's unstinting devotion and pride in her. I didn't think she was that special, anyway. 'If you insist on going in to see her, fine. It's selfish and thoughtless towards me but then that's you all over, so go ahead. I'll wait here.'

Ben frowned and shook his head. 'You really want to sit in the car while I go in and deliver my sister's birthday card? You don't want to wish her a happy birthday at all?'

'Nope.' I folded my arms across my rounded stomach and stared steadfastly ahead.

'But she'll see you when she comes to the door.'

I shrugged. 'So? I don't care.'

I could sense the cogs whirring in Ben's brain. He looked up and down the street before starting the engine again. I tried to conceal the tiny smile of triumph that was tugging at the corners of my mouth, as he pulled out of the space. But when he pulled into another space about twenty metres away, I looked at him in fury. 'What the hell are you doing?'

Ben undid his seatbelt and opened the car door. 'I'm dropping off my sister's birthday card and if you don't want to come with me, at least she's not going to see you sitting here refusing to get out of the car.'

My mouth dropped open as he slammed the door behind him and I watched as he strode back down the street towards Emma's door.

I watched the clock through narrowed eyes, the anger inside

me increasing with every minute that elapsed. Finally, after eleven minutes, I saw him coming back down the road. He got into the car and started the engine, pulling away too fast and causing me to be thrown back in my seat. I looked at him in disgust. 'Oh that's right, take your temper out on your pregnant wife.'

Ben took a deep, shuddery breath and exhaled loudly. When he glanced at me, I thought I could see tears shining in his eyes. 'I'm sorry,' he said at last. 'It's just that Emma's my sister and we've always been close. She's not had the easiest life . . .'

'Pffft!' I hissed, thinking that if Emma wanted to know what a life that wasn't easy looked like, she could try mine for size.

Ben ignored me and carried on. 'You know that she's got issues but she's a good person and I love her.'

I sighed. God, he was nauseating sometimes! 'Look,' I began, swallowing down the venom I desperately wanted to spew. 'I know all that. But she makes me feel like I'm not good enough for you. As if she looks down her nose at me . . .'

'She really doesn't . . . she's not like that at all.'

'Well, I'm just telling you how she makes me feel – and you can't argue with how I feel, can you?'

Ben gave a small, dry laugh. 'No,' he said. 'I can't.'

Ben's parents were easier to avoid as they lived in Suffolk and although I knew Ben often met Peter for lunch in London, he didn't expect me to go, too.

I had absolutely no desire to spend any more time than necessary with his twittering idiot of a mother and would always invent an illness or a hastily arranged trip that I swore I had told Ben about if he ever suggested a weekend in Suffolk.

But prising Ben away from his friends was another matter

entirely. He seemed to be obsessed with Matt, his best friend, and was always suggesting dinners with him and his wife, Freya.

When I realized that I could no longer keep making excuses, I reluctantly agreed to a night at their flat. 'You're going to love them so much!' Ben exclaimed, giving my hand a squeeze as we walked up to the front door. 'I can't wait for them to meet you.'

I smiled dutifully and pretended to be nervous, clutching the flowers I'd bought closer to my chest. 'I hope they don't hate me,' I told him, biting my lip for good measure.

Ben's eyes widened. 'Of course they won't hate you! They'll love you as much as I do.' He planted a kiss on the top of my head, causing me to grit my teeth.

Matt opened the door with a wide smile and pulled Ben into a laddish embrace. I had forgotten how attractive Matt was, actually. The only time I had seen him before, I was concentrating so hard on snaring Ben that I hadn't taken much notice of him. He also seemed to have quite a good sense of humour and was a bit less drippy than Ben. I clocked his eyes roaming over my body and thought what a shame it was that I couldn't have a pop at him, but decided that being pregnant and his best friend's new girlfriend meant that anything more was unlikely. I didn't want to look too pushy, so I just gave him a small, playful wave rather than a kiss.

Matt's wife, Freya, came out to greet us and I presented her with the flowers, which she took shyly, looking slightly overawed. I was pleased to see that, just like Ben's boring ex, she was nothing special to look at, so I wouldn't have had much competition if I did decide to make a move on Matt. Yes, she was pretty enough and had an annoyingly sexy figure, but she wasn't outstanding in any way. She certainly wasn't in my league. I knew that she and Charlotte had been very close and I could sense immediately that she was unsure about me, so decided to launch a charm offensive to win them both over.

I spent the evening asking them all about themselves and their lives, gushing over the food and admiring their perfectly ordinary flat, so that by the time we were ready to leave, I knew I had won them both over. There was a brief, slightly awkward moment when Ben told them about the pregnancy and once they had recovered from the shock, I could see Freya's eyes narrowing slightly, as if she was working something out. She was a midwife and I didn't want her asking too many questions, so I employed my usual technique of changing the subject as soon as it turned to me.

It wasn't a bad evening and I could see that Ben was enjoying himself – he certainly drank plenty – but by 11 p.m. I was exhausted from being on my best behaviour and wanted to go home. As Ben showed no signs of flagging I started looking at my watch pointedly and yawning. Finally, he took the hint and stood up. 'I suppose we'd better be making a move.'

Matt nodded. 'Fancy a quick stroll to clear your head first? To the end of the road and back?'

Ben nodded enthusiastically. 'Definitely!' He looked at me. 'I'll just be five minutes, darling.'

Irritation quivered in my chest. What the hell was this all about? I really did just want to go home now and I certainly didn't want to risk any alone time with Freya, in case she starting grilling me on the details of the pregnancy.

So I smiled as pleasantly as I could and stood up, fully aware that I was impinging on their ridiculous lads' ritual. 'Sure. I'll get my jacket.'

Ben and Matt exchanged confused glances. 'Um, no need for you to come, too, darling.' Ben nodded at me reassuringly. 'We'll only be a few minutes.'

I fixed Ben with my most determined stare. There was no way he was going anywhere without me. 'I'd like some air, too. Don't worry, you won't even know I'm there.'

There was a slightly uncomfortable pause, before Ben shrugged at Matt. The three of us let ourselves out of the house and turned into the street, where Matt and Ben stood awkwardly hopping from foot to foot, unsure what to do.

'You go on ahead,' I prompted, trying to conceal my annoyance.

'OK,' they chorused obediently, before walking ahead of me, both glancing occasionally over their shoulders to see if I was still there. I knew it was weird but I didn't want Ben saying anything he shouldn't behind my back. I needed to keep an eye on him.

I watched as Matt took a packet of cigarettes out of his pocket and offered them to Ben. Ah, so that was what this was all about. By now I had let them get a short distance in front of me and I saw Ben glance back over his shoulder. 'Nah, I'd better not,' he muttered, nodding towards me.

'She won't mind you having one, surely?' Matt also glanced over his shoulder back at me.

'She might.'

I felt like shouting out, telling Ben that yes, I absolutely did mind him having a cigarette, but that I minded him making me out to be a complete control freak much more.

Matt lit a cigarette and I saw the swirls of smoke rising above his head as he puffed on it. 'So, what do you reckon then? About the baby?'

I strained as hard as I could so that I could hear Ben's answer.

'I'm really happy about it,' he fired back instantly, a note of defiance in his voice.

Good boy I thought, pleased with his decisive response.

'That's good,' Matt replied.

'I must admit it was a bit of a shock, though,' Ben said, after a long pause.

Shut the hell up! I wanted to scream.

'I bet.' I could tell Matt was fishing by the long pauses he was leaving for Ben to fill.

Ben glanced back at me again, clearly unaware that I could hear every word, carried on the still night air. 'I keep thinking about Charlotte and me.'

Again, my ears pricked up.

'And?' Matt prompted.

Ben sighed. 'I think it must just not have been meant to be. All that time and we never had an accident. First night with Bella and . . .'

'Bingo!' Matt finished the sentence for him.

My heart began to pound. Surely he wasn't suspicious?

Ben gave a dry laugh. 'Yeah. Bingo.'

'Well, as long as you're happy about it, I'm pleased for you, mate.'

I held my breath but Ben didn't reply. Matt blew out a long trail of smoke before stubbing out his cigarette on the pavement and together, they turned back towards me. I turned, too, and tried to look as nonchalant as possible as we walked back the way we had come, this time with me in front of them.

'Does she always do that?' I heard Matt say.

'Do what?' Ben replied.

'Follow you everywhere you go.'

Ben laughed. 'No! 'Course not. I think she genuinely did just want some air.'

As if! I thought. I just wanted to make sure he wasn't saying anything he shouldn't.

'She's an absolute stunner, mate,' Matt said, loud enough for me to hear. I knew he fancied me. 'You have definitely lucked out there.'

By now I was at the gate, waiting for them to reach me. Ben looked up and met my eye. 'Yup,' he said with a smile. 'I certainly did.'

Poor Ben. He had no idea.

CHAPTER TWENTY

I had thought that one evening with his friends would be enough to stop Ben going on about us 'spending more time with Matt and Freya' but I was wrong. It became obvious that he and Charlotte had got into the habit of seeing them most weeks for an impromptu dinner or drinks and he made it clear that he was keen for us to carry on where they left off.

I had no intention of spending any more time than was absolutely necessary with them, so I would ignore the phone whenever I saw their number flash up on the caller display. I knew Matt called Ben all the time on his mobile but I also hoped that he had learned by now not to make any arrangements without me giving the go-ahead, so I felt safe in the knowledge that I wouldn't have to see them again for a while. But one Friday morning, as we were eating breakfast in the kitchen, Ben casually said, 'Oh, by the way, Matt and Freya are coming round tonight. I thought we could get a takeaway.'

He was scrolling on his iPad at the time and wasn't looking up at me.

I felt an immediate, visceral rage rising up inside me. 'No, they're not. It's not convenient.'

Ben looked up and frowned in puzzlement. 'But . . . . I've already invited them. And they've accepted.'

I couldn't believe his insolence. 'Well, you shouldn't have. Not without clearing it with me first.'

Ben took a deep breath and drew himself up to his full height, making him look ridiculous. 'I'm sorry, darling. You're right. But I've asked them now so they're coming. I'll know better next time.'

I fixed him with my hardest stare, before I stood up and threw my napkin on the table. The urge to slap his stupid face was overwhelming. I pulled my robe around me and marched out of the kitchen before I could actually inflict any physical damage.

I was so angry that I was shaking and I could feel tears of frustration welling up in my eyes. I slammed the bathroom door and switched on the shower to its hottest setting, wanting to feel some kind of sting to match my mood.

As the water hit my skin, I furiously lathered soap all over my body, thinking murderously of how I could make him pay. One thing I knew for absolute certain was that I wouldn't be joining them for their impromptu dinner tonight, so he would live to regret not consulting with me first.

I made sure I took as long as possible in the bathroom, so that Ben would be late for work and wouldn't have time for a discussion of any kind. I took particular care with my make-up and chose a dress that still looked sexy, despite my growing bump. Then I left the flat without saying goodbye, slamming the door as hard as possible for good measure.

Marcus was already in the office when I arrived. Since my marriage and pregnancy, he had cooled in his flirtations towards me, which hadn't bothered me and actually made things a bit easier. But today, I decided that maybe we could enjoy one last hurrah. My own little way of getting back at Ben.

'Morning, Marcus,' I said, placing a cup of his favourite coffee that I had bought on the way in, on his desk.

He looked up in surprise. 'Hey, Bella . . . thank you. Surely I should be buying you coffee, not the other way round?'

I flashed him my sexiest smile. 'I just remembered how much you always enjoyed it and thought it wouldn't do any harm to revisit our old habits, every once in a while . . .'

Marcus picked up the double meaning behind my words immediately. 'Well . . . what a nice thought that is. Revisiting old habits . . .' He grinned mischievously. 'I'm all in favour of that.'

With that, the mood was set and for the rest of the day we traded increasingly suggestive remarks. At 6 p.m., as I was getting ready to leave, he came and perched on my desk. One thing I had always loved about Marcus was that he was incredibly straightforward and didn't waste time with small talk when there was the promise of uncomplicated sex in the offing.

'So, am I right in thinking that we'll be spending this evening together?' he began easily.

I smiled. 'If you'd like to . . .' I locked eyes with him. 'Would you like to?'

Marcus pulled a wry face. ''Course I'd bloody well like to! Shall I book the usual place?'

'Sounds good. I'll just powder my nose and then we can go.'

'The usual' was a rather cheap and soulless hotel on the south side of the river. Marcus drove us there in his sleek Aston Martin, which he was able to drive in and park underneath the building. Unlike Peter, Marcus had always been paranoid about being caught playing away, so he made sure to go somewhere we were unlikely to run into anyone he knew.

We made our way up to the room and spent the evening having perfectly pleasant but not exactly earth-shattering sex. I felt self-conscious of my bump at first but Marcus didn't even seem to notice and it certainly didn't affect his performance. Finally, at around midnight, I decided that Matt and Freya should have gone by now and asked Marcus if he would drive me home.

He was pulling on his trousers and looked at me in horror. 'Drive you home? Don't you think your husband might have a few questions about that?'

I shook my head. 'I've already come up with a watertight cover story. You'll be fine, I promise.'

He shrugged. 'Well, as long as you're sure . . .'

After he dropped me off, I hastily squeezed in some eye-drops and rubbed hard at my eyes, causing my eye make-up to smear beneath my fingers. Then I unlocked the door to the flat and walked in.

I listened out for the sound of any movement but couldn't hear anything. I decided he must have gone to bed, so I dropped my bag in the hallway and walked through to the bedroom. I peered into the gloom but to my surprise, the bed was empty. I frowned, wondering if he might have actually gone out looking for me. It was just the sort of thing Ben might do if he was worried.

I walked around to my side of the bed and sat down, exhausted after all the exertions of the day. Suddenly, I heard footsteps and Ben marched into the room, making me jump in fright. 'Where the bloody hell have you been?' he hissed, sounding furious. I had my story all planned out but I hadn't reckoned on him being so angry. I had thought he would just be worried sick and would be so glad that I was OK, he would just make a huge fuss of me.

I took a deep breath to calm my racing heart and shook my head.

'Well?' he shouted. 'Answer me! Do you have any idea how embarrassing that was?'

I turned towards him and watched with satisfaction as he visibly recoiled. My trick with the eye-drops had clearly worked wonders. 'I've been at the hospital,' I whispered, summoning up genuine tears as I threw myself into my story. 'I thought I was losing the baby.' I put my head in my hands and was pleased to see that my face was wet.

'Oh my God! Why didn't you call me?' Immediately, Ben's tone switched from angry to distraught and he dashed over to my side of the bed. He knelt in front of me and put his arms around my shoulders, stroking my hair.

I looked up at him with an apologetic expression. 'I'm sorry, there wasn't time . . . I just wanted to get there.' I paused to let Ben take in the enormity of the situation before delivering the killer blow. 'Marcus took me.'

Immediately, I felt Ben bristle. He knew that I had had an affair with Marcus in the past and he had always been a little bit wary of him because of it. He had even once tentatively suggested that it wasn't really appropriate for me to continue working with him, until I set him straight in no uncertain terms. 'Right,' he said, looking annoyed.

'He was so lovely.' I was enjoying twisting the knife. 'He waited while they checked me over and then insisted on bringing me home.'

'That was very nice of him,' Ben said through gritted teeth.

'But of course, if you'd rung me, or not had your phone switched off, I would have come straight away.'

I nodded and wiped my eyes, further smudging my mascara, this time with genuine tears. 'I know – but I didn't want to spoil your evening with Matt and Freya . . .' I let my words hang in the air, making sure there was no doubt about tonight being his fault entirely. Without me actually saying so, I wanted him to feel guilty as hell that he had put a night of drinking with his mates above looking after his pregnant wife, with potentially tragic results. I was so outraged, I almost believed my own story.

Ben looked duly ashamed. 'So what happened? What made you think you were losing the baby . . . and is it OK?'

I shook my head and made a swatting motion with my hand. 'I don't want to talk about it,' I said, trying to sound stoic. The last thing I needed was him asking too many questions, as I actually didn't have a clue what happened if you really did have a miscarriage. 'But the main thing is that everything is OK and the baby's fine.'

'Oh, thank God!' Tears flashed into Ben's eyes and I felt a tiny bit guilty for lying about something so serious. I briefly hoped I wasn't tempting fate. 'I'm so sorry I wasn't there for you, darling.' He kissed the top of my head and pulled me towards him.

I gave him a brave smile. 'It's OK. Luckily Marcus was there, so he took care of me. Don't feel bad.'

My words landed and Ben swallowed hard. 'Well, let me look after you now,' he said, bending down to take off my shoes. 'From now on, I'm not leaving your side.'

I allowed him to help me lay down gently on the bed and smiled up at him. 'Thank you,' I whispered, confident that he wouldn't be inviting Matt and Freya round again in a hurry.

CHAPTER TWENTY-ONE

I tried to persuade Ben that we shouldn't spend Christmas with his parents but he was infuriatingly intransigent on the matter. 'I promised Mum ages ago that we'd be there and I can't let them down now.'

'Well, you shouldn't have promised anything without checking it with me first.' I couldn't believe he hadn't learned his lesson from the last incident with Matt and Freya.

'You were there!' Ben protested, a flicker of annoyance passing over his face. 'I didn't think I needed to check with you again.'

I hesitated, wracking my brains to remember any such conversation. It must have been back in the summer when I was still trying to be on my best behaviour. It was also before my body swelled up like a balloon, and. I really didn't want Peter seeing me looking like this but I could hardly tell Ben that. 'Fine!' I snapped, resigning myself to spending Christmas with them, but vowing to make it as uncomfortable as possible. It would be fun watching Peter having to bite his tongue all the time.

So on Christmas Day, Ben drove us out to Suffolk. He kept throwing nervous glances in my direction, which only served to make me feel even more bad-tempered.

Jo threw open the door as we pulled up. 'Hello, you two! Happy Christmas!' she trilled in her irritating, squawky voice. I was disappointed to see her looking glamorous, pretty and, worst of all, slim.

Ben kissed her as we joined her on the doorstep. 'Hi, Mum, happy Christmas.'

'And look at you!' Jo beamed, as she kissed me on both cheeks, before motioning towards my rounded stomach. 'You're cooking nicely.'

I wanted to slap her. 'You make me sound like a bloody turkey!'

'Oh! Well, you're certainly the most beautiful turkey I've ever seen.' Jo looked flustered and there was an awkward pause as both she and Ben watched me nervously, waiting to see what I would do next.

'Right,' I said eventually. 'Are we standing out here all day or are we allowed in?'

Jo almost gasped with shock, before gathering herself. 'Of course! Come on through. Peter's in the kitchen.'

I smiled inwardly as I followed Ben and Jo into the hallway. I was suddenly looking forward to seeing Peter again.

Ben took off his jacket and hung it on the coat rack before turning to me and reaching out to take my coat. 'Leave it!' I snapped. 'I'm cold.' I wasn't cold at all – if anything, the bump was like a permanent hot water bottle, which meant I was always very warm. But I wanted to be as difficult as possible.

'Look who's here!' Jo trilled, as we reached the kitchen. Peter had his back to us, stirring a pan on the Aga. I figured it was the mulled wine Ben had warned me about, which apparently he made every year, even though everyone hated it, but he had done it for so long that no one had the heart to tell him it was disgusting. I was glad I wouldn't have to drink it, as I was such a respectable teetotaller these days.

Peter seemed to be steeling himself to face us, as he took an overly long time to wipe his hands on a tea towel, before turning around. 'Hello, you two. Happy Christmas!'

I wished my heart didn't still flip at the sight of him but I was powerless to stop it. I moved into his reluctant embrace and gazed up at him with a massive fake smile. 'Happy Christmas, Peter! That mulled wine smells divine . . . almost makes me wish I could drink it.'

Peter flushed immediately and threw Jo a panicked look, before clearing his throat. 'Well, you'll be pleased to hear that you can . . . I made it non-alcoholic this year, knowing you didn't drink.'

'Did you? You didn't say.' For the first time ever, I thought Jo sounded annoyed, which pleased me enormously.

Peter reached for a glass and poured a generous serving, which he handed to me with the air of someone who was giving a dog a treat, whilst half-expecting it to bite their hand.

I took it from him, making sure to brush his hand with mine as I did so. I gazed deliberately at him over the rim of the heavy pewter goblet as I drank. It was possibly the most horrible concoction I had ever tasted – a cross between clove mouthwash and corked wine. 'How wonderful,' I managed, trying not to gag as I swallowed each mouthful. Peter's face was almost puce by now, as he tried to maintain his neutral expression.

'Well,' Jo cried, clapping her hands like a hyperactive 4-year-old child. 'Let's go through and make ourselves comfortable, shall we? Bella, are you sure you won't take off your coat?'

'No.' I adopted a pained look. 'I'd rather keep it on as I'm feeling a bit chilled.' I glanced up at Peter with an overly apologetic smile.

'Oh dear, I do hope you're not sickening for something?' Peter's words were loaded with sarcasm but somehow I didn't think anyone else would have picked up on it.

'Pregnancy's not an illness, is it, Bella?' Jo said sharply, confirming my theory.

'Um, no, I guess not,' I said, in what I hoped was a hurt tone, giving a little shudder for good measure.

After a stilted silence, during which Ben looked at his mum with a satisfyingly accusatory stare, the four of us made our way into the sitting room. I sat down gingerly, wincing slightly as I did so, even though there was actually nothing to wince at.

'Are you OK, darling?' Ben's face was full of concern.

'Yes, I'm fine,' I told him with a brave smile.

'What time is Emma getting here?' Ben asked Peter. I'd almost forgotten she would be here, too and I had to make a real effort to stop my lip curling.

Peter looked at his watch. 'Any time now, I should imagine. I told her she should have hitched a lift with you two. Seems a bit crazy to bring two cars to do the same journey.'

I shot Ben a warning look. He didn't need to mention that I had said it was bad enough that we were going to his parents for Christmas, there was absolutely no way I was travelling down with his sister, too.

I could feel Jo staring at me and when I turned towards her, she quickly tried to rearrange her expression, but not before I had caught the look of pure dislike in her eyes. *The feeling's entirely mutual*, I felt like yelling. She frowned, before getting up and leaving the room.

Ben and Peter didn't seem to notice Jo leaving and Ben continued chatting to his dad, completely oblivious to the undertones crackling around them. I now saw that Peter didn't look great. His colour was high and he had acquired quite a few more lines on his face, even in the couple of months since I had last seen him. He was still handsome but there were dark circles under his eyes and he looked diminished, somehow. The sexy swagger that he had used to seduce me had long gone.

I guessed that it was caused by stress but I couldn't feel any sympathy for him. He didn't worry about the stress I was under, when he vanished like a ghost and thought he could drop me without a backward glance.

I watched him now, trying to concentrate on what Ben was saying, but his eyes kept flickering nervously in my direction. I wondered if he had even the slightest trace of love remaining for me. When we were together, although I always knew that I felt more for him than he did for me, I was certain that his feelings ran deeper than just lust. I got enough back from him to make me believe that one day he would leave his wife and make a life with me and our baby.

How naïve and dumb that seemed now, bearing in mind what he did to me.

Just then, Jo came bursting back into the room. She seemed to be borderline hysterical. 'Emma's had an accident. We need to go and get her!'

Peter and Ben both immediately leaped out of their seats. 'Shit! Is she OK?' Ben looked genuinely distressed, which was a bit of an over-the-top reaction. I was fairly sure Emma couldn't have been badly hurt or she wouldn't be calling her mum and dad to go and pick her up. She would have been on her way to hospital in an ambulance.

'She's very shaken and upset and I think she's bumped her head but she was talking coherently, so hopefully she's fine. Come on, Peter, we need to hurry.' Jo gestured towards the door expectantly, chivvying him as if he was a naughty child.

Peter nodded quickly and strode out of the room. I looked up at Ben, expecting him to sit back down beside me but instead, he headed for the door.

'I'll come!' he said loudly.

'No, Ben!' I shouted, before I had time to think, causing them all to stop in their tracks. 'You can't go,' I added, as three sets of eyes turned towards me.

Ben scowled irritably. 'What? I need to go with them in case Dad and I have to pull the car out of a ditch or something.'

His insolent tone made me fizz with instant rage. 'You can't leave me here on my own!' I hissed through gritted teeth, hoping he would get the message and come back in.

'Come, don't come,' Jo snapped at Ben. 'But make your bloody mind up because we need to get to Emma.'

Ben hesitated and I glared at him murderously. He didn't need to go. He was just trying to play the hero in front of his mum and dad. I didn't want to be left in the house on my own when I wasn't feeling well. The fact that I felt fine was irrelevant – he *thought* I was unwell which was the main thing.

To my horror, he gave me an apologetic smile. 'Sorry, darling, I'll only be a few minutes. You'll be fine.'

With that, the three of them raced out of the door, leaving me sitting by myself in a fog of such violent outrage that it brought genuine tears to my eyes.

I couldn't believe that Ben would deliberately disobey me like that, trying to humiliate me and make a fool of me in front of his mum and, particularly, his dad. 'You bastard!' I screamed into the empty room.

It was almost half an hour before they came back. By that time, the upset I felt had solidified into cold, hard rage. I watched resentfully through the window as Peter and Jo tenderly helped Emma out of the back of the Range Rover. She seemed absolutely fine. Well, apart from the bump on her forehead, which probably looked a lot worse than it was. They each took an arm and steered her towards the house, as if she was about to collapse at any minute. Emma was milking it for all she was worth, shuffling along like a 90-year-old. As they reached the front door, her small green Fiat pulled onto the gravel driveway, driven by Ben. Admittedly, it was pretty badly bashed up but it was clearly drivable. Emma hadn't needed everyone to go running to her rescue – she could just as easily have driven it home herself. Bloody drama-queen that she was, she probably just wanted everyone to make a fuss of her, instead of me.

As Peter, Jo and Emma all made their way to the kitchen, Ben came into the sitting room. I fixed him with a cold stare as he stood nervously in front of me, like a schoolboy summoned to see the headmistress. 'Poor Emma – that was a pretty nasty prang she had there,' he began.

I pulled my coat around myself defensively and looked away without replying.

Ben ran a hand through his hair. 'Did you see the car? It's a right mess.'

I shrugged huffily. 'It doesn't look that bad to me. And Emma seemed fine.'

Ben frowned. 'She's actually very shaken up, Bella! And she's got a hell of a bump on her head.' He hesitated. 'Why are you being like this? You've been really off since we arrived.'

Immediately, the tears that had been threatening, spilled over and I put my face in my hands. 'I'm sorry, Ben. It's just that I'm feeling so ill and I thought I might faint but I was here on my own and I didn't know what to do. I was so worried about the baby.'

As always with any mention of the baby's wellbeing, Ben's irritation immediately melted away. He came rushing over and knelt down in front of me, pulling me into his arms. 'Oh sweetheart, you poor thing. You should have said . . .'

'I didn't want to ruin Christmas for your mum. She's gone to so much trouble!'

'You haven't ruined Christmas! There's still plenty of time to enjoy ourselves.' Ben gave my back a reassuring rub as he spoke.

I rolled my eyes. I had absolutely no intention of staying here a minute longer than I had to. 'But I just feel dreadful, Ben. I'm so sorry but all I want to do is go home to bed.'

Ben pulled away and I could see the conflict travelling over his features. It was either upset me or upset his mum. We both already knew there was no contest. 'You couldn't go to bed here?' he suggested without conviction, knowing the battle was already lost.

I shook my head sadly. 'I think it's best if I'm near the hospital . . . Just in case.'

Reluctantly, Ben nodded and stood up. 'OK, I'll just go and tell Mum.' I could see he was dreading the conversation as he trudged out of the room, his shoulders hunched.

I felt slightly guilty, leaving him to face the music alone, so I followed him out into the hallway and headed towards the kitchen, where Ben was standing in the doorway. I paused halfway along, so that I could listen to what he was saying. 'Um, Bella's not feeling too good. I'm really sorry but I think we'd better go home.'

'What?' Jo whined. 'But what about lunch, your presents . . . you were supposed to be staying the night?'

Ben glanced over his shoulder nervously and locked eyes with me, standing watching him. 'I'm sorry, Mum,' he said, walking back towards me.

'Peter, can't you speak to her?' Jo said in what she clearly thought were hushed tones but which carried down the hallway, loudly enough to be easily heard by Ben and me. 'See if you can persuade her to stay? She seems to like you more than me.'

I almost laughed at the irony of her words.

'I'd rather not,' Peter said. *That's the understatement of the century!* I thought. 'I'm not sure it'll do much good anyway and if she's genuinely not feeling well . . .'

'Please, Peter. It'll spoil everything if they leave and I can tell Ben doesn't want to. It's her . . .'

Ben looked at me in panic and tried to usher me back down the hallway out of earshot. But I shook him off and walked to the doorway of the kitchen.

Jo had her back to me and hadn't noticed I was there, but both Peter and Emma looked at me in horror. 'She can't bear the attention wandering from her for a second. She's such a little bloody madam! Honestly, Emma, you should have seen her earlier, refusing to even take her coat off!'

I felt like clapping my hands with joy. She had done exactly what I hoped and given me the perfect excuse to leave, with all the blame landing squarely on her shoulders. There was a long, agonizing pause, as Jo realized that Peter and Emma were looking over her shoulder with horrified expressions and that I must have overheard her. I saw her tense, before she turned very slowly to face me.

'Wow, thanks for that, Jo,' I said, in a tone of voice that I hoped sounded deeply wounded, aware that I needed to put a stop to the smile that was tugging at the corners of my mouth. 'It's a good job we're leaving – I certainly know where I'm not wanted.'

'Bella, I . . .' Jo's face flushed bright red. She stepped forward and reached out to take my arm but shrugged her off brusquely.

'Let go of me! Come on, Ben. We're going.'

Ben looked like he might cry. 'I'm really sorry but we have to go. Em, I hope you're OK?'

Emma nodded and raised her glass. 'Thanks, I'll be fine,' she slurred. She sounded absolutely plastered. 'Happy Christmas.'

Ben hesitated and for a horrible moment, I thought he might be going to ask if we could stay after all. I gave him my most ferocious glare. 'Ben!' I growled, leaving him in no doubt that I would not be staying in this house a minute longer.

With a final, anguished look, he gave a small wave and followed me to the front door.

As he opened the door, we heard Jo burst into noisy sobs and he threw me a pleading look. I shook my head fiercely and pushed him out, before pulling the door shut behind me with a loud bang.

We got into the car and Ben reversed out of the drive, looking distraught.

'Well, I always suspected that she didn't like me all along

and it looks like I was right,' I told him, trying not to sound too triumphant.

'She does like you . . .' he said, sounding weary. 'But you have to admit you weren't exactly friendly to her either.'

Indignation rattled through me. How dare he blame me for his mother's hurtful comments. 'Are you saying it was my fault?' My bottom lip began to wobble and I knew the tears weren't far behind.

Ben closed his eyes for a moment, before reaching over and putting his hand on my leg. 'No, of course not. Come on, darling, don't cry. Let's get you home and into bed. I'm sure you'll feel better if you have a good sleep.'

I blew my nose and nodded my agreement. I didn't need to tell him that I felt much better already.

CHAPTER TWENTY-TWO

We didn't have long to wait for the baby to arrive. I started to have contractions at around midnight on January 3rd and Ben drove me to the hospital, casting worried glances in my direction. 'Isn't it too early?' he kept saying.

I looked out of the window, counting the time between contractions and vowing to get him well out of the way when I was talking to the midwives about dates. I was sure I'd be able to fob him off easily enough. For my part, I couldn't wait to meet the little person who had been growing inside me these past nine months and felt almost giddy with excitement.

The birth was remarkably straightforward, if unbelievably painful, and Elodie arrived, looking more serene and perfect than I could ever have imagined. I held her tiny, perfect hands and counted her dainty little toes with a feeling of awe like I had never experienced before. She was mine and mine alone. I could see Peter in her but more than anything, I could see myself. It was such a strange sensation to look at another person and see yourself reflected back.

Ben was immediately smitten and it surprised me how good he was with her. It should probably have made me feel guilty but instead I just felt grateful that he was there and so supportive. When we first brought her home, we both spent hours just watching her sleep in her Moses basket. I don't think either of us could believe we had been left in charge of this tiny baby who was entirely dependent on us for her survival.

Once Ben went back to work, my mum came to stay for a week and I let her do the lion's share of the work, while I got as much sleep as possible. She was wonderful with Elodie, which I had mixed feelings about. On the one hand, I was grateful for the help but on the other, I felt it was the least she could do to make up for the crap childhood she had given me, after she accused my dad of all sorts and had him sent away.

Mum and I had always had an odd relationship. Somewhere along the line, she had become scared of me and as a result, she irritated the hell out of me. It became a vicious circle: the more I sensed her nervousness around me, the nastier I became, which only served to make her more nervous. Both of us breathed a huge sigh of relief when I moved out of our poky little house on an estate in Croydon, to move into a place of my own in London.

But after I had Elodie, it seemed like we developed a slightly uneasy truce. I thought that maybe it was because I really did need her help for the first time ever. I was bone-tired and had absolutely no clue what I was doing, so I had no choice but to watch her and learn. As well as looking after Elodie, she also mothered me – feeding me and letting me sleep whenever I wanted – which I had to admit I enjoyed. I was almost sad when she left to return home. Almost. And she must have felt the same way, because after that she began to pay more regular visits, taking over the housework and childcare the minute she walked through the door.

I waited for Ben to suggest that his parents should come to visit, but as things had settled down between us since the Christmas 'incident', it was as if he didn't want to tempt fate.

For my part, I only wanted to see Peter again once I felt like I was back to looking my best and had lost the unsightly jelly-belly that my pregnancy had left behind. So it suited me perfectly to have the excuse of the row at Christmas to avoid having to see them. Jo sent texts, letters and flowers, all apologizing profusely for what she'd said and begging my forgiveness.

Ben and I would read them in silence, before quietly carrying on with whatever we were doing, with no discussion or even acknowledgement.

The weeks ticked by and I liked that our bubble had shrunk to just Ben, me and Elodie, with only sporadic visits from my mum. I felt back in control, which is how I liked it. Matt and Freya seemed to have got the hint and their phone-calls, which I had grown expert in ignoring, had dwindled away to almost nothing. I never mentioned to Ben that they had called or left messages on the Ansaphone because I didn't want him getting any ideas about rekindling their friendship. That most definitely wasn't going to happen.

I also 'accidentally' smashed his mobile phone and then offered to get a new one for him, making sure that he got a new number in the process, so that no one from his 'old' life could contact him. When he started to complain and wail that I'd lost all his contacts, I burst into tears and he promptly shut up.

So when Ben came home from work one day and mooted the idea of finally inviting his parents to visit, it took me entirely by surprise. I had been trying to contact him at lunchtime and he wasn't answering his phone. I had a sixth sense that he was doing something he shouldn't have been doing and I was ready for a row about it by the time he came through the door. His sheepish demeanour only confirmed what I suspected.

'So, what were you doing today that was so important you ignored my calls?' I asked him, as we sat down to eat the risotto he had prepared.

'I didn't ignore your calls.' Ben took a mouthful of his risotto but seemed to struggle to swallow it and winced slightly before continuing. 'I was at work, Bella. I can't just drop everything and take a personal call every time my phone rings. It's unprofessional and it will get me into trouble. We can't afford for me to lose this job.'

There was something about his patronizing tone that annoyed me and I threw my fork down onto my plate. It landed with a clatter and made both of us jump. 'But what if it's urgent? What if it's something to do with Elodie?'

'Well, then of course I will drop everything and come running. But it wasn't about Elodie, was it?'

He was right of course but I was still furious and could feel the tears welling up.

Ben sighed, before reaching out to take my hand. 'Come on, sweetheart. Don't get upset. You are doing a fantastic job with our gorgeous baby. I'm so proud of you.'

He was so sweet sometimes. 'Thank you. I'm sorry for calling so often, it's just that I get so bloody lonely sometimes. It's really, really hard.'

Ben reached out and took my hand in his. 'Of course it is. I completely understand darling. But . . . you don't *have* to be lonely.'

Ah. I had wondered when this might come.

'I'm sure Mum is desperate to see Elodie and she'd be so happy to help out. To give you a bit of a break.' Ben was trying not to sound too eager but he wasn't succeeding. I could clearly hear the hope in his voice.

It wasn't Jo who would be most desperate to see Elodie, I thought, it was Peter. I could just imagine how badly it would have hurt him not to be able to see her before now, knowing that she was his. And he deserved every bit of pain he was going through. But now that I was back to my pre-pregnancy weight and looking pretty good, I thought that maybe it was time. It would only pile on the agony for him.

'Why don't we invite her round? Come on, Bella, otherwise it's a bit like cutting off your nose to spite your face.'

'Maybe,' I began, seeing his eyes light up instantly with anticipation. 'But you have to be here, too. I don't want to see her on my own, just in case . . .'

I thought Ben might react to my insinuation but he just nodded eagerly. 'Of course I'll be here, too. How about this weekend? Shall I ask them to come here then?'

'Them? Invite your dad, too?' I wanted to be sure.

'Well, yes. I'm sure he's as desperate to meet his first grand-child as Mum is.'

If only you knew, I thought, looking away as I pretended to ponder, prolonging the moment for as long as possible. 'I suppose so,' I said eventually.

Ben gave a sharp gasp of surprise, his eyes shining, before he picked up his fork and resumed eating, trying to seem as casual as possible.

'Why don't you go and have a relaxing bath while I clear up?' he said, once we had both finished.

I had wanted to listen to the conversation but a bath sounded very appealing and I could listen from the bathroom anyway. 'OK, that would be nice. Thanks.'

I ran the bath as quickly as I could, then turned off the taps, climbed in and listened hard.

'Mum, it's me,' I heard him say in a choked voice. I hoped he wasn't going to get all emotional. It got on my nerves and was another thing that made him so different to Peter, who was rarely anything other than calm and measured.

'Good, Mum. I'm really good . . . Well, that's why I'm calling, actually. We wondered if you and Dad would like to come and visit this weekend?'

I felt a little frisson of excitement at the thought of seeing Peter again and of him seeing his daughter for the first time. It would be agony for him not to be able to say anything. I got out of the bath and wrapped my robe around me, as Ben's voice carried through the flat.

'Of course! She'd love to see you, too.' His voice lifted an octave as he voiced the lie. Ben wasn't a good liar, unlike his father. 'Um, about midday? We'll do lunch.'

Irritation flared, causing me to grit my teeth in fury. He was so bloody useless! Elodie's routine meant I put her down for her lunchtime nap at noon. How did he not know that? I snatched open the door and glared at him as he finished the conversation and hung up.

'Midday?'

Ben spun around to face me, with a dopey frown on his face. 'Yes. What's wrong with that?'

'Oh, nothing, except that Elodie will be asleep. I thought they were coming to see her?'

Ben's frown deepened and he sighed. 'They are coming to see her,' he said, in his most patient voice. 'Surely it won't do any harm to keep her up a little bit longer for once?'

I could have slapped him. 'Oh for God's sake, Ben! That's typical of you. You aren't the one who's worked your backside off to get her into her routine. I'm not wrecking all my hard work just to suit you.'

'Fine!' Ben snapped. 'Then we'll have lunch first and they can see her when she wakes up.'

'Well, you needn't think I'm cooking lunch. I've got enough to do, thank you very much, without having to entertain your parents.'

His jaw tightened with the effort of controlling his temper. 'I'll do the cooking,' he cajoled, clearly desperate that I didn't change my mind. 'You can sit and chat to them.'

'Oh yes, that's a good idea, because we get on so well.' I knew I was being unreasonable but I couldn't help it. He just irritated the hell out of me.

Ben came over and pulled me into a hug that I didn't return. 'Please, Bella, don't turn this into a feud,' he said. 'They're my parents and they're Elodie's grandparents. I don't want them to become strangers.'

I wondered for a second how it would feel to tell him that Peter was actually Elodie's parent, rather than her grandparent. The words would literally kill him. For a second, I felt a tiny hint of sympathy for him. None of this was his fault. 'I'm sorry, Ben. I just . . . feel that your mum doesn't like me and it's really hurtful.'

'She does like you,' Ben insisted, tilting my chin up so that I was looking at him with my best doe-eyed expression. 'So don't go looking for insults and slights. Just be yourself and they will love you as much as I do.'

Unlikely, I thought, smiling at the idea. 'I love you, too. I'm just tired, I think. How about we get an early night?'

Ben grinned at me with genuine love and tenderness in his eyes. 'There was a time when that would have meant something else entirely. And do you know what? Even though I know you're only talking about going to sleep, I can't think of anything I'd love more.'

'Who says I'm only talking about going to sleep?' I gave him my best seductive look over my shoulder, as I took his hand and pulled him towards the bedroom. I needed to keep him sweet.

CHAPTER TWENTY-THREE

'They're here!' Ben called from his vantage point, looking out of the living-room window into the street beyond. He had been like a cat on hot bricks all morning, awaiting his parents' arrival. He had prepared a lasagne for lunch and made sure everything was just so in the flat, clearly desperate that nothing should go wrong.

Like Ben, I had been making preparations all morning, too. I had had a long soak in the bath, before spending almost an hour on my hair and make-up. Finally, I spritzed with the Hermès scent I knew Peter always loved and dressed in a deceptively sexy fitted shirt and my most flattering pair of skinny jeans, which showed off my long, slim legs and perfect bum. I felt pleased with what I saw in the mirror, as I put Elodie down for her lunchtime nap, buying time until I had to face Peter and Jo.

'Hi, Mum, hi, Dad,' I heard Ben say, sending a shiver of excitement through me. 'You've lost weight, Dad, are you OK?'

I held my breath waiting for Peter's answer. 'I am now.'

I waited in the gloom of Elodie's room, listening as they bustled into the flat.

'Hello, darling, these are for Bella – and Elodie.' Jo's voice still had the power to set my teeth on edge, even after all this time.

'Thanks, Mum, come on in!' Ben sounded happier than I had heard him in a long while – clearly, she didn't have the same effect on him.

'She's just put Elodie down for her lunchtime nap,' Ben said. 'She'll be out in a minute.' I decided to prolong the moment for as long as possible, so I leaned against the door, listening.

I heard Ben go into the kitchen to make tea. While he was gone, Peter and Jo didn't appear to exchange a word. Probably too scared to speak in case I overheard, I thought with satisfaction.

'So . . . how have you been?' Ben asked in an overly chirpy voice, as he returned to the living room.

'Fine . . .' Jo started to say, but Peter cut across her.

'Not great – we've been wondering when we'd finally get to meet Elodie . . .' My heart skipped at the sound of his voice, which seemed full of pent-up emotion, as his words tumbled out over each other.

'Peter . . .'

'No, Jo,' Peter cut her off. 'I want to know why you haven't been in touch. Have you any idea how upset your mother's been? How upset I've been, for that matter?'

I wished I could see his face, to see the anguish that was evident in his voice. Good. He deserved to suffer.

'I'm sorry,' Ben replied quickly. 'We've been so busy with the baby. Time ran away from me.'

'Rubbish!' Peter spat. 'You forget that we've had two children ourselves and yes, it's hard work, but it's also possible to find time to make a bloody phone-call! How could you have left it for so long? Do you have any idea how hurtful that was?'

In one movement, I opened the bedroom door and stepped over the hallway into the living room.

'It was because of me,' I said, making them all jump visibly. Jo and Peter both swung around to look at me simultaneously and both of them gave a half-gasp. Peter's eyes met mine and for a second, I could see the confusion, as lust fought against his already dwindling anger. It had been worth putting in so much effort to look as good as possible.

'I didn't want Ben to contact you. I'm sorry,' I continued, aiming for calm, yet vulnerable. 'I was just so hurt by what happened at Christmas and . . .'

'Of course you were!' Jo leaped out of her seat and for one awful moment, I thought she was going to hug me, so I wrapped my arms around my body defensively, hoping to ward her off.

It seemed to work and she stepped back slightly. 'I am so sorry for what I said, Bella. It was in the heat of the moment and I was feeling very stressed after Emma's accident . . .'

I nodded and adopted a stoic expression. 'It's fine. Let's forget about it.'

Jo nodded eagerly. 'Thank you!' she trilled. 'How are you, Bella? You look truly amazing! I can't believe how quickly you've got your figure back.'

I smiled. All the hard work had paid off. I had barely eaten for weeks. 'Apparently my mum was the same with me. Lucky, genes, I guess,' I said breezily before twisting the knife a bit more. 'She says Elodie's identical to me as a baby so hopefully she's inherited them, too.'

My words landed and Jo swallowed hard. The truth was, my mum hadn't been around that much either recently because she drove me mad, but Jo didn't need to know that.

She blinked quickly, as if to squeeze away any tears that might be threatening. 'And what's she like? Elodie, I mean? I can't wait to see her.'

I could tell she was treading on eggshells, unsure if I would take anything she said the wrong way. I decided to be beneficent for once. After all, I didn't want any of them thinking I was an unreasonable bitch.

'She's perfect. She'll be up in a little while but you can have a peep at her if you like?'

Jo's face lit up with joy. 'I'd love to!' she breathed.

Although I didn't look at him, all the while I was aware of Peter watching me with those sleepy brown eyes of his. I didn't invite him to join us, wanting to make him wait for as long as possible before he got to set eyes on his daughter.

We tiptoed together into Elodie's room, me aware that Jo was being exaggeratedly careful not to make a noise. We made our way to the white wooden cot in the corner where Elodie was lying on her back, sleeping soundly. I watched Jo's rapt expression as she peered down at her. She put her hand to her chest, clearly fighting back tears. 'She's so lovely,' she whispered. 'And she looks so much like you.'

Well, she's certainly not going to look like you, is she? I thought meanly. 'Thank you. And yes, I think she's lovely too but I'm a bit biased.'

'You're allowed to be. You're her mum,' Jo gushed, before we both tiptoed back out of the room.

In the kitchen, Peter and Ben were chatting quietly, as Ben

prepared the lunch. I deliberately avoided making eye contact with Peter as we joined them, but made sure that I was as charming as possible. I laughed at all Ben's stupid jokes and listened intently to Jo's dreary stories, knowing that Peter's eyes were on me the whole time. I wondered idly if he ever felt any regret over me. Whether he ever imagined what it would be like to set up home with just me and his new baby daughter. It killed me to know that if he just said the word, I would still run away with him in a heartbeat.

'And how has Ben been looking after you?' Jo suddenly piped up, interrupting my thoughts.

'He's been amazing,' I said, aware as I spoke of how true it was. 'But he works such long hours. I think we might need to rethink.' I could see Peter's eyes narrowing as I spoke, wondering what I might be up to now.

'Rethink what?' Ben chimed in, his mouth full of lasagne.

'Your job. It's not even as if you love it that much. A fresh start somewhere out of London might be good for all of us.' An idea was beginning to form in my mind.

'You never mentioned it before. What's brought this on?'

'Oh, I don't know. Maybe hearing your mum and dad's stories about you growing up in Suffolk. It sounds idyllic . . .' I deliberately left the words hanging for a second. 'I'd like Elodie to have that sort of upbringing.'

'What was your childhood like, Bella?' Jo asked, annoyingly interrupting my flow. 'I'm not sure I've ever heard you talk about it.'

'That's because I don't want to bore everyone rigid. It was dull as ditchwater.' I rolled my eyes to close down the conversation. 'There's honestly nothing to tell.'

'I'm sure that's not true,' Jo persisted. 'Where did you live again?'

I put a hand to my ear. 'I think I can hear a certain little someone stirring!' I stood up and left the room. It was the only way to shut her up.

I hated waking Elodie but there was no choice. I opened the blackout curtains and unzipped her sleeping bag, shaking her gently as I did so. Her eyes popped open in surprise, before she stretched out her arms and legs and gave a huge yawn. I watched her, smiling to myself. She was so beautiful it was impossible not to fall in love with her all over again.

I scooped her up, drinking in the sweet smell of sleep that still clung to her and carried her back into the kitchen where Peter and Jo were waiting with bated breath.

'Here she is!'

'Oh my word, she's just perfect!' Jo cooed, as they stood either side of me. 'Isn't she, Peter?'

I looked up at Peter, who was gazing at Elodie with undisguised awe. 'She certainly is,' he breathed. 'Can I hold her?' He looked up and met my eye with an expression that said so much.

'Of course,' I replied, after a moment. I lowered Elodie into his arms, watching him closely as I did so. It felt as though all my senses were heightened, I was so aware of his smell, his touch and the sound of his voice.

'What do you think then, Dad? Do you think she looks like me?' Ben came over and tickled Elodie's stomach, causing her to squirm and smile at the same time. I thought of all the terrible things I could say that would smash his world to smithereens.

'Not really, son,' Peter said carefully, causing my stomach to drop with fear. Was he about to blab everything in a moment of madness? I held my breath until he finished. 'She's far more beautiful than you.'

We all burst into peals of exaggerated, relieved laughter and I caught Peter's eye. He gave the tiniest of smiles. So this was how it was going to be: like a continuous jousting session, with one or other of us scoring points against the other. Well, that was fine by me.

Later, when the dishes had been cleared and we were finishing our coffee, I stood up and hoisted Elodie over my shoulder. 'I think someone needs changing,' I said by way of explanation as I turned to leave the room.

'I'll come and help,' said Peter, giving a warning look to Jo, to stop her following. It wasn't a question, it was a statement, and before I could object, we were alone together in Elodie's room.

'What do you think of your daughter, then?' I asked in a low voice, careful to make sure my words didn't carry through the flat.

Peter swallowed hard and fixed me with a fierce stare. 'I should have been able to see her before now.'

'Really?' I pretended to consider his words. 'Only, I seem to remember that you were rather keen for me to abort her. I didn't think you'd be too bothered about seeing her.'

Peter shook his head. 'It was cruel of you, particularly towards Jo.'

I gave a dry laugh. 'So? She's not actually related to her, is she?'

He reeled slightly, as if I'd struck him. 'But she doesn't know that!' he hissed. 'And of course, we've only got your word for it . . .'

'Seriously, Peter? You're still going down that route? I'd

better book a DNA test to prove it once and for all. I can get the results sent to your home . . .'

Peter's eyes slid from me to Elodie.

'But I don't think you really need a test, do you?' I turned her around so that he could see her more clearly. 'You know she's yours, don't you?'

Peter's eyes filled with tears and he nodded miserably. 'What a bloody mess.'

I laid Elodie down on her changing mat and began to change her nappy. 'There was no need, though, Peter. You could have had a happy life with me and her.' I turned to look at him. 'Just the three of us together.'

He shook his head. 'That would never have happened. I couldn't leave Jo.'

'But you could shag around behind her back with no trouble!' My voice was louder than I had intended and we both gasped slightly, straining to hear whether my words had reached Ben and Jo. But the murmuring sound of their voices burbled on uninterrupted.

Peter came to stand beside me, as I buttoned up Elodie's babygro. I cursed the renewed shiver of excitement that ran through me at his proximity. 'Look,' he said in an urgent undertone. 'We need to work out a way to make this bearable for both of us – for all of us, actually,' he added, looking at Elodie. There was genuine affection in his eyes. 'This isn't a game, Bella, this is Elodie's life we're talking about. Ben's life. I want them both to be OK.'

I didn't reply. It annoyed me that he was making it out to be my fault when it was his selfish actions that lay at the root of everything.

Peter put his hand on my shoulder, causing a crackle of electricity to shoot through me. I didn't want his touch to have any effect. I just wanted to be able to mentally shut him out, whilst making his life a living nightmare for the way he'd treated me. But he triggered such a violent reaction in me that it was impossible. To my horror, my eyes filled with tears and I blinked them away furiously.

'Bella?' he prompted, his tone slightly softer.

I nodded slowly. 'If you behave, Peter, then I will, too.'

Peter exhaled, relief flooding his features. 'Thank you . . .'

'*But*,' I continued, 'the second you put a foot out of line, I will make your life hell. Remember that.' I picked up Elodie and laid her over my shoulder, rubbing her back gently.

Peter gazed at her sadly. 'How could I ever forget? I'm glad I've finally seen her. She's beautiful. Really beautiful.'

I couldn't help smiling. 'Yes. She certainly is. Well, you might be seeing a bit more of her soon anyway.'

Peter's own smile died on his lips and his eyes narrowed slightly. He was always so suspicious around me, albeit with good reason. 'And why's that?'

I shrugged. 'I'd like Elodie to have the sort of childhood your other children had. So I think maybe we should buy a house similar to yours in Suffolk and move there.'

Peter blanched. 'Close to us, you mean?'

'Yes. Then you could get to see Elodie whenever you wanted.'

I could see the internal battle as his thoughts raced. 'But how could you ever afford a house near us?'

I wanted to laugh at his naivety. 'We couldn't. But you could.'

As understanding dawned, his expression darkened. 'You want me to buy you a house?'

'Well, you bought your other children a house, so I don't see why you wouldn't buy Elodie one.' I adopted my most annoying sing-song tone, knowing it would irritate him further.

'Ben wouldn't accept it,' Peter said at last. 'I know what he's like and he'd be too proud. It was different when he was young, just getting started, but now that he's a husband and father . . .'

I fixed him with my steeliest stare. 'Then it's your job to make him accept it.'

Peter ran his hand through his hair, looking panicked. 'And if I don't succeed?'

I smiled. 'I don't think I need to answer that one, do I, Peter?'

CHAPTER TWENTY-FOUR

He had told me. Of course he had. But I pretended that he hadn't. 'What the hell did you invite them round for?' I yelled at his retreating back, as he walked out of the bedroom, having reminded me that Matt and Freya would be arriving in about half an hour for a final, goodbye get-together. When I saw the alert pop up on his phone calendar earlier, I had deliberately gone back to bed, claiming that I didn't feel well.

Ben stopped walking and sighed heavily, his shoulders dropping before he turned back to face me. 'Because they're my friends, Bella. *Our* friends. That's what friends do – they spend time together.'

'They're not *my* bloody friends!' I spat. 'Well, anyway, I don't feel well so they will have to come another time. Or not at all, preferably.'

Ben closed his eyes in that way that really wound me up. As if he was trying desperately hard to keep his temper. 'No, Bella, it's too late to cancel them now. They'll already be on their way.'

'Well, call Matt on his mobile and tell him your wife is sick and you are going to do the right thing and look after her, rather than getting pissed with those two arseholes.'

'Bella!' Ben looked genuinely enraged and I wondered if I might have gone too far. 'They are not arseholes. Matt has been my friend since I was seven and Freya is lovely.'

I pulled a face. 'Ugh. You're not twelve, Ben!'

Ben shook his head. 'You did this the last time they came round. They'll know you're not really sick.'

My mind raced. Oh yes, that was the time he invited them round for a takeaway without consulting me. 'I think you'll find I spent the evening in hospital because I thought I was losing our baby!' I yelled, raging with genuine indignation. It didn't matter that I had actually spent the evening having sex with Marcus. The point was that Ben *believed* that I had spent the evening in hospital, yet he had the cheek to accuse me of faking it.

Ben's eyes widened with panic. 'Shhhh, Bella! Stop yelling.' His eyes kept darting towards the front door and I suspected he had heard them coming through the gate. 'OK, OK, I'll tell them it's not convenient.'

I smiled to myself as the doorbell rang, pleased with my little victory. I walked to the bedroom window and looked out from behind the curtain. Matt and Freya were having a furtive conversation and Matt seemed nervous as he shuffled from foot to foot, a large bag of supplies in his hand. Freya had a look on her face that I didn't like one bit. She looked determined. Well, I was determined too. So we'd soon wipe that look off her face.

I moved into the hallway, out of sight of Matt and Freya but just a couple of feet away from Ben. I shot him a warning look as he opened the door.

'Hey, mate!' I heard Matt say in an overly jolly voice. 'Good to see you. I've brought the usual supplies!'

'Uh, yeah. Look I'm sorry, guys, it's not a great time . . .'

Jesus, Ben was such a hopeless actor. He needed to be a lot more convincing than that.

'Oh! Sorry, mate, I must have got the date wrong,' Matt replied. 'I thought we'd arranged today.'

'We did,' Freya cut in. 'What's the problem, Ben?'

I didn't like her tone at all. Ben glanced over his shoulder at me nervously, before closing the door a fraction more. 'Bella's not feeling too good.'

'What's the matter with her?'

God, she was rude! For all she knew, I could be really unwell. 'Um,' Ben stuttered. 'She's . . . er, she's just . . .'

'She's refusing to see us, isn't she?' Although I was annoyed, a small part of me was glad that she'd got the message that I didn't like them.

'Freya!' Matt admonished her but she was having none of it.

'I'm right, aren't I, Ben?' she demanded.

Ben sighed and ran his hand through his hair the way he always did when he was flustered. 'No, Freya, you're not right . . . She's just not very well.'

'How very convenient! Ever since you met her, Ben, she's been trying to cut you off from us. And your family . . .'

'She's fine with my family, actually,' Ben interrupted, making me smile with satisfaction. Finally, he was standing up for me.

'Is she?' Freya stormed. 'Because that's not what you told me when we had lunch . . .'

I gasped. He didn't tell me he had lunch with her! As the red mist descended, I stepped into view behind him. 'Ben! Can you close the door, please, you're letting in a draught.'

'Hi, Bella, you look well?' Freya snapped, her voice dripping with sarcasm.

I felt like hitting her. She was such a bitch, acting like she owned Ben and treating me like some kind of interloper into their cosy little threesome.

I stared her out for a few seconds, just to unnerve her, before I answered, 'Actually, I'm not well. Ben, close the door, please.'

Ben hesitated. 'I'm really sorry, guys,' he said in a pathetic, pleading tone. 'Let's rearrange for another time, eh?'

Matt nodded unhappily and began to turn away but Freya stood her ground. 'There won't be another time, Ben! Don't you see what she's doing? For Christ's sake, why don't you grow a pair? Matt is your oldest friend and you're treating him like dirt! Shame on you!' With that, she reached for Matt's hand and together they walked away. Ben and I watched them go and as they reached the end of the path, I leaned over Ben's shoulder and slammed the door as hard as I could.

Ben paused for a split second, before he turned around to face me. He was so weak. I glared at him in fury. I couldn't believe that he had gone behind my back to have lunch with Freya. And more to the point, I couldn't believe that he had managed to keep it from me.

'So you had lunch with Freya, did you?' I folded my arms to quell the massive urge I had to punch his idiotic face. 'You obviously forgot to mention it.'

'I didn't forget to mention it, Bella. It was just that I knew how you'd react, so I deliberately didn't tell you. Anyway, it wasn't arranged. I just bumped into her and we had a sandwich, that's all. No big deal.'

I didn't believe that for one second. The only way they'd have bumped into each other is if they had arranged it. 'No bloody big deal? You having lunch with another woman behind my back and moaning about me?'

Ben closed his eyes, aggravating me even further. 'For a start, Freya is not "another woman". I have known her for so long that she's more like a sister. And I wasn't moaning about you.'

He obviously thought that I was born yesterday. 'Then what did she mean about your family and me not being fine with them?'

Ben's eyes slid away and he paused, as if considering whether to say what he was about to say. 'It was just that she was a bit shocked that Mum and Dad hadn't seen the baby at that point.'

My stomach dropped slightly. 'Why did you tell her?'

Ben sighed. 'Because she asked. Honestly, Bella, you're making a mountain out of a molehill here.'

'Well, I just don't like the thought of you talking about me behind my back. Anyway,' I continued, keen to get him back on the subject of how awful Matt and Freya were, 'I was obviously right about Freya and Matt not liking me. You heard the way she spoke to me.'

Ben sighed, as if he had the weight of the world on his shoulders. 'Well, they've gone now, so you can go back to bed and sleep off whatever lurgy you've picked up.'

Ha! I'd won. I was fairly certain that was the last we'd be seeing of Matt and Freya. 'No, it's fine,' I said, flashing him a brilliant smile. 'I feel much better now.'

I was sitting at the kitchen table, with Elodie lying in her baby gym, gurgling happily and kicking her legs wildly, when the landline rang. I picked up the handset and glanced idly at the caller display. Ugh, it was Jo. There was no way I was going to answer it, so I put the handset back down and carried on reading the article on my phone.

'Why are you ignoring the phone, darling?' said Ben, as he raced into the kitchen and snatched up the handset, just before it went to the Ansaphone.

I gave a tiny smile but didn't answer him.

'Hi, Mum, how are you?' he said cheerfully, before pausing to listen. 'Don't be daft.' He frowned. 'Is everything all right?'

I looked up at him, my senses suddenly on high alert, as his legs seemed to buckle and he slumped down on a chair. 'A heart attack? Shit. How serious?'

It felt as though my own heart had stopped in sympathy. Had Peter had a heart attack? He couldn't have. It just wasn't possible.

I watched Ben intently, searching for clues as to what might have happened. He was swallowing hard and trying to keep calm. 'Right, don't worry, I will be there as soon as I can. Which hospital? OK. Get yourself a coffee and I'll be there in a couple of hours. Does Emma know?'

It was obviously Peter. And it sounded serious if Ben had to dash off immediately. He spoke for a few more minutes before telling Jo he loved her and hanging up. All the colour had drained from his face and he looked as if his legs had turned to jelly.

'What's happened? Is it your dad?' I asked, slightly unnecessarily.

Ben nodded his affirmation, clearly fighting back tears. I wanted to cry myself through shock and, inexplicably, anger at Peter. How dare he do this? I walked over and wrapped my arms around Ben, as much for my own benefit as his.

Ben took a deep breath and gave me a slightly apologetic look. 'I need to call Emma and go.'

I nodded, still too stunned to take it in. 'Of course you do. Let me know the second you have any news.'

Ben nodded. 'Of course. Just keep an eye on our baby girl while I'm gone.' He knelt on the floor and kissed Elodie, who beamed up at him with a gummy smile.

'I will,' I assured him, wanting him to get out of the flat and get to the hospital as soon as possible. 'And we'll be waiting for you when you get back.'

CHAPTER TWENTY-FIVE

After Ben left, I sat at the kitchen table, staring into space until Elodie started to whinge and my coffee had gone cold. My thoughts were in turmoil, wondering what was happening with Peter. My heart pounded violently every time I remembered Ben's conversation with his mum. It sounded serious.

Eventually, I felt that I couldn't stay in the flat a moment longer. I changed and fed Elodie, then put her into her pram and strode out into the sunshine, not sure where I was going or what I was doing. I kept walking and before I knew it, I was standing outside Peter's old apartment block, where we had spent so many happy times together. It was where we had conceived Elodie.

I sat on a bench and stared up at the rather clinical façade of the building, trying to remember which window was his. I had genuinely imagined moving in here with him, us making a life together. God, I was so stupid. It felt as if there was a slab of concrete weighing heavily on my chest and I knew it was guilt. I tried to swallow it down, reassuring myself that he had behaved much worse than me. He had used me and then cast me aside when I had outlived my appeal. He had thought

I was as disposable as a piece of trash that he could bin and then forget about.

I knew without a doubt that his heart attack had been caused by the stress of his situation and I did feel bad about it. But I only did what I did because I was so hurt. He was the first man I had ever loved and, like an idiot, I thought he felt the same way, but the truth was I was just one in a long line of silly, available women who fell for his charms. The only difference was that I refused to let him get away with it, as the others had clearly done, for years.

I refused to allow a scintilla of acknowledgement that he might die seep into my thoughts. He was too fit and healthy. He would pull through, of course he would. But what would happen then? Would a brush with death force him to come clean about what he'd done? Suddenly, a horrible thought occurred to me, that he might feel the urge to confess everything with his family gathered around his bedside. Where the hell would that leave me then? Where would it leave Elodie?

And then, right at the very back of my mind, lurked a tiny hope that maybe it would cause Peter to realize that life is too short and that he should be with me and Elodie after all. He obviously wasn't happy or satisfied with Jo or he wouldn't have had so many flings behind her back. This scare might make him reassess and grab the opportunity.

Inexplicably, I felt furious with Ben. He was the biggest obstacle to that ever happening, as Peter wouldn't be able to bear to hurt him. I was beginning to hate him. He was such a drip compared to Peter and everything he did annoyed me.

Clouds were beginning to smear the pale blue sky and a strong breeze was starting to make it feel chilly. I was about to stand up to leave, when I felt the weight of someone sitting down on the bench beside me. 'Hello,' said a male voice that I didn't recognize, in a way that suggested he recognized me.

I looked over at him curiously, trying to place him. He had blond curly hair and a pleasant, vaguely familiar face. 'Hello? Do I know you?'

He smiled easily. 'No. Not really. I moved into to your boyfriend's flat.'

It took a moment for me to register that he was referring to Peter as my boyfriend. 'Ah, yes, of course. Sorry about that evening by the way. It was just a bit of a shock to find he'd gone.'

'I can imagine. And don't apologize. I'm just glad you were OK. You worried me for a moment there.' He nodded towards Elodie's pram. 'Presumably that was part of the reason you felt a bit faint, too?'

I bit the inside of my cheek, not entirely sure I wanted him to know that Peter was the father of my child. 'Uh, maybe . . .' I gave a vague wave of my hand, before changing the subject. 'I'm amazed you recognized me, after all this time.'

He grinned mischievously. 'I never forget a pretty face. And yours is prettier than most, to be honest.'

I smiled broadly. Clearly, I still had it. 'Thank you.' I dropped my eyes demurely.

'So what brings you here today, sitting on a bench, staring up at my windows?'

I wondered whether to tell him the truth but something stopped me. It made me sound a bit weird. Like a stalker. 'I was just out for a walk and needed to sit down. It was only when I looked up that I remembered that this was where Pe— um, my ex, used to live.'

He nodded. 'And did you ever see him again, after he moved out?'

I laughed and nodded. 'Well, yes, actually. Yes, I did.' Our eyes met and we both grinned. He had a nice face, if a little bit haughty-looking. 'It's complicated.'

He squinted at me curiously, as if deciding whether to probe further. 'But you referred to him as your "ex", so presumably you're not together now?'

'Um, no. Not exactly. He's still in my life . . . but as I said, it's complicated.'

He nodded, apparently satisfied. 'I'm not sure you ever told me your name?' He raised his eyebrows quizzically as he spoke.

'Bella.'

He nodded. 'Of course it is. It means "beautiful" in Italian.'

If I'd had a pound for every man who'd used that line on me, I would be a multi-millionaire. But after so long, it felt good to have someone hitting on me again, so I smiled encouragingly. 'It does indeed. And what's your name? Bello?'

He laughed, showing straight, white teeth. 'My name apparently means "brave lion" – I'm Leo.'

He looked like a Leo with his mane of blond curls. 'Kind of appropriate, I'd say. It suits you.'

He gave me a sidelong glance, as if to gauge whether I was giving him the come-on or not. 'Thanks. So, listen, Bella, it's getting a bit chilly. Would you like me to buy you lunch somewhere nice?'

I thought for a moment. The day was suddenly taking a very surreal turn but at least it took my mind off Peter for a while. 'Sure, as long as you don't mind having a chaperone in a pram?'

His eyes darted towards Elodie, as if he had completely

forgotten she was there and for a second, there was a flicker of doubt. My heart sank. I had begun to feel excited at the prospect of a flirtatious lunch with a handsome stranger. But just as quickly, the doubt faded and he stood up. 'Of course I don't mind,' he said. 'Who could possibly object to dining with two beautiful women instead of one? Would you like me to push?' he offered, gesturing towards the pram.

I smiled, amazed at how the day was panning out. 'I'd like that very much,' I said, falling into step beside him, all thoughts of Peter now pushed firmly to the back of my mind.

'I suppose I had better be getting back . . .' I propped myself up on one elbow and looked at the bedside clock, shocked to see that it was almost 7 p.m.

Leo traced a finger from my breast down to my hip, gazing appreciatively at my body with hungry eyes. We had enjoyed a long, champagne-fuelled lunch at a beautiful restaurant in the shadow of Tower Bridge, then walked back to his apartment, without either of us questioning that we would be going to bed together. I parked Elodie's pram in the spare room, where, exhausted from missing her usual lunchtime nap, she promptly fell asleep, leaving Leo and me to indulge in a surprisingly energetic and erotically charged few hours of sex. It felt so good to have sex with someone new and exciting, after putting up with Ben's infuriatingly tender advances for all this time, and it had enhanced my mood enormously.

'Don't go yet.' Leo fixed me with a wolfish stare and I could see that he was already erect again. His athleticism was impressive, considering we had already made love four times. He leaned over to kiss me and I just was succumbing to him once more, when Elodie's cries rang out through the flat.

'Sorry. I'm afraid that's my alarm call.' I rolled away from him and swung my legs over the side of the bed. 'But thank you for today, it was just what I needed.'

Leo smiled sleepily. 'Me too. Maybe we could do it again sometime?'

I looked down at him with a non-committal shrug. 'Maybe.'

He sat up in bed and reached for a pack of cigarettes on the bedside table. He lit one and inhaled deeply. 'Is there someone waiting for you at home?' he looked up at me through a veil of smoke as he exhaled.

'There might be,' I replied, adopting a casual tone and glancing down at my wedding ring. 'Depends whether he's home yet.'

Leo smiled and nodded his understanding. 'Gotcha.'

As I left the flat, pushing Elodie in her pram along the hallway towards the lift, I pulled my phone out of my bag. I had one missed called from Ben and I felt a spike of relief. If there had been anything seriously wrong with Peter, he would have called more than once.

I stood in the lift, staring at myself in the mirrored walls, thinking about all the other times I had left this flat after an afternoon or evening of illicit sex. Today with Leo had been a fun distraction but still, even now, no one compared to Peter. I wondered if anyone ever would. There was something about him that just clicked for me and I still felt a physical ache for him, even after all this time.

Back home, I bathed Elodie and put her to bed, then had a long, hot shower myself, washing away all traces of Leo, just in case Ben came home without warning. As it seemed as if Peter was OK, there was no reason for him to stay overnight.

The phone rang, just as I was thinking of going to bed.

'Ben?' I said, wondering why he was calling, rather than just coming home. I hoped he hadn't somehow found out what I'd been up to.

'Yes.' He sounded slightly tearful but not angry.

'How is he?'

There was a weird pause and I could tell he was struggling to speak. My heart began to pound with alarm and I suddenly knew what he was going to say before he said it: 'He's dead. He died, Bella.'

'What? Oh my God!' I could barely breathe for shock. It just wasn't possible. Peter was too young and fit to have died. My throat dried and a wave of genuine sorrow swept through my whole body, causing me to start shaking. 'Jesus, I can't believe it.'

'I know. I've just arrived back at Mum and Dad's—' Ben stopped speaking abruptly.

There was a long silence as we both tried to digest what Ben had just said. For a fleeting moment, I wondered if he had found out the truth about me and Peter and was making it up to punish me but I dismissed it just as quickly. I could hear the raw grief in his voice.

'Are you coming home?' I didn't want him to. I wanted him to stay away, so that I could process my own feelings without having to worry about him or comfort him in any way. I just didn't have the strength to put on my usual Oscar-winning performance.

'Not tonight,' he replied and I exhaled with relief. 'I need to stay here with Mum and Emma, to make sure they're OK.' Of course he did. His bloody mother would milk this for all it was worth, playing the grieving widow of a devoted husband and father. Only I knew the truth about him. Which was that he was about as far from devoted as it was possible to be. He was a liar and a cheat and a user, who had spent his whole life pretending to be something he wasn't. But, despite all of that, I had loved the bastard.

'Just look after Elodie and I'll call you in the morning,' Ben said, cutting through my thoughts.

'OK,' I whispered, before hanging up. I didn't want to speak to Ben, or hear his voice for a second longer. I was stuck with him now and it had all been for nothing. He had served his purpose and been the perfect way to punish Peter for what he had done but I didn't need him anymore and I certainly didn't want him. The thought of him coming anywhere near me already made me feel physically sick and my mind raced with thoughts of how the hell I was going to get out of this mess I was in.

I switched on the coffee machine and waited impatiently for it to heat. I already knew that wouldn't be sleeping a wink tonight so it wouldn't matter if I made myself the strongest possible cup of coffee, to steady my nerves. I lifted the cup to my lips and flinched as the boiling liquid burnt my tongue. With a wail of pain and anguish, I flung the cup at the wall, smashing it and sending liquid exploding everywhere. 'Screw you, Peter!' I yelled. 'Screw you!'

CHAPTER TWENTY-SIX

'Hurry up, Bella!' Ben yelled from the hallway. 'We need to go!'

'Piss off!' I muttered at my reflection in the mirror of my dressing table. I was dreading today in so many ways. Ben was absolutely distraught about the death of his father and I was finding it increasingly difficult to be sympathetic to his grief. Every time he broke down or became maudlin, I just wanted to scream at him that it was worse for me.

I felt so many emotions towards Peter – anger, grief, love, hate and sometimes all of them at once. But the overriding emotion was disbelief. I still couldn't accept that he had really gone.

Ben strapped Elodie into her car-seat and I climbed into the back beside her, not wanting to sit beside Ben or have to communicate in any way. He frowned at me in the rear-view mirror but said nothing. We had barely spoken since he came home the day after Peter's death, which suited me just fine. We were both locked in our own intense thoughts and for my part, I didn't want to risk letting anything slip. I knew I should try to comfort and support him but I couldn't bring myself to say anything good, so decided it was best to say nothing. Ben probably thought I was feeling guilty about my behaviour towards Peter but that couldn't have been further from the truth.

Elodie fell asleep almost immediately, as she always did in her car-seat, so the journey progressed in silence, with me staring out of the window, as the pretty Suffolk countryside rolled by.

We had had an offer accepted on a house less than a mile from Ben's parents' home. Peter had been true to his word and stumped up the extra cash, not that he had had much choice. It had seemed like a good idea at the time, when I thought we would be living so close to Peter. But now that it was going to be just Jo, I had no intention of going through with it. She drove me mad just seeing her once every few months. Her being on the doorstep would be a nightmare.

Ben pulled up on the gravel driveway and turned off the engine. As he did so, Elodie's eyes popped wide open and she made herself jump with a giant hiccup. Ben and I both laughed and it broke the tension that had enveloped us for the whole journey. Ben hopped out and unstrapped her, lifting her out in one deft movement. I watched him tickling her for a moment before climbing out myself. He really did love her. How devastated he would be to know the truth, that he was her brother, not her father.

I put my arms out and took her from him, noting with satisfaction how she squealed with genuine delight when I lifted her up and blew raspberries on her belly. Ben couldn't even make her laugh the way I could.

Jo opened the front door before we reached it and I was slightly taken aback by how diminished she looked. She wasn't a big woman anyway, but she seemed to have shrunk into herself since I last saw her. Her eyes looked slightly glazed and there were dark shadows beneath them. She reached up to hug Ben and clung to him for a few seconds, as if she was hanging onto a lifebelt. As she released him, she gave me a cursory glance and attempted a half-smile. 'Hello, Bella,' she said, in what I thought was a very cold way.

I felt a creeping sense of unease. Usually, she would be excessively friendly, rather than offhand and distant. I wondered if she knew anything. Maybe Peter had confessed all on his deathbed, however unlikely that seemed. 'Hello, Jo.' I swallowed hard so that I could continue. 'I'm sorry about Peter,' I managed, distracting myself by gently rocking Elodie.

'Thank you,' Jo said, before turning away abruptly, without even so much as a glance at Elodie. I couldn't believe that she could be so disinterested and looked at Ben in disgust, but he was already following his mum into the kitchen like an obedient puppy. So this was how today was going to be then, I thought murderously. Everyone fussing around Jo and pretty much ignoring Elodie and me.

I took a seat at the island with Elodie on my lap and watched as Emma bustled about, issuing orders and bossing everyone around, whilst preparing tea and coffee. She put a coffee in front of me without asking what I wanted or even acknowledging that I was there. I deliberately left it to go cold. Annoyingly, Elodie was as good as gold and sat quietly watching the goings-on without making even a whimper, which would have given me an excuse to leave.

Finally, we heard the cars arriving on the gravel driveway and my heart lurched. It was only now that it felt real for the first time. We all stood up and Jo reached for Ben's arm.

'Are you OK, Mum?' he asked with a look of genuine concern, as we all began to walk down the hallway.

Jo nodded and gazed up at him with a wan smile. 'Yes. My legs are just a bit wobbly, that's all.'

Ben nodded and rubbed her hand tenderly.

At that moment, Elodie started to cry in my arms, no doubt unsettled by the tense, strange atmosphere. Ben turned back towards us. 'Shhhh, don't cry, sweetie,' he whispered.

God, he was so wet sometimes. 'She's a baby, Ben,' I snapped. 'That's what babies do!'

Ben looked hurt but didn't reply and kept leading Jo out into the driveway where the hearse and the family car were waiting. We all stopped sharply at the sight of the coffin and my stomach dropped. He really was dead. Until this moment, I had felt as if he might just be playing some kind of cruel trick, but seeing the coffin, decked with a simple bouquet of beautiful white lilies, put all doubt to one side. This was no trick. He was gone for ever.

As if reflecting all our thoughts, Ben let out a guttural moan, before putting his hand over his mouth. I thought about comforting him but he was holding Jo's hand and I couldn't see a way to break into their huddle, especially when Emma came and took hold of Jo's other hand. Instead, I stood off to one side holding Elodie, aware that we were being deliberately excluded from this private family moment, which struck me as ironic.

They climbed into the car, which only had seats for the three of them. 'What about Bella?' I heard Jo say.

'She's driving our car so that she can put Elodie in the carseat,' Ben replied.

I stood watching them pointedly, until the hearse began to

move off, when I climbed into our car and we drove in a slow convoy towards the church, which was less than a mile away. I imagined what they were talking about in the car in front of me and decided that they would no doubt be eulogizing Peter, gushing over what a saint he had been. If only they knew.

I was slightly surprised that he was being buried and having a church service at all, as he had never struck me as the religious type but I reasoned that it just showed what a great actor he had been. Not unlike myself, I thought ruefully, as we pulled up in front of a large crowd of mourners outside the church. I wondered vaguely how many of the assembled throng knew what Peter was really like.

Again, no one seemed to give much thought to Elodie and me, as Ben helped Jo and Emma out of the car and led the way towards the church doorway. He stopped abruptly as someone stepped forward from the crowd to hug him. I narrowed my eyes, as I realized it was Matt. I might have known they'd be here. I stepped back slightly and pretended to attend to Elodie, in order to avoid having to talk to them. Just then, Freya and another woman walked over to Jo and Emma, embracing them both. 'I'm so sorry,' the woman said, taking Jo's hand in hers. 'You must feel so lost without him. I know how much you loved him.'

'Thank you, Charlie,' Jo gushed, gripping her hand tightly. I watched out of the corner of my eye. Ah. So this was the famous Charlotte. She was slimmer than I thought she'd be and she wasn't unattractive but, a bit like Freya, she wasn't exactly a head-turner, either. She certainly wasn't in my league.

'I don't even know where to begin,' Jo whined on. 'I already miss him so, so much. I feel so alone.'

'I know, I really do,' Charlotte told her earnestly. She sounded every bit as wet as Ben. It wasn't much wonder they had been together for so long. 'But you have Ben and Emma and they will be there for you. You aren't alone, I promise you.'

Jo nodded. 'Thank you for coming, Charlie, it means a lot.' I resisted the urge to stamp my foot. She had barely said hello to Elodie and me, yet she couldn't fawn over Ben's stupid ex enough.

Charlotte shook her head. 'We all loved Peter. There is no way we wouldn't have been here today.' Ugh. I wasn't surprised she had got on so well with Jo. She was nauseating.

'Please make sure you sit with us at the front. We'd all appreciate it.' I could have sworn Jo's voice became a little bit louder, to make sure that I would hear.

'Are you sure?' Charlotte replied uncertainly, her eyes flickering towards Elodie and me. 'We wouldn't want to take anyone else's seat . . .'

'No, Mum's right,' said Ben, appearing at their side. 'You should sit with us. It would help, especially Emma,' he added, gesturing towards Emma, who was wailing away and being comforted by one of her relatives.

'OK,' Charlotte said, before stepping back. 'We'll see you in there.'

A swell of indignation and anger swept through me, so strongly that I contemplated not going into the church at all. How dare they! They were behaving as if I wasn't even there. At that moment, I truly felt pure hatred for both Jo and Ben.

It was quite a small country church and it was already packed by the time we took our seats in the front pew. Ben reached out to take my hand as I sat down beside him, but I snatched it away and pointedly wrapped both arms around Elodie instead. Jo sat between Ben and a weeping Emma, with Charlotte on Emma's other side, rubbing her back to comfort her.

Charlotte had tried to meet my eye but I refused to look in her direction. I had absolutely no interest in making any kind of connection with her and I also avoided looking at Matt and Freya, who were in the row behind her. We all knew where we stood after their last visit to our flat, so I didn't see any point in pretending to be civil.

Suddenly, the organ music changed and the church was filled with the sound of singing. Only then did I realize how many people were there, filling the aisles and any available spaces. Peter had clearly been very popular. I glanced around me, wondering idly how many of the women present had also succumbed to his charms.

When the vicar invited Ben to give the eulogy, he stood up shakily and made his way to the lectern. After swallowing several times, he started to speak in a trembling voice. 'My dad was my best friend,' he began. 'He never, ever let me down and was always there when I needed him.' I stared straight ahead, resolutely resisting the urge to yell out that his father had let him down in ways that were unimaginable.

'And I honestly don't know how any of us are going to cope with losing him.' Tears rolled down his cheeks and when he opened his mouth to speak again, he emitted a loud sob, before breaking down completely. To my surprise, I felt the tears welling up in my own eyes, not out of sympathy for Ben but because I felt sorry for myself. Why the hell did Peter have to die?

Matt stood up and walked calmly towards the altar.

I watched him with a murderous glare. Trust him to act like the conquering hero. 'Would you like me to continue for you?' he asked Ben, who was weeping like a baby.

Ben nodded, so Matt took the paper he was holding and read the eulogy without faltering. When he had finished, they looked at each other and Ben mouthed, 'thank you' as the two of them walked back to their seats.

I looked down, unable to meet Ben's eye or offer him any kind of comfort. 'I'm sorry, Mum,' he whispered, as he sat back down. 'I just couldn't do it.'

'I know, darling, we all understand,' she replied, taking his hand in hers. She didn't let go for the rest of the service. At the end, we all filed out, with everyone ignoring Elodie and me. It was as if we were invisible. I stood off to one side and watched, as the mourners fussed around Jo, offering her their condolences. Yet again, I thought about how much trouble I could cause with just a few words.

Matt, Freya and Charlotte all came out together. Matt tried to catch my eye but I pretended not to see and focused on Elodie instead.

Jo reached out and gave Matt a hug. 'Thank you so much for helping Ben, Matt. It means the world to us.'

Matt hugged her back. 'We'll always be here for him, Jo. And for you and Emma, too. Don't ever forget that.'

He had pointedly not mentioned me and was speaking loud enough for me to hear. I smiled inwardly. He wouldn't be having anything to do with me in future, so I couldn't have cared less.

The burial was supposed to be family only, so the plan was for Ben, Jo and Emma to go in the funeral car and I would again drive Elodie in our car. But as I started the engine and prepared to follow the cortege, I changed my mind. I had no desire to see Peter lowered into a hole in the ground and I didn't think it was appropriate for Elodie, either. So instead, I turned off the road and took a detour past the house Ben and I were supposed to be buying.

It was a grand, elegant, Georgian building, set back from the road behind well-kept hedging, with a large, beautifully landscaped garden. It would have been a gorgeous place for Elodie to grow up but now that Peter had gone, there didn't seem to be any point in moving to somewhere so close to his mum. She would no doubt want to be hanging around with us all the time, getting on my nerves and interfering with Elodie. She wasn't even related to her, not that she had any idea about that, of course.

A large number of people had gathered back at the house by the time I arrived. Ben came over as we walked in. 'Are you OK, darling? I was worried about you.'

I nodded, aware that people were watching. 'Yes. Sorry I didn't come to the burial – it's just that Elodie had fallen asleep and I didn't think it was wise to wake her.'

Ben nodded but I could tell that he didn't believe me. 'Oh, OK. Would you like a drink?'

I glanced at the glass of red wine in his hand. 'Um, well, actually maybe I will . . . I'll have a red wine.'

I could see the panic flare up in his eyes. 'Really? But you don't drink alcohol.'

'I know. It's just that it's been such a stressful day, I think maybe I will for a change. Oh, you haven't been drinking yourself, have you?'

Ben frowned and handed me his glass reluctantly. 'No. Well,

just a couple of sips. I thought you might drive, given the circumstances.'

I raised my eyebrows. 'I think, given the circumstances, it might be best if you don't drink today. It'll make you all maudlin. And anyway,' I added, taking a long sip of wine, which tasted revolting. 'I've done enough driving around for one day.'

CHAPTER TWENTY-SEVEN

I finally persuaded Ben to leave, although he was reluctant. He hadn't wanted to leave Jo. He started the car, then turned back towards her, standing on the doorstep, looking all forlorn. 'Should we stay? I feel bad leaving her.'

I had no intention of staying a moment longer than we had to. I gave him my fiercest scowl. 'No. She'll be fine. We need to get Elodie home.'

After another brief hesitation, Ben finally drove away, looking as though he might break down at any moment. I waited for him to ask me how the day had been for me but he didn't speak at all. I decided that he was sulking because I had made him drive. He was so selfish sometimes. I gave a huge sigh.

'OK,' he said at last, looking bored and annoyed. 'What's the matter?'

I looked at him in disbelief. 'I can't believe you didn't notice the way your mum treated me today. She made me feel like a piece of shit! And she barely even looked at Elodie . . .'

Ben frowned. 'That's not fair, Bella. It was her husband's funeral – she's in shock.'

'She wasn't in so much shock that she couldn't fawn over

Matt and Freya, not to mention how she acted like Charlotte was her daughter-in-law instead of me! Honestly, Ben, you have no idea how hard today was for me.'

Ben rubbed his forehead wearily. 'I don't think Mum would have done anything to upset you deliberately.'

'Pah!' I snorted. She couldn't have been more deliberate in the way she had excluded me today. 'She was off with me from the minute we arrived. She barely said "hello" then turned her back on me and stomped into the kitchen without attempting to take Elodie. You'd think she'd have been desperate to see her.'

'As I said, I think she had other things on her mind. Come on, Bella, give her a break.'

Ben sounded exhausted and upset but I couldn't feel sympathy for him. 'She didn't worry about how I was feeling when she insisted that your ex come and sit with us and went out of her way to make me feel left out.' I could feel the tears welling up.

Ben gave an irritated sigh. 'You didn't exactly try to integrate, though, did you?'

'I did!' I shouted, swiping at the tears that were now rolling down my cheeks. 'But you were too busy ignoring me to notice!' I looked at him defiantly, waiting for a reply, but he just gripped the steering wheel and stared at the road ahead. 'You can't even deny it!' I added, knowing that I was pushing him to the edge.

'Oh, for Christ's sake!' Ben slammed the steering wheel with the flat of his hand. 'It was my dad's funeral, Bella! Why are you being like this?'

I had never seen Ben lose it like that and I jumped with surprise. 'Ben! Stop being so aggressive! You're scaring me and you're scaring Elodie.'

As if to illustrate my words, Elodie, who had been sleeping

soundly in her car-seat, began to cry. I twisted around so that I could shush her and calm her down and after a few moments, she began to drop off to sleep again. I looked at Ben in disgust. He really didn't think about anyone other than himself and he had hardly glanced at Elodie all day.

I sat back in my seat, waiting for Ben to do what he usually did and apologize but he just drove in silence. In front of us, the sun was a heavy ball of orange, sinking fast in the purple sky. It was a stunningly beautiful view, but I hardly noticed, as my thoughts raced. 'So you're sulking now, then?'

Ben sighed. 'No, Bella, I'm not sulking. I'm just trying to get my head around today. It's been a horrible day.'

'Yes, it has,' I agreed quietly, folding my hands in my lap. 'I'm glad it's over.'

Ben didn't reply.

'And at least we've got the move to focus on now.'

'Yes.'

Ben couldn't have sounded less interested if he'd tried. I wondered whether I should let it drop for now and discuss it later but I didn't want to. I needed to let him know that I had had a change of heart, so I continued. 'You know, maybe we shouldn't move to Suffolk, after all? Maybe Surrey would be better.'

Ben frowned and I saw his body stiffen, as if bracing himself to answer.

'No, Bella. You were super-keen on Suffolk and being near my parents, so I don't know why you'd suddenly change your mind.'

I mentally rolled my eyes. Of course he didn't know why I would suddenly change my mind. It would change everything if he did.

'Anyway,' he added. 'It's too late.'

'Not necessarily,' I said with a wave of my hand. We hadn't yet exchanged contracts so there was nothing set in stone. 'We can still pull out of the Suffolk house.'

'No. You insisted on Suffolk, so that's where we're going. And I like the house. Plus, it'll be good being so close to Mum, now that she's on her own . . .'

I didn't like the unusually defiant tone in his voice. Normally, he would just agree with whatever I said but he sounded worryingly determined.

'It should be a joint decision,' I snapped, aware that actually it had all been down to me so far. I hadn't given Ben any say on the houses we looked at, or, come to think of it, the one I eventually plumped for.

'It is a joint decision, we chose it together, remember?' Ben said. 'Although, to be honest, you didn't really give me much say in the choice, did you?'

I didn't think he had been so aware that I wasn't giving him any say. 'Don't play that card with me, Ben,' I said, trying to deflect his words with my defensiveness. 'While you've been dashing off to be at your mother's beck and call, I've had to sort everything out by myself. So now I've decided that Surrey would be better instead.'

'And remind me how far it is from your mum's house?'

I rolled my eyes dramatically. 'Oh, for Christ's sake! We will need my mum's help with Elodie, so it's a good thing that she'll be so close.'

'My mum would be just as much help, especially now that she's on her own. It would give her a focus.'

I couldn't believe my ears. Ben had never defied me before

and I didn't like it one bit. 'She's not as good with Elodie as my mum. I wouldn't feel happy leaving her. Your mum seemed completely disinterested in her today . . .'

'Well, I expect burying her husband might have meant her mind wasn't fully on Elodie today.'

'There's no need to be sarcastic, Ben.' I threw him my angriest stare, hoping that he would do his usual and just roll over. But he was in a strange, surly mood and didn't seem to be prepared to give in so easily.

'Of course my mum isn't as good with Elodie as yours,' he said through gritted teeth. 'Because she hasn't had a chance. If she'd spent as much time with her as your mum, she would be just as capable. It's not her fault that she was banned from seeing her for the first few months of Elodie's life.'

He stopped speaking and swallowed hard. I hoped he wasn't going to start weeping and wailing. 'That was her own fault for the way she attacked me at Christmas,' I replied, knowing that in that respect at least, I had right on my side. 'And she hasn't exactly tried to make it up to me since. No, considering how strained our relationship is now, I definitely think Surrey is the best option.' I adopted a decisive tone that made it clear that I wasn't going to change my mind. There was no way I was moving to live so close to his mum now and that was that.

Ben pursed his lips. I could tell he was thinking about arguing but he seemed to have run out of energy and drove in virtual silence for the rest of the journey, giving just one-syllable answers to my questions. In the end, I gave up and decided to have a little sleep instead. The wine I had drunk had made me drowsy because I was so unused to it.

After we arrived home at the flat in London, I put Elodie

straight to bed, then returned to the kitchen to find Ben sitting at the kitchen table, nursing a glass of red wine and looking deep in thought. I took a glass out of the cupboard and poured myself a glass of iced water. It felt good to have got today over with and I tapped my glass against Ben's. 'Well, cheers!' I said, giving him an encouraging smile.

Ben lifted his glass without enthusiasm and refused to meet my eye.

'Oh come on, Ben. Please stop sulking.' I was running out of patience with him.

'I'm not,' he said, his voice choked. 'I'm just upset. I still can't believe that Dad has gone. That I'll never, ever see him again. That Elodie won't know him growing up. It all just makes me feel unbearably sad.'

I didn't want to dwell on Peter's absence from Elodie's life, for reasons that Ben would never understand. 'Well, she won't know mine either, so we're sort of even, aren't we?'

'Good God, Bella, it's not a competition!'

My mouth dropped open in shock. I couldn't believe how insolent he was being. 'I never said it was. Stop putting words into my mouth.'

Ben tutted and shook his head.

An unstoppable tidal wave of rage swept over me. 'Don't you dare tut at me! I've had just about enough of this shit!'

'Well, that makes two of us!'

I didn't remember doing it. I didn't remember the glass leaving my hand. I just remember watching, as if from above, as the glass hit the wall above Ben's head and exploded in a beautiful, iridescent shower of fragments. Then, as if in slow motion, I was pulling at his hair and pummelling his body with a strength that came from somewhere deep inside. Every blow seemed to encapsulate all my hurt at Peter's betrayal.

Ben's arms were up, as he tried to defend himself. 'Stop it, Bella!' he was yelling but I couldn't hear him. It was as if I was underwater, with everything happening in muffled, slow motion.

Finally, I ran out of energy and stopped, aware that I was actually panting with the effort of it. My senses seemed to snap back into focus and I stared at him, cowering pathetically, before I turned on my heel and headed for the bathroom. I slammed the door and locked it, then perched on the edge of the bath, as I reached with shaking hands for the taps, and turned them on full.

I stared at my knuckles, which were red and already starting to bruise. I wasn't sure what I had done. Had I injured him? Surely not. I was far too small to have inflicted any real damage on someone as big as him. I waited for the bath to fill, calming myself with deep breaths. I climbed into the frothy water and sank gratefully down into it, hardly daring to look at my hands, as I lathered soap all over my body.

After a few minutes, my heart had stopped racing and I was calm again. I relaxed back and closed my eyes, telling myself I must have imagined it. Maybe I had dropped off to sleep in the bath briefly and dreamed it? It seemed the most likely explanation.

I lay there for a while, until I felt calm, relaxed and rejuvenated. I stepped out of the bath and wrapped a towel around my body, and another one as a turban around my head. I rubbed at the steamed-up mirror so that I could see my reflection and smiled when I saw that I looked the same as usual. Nothing had happened, it was just a dream. At least, that's what I was going to believe.

I unlocked the door and walked out into the hallway. I was about to go into the bedroom, when I became aware that Ben was standing in the doorway to the kitchen, watching me with a look of sheer terror in his eyes. 'What are you doing standing there like that?' I said, smiling warmly at him. 'You look like you've seen a ghost!'

Ben frowned, wrong-footed. 'Bella, we really need to talk about what just happened.' His voice was trembling and there was a flash of tears visible in his eyes.

I raised my eyebrows in surprise. 'What are you on about? Nothing happened.'

Ben shook his head incredulously. 'You attacked me!'

'No, I didn't. Don't be so ridiculous! As if someone the size of me could attack anyone, let alone a six-foot-two hulk like you. You must be having some kind of hallucination. Listen,' I said, adopting a softer, more sympathetic tone of voice. 'It's been a long, stressful day – for both of us.'

Ben's mouth dropped open and he winced slightly as I put my hand on his arm.

'So why don't we get an early night and try to put everything else to the back of our minds? Let's remind ourselves why it's just you and me that matters. We don't need anyone else. It's better when it's just us.'

Ben gazed at me for a few seconds before he nodded slowly and allowed me to take his hand and lead him into the bedroom.

PART THREE

PART THREE

CHAPTER TWENTY-EIGHT

One Year Later

Jo stared at the screen of her mobile, willing it to spring into life with a reply from Ben. She would much rather have called than texted, so that she could at least hear his voice but she knew there was no point. Bella was obviously screening his calls, whether she rang the landline or the mobile.

Sighing as the screen stayed resolutely blank, Jo put the phone down and rested her forehead on the cool granite surface of the island worktop, as the heavy weight in her chest became just a tiny bit heavier. After a while, she looked up and stared out of the window, across the undulating green lawns, speckled with the first leaves of autumn, the sky a sulky shade of grey. She could almost hear her own breath echoing back at her from the four walls of the empty kitchen.

The pain of losing Peter was never far away and although she was beginning to learn how to survive without him, she sometimes thought it hurt more now than on the day he died. So many times, the grief assaulted her when she was least expecting it: she would start to dial his number automatically; or a diary entry would pop up on her phone for something he had put in as a yearly event; or she would put something in her basket at the supermarket that only he ever ate. Each time, it was like a punch in the face.

But she also knew that she would be coping far better if she hadn't also lost Ben. He had all but disappeared from her life as soon as the funeral was over. He and Bella immediately pulled out of buying the beautiful house they had found nearby and had moved to Surrey instead, 'to be near to Bella's mother', Ben had told her, sounding embarrassed. His words caused her heart to splinter just a tiny bit more.

Despite Bella's prickliness, Jo had looked forward to them moving closer. She had imagined balmy summer days full of fun, when she would take Elodie off to the beach or for walks in the beautiful countryside, hoping that the little girl would be just the tonic she needed, to fill the void left by Peter. But those dreams were quickly buried, along with him.

Whenever Ben did call her these days, which wasn't often, he was furtive and rushed, as if he was terrified that Bella might catch him doing something he shouldn't. At first, he had been able to call her from work, but once they moved, Bella had insisted he give up his job to stay at home with Elodie, while she returned to her job in the city. Apparently, she had been promoted within the company, so wanted to focus on her career. Jo knew that Peter would have hated Ben giving up his job but she was pretty relaxed about it and proud that he was happy to be a house-husband for a while.

Thanks to Peter buying them a house, plus a large inheritance from his estate, Ben didn't really need a salary, so he had acquiesced to Bella's demands without any argument. Jo had barely seen Elodie since the funeral, except on FaceTime. When she tentatively invited them to spend Christmas with her, Ben's eyes had widened in alarm and Jo knew that he was too scared to even broach the subject with Bella, so she had brushed it off with a nonchalant wave of the hand and a cheery, 'Never mind!' She didn't want to do anything to put him in an awkward position with Bella.

The worry she felt for him was like rust gradually eating away at metal. He looked thin – too thin – and his eyes were clouded with anxiety. He had always had beautiful, soulful eyes that danced with mischief but now they just peered at her through the screen with a blank stare. He looked lonely, which she recognized all too well because she was lonely too.

Emma did her best to keep in touch as much as possible, but her job meant she was away travelling a lot and Jo didn't want to burden her with her own worries and upset, so she put on a brave front whenever they spoke. Only when she came to visit could Jo really let her guard down and tell Emma how worried she was. They would sit across from each other, shaking their heads helplessly, as they tried to understand why Ben had allowed Bella to rent their family apart the way she had.

Jo took a deep breath and looked again at her stubbornly silent phone. Before she knew what she was doing, she was dialling Charlotte's number.

'Hi, Jo!' Charlotte sounded a mixture of pleased and nervous. 'Is everything OK?'

Tears sprang into Jo's eyes at the sound of Charlotte's sweet, lovely voice and for a moment she was too choked to speak.

'Jo?' Charlotte prompted. 'What's wrong?'

'Oh, Charlotte!' Jo burst into a torrent of terrifyingly

powerful sobs that she couldn't contain. Months of grief and sorrow came pouring out in an unstoppable wave.

'Oh, Jo, what's happened? Don't worry, just take your time . . .' Charlotte's sympathetic tone and the warmth of her words caused Jo to cry even harder. It felt like so long since someone had shown her any kindness.

After a few moments, the worst of her sobs had subsided and she was able to speak through a succession of hiccups and gasps. 'It's Ben,' she managed at last. 'I'm so worried about him.'

There was a long beat of silence before Charlotte replied. 'I know, Jo. We all are.'

Jo blinked away the last vestiges of tears, relieved at hearing someone else echo what she felt. 'Really? I was sure it was just me.'

Charlotte sighed heavily. 'No. Matt and Freya feel exactly the same. We never hear from him anymore. He's like a ghost that just vanished overnight.'

Jo thought back to Peter's words when talking about Bella: 'She's like a ghost that just appeared out of nowhere.' And now Ben was like a ghost that just vanished overnight. There was some sort of irony in there somewhere. 'It's her,' Jo said quietly.

'I know. She's managed to prise him away from everyone who loved him.' Charlotte's own voice wobbled. 'I'm so sorry, Jo. This is all my fault!'

'No!' Jo shot back. 'Of course it's not. It's her fault.'

'But if I hadn't been stupid enough to walk away from him, he would never have met her and we would be happily married by now, maybe even with our first baby . . .' Her voice tailed off.

Jo closed her eyes for a moment, imagining what might have been. She knew, without even the tiniest of doubts, that Peter would still be alive. It was the stress of the situation with Bella that had caused his death, of that she was certain. 'Well, there's no point in thinking of what might have been, it doesn't help anyone,' she sighed.

'No,' Charlotte agreed. 'I suppose not. Jo, what can I do? What can Matt and Freya do? We must be able to do something.'

'I honestly don't know.' Jo wracked her brains, thinking over the possibilities. 'It's such a horrible, odd situation. I've got no idea how we tackle it.'

'Why don't we come and see you at the weekend? We could try to work out a game-plan.'

Jo's spirits soared instantly. 'Oh, Charlie, I would love that! Do you think Matt and Freya would be able to make it, too?'

'I'll ask them. I know they're as worried as we are, so I'm sure they'll do their best.'

'And it would be so lovely to meet Bertie!' Jo cried, instantly revived by the thought of meeting Matt and Freya's 3-month-old baby boy.

'Leave it with me and I'll organize it all,' Charlotte said, now back to her usual, no-nonsense, clear-headed self.

'Oh, thank you so much, Charlie – you have no idea how much this has helped already.'

Jo hung up, feeling lighter than she had done for weeks and wishing she had thought to call Charlotte sooner. If only . . . she started to think, before swatting the thought away quickly. There was nothing to be gained by dwelling on the past. Right now she needed to focus on the future and finding a way to get her son back.

CHAPTER TWENTY-NINE

I looked at the clock on the office wall. It was just before noon, almost time for Elodie's lunchtime nap. I called Ben's mobile, listening with increasing annoyance as it rang six times, before cutting to voicemail. 'Where the fuck are you?' I hissed into the Ansaphone, before hanging up, the urge to smash the phone onto my desk almost irresistible.

I clicked on Find Friends and was furious to see that he was in town, rather than at home where he should be. So bloody typical of him to be gadding about shopping when it was time for Elodie's nap. He had never understood the importance of keeping rigidly to her routine. The few times in the past that we had deviated, she invariably woke in the night and caused us all a sleepless night. Well, he would be the one getting up to her tonight, the selfish pig.

Just as I was contemplating ringing again, Marcus appeared at my office door, beaming broadly. I quickly rearranged my scowl into a smile. 'Someone's in a good mood.'

He walked into the office and perched on the edge of my desk the way he used to when I was his PA. I didn't know whether to be annoyed and point out that since my promotion, he should stop doing it. 'Yes, I bloody well am! Turns out that new client you brought in is proving extremely lucrative.'

'Leo?' I raised my eyebrows, as if I was surprised by the news. 'That's good to hear.'

'Remind me how you met him again?' Marcus narrowed his eyes slightly. He obviously suspected that my relationship with Leo was more than just platonic and he made no secret of his jealousy.

I gave a dismissive wave of my hand. 'It's a long story . . . But I'm delighted that he's proving such an asset to Norton.' I didn't want Marcus knowing too much about my relationship with Leo, in case he started questioning how much confidential information I might have passed on, in my efforts to get him to invest his considerable wealth with Norton. It was what had eventually secured my promotion.

I genuinely hadn't planned to see Leo again and had consigned our illicit afternoon together to the back of my mind. But following Peter's funeral, with Ben tiptoeing around me like a frightened deer one minute, and sobbing pathetically whenever he locked himself in the bathroom the next, I felt in need of a bit of a boost.

In what had proved to be a master-stroke on my part, I had insisted that Ben give up his job when we moved to Surrey, while I went back to work. Thanks to the money Peter had already given us for the house, plus a substantial inheritance from his estate, we were rolling in cash. But, I told Ben earnestly, I still needed to work for my own self-esteem and so that I didn't feel like I was sponging off him.

And although in truth I had absolutely no qualms about sponging off him, it certainly had helped my self-esteem, as it meant that I had ample opportunity to hook up with Leo during the week.

His reaction to my call was instantly uplifting. 'Beautiful Bella!' he exclaimed. 'I was hoping you might call one day.'

I smiled to myself, aware that it was the first time in ages that I had worn anything other than a frown on my face. 'I'm not sure it's a good idea but . . .'

Leo chuckled. 'Couldn't resist me, eh?'

I laughed, already feeling a frisson of excitement at the prospect of seeing him again. 'Something like that.'

'I have to say it was one of the more pleasurable afternoons I've enjoyed . . .' Leo's tone was a mixture of amusement and mischief. I liked that we could be so upfront with each other. There was no need to dance around the real meaning of our conversation.

'So, I was wondering . . . do you fancy a rematch?' I asked, adopting my most seductive tone.

There was a very slight intake of breath from Leo. 'I certainly do . . .' he began. 'And, would our mini-chaperone be joining us again? Not that it's a problem, of course,' he added hastily.

I grinned. 'No, our little chaperone is otherwise engaged. So we're free to be as badly behaved as we like, although it will have to be outside of office hours this time . . .'

'Excellent! That suits me just fine . . .'

Usually, we went to Leo's flat after work. Working in the City, he started early and finished early, which fitted with my schedule perfectly. On the evenings we met, I could spend a couple of hours with him, before getting on the train back to Surrey with a spring in my step.

He was an exciting and voracious lover, with a dangerous

edge to him that only added to the excitement of our trysts. He pushed me further than anyone ever had before and I found it addictive and electrifying.

Returning home to Ben after I'd seen Leo was like coming down from a drug-induced high. He was so tentative and wary around me that it just made me despise him even more. I had thought about leaving him numerous times but he was too useful with Elodie, allowing me to indulge my needs and get away from the claustrophobia of the house during the day. I loved Elodie, but found being at home with her boring and stultifying, whereas Ben didn't seem to mind. Not that I gave him any choice.

Ben and I rarely had sex these days, which suited me just fine. The only times I forced myself to let him anywhere near me were after we had had a particularly vicious, often violent, row. I knew I needed to keep him sweet, so I would work my magic on him until he was back onside, knowing he would stay because of Elodie.

He was undoubtedly a good father and he and Elodie were becoming increasingly close. It used to irritate and upset me when she turned to him first for comfort, but I also knew that it benefitted me in the long run, as she stopped being clingy and tearful about me going out to work each day.

Thankfully, moving to Surrey meant we now had almost no contact with his awful family or nosy, horrible friends. I kept a close eye on his movements to make sure that he wasn't seeing them behind my back or getting friendly with anyone new in the area. To begin with, he would whine that he didn't want Elodie to lose touch with her grandmother and suggest that we should visit her. But I would create such a scene that he gradually stopped mentioning it. In fact, the last time resulted in a physical fight so violent that it left him nursing a black eye and cracked cheekbone, so perhaps it wasn't surprising that he didn't want to risk it.

There was another reason that I didn't want Ben seeing his family or friends but I could barely admit it, even to myself. His appearance had changed so dramatically over the past year that I didn't want them to start asking any awkward questions. He was like a balloon that had been popped. Everything about him seemed to sag inwards and his eyes had taken on a haunted, defeated look. Sometimes I would catch him staring into space with such a grief-stricken expression that I almost felt sorry for him. But then he would do something to annoy me and all sympathy was lost.

I arrived home that evening and parked on our sweeping drive-way, looking up at the large, white, modern house we had bought with Peter's money. It was what I had wanted for Elodie and it always gave me a surge of satisfaction knowing that her upbringing would be a damn sight more privileged than mine. That was one thing at least her father had provided for her.

I let myself into the house and listened for a while to Ben and Elodie, who were in the kitchen, chatting and giggling at CBeebies, which was blaring from the TV on the kitchen wall.

'Haha, look, Daddy!' Elodie said with the precision of a toddler who was still new to speaking.

I walked to the kitchen door, in time to see Elodie pointing to a character on the screen who was rolling his extra-long tongue around his mouth.

'Daddy do it!' she demanded bossily. She was certainly her mother's daughter, I thought with a rueful grin.

Ben glanced at the screen, before copying the character and sticking his tongue out as far as possible, before rolling it around in a huge circle, eliciting squeals of delight from Elodie. Ben beamed and turned back to the worktop, where he was preparing a Jamie Oliver chicken dish that I had once mentioned was my favourite.

'Hello, you two,' I said, making them both jump with surprise. Elodie beamed and put her arms out from her high chair. 'Mummy!' she cried delightedly, agitating to be lifted out. I walked over and scooped her up into a hug, trying to avoid my hair making contact with her sticky little hands.

Ben eyed me nervously. 'Hi, darling. You're home early.'

'I thought I'd get home in time to put Elodie to bed. Ooh, you smell gorgeous,' I told her, kissing her chubby red cheeks, which were hot from where she was teething. I omitted to mention that I had been supposed to meet Leo tonight but he had had to cancel due to a work crisis of some sort.

Ben nodded, relief at my apparent good mood flooding his features. 'That's nice. Well, I'll get dinner ready while you bath her and it'll be ready by the time she's in bed.'

'Lovely,' I said, taking Elodie upstairs. I ran the bath and sat on the floor while she splashed around with her toys and told me several nonsensical stories about her day. I wasn't required to speak, so I scrolled through my phone and filled in any gaps with an obliging 'Oooh' or 'Wow'.

Leo had texted me: *Sorry about tonight – wish I was fucking your brains out as usual rather than being stuck here in my office!*

God, he wasn't the only one. Even his texts turned me on. *You'll just have to fuck me twice as hard next time,* I replied.

Just then, Elodie leaned over the side of the bath and with a delighted giggle, tipped a huge bucket full of water over my phone. 'Shit!' I yelled in panic, causing her to sit back down suddenly and look at me in shock. 'Fuck, fuck, fuck!' I shouted, before I heard Ben's footsteps pounding on the stairs.

'What's happened?' he gasped, running into the bathroom with a stricken expression, which immediately relaxed with relief when he saw Elodie sitting up safely in the bath.

'She tipped water over my bloody phone!' I snapped, wiping it furiously with a towel.

Ben sighed and took the phone out of my hand. 'Christ, is that all? I thought she'd been electrocuted or something. It'll be fine, I'll sort it.'

I exhaled with relief. One thing Ben was good at was technology. He could usually fix most things. That was another reason for not leaving him.

'It's OK,' I told Elodie, who was watching me with a worried frown. 'Sorry Mummy shouted – but you mustn't throw water. It's naughty and you might have broken my phone.'

Elodie gave me a tentative smile. 'Sorry, Mummy.'

I nodded and lifted her up and into her bathrobe. 'Right, let's get you dry and into beddy-bies, shall we?'

By the time I got downstairs, Ben was putting dinner on the table. It did look good and I was suddenly ravenous, not having eaten all day. I sat down and picked up my fork, before remembering my phone. 'Oh! Did you manage to fix my phone?' I looked up at him expectantly.

Ben was staring at me in an odd way, as if he was making up his mind about something. 'I did actually . . .'

I speared a forkful of chicken and nodded as I ate it. 'Great. Thanks.'

Still Ben kept watching me. He didn't touch his food.

'Aren't you going to eat?' I motioned to his plate. It was delicious, I had to admit. Ben was a pretty good cook. Certainly a lot better than me. I could never be bothered with anything more than an omelette or a piece of toast.

Ben took a deep breath. 'I sorted your phone . . .'

'I know you sorted my phone . . . you told me already. Why are you being so weird, Ben?'

Ben turned and picked up my phone from the worktop, then he tapped something in and looked at it for second before handing it over to me.

Shit. The messages from Leo. They would still have been on the screen. I put down my fork and took the phone as slowly as possible, trying to buy some time.

'I read them,' Ben said quietly.

I rolled my eyes and shrugged. 'So? They were just banter.'

Ben pursed his lips. 'Really? They looked like a lot more than that. And now it all makes sense, of course. Why you're so keen for me to stay at home with Elodie while you go out to work, even though we don't need the money . . .'

I could feel the heat in my cheeks and knew that I was blushing furiously. 'Oh, stop being so dramatic!' I blustered. 'There's a perfectly innocent explanation . . .' I wracked my brains to think of something plausible.

'Which is?' Ben's eyes met mine and I could see a spark of defiance that I thought had gone completely.

'It was a joke. That's all.' I adopted my sternest tone in the hope that he would let it drop.

'And all the other messages from Leo? Are they jokes, too? Only they're not very funny and they look a lot like arrangements to meet.'

Damn, I didn't think that he might have read them all. I bit my lip, my mind racing. Eventually I decided that there was no point in denying it. I had been caught red-handed. 'OK, so what? It's just sex, nothing more. It means nothing.'

Tears sprang into Ben's dark eyes, which surprised me slightly. 'How long?' he whispered.

I exhaled loudly, not wanting to discuss this now – or ever. 'Not long. Look, Ben, don't make a big deal out of it. You never seem to want to have sex so what am I supposed to do? Live like a bloody nun?' It was deeply unfair of me but guilt was making me bluster.

Ben recoiled at my words and shook his head. 'Why didn't you talk to me about it? Instead of skulking around behind my back? Behind Elodie's back.' His voice wobbled slightly at the mention of Elodie's name.

'Oh, for Christ's sake, Ben!' I snapped. 'Stop being such a bloody wimp!' I stood up crossly and picked up my plate, all hunger now completely gone.

'Promise me you won't see him again.' Ben's voice lacked conviction but he was clearly trying to sound as manly as possible.

I hesitated. 'Oh, whatever! Fine!' He didn't need to know whether I saw Leo or not and I wouldn't be making the mistake of giving him access to my phone again.

Ben watched me silently as I scraped the food into the bin. 'You haven't even said sorry,' he murmured.

I gritted my teeth, as a wave of rage swept through me. 'Ben, please stop making this into such a big drama. You're blowing it all out of proportion.'

'I'd like to see how you'd react if it was me you caught having an affair!'

I looked up at him, surprised by his outburst. I couldn't remember the last time he had raised his voice to me. 'As if anyone would want to have an affair with you!' The words flew out of my mouth like the rattle of a machine gun.

Ben's face creased in pain and he stood up slowly. 'You are such a bitch sometimes,' he whispered, shaking his head, before turning his back on me and heading towards the door.

Instinctively, without registering what I was doing, the plate I was holding had left my hand and sailed across the room, landing with a sickening thud against the back of Ben's head, before crashing into pieces on the kitchen floor. His legs gave way and he seemed to melt down onto the cold, tiled floor, where he lay very still.

My mouth dried instantly. What if I'd killed him? I made my way over to him, stepping tentatively over the pieces of smashed crockery. 'Ben?' I said, rolling him over onto his back. His face was deathly pale but I could see that he was breathing. 'Oh, thank God,' I said, stroking his face. 'Come on, Ben, wake up, darling. You've fallen over.' I gave him a small shake.

After what seemed like an eternity but was probably no more than a minute, his eyes flickered open. He looked at me unseeingly, before he seemed to regain focus.

'You're OK,' I told him gently, making a promise to myself there and then that I would never hurt him again. This had been too much of a fright. But I didn't seem able to control it. The anger inside me just bubbled up out of nowhere. 'You're OK,' I repeated, as much for his benefit as for mine.

Ben reached up to touch his head and winced.

I helped him into a sitting position and got an ice-pack from the freezer. 'Here, put this where it hurts. You'll be fine.'

Ben did as he was told and sat quietly while I swept up the broken pieces of plate.

'Right, let's get you upstairs.' He allowed me to help him stand and lead him up the stairs to the bedroom. I lay him on the bed and perched beside him, taking his hand in mine. 'What can I get you?' Relief that he seemed to be OK was making me solicitous.

Ben gave me a wan smile. 'Nothing. Just lie with me for a little while.'

I took off my shoes and lay down with my head on his chest and my arm across his body. It felt surprisingly nice. For the time being at least, the storm had passed.

CHAPTER THIRTY

Charlotte pulled onto the driveway of Jo's house, which had once been as familiar to her as her own. The last time she'd been here was the day of Peter's funeral and it had been such a bittersweet experience to be back, in the home where she had spent so many happy times with Ben and his parents.

It had always been such a warm, vibrant and inviting place, full of laughter, celebration and fun. But even by the time of the funeral, it already felt like a shell of its former self. With Peter gone, it was as if the heart and soul had been ripped from its beautiful walls and it was just a building where a pall of sadness hung in the air. At least back then, the summer sun provided some warmth, but with autumn's smoky dampness now in the air, it looked as cold as it felt.

Shivering, Charlotte took her bag from the boot and crunched her way over the gravel towards the heavy, grey-painted front door. Just as she was about to ring the bell, it swung open and Jo stood in front of her. 'Charlie!' she cried, reaching out to embrace Charlotte in a tight hug. 'I am so happy to see you.'

Charlotte hugged her in return, aware of how diminished Jo seemed since she had last seen her. She pulled back and looked at her closely. 'Hello, Jo. It's good to see you too, although you've lost too much weight.'

Jo smiled, but the smile didn't reach her blue eyes, which had dulled and lost their sparkle. 'You sound like Emma. She's always telling me that, too – talk about ironic.'

Charlotte grinned ruefully. Emma's anorexia had stabilized in recent years and she seemed to have got it under control but none of them would ever forget the horror of when she was in its fiercest grip.

'Anyway, come on in!' Jo motioned with her arm and ushered Charlotte into the cool flag-stoned entrance.

Charlotte followed her down the long hallway towards the kitchen, thinking how tiny she looked in such a vast space. The house had never seemed too big when there were lots of them to fill it but with just Jo there, it felt enormous and echoey.

Charlotte perched at the island while Jo made her a cup of tea. 'Matt and Freya aren't far behind me. They'll be here in about an hour.'

Jo nodded as she put a mug in front of Charlotte. 'I can't wait to see them. And meet Bertie – it'll be so lovely to have children here again . . .' Her voice dropped away and Charlotte could tell that she was thinking about Elodie.

'Do you not see much of Elodie?' Charlotte took a sip of her tea, savouring its comforting warmth. Jo always did make the best cup of tea.

Jo perched on a stool and shook her head sadly. 'Only on FaceTime. When Bella's out, presumably.'

Charlotte's insides constricted with guilt. 'I'm so sorry, Jo. I don't know what to say.'

Jo shrugged. 'There's nothing anyone can say. But,' she

adopted a stoic expression, 'you being here is such a wonderful tonic. Makes me feel like I'm not completely alone.'

'I wish you'd called me sooner.'

Jo nodded. 'So do I, but I couldn't face the embarrassment of admitting that I haven't seen my own son for months.'

'You must have seen them at Christmas, though?'

Jo shook her head. 'No. Ben got so panicked when I suggested that they might come here that I didn't push it. He seems in such a bad way, Charlie . . .' Tears that Charlotte could see were never far from the surface spilled down Jo's cheeks and she swept them away, looking defeated.

'In a bad way . . . how? Do you mean he seems depressed?' Charlotte pictured Ben on the day of the funeral. Even back then he had looked different but she couldn't put her finger on exactly what had changed. He seemed anxious, which was understandable on the day of his father's funeral. But it was more than that.

Jo sighed and blew her nose. 'Yes, he does seem depressed. But he also looks haunted, somehow. Even a bit scared.'

'Scared of what? Bella?' Charlotte couldn't comprehend how a big man like Ben could possibly be scared of someone as slim and delicate-looking as Bella.

Jo nodded. 'Yes, Bella. I know it sounds crazy but I've been on the receiving end of her tongue and she is pretty terrifying when she wants to be.'

'She was certainly very cold and unfriendly at the funeral,' Charlotte agreed. 'I thought it might just be because she didn't want to engage with an ex, which is fair enough, I suppose.'

Jo gave a mirthless laugh. 'It's not just you, believe me. She doesn't want to engage with anyone from Ben's side of the family. Or his friends.'

Charlotte nodded. 'Yes, that's true. Matt and Freya are so upset at the way he allowed her to cut them out of his life. Well, Matt's upset. Freya's just absolutely bloody furious.'

'Have they not heard from him at all? Even since Bertie was born?'

Charlotte shook her head. 'Nope. Not a word. Matt is unbelievably hurt.' She stopped talking, suddenly aware that it must be so much worse for Jo.

There was a moment of silence, as they both contemplated the situation.

'Do you think he seems happy with her?' Charlotte wanted to see if she could find some ray of light to give Jo, who looked utterly desperate and forlorn.

Jo shook her head. 'No. After the first time he brought her home, he never seemed happy again.'

'God. That's so sad.' Charlotte could feel the tears welling up and for the millionth time, cursed herself for letting him go. Jo, noticing her tears, handed her a tissue, which she took gratefully. 'And what was she like towards you and Peter?'

Jo paused, thinking. 'Well, Peter didn't like her.'

Charlotte wiped her eyes. 'Really?' She took some satisfaction in that. Peter had loved Charlotte and she had loved him. 'I never knew Peter have a bad word to say about anyone.'

'No,' Jo agreed. 'Even from that first visit, when she was on her best behaviour, he said he didn't like her. I didn't like her either, but I ignored the signs, for Ben's sake . . .' She looked into the distance. 'I couldn't bear to see him hurt any more. That was a mistake. I should have told him then and there.'

Charlotte reached out and took Jo's hand across the island.

'What difference would it have made? Ben's a grown man and you can't tell him who to love and not love.'

'No, I suppose you're right. But I really do believe that the stress of it all is what killed Peter. I just know that if you two had stayed together, then he'd still be alive today.'

'Oh God, don't say that!' Charlotte cried. 'I feel bad enough as it is without having Peter's death on my conscience too!'

Jo squeezed Charlotte's hand. 'I'm sorry, I didn't mean it like that, Charlie. I don't blame you. I've never blamed you for any of it. I blame her.'

'Well,' Charlotte sighed heavily. 'You might not blame me but I do blame myself for breaking up with Ben in the first place. I never stopped loving him, so I promise you, Jo, I am going to do everything I can to help put things right.'

Jo smiled and for the first time, Charlotte could see a spark of hope in her eyes.

Jo and Charlotte had prepared a huge pan of spaghetti bolognese and were halfway through a bottle of red wine, by the time the doorbell chimed, heralding Matt and Freya's arrival.

'I'll go!' Jo leaped off her stool and raced towards the front door.

Charlotte smiled to herself. Jo's loneliness clung to her like a cloak of cobwebs and it was lovely to see her shaking them off, even for a short while.

'Well, this is a sight for sore eyes!' Matt came bustling into the kitchen, along with a sleeping Bertie in his car-seat and what seemed like dozens of bags stuffed with baby-themed paraphernalia. Freya followed behind him, beaming proudly.

Charlotte hugged them both tightly, before crouching down

to look at Bertie. Even in the two weeks since she had last seen him, he seemed to have grown and his downy dark hair was becoming fairer and thicker. 'Oh, I could eat him!' she exclaimed, stroking his velvety cheek.

'Yeah, I could too, I'm so bloody hungry!' Matt laughed.

Jo walked over to the Aga, where she stirred the simmering sauce. 'Good, because I am counting on you guys to eat me out of house and home this weekend. It's been too long since I've had a houseful to feed and I'm going to make the most of it!'

Matt clapped his hands together. 'Well, if you insist, Jo,' he said, as they all burst out laughing.

'So,' Freya took a sip of her coffee and looked across the vast dining table at Jo. 'Let's talk about the elephant in the room. What's going on with Ben, then?'

Jo's expression, which had lightened from the moment they arrived, suddenly dropped again. She stirred her coffee in its china cup and pursed her lips in contemplation. 'I'm not entirely sure . . .'

'Tell them what you've told me, Jo,' Charlotte prompted her gently.

Jo nodded. 'I haven't seen him since the funeral . . .' she began.

'What!' Freya gasped and looked aghast at Matt. 'Not at all?'

'Not in person, no,' Jo said quietly. 'The only time I see him – and Elodie – is when he calls on FaceTime. And even then it's always very rushed. Bella is never there, which makes me think he waits until she's gone out before calling me. If I ever call him, he only answers when he's alone. I think she screens his calls to stop him speaking to me.'

Matt and Freya exchanged a knowing look. 'That sounds familiar,' Freya muttered under her breath.

'And how does he seem, in himself?' Matt cut in.

Jo sighed. 'Unhappy. Anxious. Scared.'

Matt shook his head in disgust. 'Jesus.'

'Why doesn't he just leave her?' Freya threw her arms up in the air in exasperation.

'Because of Elodie. He adores her.' Jo looked from Freya to Matt. 'As you both know, having a child changes everything.'

'It didn't change everything for me and Freya, though, did it, Charlie?' Matt looked at Charlotte for affirmation. 'We're still the same as we were before we had Bertie, aren't we?'

Charlotte nodded. 'You are, but then again, you're not married to Bella.'

'Thank God!' Matt snapped, before looking sheepishly at Jo. 'Sorry, Jo.'

Jo waved away his apology. 'No, don't apologize, Matt. It's the truth. She is a terrifying person and I think he's genuinely scared of her, which just breaks my heart . . .' She stopped speaking abruptly and put a hand over her mouth.

Matt shook his head, a grim expression on his face. 'It's a bad, bad situation. So what are we going to do about it?'

They all looked at each other across the table. Eventually Charlotte spoke. 'Well, I think maybe we need to stage some sort of intervention, don't we? We need to see him in person to find out what's really going on.'

'Pah, how do we do that if he's never on his own without her?' Freya replied.

'He's not with her when she's at work all day, is he? We just need to get to him alone, so that we can suss out if he truly is unhappy, or scared, or whatever.' Charlotte stopped to look at the others. 'I know none of us wants to hear this, but there's a possibility that he's quite happy with how things are.'

'No.' Jo shook her head firmly. 'I know Ben so well and I can see it in his eyes. He's definitely not happy.'

'OK, so let's figure out how we're going to get to him, then.' Matt glanced at Freya. 'One of us is going to have to go and see him while she's at work. It can't be Freya because she's got Bertie in tow at the moment. I would love to do it but to be honest, I'm not sure he'll want to see me. I think he might be too embarrassed.'

'I agree,' Jo cut in. 'Which leaves Charlie and me.' She paused and looked at Charlotte. 'I think you might be the best option, Charlie, as he seems terrified of her finding out that he's had any contact with me.'

'I'm not sure she'll be wild about him seeing me, either! So it will definitely have to be a covert operation.' Charlotte tried to analyse how she felt about the prospect of seeing Ben again. She felt desperately sorry for him, if he was in a situation that he couldn't get out of that was making him unhappy. But a small part of her felt angry with him, too, for cutting his mother out of his life when she needed him most. She couldn't understand why he didn't stand up to Bella more.

'You live so much closer to them, too,' Jo continued, clearly desperate for Charlotte to agree. 'So you could just pop down and if Bella's there, you can try again the next day. It's not such a mammoth exercise.'

'I suppose not,' Charlotte conceded, already feeling a frisson of excitement. She felt certain that only she would be able to tell if he was happy or not. She had always been able to read him so well. 'OK, I'll do it,' she said, her heart already beginning to race.

CHAPTER THIRTY-ONE

Ben was even quieter than usual, as we ate breakfast the morning after his 'accident' with the plate. He gently tended to Elodie and made me coffee exactly as I like it, but he barely spoke and seemed deep in thought.

I watched him out of the corner of my eye, looking for any physical signs of injury and was relieved to see that there were none, although he kept touching the back of his head and wincing slightly. 'What have you got planned today?' I asked him, as I prepared to leave the house.

He lifted his dark eyes to meet mine and shrugged. 'Not much. I think we'll go to the park after breakfast if it's not too cold.'

I nodded, grateful that I wasn't the one who had to fill my days trying to keep a toddler entertained. I felt a sudden burst of affection for him and reached up to hug him. Instinctively, he flinched. 'For God's sake, Ben, don't be so jumpy! I was just going to kiss you goodbye.'

A nervous half-smile played around his lips as he stepped forward, allowing me to embrace him.

'Mummy hug!' Elodie demanded from her high chair, making both Ben and I laugh.

I walked over and kissed the top of her head. ''Bye 'bye, my little missy-moo. Love you!'

'Love 'oo,' she parroted back, beaming through her mouthful of cereal.

'What about you?' Ben asked, as he walked me to the front door. 'What are you up to today?'

It sounded like a loaded question. I fixed him with my brightest smile. 'Oh, same old, same old . . . I won't be late, though,' I added, meaningfully.

He nodded his understanding and, in a move that was extremely rare these days, he bent to kiss me. I wrapped my arms around his neck and kissed him back, glad that he didn't seem to be holding a grudge. After he closed the door behind me, I hesitated on the step, feeling guilty. I had come perilously close to inflicting a serious injury on him last night and I needed to be careful. I didn't love Ben but I didn't quite hate him either. I just despised him. I decided that I needed to do some damage limitation for a while, just to make sure that I kept him where I wanted him.

After driving to the station, I caught the train into London, thinking about Leo. I would have to tell him that we needed to cool it for a little while. I didn't want to. He was sexy, exciting and dangerous – all of the things that Ben wasn't. But after last night, I needed to launch a charm offensive to get Ben back onside and if he thought I was still seeing Leo, it wouldn't work. I needed to show him that I was serious about us as a couple. In the past, I had always been able to work my magic, but I somehow felt that the seriousness of last night's fight could be harder to put behind us, not to mention the texts from Leo.

I rang Leo as I was walking from the station to the office. 'I hope you're calling to tell me that we should meet at lunchtime to make up for last night,' he purred. 'Don't bother wearing knickers.'

Just the sound of his deep, husky voice made my legs go weak. The thought of a lunchtime session at his flat was desperately appealing. 'Sadly not. I've got a little, uh, problem at home . . . we might need to stop meeting for a while.'

There was a long, ominous pause. 'I'm sure it's nothing you can't charm your way out of.'

'Not easily. He saw your messages on my phone last night.'

There was another pause. 'Ah, I see. So what did you do?'

'I told him the truth. There wasn't much else I could do, seeing as I was caught, quite literally, with my pants down.'

Leo gave a mirthless laugh. 'No, I suppose not. But there's no need for us to stop seeing each other. We'll just be more careful to make sure he doesn't find out next time and even if he does, what's he going to do? Kick you out? Leaving him with the baby that isn't even his?'

I stopped walking, aware of tuts from other commuters, as they had to swerve to avoid me. A shudder of alarm passed through me. I had told Leo the truth about Elodie's paternity one drunken evening when we were in bed together. Alcohol had loosened my tongue and when Leo asked how I'd ended up with Ben, when he clearly bored me rigid, I replied without thinking that I only got together with him to punish Peter for dumping me when I was pregnant with his child. He didn't seem to register it at the time and hadn't mentioned it since, so I'd hoped he'd forgotten, but clearly not.

'I just think I need to be on my best behaviour for a few

weeks, until it all blows over.' I tried to keep the quaver out of my voice and sound more in control than I felt.

'I don't think you need to do any such thing. I think we should carry on exactly as we are.'

I didn't like Leo's tone. There was a hint of menace about it. 'Not a good idea, Leo. At the moment, anyway. I'll give you a call in a couple of weeks when everything has settled down.'

'What makes you think I'm prepared to sit around waiting for you?'

Now there was more of a note of amusement in his voice and I breathed a sigh of relief. 'I'll just have to take my chances.'

I arrived in my office to find Marcus waiting for me, perched on my desk. I really needed to tell him to stop doing that. I wasn't his bloody PA anymore. 'Morning.' I dropped my bag and sat down, eyeing him warily. 'What's up?'

Marcus examined his fingernails. 'I just had a called from Leo Fox.'

I tried to look nonchalant as I logged into my computer. I had actively encouraged Leo to invest with our company by passing him information that I shouldn't have done and as a result, I had secured a hefty bonus, to go along with my promotion. Money wasn't really the incentive for me – it was more about power. I had always felt that I could outsmart all of the men I worked with, Marcus included. He didn't realize it but I had used my relationship with him to learn as much as possible about the business, with a view to one day elbowing him out of the way and taking his job. 'What did he want?'

Marcus hesitated. 'Well, it's slightly awkward.' He looked at me and I could see a slight flush spreading up his neck. The prickle of unease that I had felt when I spoke to Leo earlier intensified.

'Go on,' I urged, with an impatient wave of my hand.

Marcus's eyes slid away. 'He said he's thinking of withdrawing his capital.'

My mouth dried slightly and I cleared my throat, playing for time. 'Oh?'

'Yes,' Marcus continued. 'Which would not be good for Norton.'

'No,' I agreed. 'It wouldn't.'

'So, I was wondering . . .' Marcus stood up and put his hands in his pockets. 'Do you have any idea why he might be considering that?'

I shook my head slowly. 'No. How would I know?'

'Well, he did mention you. I may be wrong but I got the impression that you might have had some sort of . . . tiff.'

I wrinkled my nose in disdain. 'Marcus, don't be ridiculous. Leo is just a friend. We haven't had any sort of "tiff" and whatever his reasons for threatening to withdraw his investment, I'm pretty sure it has nothing to do with me.'

'Hmmm.' Marcus nodded contemplatively. I could tell that he didn't believe me for one second. He knew damn well that I had been having a relationship with Leo for months and that I must have passed him confidential information about a big merger that I knew about, in order to encourage him to invest. As if reading my mind, he added, 'As you know, Bella, you are party to some highly confidential information, especially around the merger, and if Leo Fox invested because of anything you told him during his, ahem, "friendship" with you,' he made imaginary speech marks with his fingers, 'you might find yourself in a spot of trouble if you upset him.'

My heart began to pound and my mind was racing back over the various things I had told Leo. There was absolutely no doubt that I had persuaded Leo to invest by passing him details about the forthcoming merger, which would be considered insider dealing and was highly illegal.

I must have looked panicked because Marcus flashed me a reassuring smile. 'Don't worry, I'm sure it's not going to be a problem. All you have to do is keep him sweet.'

I nodded, his meaning all too clear. Leo Fox was not a man used to being sidelined and he clearly had no intention of letting me go that easily. I looked up at Marcus and nodded confidently. 'It'll be fine,' I said with a confident smile. 'I'll sort it.'

Marcus grinned back wolfishly. 'Good girl.'

CHAPTER THIRTY-TWO

Charlotte pulled up across the road from the address Jo had given her and turned off the engine. It was only a ten-minute drive from the slightly scruffy terraced house she shared with Joe, but it seemed like a world away. She looked up at the grand white façade, set back behind ornate black iron gates. It was a hell of a house for a small family of three, especially in this part of Surrey, which was known for its expensive properties.

There were two cars parked on the luxuriously paved driveway – a pale blue Mercedes sports car and a large Jaguar SUV. Charlotte pictured the scene inside the house as they sat around the table, eating breakfast together. Were they a happy little family unit, laughing and chatting as they ate? She somehow doubted it, having seen the three of them together at the funeral. Bella definitely didn't seem like a laughing or chatting kind of person.

As she watched, the heavy black front door opened. Instinctively, she ducked down, even though they couldn't possibly have seen her from where they were. Bella emerged first, looking glamorous and beautiful in a designer grey skirt-suit. Then, behind her, Ben appeared. Charlotte's heart skipped at the sight of him. He had lost a lot of weight and his cheekbones were far more chiselled than she remembered. From a distance, she couldn't see his eyes properly but she could certainly see the dark circles beneath them.

Bella turned to say something to him and he bent down to kiss her. Charlotte's stomach churned, as she watched Bella wrap her arms around his neck and kiss him back, before closing the door and, after a brief hesitation, striding over to the blue sports car and climbing in.

As Bella pulled out through the electric gates and headed down the road, Charlotte sat up in her seat again. She hadn't been expecting the scene that she had just witnessed and it had thrown her. They looked pretty happy together and if that was how Bella kissed him goodbye each morning, there couldn't be too much wrong with their relationship.

It had clearly been a waste of time coming here. Charlotte knew that Jo was genuine in her concern for Ben, but she also knew that she might also be looking for a reason why he had cut her out of his life that didn't involve him simply deciding that he didn't want to see her. It was desperately unfair, but Ben seemed to have made his choice and there wasn't much anyone could do about it.

She sat for a while, thinking about how to break the news to Jo, before she started up her car again. She was about to drive off, when the front door opened once more and Ben emerged, this time leading Elodie by the hand towards the SUV. Charlotte smiled at the sight of them together. They seemed to be locked in their own happy little bubble and Ben was obviously a devoted father. Just as she had always known he would be.

As the gates opened for the second time that morning and

Ben drove out of the driveway, he looked straight towards Charlotte and their eyes locked. Flushing bright red with embarrassment, she scrambled to duck down in her seat again but it was too late. He'd definitely seen her. Hardly daring to look, she raised her eyes to see that he had pulled up in front of her and was getting out of the car.

'Oh shit, oh shit,' she murmured to herself, her mind racing for a plausible explanation as to why she was sitting outside his house like some sort of creepy stalker. Ben walked up to her window and knocked, a look of suspicion on his face.

Charlotte lowered the window, well aware that by now her face was a deep shade of crimson. She felt momentarily weak with humiliation. 'Hi, Ben,' she managed, unable to meet his eye.

'Hi.' He frowned and bent forward slightly, looking into the car to see if there was anyone else there. 'Um, what are you doing here, Charlotte?'

Still, nothing plausible would come to mind, so Charlotte made a snap decision that honesty was the best – and only – policy. 'I've come to see you.'

Ben frowned again. 'OK.' He paused before continuing. 'Well, two things,' he began, frowning. 'Firstly, why didn't you text me to say you were coming? And secondly, why are you sitting out here, rather than just, say, ringing the doorbell?'

There was a slight flicker of amusement in his eyes and Charlotte couldn't help smiling. 'I'm sorry. It's a long story. I was worried about you. We all are,' she added. 'So I volunteered to come and see you, as I live the closest, just to make sure you were OK. But as soon as I got here, I realized it was a daft idea and I shouldn't have come. Sorry,' she said again.

Ben nodded slowly and glanced back towards his own car.

'OK.' He hesitated again. 'Look, we were just off to the park. Do you want to join us?'

Charlotte cleared her throat. She really didn't want to stay now that she had seen Ben and noted that he and Bella seemed fine together, but she couldn't think of a way to say so. 'Um . . . OK,' she said instead. 'You lead the way and I'll follow.'

Ben smiled and nodded. 'It's not far, only a few minutes' drive, so I guess I'll see you there?'

Charlotte nodded, still hot with shame. 'See you there.'

By the time she got out of the car at the deserted park, Elodie was already on a little rocking horse, laughing and chattering to no one in particular, as she rocked backwards and forwards. Ben was standing beside her, looking on proudly.

'Looks like you might have a little jockey in the making there!' Charlotte said, as she joined him. It was a bright but chilly day and she stamped her feet a couple of times to try to kick-start some body heat.

'She loves this little horse. I'm just dreading the day she finally gets on the real thing! Then the proper worry starts.' Ben gazed at Elodie as he spoke, his love for her coming off him in waves.

'Yes, I bet.' Charlotte smiled at Elodie. She was an adorable little girl, with her mother's huge brown eyes and silky black hair. But unlike her mother, she wore a permanent smile that stretched from one side of her face to the other, showing milky white teeth.

'Who dat?' Elodie demanded, pointing at Charlotte rudely.

Ben laughed. 'It's Charlie.'

Elodie gaped at Charlotte with the unembarrassed stare that

only toddlers are capable of. 'Charlie,' she said at last, seemingly delighted to have got her tongue around the word, before she resumed her rocking with renewed vigour, both Charlie and Ben apparently dismissed.

'Shall we sit down?' Ben motioned to a bench next to them.

Charlotte nodded and they both sat down. They watched Elodie in silence until Ben finally spoke: 'So, how are things, Charlie? You look well.'

Charlotte smiled up at him and their eyes met, causing her heart to skip. 'I'm fine. More to the point, how are you?' Up close, she could see that he didn't look good at all. Jo was right that he had a haunted air about him and he almost seemed to have caved in on himself. There was none of the old Ben twinkle that she used to love so much.

'I'm fine.' Ben's eyes slid away from hers and returned to watching Elodie, but not before she had seen the threat of tears lurking. 'I don't know why they sent you to check up on me.'

Charlotte bit her lip, wondering whether to say what she had come here to say. 'Nobody sent me, Ben. Not really. I volunteered. We're all worried about you. No one ever sees you anymore and they all miss you, especially your mum.'

Ben flinched slightly at her words. 'When did you see her?' He stared into the distance as he spoke.

'Last weekend. I went to stay with her, along with Matt, Freya and baby Bertie.'

Ben gave a sad smile, filled with longing. Charlotte could tell that he was wishing he had been there too. 'How old is he?'

Charlotte felt a spike of irritation. 'He's 3 months old, Ben. How could you not know that? Matt is your oldest friend!'

Ben recoiled slightly at the harshness of her words and wrapped his arms around himself in a gesture that could either have been defensiveness or just to keep warm. Whatever it was, Charlotte's antennae prickled. Why was he being so edgy? He gave a deep sigh. 'It's difficult to keep in contact.'

'Is it?' Charlotte shot back. 'Why? All it takes is a phone-call? Or even a bloody text would do!'

Again, Ben recoiled physically at her words. He seemed so fearful and jumpy, which wasn't like him at all. Something flickered at the edge of Charlotte's brain. She had seen a man like this before, in this heightened state of alert, terrified in case he said or did the wrong thing.

'Don't you miss them?' Charlotte prompted, adopting a more gentle tone. 'You and Matt were inseparable. What's changed?' She already knew the answer but wanted to see if he would acknowledge Bella's influence.

Ben pursed his lips slightly and sighed heavily. 'I do miss them. But sometimes in life you have to make choices. My life now is all about Elodie . . . and Bella,' he added, more quietly.

'I get that Elodie is a priority. Of course she is. But, Ben, what about your mum? She's so lonely without your dad and now she's lost you, too . . .'

'She hasn't lost me!' he cut in fiercely. 'I still speak to her.'

Charlotte knew she had to tread carefully. She didn't want to get into a row with him and make things even worse than before. 'OK, well, that's good, obviously. But speaking on the phone is no substitute for actually spending time with her, is it? For her being able to hug Elodie? Why don't you ever visit?'

Ben hesitated. 'It's complicated. Bella's job is quite busy . . .'

he tailed off and Charlotte could see that even he knew it was a lame excuse.

'My job's busy, Ben. Your job was busy. But we still found time to visit your parents and we didn't even have the added incentive of a baby in tow.' She glanced towards Elodie, thinking how much Jo would love spending time with her. 'If Bella's job is too demanding, maybe you could take Elodie and go on your own?' She thought, but didn't add, that Jo would much prefer it that way.

Ben sighed again, looking exhausted and defeated. 'Maybe. I'll see what Bella thinks.'

Charlotte shook her head. She had spent twelve years with this man and yet she felt like she didn't recognize him at all. He had always been so funny and outgoing. Now he seemed cowed and beaten. He loved his friends and he loved his family. Yet he never saw any of them anymore. It was inconceivable that he could have lost touch with everyone from his old life. But somehow he had. 'Can I ask you something?' Charlotte had a desperate urge to reach out and take his hand but he still had his arms firmly wrapped around his body.

Ben gave a small shrug by way of reply.

'Are you happy?'

'Of course.' The reply was as quick as it was automatic. But it didn't ring true. His face gave him away.

'It's just . . .' Charlotte hesitated, unsure whether or not to continue. 'You seem so different to how you used to be. Do you remember, Ben? Do you remember how you used to be? You were the life and soul of every party. We couldn't shut you up!'

Ben smiled and picked at an imaginary piece of fluff on his jeans, before wrapping his arms around his body again. 'I was a nightmare,' he murmured, shaking his head. 'I don't know how you put up with me for so long.'

Charlotte frowned. 'No, Ben. You weren't a nightmare at all. You were great.'

Ben sighed before looking up and meeting her eye. 'I wasn't great enough for you to stay, though, was I?'

His words cut through Charlotte like a knife. 'There was never anything wrong with you, Ben. It was me. I just went a bit loopy after dad died. It made me question everything, including our relationship. I can't explain it, but I can promise you that it was nothing you did wrong.'

Ben nodded slowly. 'Good to know, I guess.'

'So why do you think you've changed so much?' Charlotte prompted, wanting to keep him talking, sensing that he desperately needed to talk to someone.

'I don't think I've changed *that* much,' Ben said, frowning to himself. 'And even if I have, it's probably due to having a child. Having a wife. It changes you. You can't just carry on as you were – you have to adapt to your different circumstances.'

'Matt and Freya don't seem any different since Bertie came along,' Charlotte countered.

'Don't they?' Ben's tone was wistful, full of longing and regret.

'No. They're just the same, with the addition of another little person. The only difference is that they miss you, particularly Matt.'

'I miss them, too.' The words came out automatically and Ben instinctively put a finger to his lips, as if to silence himself.

'You don't have to miss them, Ben. All you have to do is pick up the phone and they'll be there, just like they always were.'

Ben gave a wan smile. 'It's not that simple.'

'It is!' Charlotte shot back. 'It's as simple as you want to make it.'

Ben didn't reply and Charlotte could tell that his thoughts were rampaging through his head. Bella's control and influence over him were clearly stronger than she had ever imagined and Charlotte knew from experience that you didn't manage to exert that kind of control over another person without using something stronger than just words.

They sat in silence for a while longer, listening to the rustle of the autumn breeze blowing through the trees, dislodging reddened leaves that floated down and carpeted the damp grass. There wasn't much more she could do, other than reassure him that she would be there for him if he ever needed her. She started to get up and Ben's hand flew to her arm. 'Are you going?' His eyes widened in panic.

'Yes, I think I probably should.' Charlotte stood up and put her cold hands deep into her pockets. She fixed Ben with a sympathetic look. 'But, please will you promise to call me if you ever need to talk? You've got my number and I will always, *always* take your call. And text me so that I've got your new number, too, eh?'

Ben's face creased and she thought for a moment that he might cry. 'What? What's the matter, Ben? Talk to me.' She sat back down beside him and this time, she took his hand in hers. She could feel him trembling.

Ben shook his head, looking into his lap. 'Nothing. I'm fine. Sorry.'

Charlotte rubbed his hand. The hand that had been so familiar to her for all those years. 'Ben, is Bella . . . um, does she ever hurt you? Physically, I mean?'

Immediately, Ben tensed but he didn't reply. He wouldn't meet Charlotte's eye and he had reddened slightly.

'Remember that I've seen it before, Ben. At work. I've done stories on it in the past and you remind me of a man I once interviewed, who was in that situation. You don't seem right, Ben. You seem unhappy. Worse, you seem scared.'

The fact that Ben didn't immediately respond told Charlotte everything she needed to know. 'I'm OK,' he muttered.

Charlotte took a deep breath. 'You have nothing to be embarrassed about, Ben. This is not your fault. But you don't have to stay in this situation, either. You can leave.'

Ben gave a sad smile. 'No, actually. I can't. And that's the reason why.' He motioned towards Elodie, who was finally beginning to tire. She drew to a stop and slid off the horse, before running to Ben, who scooped her up onto his lap, where she snuggled into him, her thumb sliding into her mouth.

Charlotte nodded her understanding. Leaving wasn't an easy option, if it meant being parted from his child. And Bella was definitely the type to use the child as a weapon 'OK,' she sighed, once more standing up. 'But Ben, will you promise to call me anytime you feel unsafe? I'm only ten minutes away and I will be there for you whenever you need me.'

Ben nodded but Charlotte noticed that he didn't promise anything. 'And could you try to visit your mum one day? Even if it was just while Bella was at work – maybe she doesn't even have to know? It would mean the world to Jo. And I think it would mean the world to you, too, wouldn't it?'

Ben kissed the top of Elodie's head and looked up at Charlotte with a tired smile. 'I'll try.'

Charlotte knew he wouldn't do it but at least she had given it her best shot. 'Well, as I said, call me anytime, day or night.'

'Thanks.' Ben leaned in and whispered something into Elodie's ear. ''Bye 'bye!' Elodie shouted, waving frantically at Charlotte.

Charlotte waved back, as she walked away, wishing she could scoop the two of them up and take them home with her. ''Bye 'bye, Elodie. Goodbye, Ben.'

CHAPTER THIRTY-THREE

I picked up my bag from under my desk and walked out of my office, just as Marcus was emerging from his. 'You off home?' he said, gesturing towards my bag.

I nodded. 'Yes. Promised I'd be home in time to put the little one to bed.'

Marcus smiled. 'I always make sure mine are fast asleep by the time I get home, so I don't have to do any of that.'

I raised my eyebrows. 'Why doesn't that surprise me? Anyway, I'll see you tomorrow.'

'Yes, see you tomorrow. Oh, and by the way, did you get a speak to Leo Fox?'

'Yes, everything's fine,' I assured him breezily, as I left the office and closed the door behind me with a sigh of relief. I had called Leo this morning and told him I'd had a change of heart, suggesting we meet at lunchtime instead.

'Well, I've got a lunch in the diary but I can definitely move it,' Leo drawled and I could picture him smiling lasciviously. I got a cab to his flat to find him already waiting. I put my hand up to knock on his door but it opened before my knuckles could make contact with the wood and he pulled me inside.

Before I had a chance to catch my breath, he had pushed me up against the wall and lifted my skirt. I was naked underneath, which is how I knew he liked it, so he slammed straight into me and thrust hard and fast until he came with an almighty groan, matched only by own breathless gasping.

Feeling stunned and with a growing knot in my stomach, I pulled down my skirt and exhaled as I looked up at him. My legs were shaking but for once with Leo, it had nothing to do with his sexual prowess.

Leo smiled and ran his finger down the side of my face, with the air of a lion contemplating its prey. 'You see? You don't want to give this up, do you?'

'No,' I admitted, truthfully. Sex with Leo was unpredictable, dangerous, exciting and addictive. But increasingly, he also scared me slightly and his reaction to me trying to cool things off had planted a seed of doubt that I knew could only grow.

There was no way out of this. If I stopped seeing him, he had made it clear that he could make serious trouble for me at work. Yes, it would cause problems for him, too, but I didn't trust that he wasn't volatile enough to risk it. And worse, I didn't trust him not to cause problems for me at home, by telling Ben the truth about Elodie. I had to do everything I could to keep him sweet.

Leo bent down and kissed me. 'That was so much more fun than the boring lunch I had lined up. Let's do it again tomorrow. I'll make it a bit longer next time and we can make use of my new . . . toys,' he finished, with a dangerous gleam in his eye.

I hesitated, guessing what toys he was referring to, as our relationship had been growing increasingly sadomasochistic, before nodding. 'Sure.' It was the only possible answer I could give, if I wanted to keep the status quo.

As I caught the train home to Surrey, I gazed unseeingly out of the window at the wild rolling countryside, wondering how I had managed to get myself into this mess. I was married to a man I despised but needed to look after my child, and having fantastic, erotic sex with one that I also needed physically but who scared me. While the one man I loved and desired above any other, was dead and buried.

I knew that there was absolutely no future with Leo and I didn't want there to be. He wouldn't be interested in being a father to Elodie, or even being a faithful husband. I was well aware of the old adage that when a man marries his mistress, he creates a vacancy. I wasn't even sure he considered me his mistress. He was handsome, dynamic and filthy rich, so he could have his pick of women and it gave me a secret thrill that it was me he seemingly wanted. Even if it was only for sex.

I thought about Ben, waiting for me at home with Elodie. He was the complete opposite of Leo. He was nervous, drippy and weak. But he was a good father and there was no doubting his devotion to Elodie. I imagined for the millionth time what it would do to him to discover the truth and knew for certain that it would crucify him. I had to do everything I could to make sure he never found out. If that meant that I had to keep seeing Leo on the quiet, then so be it. At least I would get something out of it.

The skies were darkening by the time I drove home from the station. I hated autumn. I always had. I think it was because it was autumn when my dad disappeared from my life and ever since, I had associated it with misery and gloom. There was nothing to look forward to for months on end, until spring arrived, bringing with it the promise of new beginnings and sunshine.

As I let myself into the house, I could hear Ben and Elodie in the kitchen. She was chattering away at top volume, while Ben would chip in occasionally with a 'hmmm', or a 'wow' whenever she drew breath.

They both looked up as I walked in – Elodie with a wide, delighted smile that revealed the remnants of her boiled egg tea and Ben with a wary one. I walked over to Elodie's high-chair and scooped her up, covering her face in kisses and savouring the smell of her silky hair. Then I carried her over to Ben and kissed him on the cheek.

'You're home early. That's twice in a row.' He briefly touched the back of his head as he spoke and I knew he was thinking about last night.

Our eyes locked for a moment, before I looked away, not wanting to feel irritated by his fearful expression. God, anyone would think I was some kind of monster. 'Yes, I'm missing Elodie so much at the moment for some reason . . . I thought it would be lovely to get home and see her in time for bath and bed.'

I dropped down onto one of the kitchen chairs and pulled Elodie in for a cuddle. She put her thumb into her mouth and curled her little body into me so sweetly that it made my heart constrict. I felt such a wave of love for her that for a second, I imagined what it would be like if it was just the two of us and I gave up work to look after her.

Money wasn't ever going to be an issue, so it was a possibility. But at the same time as the thought passed through my head, I also considered how bored I'd be, with my only job trying to keep a child permanently entertained, with no Leo to break up the monotony. No, that wasn't ever going to happen, however much I adored her.

'How was your day, then?' I looked up at Ben, who was starting to prepare dinner. 'You weren't in when I called.' I had tried calling several times but there had been no answer on the home phone. It always annoyed me hugely when I called and they weren't in and we had rowed about it many times in the past.

I saw Ben's shoulder tense. 'Oh. No, we were out, sorry about that. We went to the park. Then into town to get a few bits of shopping.'

'Was the park fun?' I asked Elodie, who was starting to fidget on my lap.

She nodded vigorously. 'Horsey.'

Ah yes, I remembered now. There were loads of great rides in that park but the only one she liked was a boring little rocking horse. Once she was on it, it was almost impossible to get her off. Any thoughts of me staying home full-time to look after her evaporated instantly.

'Charlie,' Elodie added, looking up at me as if I would know what she was talking about.

'Charlie?' I replied, already losing interest. 'Is that the name of your little horse?'

Elodie frowned dramatically and shook her head. 'No!' she cried. 'Silly Mummy.'

I wouldn't have thought anything of her words, if I hadn't seen Ben's head shoot up out of the corner of my eye. I glanced up at him curiously. He seemed to be holding his breath and his whole body was frozen. 'Who's Charlie, then?' I asked Elodie, as casually as I could.

She slid off my lap onto the floor and walked over to Ben, wrapping her arms around his leg and leaning against him nonchalantly, as he remained stock-still. 'Daddy friend Charlie.' She nodded slightly, pleased with her little speech. She was a brilliant talker for her age. She said her first words at just 8 months and hadn't stopped gabbling since.

There was a long, tense silence as I waited for Ben to correct her or clarify what she had said but he didn't. He just stood with his back to me, staring out of the kitchen window. I could see his reflection in the dusky light and he looked eerily pale. 'Is Charlie a regular visitor?' I asked eventually, trying to keep the quiver of anger out of my voice. I couldn't believe that she had been here, in my house. That he had kept it a secret from me.

Ben took a deep, shuddery breath, before turning reluctantly to face me. 'No. It was the first time. I didn't know she was coming.'

There was a whiny, pleading tone to his voice that seemed to ignite the spark of fury within me again. 'Don't fucking lie to me, Ben! What sort of an idiot do you take me for?'

Ben's eyes widened and he automatically reached down to touch Elodie, who was scowling at me crossly. 'Don't shout, Mummy!' she ordered, with a stern wag of her finger.

I hesitated. Elodie had never seen us fight before. I was usually very careful to protect her from it but it was as if a red mist had descended and I couldn't do anything to control it. 'Shut up!' I snapped. 'If I want to shout, I will! Come on, Elodie, let's get you bathed before dinner and then Daddy and I can finish our conversation.' I threw him a meaningful look, before taking Elodie's hand and pulling her towards the door.

'Daddy bath me!' she whined, twisting back towards Ben and trying to pull her hand away from mine.

'No!' I bent down and scooped her up into my arms, where she wriggled and writhed.

I tightened my grip, to stop her moving and to get a firmer hold. 'Ow!' she wailed, bursting into tears.

I looked up at Ben, who was gaping back at me in horror. 'I'll bath her,' he said quietly, reaching out his arms.

'No,' I insisted. 'I've come home early especially to bath her, so that's what I'm going to bloody well do!'

I stomped out of the room with Elodie in my arms, by now almost hysterical. I managed to get her up the stairs to the bedroom, where I half threw her onto the bed.

'Now, come on, darling,' I soothed, wiping away a sheen of sweat from my forehead. 'Mummy's sorry for shouting, I'm just very, very tired.' I sat down on the bed and stroked her hair. Gradually, her sobs subsided, leaving her hiccupping as she looked up at me warily, sucking furiously on her thumb. 'It's OK, sweetie. Come on, let's get you into that lovely bath. Do you know how to run it? Because I've forgotten . . .'

Immediately, Elodie's face melted into a smile and she nodded drowsily. 'I do it,' she murmured sweetly, her tears seemingly forgotten.

Once she was bathed, I took her into her room, where I dressed her in her pyjamas and lay her gently into bed. She gazed up at me with an expression of such innocence and pure love that my eyes filled. I reached down and stroked my thumb from the bridge of her nose to the tip, like I used to do when she was a tiny baby. Immediately, her eyes began to droop shut. I smiled to myself, pleased that my little trick still worked. 'I love you,' I whispered, before tiptoeing out of the room.

At the top of the stairs I paused, needing to regain my composure before confronting Ben. From somewhere in the distance, possibly the garden, I could hear Ben's voice. My antennae crackled. He was speaking too quietly to hear what was being said but it didn't take much to figure out who he was on the phone to.

I crept down the stairs and into the kitchen. By now it was completely dark outside but the kitchen door was swinging open and I could see Ben talking into his mobile, while pacing up and down the patio. I walked to the window and looked out at him pointedly, my arms folded and my lips pursed.

He was so engrossed in his conversation that he didn't see me at first but when he finally glanced up and spotted me, he froze in shock. After a moment, he hung up his phone and walked stiffly towards the kitchen door, looking like a lamb to the slaughter.

He took as long as possible closing and locking the door behind him, before trudging towards the table, where he slumped down with a weary sigh. I remained standing. 'So?' I tilted my head expectantly.

Ben closed his eyes for a second before looking up to meet mine. He took a deep breath. 'Look, Charlie just turned up here this morning . . . I didn't invite her.'

I smiled incredulously. 'Really? You expect me to believe that you haven't seen her or spoken to her since the funeral and yet she appears one morning, as if by magic, in our house?'

'She wasn't in our house.' Ben sighed and ran his hands through his hair in a way that reminded me of Peter. 'She was waiting in her car outside and I spotted her as we went to the park.'

'So, she's stalking you? God, what a pathetic cow.' I couldn't keep the disbelief out of my voice. I was tempted to tell him that she was welcome to him, if I wasn't so reliant on him myself.

Ben flushed and I saw a flash of anger in his eyes. 'No! She . . . well, she'd been asked by mum.' He paused and dropped his eyes briefly, before looking up again. 'And Matt and Freya . . .'

I tutted and screwed up my face in disgust. Why couldn't they just back off and let us get on with our lives?

Ben swallowed. 'To make sure that I was OK. They were worried about me, apparently.'

'Jesus, you're not 4 years old! Why can't they just mind their own bloody business and leave us alone!'

Ben half-nodded. 'Well, I told her I was fine and she left. I don't think she'll be visiting again anytime soon.'

I frowned. 'But Elodie saw her, so she must have come to the park with you?'

'Yes, but I figured you'd probably prefer that to me inviting her in here!'

'You could have told her to fuck off home! I'd have preferred that most of all!'

Ben shook his head. 'Yes, because that would have gone down well with my mum, wouldn't it?'

'Who cares what your mum thinks? I certainly don't.'

Ben's eyes filled with tears, making me grit my teeth with annoyance. 'Actually, *I* care, Bella. I miss her. I'd like to see her. And take Elodie to visit her.' I could tell that he was summoning up all the courage he could muster and he was becoming more emboldened with each word.

'No!' I fixed him with what I hoped was my sternest expression. 'We don't need anyone else, Ben. It's better when it's just the three of us.'

He gave a small, mirthless laugh. 'It's not just the three of us, though, is it? There's four of us, if you include your lover . . .'

I couldn't believe that he was being so insolent. 'Don't even try that one, Ben! Anyway, I've told him I can't see him anymore.' Practised though I was at lying, I could feel myself reddening as I spoke.

'Until the next time, anyway,' Ben muttered under his breath.

I didn't want to do it. I had vowed to myself not to hurt him again but I just felt such an inexplicable rage boil up inside me that I couldn't help it. I lurched forward and grabbed a handful of his hair, pulling and twisting as hard as I could, so that he was forced onto his knees on the floor.

'Bella!' he cried, trying to squirm his way out of my grasp. 'You're hurting me! Stop it! Please!'

He looked so pathetic, kneeling on the floor and begging me to let go, that all my anger drained away at once. I released the clump of hair I was holding, slightly shocked by how much hair remained in my hand. Then I stepped back and looked down at him with my lip curled. 'Don't ever question me, Ben! OK?'

He didn't reply, so I stretched out my leg and tilted his chin up with my foot. 'I said, OK?'

Ben nodded, holding his breath. His eyes were glassy with tears. I dropped my foot and put my hand on my hips. 'Who were you on the phone to?'

He blinked several times before replying. 'Charlie.' His voice was barely audible.

'I thought so. What were you saying?'

Again, he blinked quickly, as if trying to think of an answer. 'She called me.'

'Liar!' I spat.

'I'm not lying, really I'm not!' He got up off the floor and sat back on his chair. 'She just wanted to let me know that she had told my mum everything was fine but asked if I could go to see her sometime. She said she's very lonely and she's desperate to see Elodie.'

'Hmmm. Well, I don't want you having anything to do with your ex-girlfriend. If she calls again, tell her to fuck off!'

'OK, fine, I will. But . . .' Ben paused again, then looked up with that annoying, pleading expression of his. 'What about going to see Mum? I really think I should.'

I didn't want him to. And I certainly didn't want Elodie to, but I had already broken my vow to myself that I wouldn't hurt him again, so I was feeling generous. 'OK. But you're going alone. I'm not coming with you. And only for one night.'

I thought I saw a wave of relief pass over his face but decided to ignore it.

Ben nodded. 'Great. Thank you, Bella.'

I scowled at his overly gushy tone, making me sound like some kind of tyrannical bitch. 'But no more furtive calls with your saddo ex-girlfriend, OK? She needs to leave you alone and move on with her own life.'

Ben nodded his agreement eagerly. 'Yes, yes, of course.'

God, he was like a puppy, grateful for not being kicked again. Actually, now I thought about it, the idea of a night by myself was quite appealing. I could stay over with Leo for a change, instead of always having to run off home or back to work. 'And don't be making up any stories about what a big, bad wolf I am, either.'

Ben bit his lip.

'Because I'll find out if you do,' I added, adopting my most menacing tone. 'And I won't be very happy.'

'Don't worry,' he attempted a smile, 'I won't tell her anything.'

'Good, because there's nothing to tell, is there?'

'No.'

'Right, well you'd better get on and finish making my dinner,' I said, heading out of the kitchen. 'I'm going to have a bath. Let me know when it's ready.'

Ben leaped up, already so much more energized. I pressed Leo's number as I walked up the stairs.

CHAPTER THIRTY-FOUR

Ben waited until she had safely left for work before he packed. He didn't want her to criticize or comment on what he was taking. 'Remember what I said – don't be telling any lies about me!' she threw over her shoulder, as she walked out of the door.

Ben exhaled with relief as he watched her car pulling out of the drive, still not quite daring to believe that she was actually letting him go. He sensed that she might have an ulterior motive that involved Leo, but right now he didn't care. If that was the price he had to pay for seeing his mum, then so be it.

He shook his head, remembering her instruction to him not to tell any lies about her. He'd be doing nothing BUT telling lies for the next twenty-four hours. He'd be making out that he was fulfilled and happy and that his life wasn't an absolute misery. He'd be hiding the fact that he was married to a woman who thought nothing of punching him, kicking him or – her current favourite – pulling his hair, if he committed any sort of minor transgression that provoked her fury. Sometimes, she just seemed to be in the mood for a fight, so she would pick an argument just to provide her with an excuse for lashing out.

Yes, he thought, as he loaded Elodie and their bags into the car, it was telling the truth that he needed to avoid.

'See Granny!' Elodie chirped excitedly from the back seat.

Ben looked at her in the rear-view mirror and smiled. 'Yes, you are, sweetheart. And about time, too,' he muttered under his breath.

''Bout time too!' she parroted and Ben made a mental note to be careful what he said and did in front of her, now that she was able to repeat any conversations that she overheard.

The two-hour journey seemed to take an eternity. Now that they were finally going, Ben was physically aching to get there as quickly as possible and every traffic hold-up had him clenching his teeth with anxiety.

Finally, they pulled onto the old, familiar gravel driveway. Ben lifted Elodie out of her car-seat and gazed up at the beautiful sandstone façade of the house where he'd grown up. Even before stepping inside, he had the feeling that it had changed a great deal in the time since he was last here. It looked slightly tired and a bit sorry for itself, much like his mum who, at that very moment, opened the door and ran out to greet them.

'Oh, my darlings!' she cried, her cheeks already damp with tears. 'It is so good to see you!' She crouched down so that she was at eye-level with Elodie. 'Hello, you little poppet!' She threw her arms wide so that Elodie could step into her embrace and pulled her into a tight hug. 'You are so, so pretty!'

Elodie beamed, but had a sudden bout of shyness and pulled away, before gripping Ben's leg and pressing her face into his thigh. There was a fleeting glimmer of sadness in Jo's eyes before she recovered herself and stood up to hug Ben. She held him tightly for several seconds and Ben was momentarily overcome by the familiar, soapy smell of her hair and the light, citrusy scent that she had worn for as long as he could remember. 'Hello, my darling boy,' she murmured, before pulling away and holding him at arm's length, where she looked at him appraisingly. 'You look thin.'

Ben smiled ruefully. 'So do you, Mum.' It was true. Although Jo had always been slim, she had still had a curvy figure and cute apple cheeks. Now, the curves were gone and her cheekbones were razor-sharp. It aged her.

Jo smiled and Ben was struck by the fact that her eyes no longer shone the way they used to. It was like a light had gone out. 'Well, it's a good job I've bought enough food to fatten a family of ten then, isn't it? We can both work on putting on some weight while you're here. Come on in!'

Ben took Elodie's hand and led her up the steps and through the front door. As soon as they stepped over the threshold, Ben stopped abruptly, as a wall of grief, triggered by a lifetime of memories, threatened to overwhelm him.

Jo, who was walking ahead of them along the hallway, turned and looked at him in concern. 'What's the matter, Ben? Are you OK?'

Ben shook his head, the urge to cry was unstoppable but he didn't want to alarm Elodie. Jo seemed to understand and reached out her hand. 'Hey, Elodie, do you want to see what sweeties I've got especially for you?'

Elodie immediately dropped Ben's hand and took Jo's, before toddling happily with her into the kitchen, all shyness forgotten with the promise of sweets.

Ben took several deep breaths but there was no stopping the torrent of tears that had been lying dormant, waiting for their moment to fall. He crouched down and put his hands over his face, letting the grief for his father that he had never really acknowledged, had never been allowed to acknowledge, finally pour out.

After a while, he felt steady enough to stand. He stumbled into the cloakroom and leaned over the sink, where he splashed his hot face with soothing cold water and washed away the last vestiges of tears. He looked up and gazed at himself in the mirror, imagining how he must look through his mum's eyes. He had certainly changed a lot physically, since the last time he was here for his father's funeral.

Thinking about it now, it was as if Peter's death had unleashed something in Bella that was impossible to even identify. Yes, she had been controlling and difficult before then, but for the most part, he had felt happy with her. The good times still outweighed the bad back then. Now, she seemed to hate and despise him, but still wanted to keep him under her control. It didn't make any sense. Why had Peter's death triggered such a darkness within her?

He wiped his face with a towel and, satisfied that he had regained his composure, he joined Jo and Elodie in the kitchen.

Elodie was sitting up on the island while Jo displayed an array of different sweets she had bought, like a waiter proudly presenting the best dessert trolley. 'Dat one!' Elodie cried delightedly, jiggling up and down as she pointed to the packet of Percy Pigs, which were her favourite sweets.

Jo opened the bag and held one aloft. 'Open wide . . . Percy's heading for Elodie's tummy!' Then she pretended to fly the candy pig through the air, before popping it into Elodie's waiting, open mouth.

Ben smiled and walked over to join them. He sat on a bar stool and watched contentedly as they demolished half the packet of sweets, Elodie giggling between mouthfuls, then moved on to discussing what they were going to cook for dinner. 'Want bread!' Elodie yelled, clearly sensing that she could demand just about anything from Jo and it would be granted.

'Then bread you shall have!' Jo replied. She scooped Elodie down off the island. 'But first, shall we go and play with some toys I've found for you?'

Ben followed as Jo led Elodie into the adjoining sitting room, where there was an assortment of old toys spread out, some of which he vaguely remembered from his childhood. Elodie bumped down onto the rug and was immediately engrossed in playing with an old Fisher Price schoolhouse.

Ben put his arm around Jo's frail shoulders as they watched her, already feeling the tension he had been bottling up for so long seeping out of his body. 'Was that mine?' he asked, nodding towards the schoolhouse.

Jo nodded. 'You got it for your second birthday. You wanted a doll's house but we weren't very progressive back then, so I got you this instead. I knew there was a good reason for keeping it all, not that I could ever have thrown it out, anyway. Your dad thought I was mad.'

Ben smiled at the wistful fondness in her voice. 'You must miss him.'

'God, you've got no idea how much! It's funny . . . he wasn't a loud person but the house is so, so quiet without him.'

Ben nodded. 'I bet.'

'That's why it's such a tonic to have you here, Ben' – she

looked down at Elodie, still happily arranging the desks and chairs and sitting the little characters on them – 'to have you both here. Obviously I love speaking to you on FaceTime but it's not the same, is it?'

'No,' Ben agreed. 'Shall we have a cup of tea? We can still keep an eye on Elodie from the kitchen, not that she'll even notice we've moved.' He smiled indulgently at Elodie, who seemed transfixed by her new toy.

Jo scurried back into the kitchen and made two mugs of tea. She put them on the island and perched opposite Ben. 'So how are you, darling? How are you coping with everything?'

Ben took a sip of his tea, which was exactly how he loved it – strong, not much milk and very hot. It struck him that he couldn't remember Bella ever making him a cup of tea. It was always the other way round. 'I'm OK, Mum. Look, I'm sorry I haven't been to see you. It's . . .' he paused, wondering how much to say. 'It's difficult sometimes.'

'Bella doesn't like me.' Jo's voice was flat with resignation.

Ben sighed. 'To be fair, Bella doesn't really know you. But she has . . . well, I guess you'd say she has issues. I don't know for sure because she never talks about it, but probably relating to her childhood and her dad, I think. She needs to feel in control . . . When other people are in the picture, it makes her feel unsettled and insecure. She just wants the three of us to be in our own little cocoon, I suppose.' He thought back to the night when he had suggested that there were four of them in that cocoon, if you included Bella's lover, and the rage it had provoked in her. The memory made him shudder.

'And what about you? Is that what you want?' There was

a deep frown line between Jo's eyebrows, as she gazed at him intently.

Ben chewed the inside of his cheek as he thought about what to say. 'I want Elodie to feel secure. To have two parents in her life.' He took a sip of tea to buy him some thinking time. He was struggling to answer the question without giving away that he had absolutely no choice in the matter. What he wanted was irrelevant – Bella had always made that perfectly clear. 'So in order to maintain the status quo, I've learned that it's probably best to go along with what Bella wants, rather than causing an argument. It's just not worth the hassle that follows.'

'Hassle' was such an inappropriately lightweight word to describe what happened when he put a foot out of line. For a moment, he imagined the delicious relief of telling Jo everything, but it would cause her unimaginable worry and he couldn't bear to hurt her any more. The pain of not seeing them very often wasn't a fraction of what she'd feel if she knew the reality of his day-to-day life.

Jo dropped her gaze and looked into her mug. Ben could see that her lip was quivering. 'I can cope with not seeing you . . .' she began, choosing her words carefully. 'But only if I think you're happy.' She looked back up and met Ben's eye. 'Are you happy, Ben?'

Ben's eyes filled with tears, which he blinked away in frustration. Why were his emotions on such a hair-trigger all the time? Bella was right. He had become so incredibly wet, even to himself.

'I think you've just answered my question.' Jo watched him sadly, shaking her head with a helpless expression.

'No!' Ben cut in quickly. 'No, I'm just feeling a bit emotional being back here for the first time since Dad . . . well, since the funeral.' He couldn't bring himself to use the word 'died'. 'Honestly, for the most part, Mum, I am happy. I mean, no one's happy all the time, are they?'

As he spoke, he wondered when he last had truly felt happy. With a start, he realized that it was when he was still with Charlotte. Even on what should have been the happiest days with Bella, such as Elodie's birth, there was always an undercurrent of tension that meant he was constantly treading on eggshells, in case he stepped onto the invisible trip-wire that would set her off.

'Charlie doesn't think you're happy.' Jo's voice cut through his thoughts. 'She's really worried about you, Ben. We all are. Matt, Freya, Emma . . .'

Ben looked up at Jo again. 'I wasn't happy the day that Charlie paid us a visit. She laid it on pretty thick about you being so lonely and it made me feel terrible, to think that you had all been discussing me behind my back.'

Jo smiled wryly. 'We'd have discussed you to your face if we'd had the chance, Ben!'

Ben laughed softly. 'Fair enough, I suppose. Anyway, it wasn't a great day and she caught me at a bad moment.'

'Look,' Jo reached out to take Ben's hand. 'I'm sorry if you were caught off-guard. We just didn't know what else to do. We all miss you so much and if you can't come to us, the only other option was for one of us to come to you. We just needed to see for ourselves that you were OK. And for my part, I'm glad she came to see you or I don't think we'd be sitting here now, would we?'

'Maybe not,' Ben agreed. 'I suppose I'm glad she came, too. It was nice to see her.'

In truth, seeing Charlie had been incredibly painful. It had re-ignited feelings that he thought were long-buried. She was so warm compared to Bella's coldness. So easy-going in contrast to Bella's exhausting testiness. He could still feel her love. She knew everything about him and their connection was as strong as ever. Without having to say a word about what was happening to him, he could tell that she knew. Because she knew him.

Jo tilted her head slightly. 'I think she will always regret letting you go.'

'Don't,' Ben cut in with a warning tone, shaking his head. 'Don't go there.' He couldn't bear to think of what might have been, if he hadn't met up with Bella that night and put an end to all hopes of a reconciliation with Charlotte.

Jo put her hands up defensively. 'OK . . . I'm sorry. You're right. There's no point in dwelling on the past.'

Ben gave her a reassuring smile. 'Tell me about Emma. And Matt and Freya. How are they all?'

Jo beamed. 'Oh, you should see baby Bertie!' she said, clapping her hands with delight and obviously happy to change the subject. 'He's gorgeous. Absolutely enormous, too . . . honestly, God know what they're feeding him but . . .'

Ben listened with a smile as Jo regaled him stories about the lives that had carried on without him, while he was out of the picture. Emma was still travelling far too much in Jo's opinion, but the good news was that she had met someone in Singapore, a fellow lawyer, and they seemed very happy. Apparently, she was bringing him home to meet Jo at Christmas and Jo was hopeful that an engagement might be on the cards.

Matt and Freya were both besotted with their little boy and Freya had decided that she wouldn't go back to nursing after her maternity leave as Matt was doing so well at work that she was lucky enough to have the choice to stay at home . . .

As he listened, Ben felt more and more disconnected from the world. Everyone else seemed to lead such *normal* lives. How had he ended up in a real-life version of a horror movie? Actually, he thought, the plot of his movie was so far-fetched that there was no way it would ever get made. How many other men found themselves cowering on their knees in terror, while their slim, beautiful, charming wife twisted clumps of hair from their head and cracked their jaw by kneeing them under the chin?

After an early dinner – bread for Elodie, coq au vin for them – Jo and Ben put Elodie to bed together in the white-painted little nursery that had been waiting for her since the day she was born, but had never been used.

Ben watched Jo delightedly showing Elodie all the books and toys she had lovingly collected for her, in the hope of being able to use them one day and had to swallow down the sour taste of shame that was in his throat. It must have killed Jo to have no contact with her first grandchild, when she would have been willing and able to offer her so much love. For the millionth time, he cursed himself for not being strong enough to stand up to Bella.

As Jo finished reading her a fourth story, Elodie's eyelids began to droop shut. She looked so sweet and snug, sitting on Jo's lap on the large wooden rocking chair, sucking lazily on her thumb, that Ben leaped up.

'What's wrong?' Jo asked in alarm. 'Where are you going?'

'To get my phone. I need to get a picture of this.'

Ben jogged down the stairs, two at a time like he always used to, feeling lighter and happier than he had done for years. It had been good for both him and Jo to spend time together with Elodie and he vowed that he was going to make it a regular occurrence from now on. It was ridiculous to have let so much time pass without a visit.

His phone lay on the granite-topped island in the middle of the kitchen and even before he reached it, he could see it buzzing angrily with messages. All the new-found happiness drained out of him in an instant and his mouth dried. He picked it up with a shaking hand and steeled himself to unlock the screen and read what was there.

WHY HAVEN'T YOU ANSWERED YOUR PHONE?!!!!!
WHERE ARE YOU??!
PLEASE ANSWER YOUR PHONE!!!!

The red circle beside the phone symbol told him he had forty-seven missed calls. Ben shook his head in disbelief. How had she managed to make so many calls in the time he'd been upstairs? He was about to call her back with profuse apologies, when he remembered that his mum was expecting him back upstairs to take a photo of her and Elodie.

The damage was already done, he decided. Missing another few calls wouldn't make any difference. She could wait. He climbed back up the stairs, his mood dampened by Bella's messages. He walked back into the darkened nursery and forced a smile back on his face. 'Sorry, I couldn't find my phone. Right, let's take some lovely pictures, shall we?'

Elodie was already dropping off to sleep in Jo's arms and the sight of the two of them looking so sweet together made his heart clench with love. He clicked away, as Jo gently lifted her and placed her carefully into the cot-bed, as if she was handling the most delicate package in the world. When she had tucked her in, Jo leaned over and kissed her on the cheek, then ran her hand down the side of her tiny face, gazing at her in awe.

'She's perfect,' she told Ben, as they crept out of the room and pulled the door behind them.

'I think so,' Ben agreed, smiling proudly, despite the gnawing worry about the messages that were waiting on his phone like an unexploded bomb.

As they reached the bottom of the stairs, his phone began to vibrate and he looked at Jo apologetically.

'You answer it. I'll make us some tea,' she said, already heading for the kitchen.

Ben pressed the 'accept' button and raised the phone to his ear. 'Hi, Bella,' he began, in what he hoped was a steady voice.

'Where are you? Why didn't you answer your phone? I've been trying to call you!' Bella sounded tearful and slightly panicked. But she also sounded muffled, as if she was in a bathroom or toilet.

'What do you mean: "Where am I?" You know where I am. I'm at my mum's.' He glanced towards the kitchen where Jo was busy clattering cups and plates about, before heading into the dining room and closing the door behind him, preparing for the onslaught.

'Why didn't you answer your phone? I was trying to get hold of you.' Ben could picture her narrowing her eyes with suspicion as she spoke.

'Because I was upstairs with Mum, putting Elodie to bed and my phone was on silent downstairs. I didn't hear it, that's all.' He tried to make his tone as non-confrontational as possible, to try to diffuse the situation. He couldn't cope with a full-on row while his mum was in the next room.

There was a moment of hesitation. 'Sorry, I was just worried. Ben, listen, I desperately need you to come home now.'

'What?'

'I need you to come home. I'm feeling so ill, Ben.'

There was a vulnerable, pleading tone to her voice. She sounded like a completely different person to the woman he had come to know – and fear – over the past year, and it threw him. 'Well, what sort of ill?'

'I've got terrible pains in my stomach and . . .' There was a slight pause. 'I've started bleeding.' She paused again to let out a groan of agony. 'I wonder if . . . if I might be having a miscarriage. Please, Ben, please could you come home? I wouldn't ask if I didn't really, really need you.'

Ben reeled backwards, suddenly light-headed. 'A . . . *miscarriage?*' His mind whirred, trying to make sense of her words. How could she possibly be pregnant? But he already knew the answer, remembering now how every time she lost it with him, she would follow it up by seducing him, messing with his mind a tiny bit more every time.

'I know,' she whispered. 'Oh, Ben, I just need you here with me as soon as possible. I'm so worried!'

Ben leaned heavily against the wall, blindsided by her sudden show of vulnerability. 'But . . . I can't come home,' he managed. 'We've just put Elodie to bed.'

Bella started to cry pitifully. 'I'm sorry, Ben. I know it's bad of me to ask but please would you just get her up and put her in her car-seat? She won't even wake up . . . you know what she's like. Please, Ben?'

Her tone had changed completely, from the aggressive and mean one he was so used to, to pleading, tearful and vulnerable. He couldn't remember the last time she had sounded so helpless.

His mind raced. He didn't want to leave Jo but he didn't feel that he had any other choice, especially if Bella could be having a miscarriage. He needed to be with her. 'Maybe you should call an ambulance?' he suggested, stalling for time.

Bella groaned in pain again on the other end of the line. 'Yes, maybe, but I want you to be with me. I don't want to go on my own. Please, Ben,' she prompted, 'I really need you here to help me. I can't manage without you.' Again, she dissolved into tears.

That decided him. 'OK,' he said. 'I'll come.'

'Oh, thank you Ben!' Bella gushed. 'Thank you so much!'

'I'll see you in a couple of hours,' he told her, feeling as if he had grown in stature by at least a couple of inches over the past few minutes. He could hear the genuine gratitude in her voice and it felt good to be needed for once. He had a feeling this would mark a turning point in their relationship. 'I'll be as quick as I can.'

He hung up the phone and steeled himself to tell Jo, knowing how upset she would be. But, he reasoned, if doing this one thing meant that the balance of his relationship with Bella was redressed, it would mean that he would be able to come and see Jo as often as he liked from now on. He was already determined to insist on it and judging by Bella's grateful tone, he didn't think she would be arguing in future.

Jo was in the kitchen, sitting at the island with two mugs of tea in front of her. The smile died on her lips as soon as she looked up and saw Ben's face. 'What's happened?' she asked, in voice that was heavy with dread.

Ben ran his hands through his hair. 'That was Bella on the phone . . .'

'I gathered,' Jo cut in, her face rigid.

Ben swallowed. 'Well, she's got terrible pains in her stomach and she's feeling really unwell. She thinks she may be having a miscarriage.'

A wave of different emotions passed over Jo's face. Shock, followed by fear, followed by horror. 'She's pregnant?' she whispered, her eyes wide.

Ben swallowed hard, still hardly able to comprehend it himself, let alone digest how he felt about it. 'Well, we don't know for sure . . . We didn't know,' he corrected himself. 'But she thinks she could be having a miscarriage and she's begged me to come home . . .' he tailed off apologetically.

Jo looked aghast. 'What, now?'

Ben nodded. 'I'm afraid so. I'm so sorry, Mum, but she did sound like she's in a bad way and I can't not be with her if . . . if she's losing our baby.' He didn't want Jo to argue with him. Now that he had agreed to go home, he just wanted to get in his car and get there as quickly as possible.

'But Elodie's in bed asleep. You can't wake her up and cart her off, it's not fair!' Jo's expression was a mixture of anger and confusion, as if she had been disturbed in the middle of the night and was trying to comprehend what was happening through the deep fog of sleep.

'She won't wake up. I'll transfer her to her car-seat and she won't know any different. She always sleeps like a log in the car.'

Jo's face crumpled. 'Oh, Ben!' she cried piteously. 'Please don't go. It took so long to get you here and I feel like if you leave, you'll never come back!' She put her hands over her face as the tears began to flow.

Ben's resolve immediately wavered, torn between hurting his

mum and racing to the aid of his sick wife. He walked over to Jo and put his arms around her heaving shoulders. 'Mum, look at me.' He put one hand under her chin and forced her to look up at him, as the tears poured down her cheeks. 'I *promise* you that I will be back for another visit within the month. I am never letting this situation happen again. Seeing how amazing you are with Elodie has shown me how ridiculous it was to leave it so long. I am going to make sure we visit regularly from now on.'

'But Bella . . .' Jo shook her head helplessly. 'She won't let you. She hates me and she doesn't want you to have anything to do with me.' She broke down sobbing again.

Ben's insides twisted in anguish. 'Please don't get upset, Mum. I'm going to sort things out with Bella and tell her in no uncertain terms that even if she doesn't come with us, Elodie and I are going to be seeing you once a month from now on. It's non-negotiable.' He gave her shoulders a reassuring squeeze. 'OK?'

Jo stopped crying and attempted a watery smile. 'Really?'

Ben nodded, feeling stronger and more confident than he had done in years. 'Really.'

'But, how? I know what Bella's like . . .' Jo was shaking her head again. 'She won't let you.'

Ben tried to pull himself up to his full height. 'I honestly think that me going home tonight to be with her will help to get us back on an even keel, Mum. I admit, things haven't been great before now, but I'm going to put that right. From now on, things will be different. Better. OK?' Ben tilted his head, waiting for Jo's confirmation.

Jo held his gaze for a few seconds, before she nodded, apparently convinced. 'OK.'

Together, they made their way upstairs and into the nursery, where Elodie was sleeping soundly. Ben packed her things into her little pink suitcase and gave it to Jo to carry. Then they both peered into the cot, watching her sleep. 'It seems so awful to wake her,' Jo whispered.

Ben smiled. 'She won't wake up. Watch this.' With that, he leaned into the cot and un-tucked her bedding, before scooping her up into the crook of his arm in one fluid movement. She squirmed slightly and emitted a loud sigh but, as Ben had predicted, she barely stirred.

He carried her downstairs and allowed Jo to open the front door and the car door, so that he could gently deposit her into her car-seat and strap her in. Still, she didn't wake. Ben turned to take her suitcase from Jo. 'See? It takes a lot to wake her once she's asleep.'

Jo smiled and peered hungrily into the back seat, while Ben loaded their things into the boot.

When he was ready to go, he bent down and hugged Jo as tightly as he could. 'I'm so sorry about this but we will be back really, really soon.'

He felt Jo nod into his chest. 'And you'll let me know what happens? Whether she's lost the baby?'

'Of course I will.'

'Promise?' Jo said in a muffled voice.

Ben released his grip and held her at arm's length. He tilted his head so that he could look her properly in the eye. 'I promise,' he said fiercely.

CHAPTER THIRTY-FIVE

I opened the bathroom door and walked out into the bedroom, smiling to myself. I should never have agreed to Ben taking Elodie to visit Jo. She would no doubt be spending the whole time poisoning him against me and persuading him not to return. It was only when I got to work this morning that it hit me what a mistake it had been and how potentially dangerous it was. I needed to think of something that would get him home as quickly as possible, so that I could re-assert my authority and I knew that the suggestion of a potential miscarriage would bring him running. I could easily fake it when he got here.

'What are you smiling at?' Leo drawled from his bed, where he was propped up against his headboard, smoking a cigarette.

I turned to look at him, entirely confident and unembarrassed by his nakedness, the veil of smoke lending a vaguely film-star appearance to his narrowed eyes and tousled blond hair. 'Oh, nothing much.'

'Been on the phone to the little husband, have you?' He threw me a mischievous look. 'Checking up on him?'

I shrugged noncomitally and unbuttoned the crisp, white shirt I had found in Leo's wardrobe. I was planning to go straight home, but then I looked at Leo and decided that I had a bit more time before I needed to leave. He looked too irresistible.

I walked over to the bed and straddled him, before taking the cigarette out of his hand and inhaling deeply. Leo smiled as I blew the smoke, slowly and deliberately into his face. I could feel him hardening beneath me. 'You're so damned sexy.'

'I know.' I eased him into me and moved rhythmically back and forth, watching his eyes glaze over with lust. Then I leaned down and placed the burning tip of the cigarette next to the side of his torso, holding it just long enough to create a sizzling sound, as it made brief contact with his skin.

Leo held his breath, watching me with a half-smile, half-grimace. 'Do it,' he whispered in a thick voice. I increased the pressure until I had left a satisfyingly symmetrical blister of red.

Leo exhaled with an agonized groan and gripped me tightly, his fingers digging into my flesh, before flipping me off him and rolling on top of me. He pinned my hands to the bed and thrust hard until he came with an almighty shudder.

We lay in silence for a few minutes, until Leo lifted his head and looked at me with a gleam in his eye. 'You are a bad, bad girl, Bella.'

I pushed him off me and shuffled to sit up. 'I know. That's why you like me so much.'

'It is,' Leo agreed, also sitting up. He lit another cigarette, gazing at it for a second, clearly thinking about what had just happened. 'So what have you told him, about where you are tonight?'

'He thinks I'm at home. He's gone to visit his bitch of a mother, so he doesn't know I'm not there. Or at least he didn't, until I called a few minutes ago and told him I needed him to come home as soon as possible because I was ill.'

Leo looked at me with a combination of horror and admiration. 'Jesus. You're such a bitch.'

'I know. I surprise myself sometimes.' I paused. 'But he shouldn't have gone to see her in the first place. And he certainly shouldn't have taken my daughter with him.'

'Ah, yes. The daughter that isn't his . . .' He tilted his head and looked at me with one eyebrow raised. 'So that means the mother isn't related to her at all, then?'

I shifted uncomfortably. I had always felt nervous about Leo knowing the truth and wished for the hundredth time that I hadn't drunkenly blurted it out that night. But I had been missing Peter and feeling maudlin, so the alcohol had loosened my tongue, along with my inhibitions. 'No.'

I could see the cogs of Leo's brain whirring and wished I could shake the sense of unease that I felt, knowing that if I put a foot wrong, or tried to end it with him, he was armed with some dangerous information that could destroy me. I stood up and headed for the bathroom, feeling Leo's eyes on me. 'Are you going home, then? I thought you were staying the night.'

I turned to face him. 'I was, but now that he's coming home, I need to be there to make it plausible. You're not upset with me, are you?' I fixed him with wide-eyed stare.

Leo thought about it for a few seconds before he shrugged. 'Not really, no. You've worn me out anyway,' he added, with a wolfish grin.

'Good. Now be a good boy and call me a cab while I remove all traces of my outrageous behaviour tonight.'

I heard Leo laughing as I closed the bathroom door behind

me. I looked at the time on my phone. It was just gone eight. Ben would have left his mother's house at around 7.45, so I had about an hour and a half to shower and get home before he did. It was cutting it fine but I should just about make it.

The limo Leo had booked crawled through the London traffic, making me grit my teeth with anxiety. I had forgotten that getting from East to West London was always a mission, even when the rush hour had supposedly finished, and I wished I had just caught my usual train instead. My car was parked at the station in Surrey, so I would need to go there first anyway. 'Don't you know any quicker routes?' I asked the driver, as we drew to a halt at yet another set of traffic lights.

'This is the quickest route,' he replied, his voice clipped with an Eastern European accent and a level stare in the rear-view mirror.

I sighed and leaned back against the plush leather seat, drumming my fingers on my leg. I clicked on Find Friends. Ben was only just approaching the M25, so I was still on track to get home before him, as long as there weren't any more hold-ups. There was nothing more I could do, so I closed my eyes for a moment and took a long, soothing breath, trying to block out everything around me and relax instead . . .

I woke with a jolt and sat bolt upright. 'Where are we?' I demanded, looking around me in a panic, trying to get my bearings. I didn't recognize the houses and fields, as they sped by outside my window, although in the dark it was hard to tell anyway.

'There was an accident. We had to take a diversion.' The

driver sounded unapologetic and bored, which immediately caused my hackles to rise.

'For God's sake! Why didn't you know how to avoid it in the first place? Don't you get traffic updates on that thing?' I gestured to the electronic map he had on his dashboard.

The driver shrugged and gave a dismissive wave of his hand by way of an answer.

I wanted to scream. With a shaking hand and hardly daring to look, I pressed the home button on my phone. The time flashed up in giant numbers on the screen: 21.25.

'Shit!' I muttered, furiously clicking on Find Friends. My mouth dried as I watched the little green circle that signified Ben's location move jauntily towards our road, before drawing to a stop as it arrived at our house.

CHAPTER THIRTY-SIX

Ben pressed the fob that opened the electric gate and frowned as he pulled onto the empty driveway, unease immediately seeping through him. Where was Bella's car? The house itself was in darkness, except for the usual security lights that were on a timer. His mind raced wildly and his heart began to pound. There was no sign of any activity. Had she taken herself to hospital after all? It seemed unlikely, given the state she was in when she called. Or had her car been stolen? Whatever the explanation, he knew it was something bad. He could just sense it.

Leaving Elodie asleep in the car, he opened the front door and let himself in, keeping it ajar as he tiptoed into the hallway, adrenaline and fear racing through his veins. He glanced at the alarm system control box and frowned as he realized it was still armed. He tapped in the code and stood very still, listening for any signs of life in the house. Apart from the faint click and whirr of the heating system, there was nothing.

Still not convinced that she wasn't there, he moved from room to room looking for her, before remembering that she had sounded like she was in the bathroom when she called. He climbed the stairs two at a time and raced into their en-suite bathroom. But, like every other room in the house, it was empty and in darkness. Ben stood with his hands on his hips, looking around him in confusion. None of it made any sense.

When he had searched every room a second time and was satisfied that she wasn't in the house, Ben walked out into the back garden, straining his eyes and ears for any kind of movement. Suddenly, there was a sharp crack as something moved in the bushes and he jumped with fright.

Not wanting to, but knowing he had no choice, he made his way as noiselessly as he could in the direction of the sound. When he was just a couple of metres away from the bush, something sprang out at him and instinctively, he leaped backwards, losing his balance as he did so and falling in an ungainly heap onto the damp grass. A large fox darted past him, its eyes gleaming eerily in the moonlight and disappeared through the hedge into the garden beyond.

Panting with shock, Ben stood up shakily and brushed himself down, still trying to comprehend what was going on. Bella had definitely been at home when she called him and she had sounded genuinely distressed and in pain. So where the hell had she gone since? She must have taken herself to hospital, but if that was the case, why hadn't she rung him and asked him to meet her there?

He walked back into the house and locked the back door, looking around him as he tried to figure out what to do next. A niggling doubt tugged at the back of his brain. He walked slowly back down the hallway trying to figure out what it was.

As he reached the still-open front door, the answer came to him. There were no lights on. It would have been dark by the time she called him earlier and, even if she had left the house to take herself to hospital, she wouldn't have gone around switching off all the lights first, especially not if she was in a rush or in pain. She didn't tend to turn lights off anyway, and would quite happily leave every light in the house on if they went out in the evening.

With a creeping, sickeningly vivid realization, it dawned on Ben that Bella must have been lying. That she hadn't even been in the house when she called him. She just wanted to ruin his visit to see Jo and get him back home, where she could carry on making his life a misery and treating him like a slave that she could use and abuse whenever she liked.

He sank down onto the doorstep and put his head in his hands. All the way through the car journey from Suffolk, he had imagined the ways in which his life was going to change from now on. How this experience would have made Bella realize how much she needed him and he had actually visualized her greeting him with open arms and a tearful smile of gratitude.

He had felt bad in the past. Really bad. But nothing compared to the abject humiliation and hurt he was feeling right now. All the blows she had inflicted, all the times she had hurt and abused him were as nothing to the fatal blow she had just delivered. It was like a switch in his brain. He couldn't even cry any more. He had crossed a threshold of pain and there was no coming back from it.

He looked at his phone, trying to work out what to do. He thought about calling her, but he couldn't bear to hear her voice, lying to him as easily as breathing. She would come up with some ridiculous explanation for her behaviour but he wasn't going to let her dupe him again. Not now. Not ever.

He scrolled through his contacts, coming to a halt at the number for Bella's lover, Leo. He had copied it down the night he had fixed her phone, somehow knowing that he might need it one day. He had absolutely no doubt that that was where she would have been tonight. Where she had called him from, pleading with him to come home and look after her. He pressed on the number before he could change his mind.

'Leo Fox,' a deep voice drawled, as the phone was answered.

Ben closed his eyes and took a deep, steadying breath. 'It's Ben. Ben Gordon.'

There was a long pause. 'I'm sorry. I don't recognize that name . . . you must have the wrong number.' Leo already sounded bored.

'Bella's husband.' Ben waited for the words to land before continuing. 'Is she there?'

There was a brief pause, before he answered. 'No. She left a couple of hours ago.'

Although he had been fairly sure that Bella was with Leo, hearing it confirmed was like a blow to the stomach. He felt the bile rise in his throat. He opened his mouth to speak, but no words would come out.

'Look, mate,' said Leo. 'I'm not interested in getting involved in your relationship. But she's playing you for a fool. You need to toughen up a bit and have some respect for yourself.'

Ben gasped, hurt and anger still rendering him speechless. Bella having an affair with this guy was one thing, but discussing Ben's failings with him was a whole other level of humiliation. Finally, he found his voice: 'You don't know anything about me, so don't you dare tell me what I should and shouldn't do!' A deeply buried, boiling rage was bubbling up inside him and he was glad that Leo wasn't standing within reach, or he would have been in serious danger.

'Actually,' Leo said, with a malicious-sounding roll of his tongue. 'I think you'll find that I know *everything* about you, mate. Even more than you know yourself.'

'Bullshit!' Ben fired back, overwhelmed with hatred for this pompous-sounding creep.

'Oh yeah? Bullshit, is it? Well, how about if I tell you that I knew your father, for starters?'

'So what?' Ben thought about hanging up, not wanting to let anything Leo said get to him. It had been a mistake calling him in the first place.

'But obviously I didn't know him as well as Bella knew him . . .'

Something about his tone of voice made Ben's blood run cold but he refused to acknowledge it. 'Of course she knew him! He was her father-in-law.'

Leo chuckled and Ben could hear him lighting a cigarette. Somewhere in the back of his brain he registered that Bella had sometimes come home smelling of smoke. 'He was a bit more than that,' Leo said, exhaling slowly and deliberately.

Ben's mouth dropped open in shock.

'Oh, come on!' Leo continued, when Ben didn't reply. 'Seriously, mate, don't tell me you never suspected?'

Ben closed his eyes, as if by doing so, he could somehow make the words go away. Make them unheard. 'No,' he heard himself whisper hoarsely. 'You're lying.'

'You know I'm not. She only ever got with you to get back at him for dumping her.'

There was a sudden tightness in Ben's chest and he knew he

needed to stop Leo talking, before he could inflict any more damage. 'I'm hanging up,' he hissed, dizzy with the sheer horror of it.

With shaking hands, he reached for the 'end call' button, but before he could get to it, he heard Leo's voice, as he shouted his final onslaught: 'And to make him pay for his kid! It's not even your kid, mate. It's your father's!'

The line went dead and Ben stared at the handset in shock, unable to absorb what he had just heard.

He was struggling for breath and gulped down lungfuls of air to try to steady himself but he felt as though his brain was frying. He couldn't seem to form any kind of coherent thought.

It couldn't be right, he told himself. Elodie *was* his child. Of course she was. Even without the incredible emotional bond between them, he just knew that she was his child. He could *feel* it.

Without really thinking about it, he was dialling Charlotte's number. She answered immediately. 'Ben, is that you? Are you OK?'

'No, Charlie, I'm not OK.' He could hardly get his breath to speak. He felt winded and sick.

'What's wrong? What's happened? Are you still at your mum's?'

Ben tried to speak, but he couldn't manage to get any words out.

'It's OK, Ben,' Charlotte coaxed him. 'Take a couple of deep breaths and try to tell me what's happened.'

Ben did as she said before speaking. 'Bella tricked me into coming home,' he managed at last. 'She said she thought she was having a miscarriage. She needed me to come home immediately.'

'Oh no, Ben . . . And you did?'

Ben nodded, sick with humiliation. 'She was so convincing. I thought maybe it would be a turning point for us, if I came to her aid when she needed me most. I'm such an idiot . . . I should have known.'

'So . . . she wasn't having a miscarriage?' Charlotte's tone was now one of disbelief.

'No. She wasn't even here. She was in London.'

Charlotte gasped. 'Jesus, what a vile thing to do. Of all the things to lie about . . . I'm not surprised you're so upset.'

'That's not why I'm upset. It's so much worse than that.'

'What? How could it be worse?'

Ben swallowed back the tears that were thick in his throat. He didn't know if he would be able to say the words. 'When I got back and she wasn't here, I knew where she'd be . . . So I called the guy.'

There was silence on the end of the line and Ben could tell that Charlotte was holding her breath.

'He was so horrible. He said that Dad . . . Peter . . .' He corrected himself, somehow feeling that the word 'dad' no longer fitted. 'He said Peter is Elodie's real father.' Ben's face crumpled as he spoke and he couldn't hold back the tears any longer.

Charlotte gasped. 'What? But that's ridiculous! It's not possible!'

Ben wished more than anything that she was right. But not only was it possible, it made sense. It explained so many things.

'He's making it up, Ben! Don't fall for it!' Charlotte sounded anguished and outraged on his behalf.

Ben's heart leaped momentarily. *Could* she be right? *Could* he have been making it up? But almost immediately, the doubt started to crawl back into his brain.

'No. There was just something about the way he said it, Charlie. He was enjoying it too much. And he sounded so sure of himself.'

'He's probably a great liar, Ben. How do you even know this guy? Who is he?'

Ben hesitated. 'He's Bella's lover.'

There was a sharp intake of breath from Charlotte, before she spoke. 'Oh, Ben. I'm so sorry.'

Ben bit his lip and closed his eyes, trying to stop the tears. It was the kindness in her voice that did it. That, and the pity. 'I don't even care about that. It's been going on for ages, anyway. But it's what he said that's killing me. He couldn't possibly make up something like that, Charlie. It's not like it's an obvious scenario that he could invent.'

As his thinking became clearer, memories began to float to the front of his mind: how uncharacteristically flustered Peter had seemed on the day he'd first brought Bella home; how they had both disappeared for a suspiciously long time while he was supposedly showing her to the bathroom; how he had been so insistent about buying them a house. And, most of all, the darkness his death had unleashed in her.

'It's true,' Ben said, his voice muffled by the tears that were streaming down his face. 'I know it's true, Charlie. It all makes sense now.'

There was a long pause as Charlotte absorbed what he had said. 'Right, I'm going to come and get you. Are you at home?' She was instantly practical, but her voice was kind and tender, making Ben cry even harder.

'I'm at home,' Ben sobbed. 'I need you to take Elodie for me.'

There was a pause. 'Take her where, Ben?' Charlotte sounded scared.

A plan was forming in Ben's head, but he still wasn't entirely sure what it was. He just knew that he needed to get Elodie as far away from Bella as possible. 'I'll explain when you get here. Just come, Charlie. I really need you to come.'

'OK, OK, I'm coming. Give me ten minutes. Oh, and Ben?'

Ben wiped his face with the back of his hand, wanting to get off the phone as quickly as possible. 'Yes?'

'Please don't do anything until I get there.'

CHAPTER THIRTY-SEVEN

I drove like a maniac from the station towards home, breaking every speed limit and cursing the ignorant limo driver, who I was convinced had deliberately taken a longer route than necessary. The palms of my hands were sweating and slid on the steering wheel, as I careered at breakneck speed around a sharp bend, almost colliding head-on with a car coming in the opposite direction. As the furious beeping of the oncoming driver's horn receded into the distance, I took a deep, shaky breath and pressed my foot on the brake to slow down.

Ben was already home, so there was no point in rushing now, I told myself sternly. I just needed to concentrate on coming up with a plausible explanation as to where I'd been. Although I had always insisted that Ben was on Find Friends, so that I could follow his movements at all times, I was grateful now that I had made sure he wasn't able to track me in the same way, so he wouldn't have known that I was at Leo's flat when I called him earlier.

At that moment, I passed a petrol station and an idea flashed into my mind. I turned the car around and parked on the forecourt, before heading into the shop. I could pretend that

I went out to buy Ben something to thank him for coming home to look after me. Scanning the shelves, I picked up a packet of sweets for Elodie and a bottle of champagne for Ben. He didn't really like champagne but there was nothing else suitable, so it would have to do.

Feeling more confident, I drove the final five minutes of the journey towards home, rehearsing what I was going to say when I arrived. By the time I pulled into the driveway, I was calm and prepared.

I parked beside Ben's car and got out, reaching back into the passenger seat for the champagne and sweets. The house seemed to be in darkness as I approached the front door and I frowned, as a prickle of unease caused me to stop in my tracks. Why would he have turned all the lights out?

'Hello, Bella,' said a voice behind me, making me yelp in shock and drop the champagne. The bottle smashed and the fizzy liquid pooled out over the block paving. I swung around to find Ben staring at me with a strange, slightly crazed look in his eye.

'Ben!' I cried, clutching my hand to my chest. 'You scared the shit out of me!'

Ben didn't answer. He was standing very still and his face was rigid.

'Thank you so much for coming home, darling,' I gushed, recovering my composure and approaching him with a grateful smile. 'I felt so ill but I took some paracetamol and had a sleep and felt a bit better, so I went to the petrol station to get you something.' I motioned to the remains of the champagne bottle strewn across the drive behind me. 'Sorry I dropped it . . .'

'Shut up!' he hissed, his eyes narrowing. I could see a faint sheen of sweat on his upper lip.

I stopped and frowned. 'Ben! Come on! Don't be like this. You're being ridiculous.' I moved a bit closer to him, starting to feel more irritated than alarmed. He was acting like some kind of big-time gangster, instead of the pathetic wimp I knew he was.

'Don't. Come. Any. Closer.' Ben had one hand hidden behind his back and I somehow knew what he was going to do before he did it. With a fluid movement, he pulled his arm forward and the blade of the kitchen knife he was holding glinted as the moonlight caught it.

I stopped dead, my eyes fixed on the knife. Gradually, I began to step backwards with my hands up in a gesture of surrender. 'OK, Ben, calm down. Don't do anything stupid . . .' I knew damn well that he didn't have the guts to use it and was just trying to freak me out, but I thought I would play along to keep him calm.

Ben looked at me incredulously. 'Don't do anything stupid? I've already done the stupidest thing I could ever have done, which is let you into my life.'

He paused and took a step towards me, his expression setting hard again and his knuckles white, as he tightened his grip on the shaft of the knife.

'You've destroyed me. You've destroyed my family . . . you even killed my dad!' His voice cracked in pain as he spoke and his face crumpled as tears began to roll down his cheeks.

My stomach lurched slightly at his words and I swallowed hard and forced myself to meet his eye. 'Listen, Ben,' I said as calmly as I could. 'You're not thinking straight. I know you're upset but you're wrong. I didn't kill Peter! He had a heart attack . . .'

'He had a heart attack because of what you did to him!' Ben's words were hissed through gritted teeth and he seemed to be working himself up into a frenzy.

Again, I felt a ripple of unease. There was something about the way he said it that made me think he had been speaking to someone. But who? No one knew the truth except Leo, and I was fairly sure he wouldn't have been speaking to him. He would have no way of contacting him. I took another step backwards, and felt the crunch of glass under my shoe, as I stepped onto one of the shards from the broken champagne bottle.

'You've taken everything away from me,' Ben continued, now weeping openly. 'I left my mum in pieces tonight to come racing back here for you because I stupidly thought it might make you appreciate me for once. Even after everything you've done . . . all the lies, the cheating, the violence . . .' He shook his head in disbelief. 'Even after everything you've done to me, I was still hoping we might be able to salvage our relationship. For Elodie's sake.'

'We can, Ben, of course we can . . .' I started to say, but he put his other hand up to silence me.

'No! We can't. I should have known it was just another of your sick little games. God, I've been such an idiot letting you wreck my life!' He swiped away the tears from his face. 'Letting you wreck my family's lives . . . Well, I've had enough. I've taken Elodie and I'm leaving you.'

My heart thudded in my chest and I looked around me in panic. It was only now that it occurred to me that I hadn't seen her. 'Where is she? Where's Elodie?' My throat had dried and I struggled to speak. What if he'd harmed her to get back at me? The sensible part of my brain told me that he would never hurt her but I had never seen Ben like this before. He was unstable enough to have got a knife from the kitchen, which was unimaginable in itself. What if he'd used it on Elodie? My legs felt weak and I let out a whimper of pure fear. 'What have you done to her?' I whispered, shaking my head, as I willed him to tell me she was OK.

'She's safe,' Ben snarled, his lip curling with contempt, as relief flooded my whole body. 'God, I can't believe you would think for one minute that I would hurt her! You're disgusting!'

I didn't care what he called me. As long as Elodie was alive and well, he could throw whatever insults he wanted. I nodded and took a deep breath. 'So where is she, then?'

Ben's eyes glittered with tears in the moonlight. When he spoke, his voice was thick with emotion. 'All you need to know is that she's safe. From now on, we're both safe. From you. Come anywhere near either of us again and I will kill you.' He thrust the blade forward to emphasize his words. 'I know you don't think I'd do it. That I'm too much of a wimp. But believe me, I would. I will do whatever it takes to keep her safe and get you out of our lives.'

A mixture of shock and relief had once again turned my legs to jelly and I briefly thought I might faint, but I took another deep, calming breath and tried to think clearly. 'Ben, tell me where Elodie is . . . Please, Ben, I need to see Elodie.'

Ben's face contorted into a look of contempt. '*You need to see Elodie?*' He gave a half-laugh and rolled his eyes. 'Well, that's strange, because you didn't seem to need to see her earlier tonight when you were in your lover's bed!'

My mouth dropped open in disbelief. How could he possibly

know about Leo? In the few seconds I had to collect my thoughts, I decided that he couldn't know for sure and that it was just a lucky guess. I needed to brazen it out. 'I wasn't . . .'

'Stop fucking lying!' Ben yelled. 'I know you were with him because I called *Leo* . . .' He rolled his tongue around the word to emphasize the name. 'And *Leo* told me that you'd left nearly two hours ago!'

I opened my mouth to reply but no words would come out. I was frantically trying to assimilate my thoughts but they were tumbling over each other and I couldn't seem to hold onto anything concrete. He knew. He knew everything.

Ben took a step closer to me and squeezed hard on the shaft of the knife. A muscle pulsed furiously in his cheek and beads of sweat trickled down the side of his face, mixing with the trail of tears. He had a crazed look in his eyes that I had never seen before. 'You promised me that you'd stopped seeing him but you were lying, like you lie about everything.'

'How . . .?' I managed to gasp. 'How did you call him?'

'Really? *That*'s what you're most concerned about? How I got Leo's number?'

I didn't reply, fear rendering me mute. The terrifying look in Ben's eyes was even scarier than the knife he was holding.

Ben shook his head in disbelief. 'OK,' he began in a sing-song voice. 'So remember that night, when I saw the messages on your phone between you and him?'

I nodded slowly, as realization dawned.

'Well, obviously, I took the precaution of copying his number. In case I ever needed it,' he added.

I closed my eyes, unable to stand the way he was looking at me for a second longer. Leo would have told Ben everything.

Worse, he would have enjoyed it. I had always regretted telling Leo the truth in a drunken moment of madness. I somehow always knew that it would come out eventually.

As if reading my mind, Ben continued. 'We had quite a long chat in the end, me and Leo . . .'

I opened my eyes to see Ben looking at me with an expression of pure hatred, before his face crumpled and fresh tears began to pour down his cheeks again. He wiped them away furiously with his free hand and gave an anguished howl. 'And the one word that keeps going round and round in my brain, is "why"? Why did you have to wreck our lives, Bella? Why couldn't you just have stayed away from us and got on with your own life, instead of stealing ours?'

A volcanic wave of rage exploded within me. 'To make your fucking father pay for what he did!' I screamed, all control now lost. 'He thought he could dump me like a sack of rubbish. Like I meant *nothing*! When he knew I was pregnant with his child! He thought he could pay me off like some kind of prostitute and that I'd just take the money and run. That I'd kill our baby!'

Ben visibly recoiled at my words.

'Well, I wasn't going to just go away! I wasn't going to make it easy for him! I decided that the best way to make him pay for what he'd done was for him to be forced to have me in his life for ever.'

Ben's eyes narrowed, as if steeling himself as I delivered the killer blow. 'And you were just the convenient idiot to make that happen!'

There was a stunned, heavy silence as my words landed with a sickening, heavy thud, before Ben looked up at me with an agonized, haunted expression. 'You never felt anything for me,' he said, his voice filled with pain.

'No! I never wanted you!' I yelled. 'I just wanted him! I couldn't believe it when the bastard died and I was left alone and stuck with you!' Rage drove the words out of me with reckless abandon.

'You're sick!' Ben shouted back, anger helping him to recover his strength. 'You're a bloody psychopath! I don't care if I'm not Elodie's biological father! She loves me and I love her. I'm taking her as far away from you as possible where she'll be safe. I'm going to make sure you never see her again, you evil bitch!'

I didn't remember doing it. All I knew was that when I came to, Ben was lying motionless on the ground and I was on top of him, still holding onto a shard of glass that seemed to be embedded in his chest.

As if in slow motion, I climbed off him and stood up. I looked down at myself, frowning at the deep, dark stains on the front of the pale green mac I was wearing. I didn't understand what the stains were or how they had come to be there. I unbuckled the mac and carefully folded it in on itself, so that the stains weren't visible. I didn't want to be able to see them.

I looked down at Ben. His eyes were closed and he seemed as if he was sleeping peacefully. All the angst had left his face, despite the tracks of sweat and tears that remained on his skin. Feeling a sudden tug of affection for him. I knelt down beside him and kissed his cheek. 'Goodbye, Ben,' I whispered.

The sound of a car pulling up in front of the gate caused me to snap back into focus, my heart suddenly racing with panic that it might be the police. I look around me wildly, checking that we weren't overlooked by anyone who might have witnessed what happened and dialled 999. But I already knew we weren't and mentally said a prayer of thanks that I had insisted on such a private and secluded property.

Stay calm, I told myself. *He had a knife. It was self-defence.* I would say he had battered me for the past two years and I'd had enough. No jury in the land would convict me. Now I just needed to find out where Elodie was and get her back so that we could disappear. Just the two of us, like it always should have been.

I crept towards the large, wrought-iron gates, trying to see who was in the car, without them seeing me. Although it was dark and I didn't recognize the small Volkswagen hatchback, from the brightness of the streetlights, I could just about make out the silhouette of a woman sitting at the wheel. I could see that she had shoulder-length, straight hair but as she was facing slightly away from me, I couldn't see her face.

Just as I was straining to get a better look, she reached up and switched on the internal light, revealing that it was Ben's ex-girlfriend. I jumped in shock, which was quickly replaced by blind rage, as she turned to hand something to a child sitting in a car-seat in the back. It was Elodie. What the hell was she doing with my child?

Instinctively, I grabbed the knife that Ben had dropped when he fell and pressed the release button to open the gates. I waited impatiently for them to glide open, before striding through them towards the car.

The smile died on Charlotte's lips as she caught sight of me and she reached for the lock button, her eyes wide with panic, but I was too quick for her.

I wrenched open the passenger door and leaned in.

'Get out!' I screamed, pointing the knife in her direction.

'Mummy!' Elodie cried in alarm from the back seat.

Charlotte's eyes flickered towards the knife, before looking up at me defiantly, as if she was weighing up her odds. 'No,' she said, her voice quiet but fierce. 'Where's Ben?'

'Get out of this car now or I will kill you.'

A wave of fear crossed Charlotte's face but she remained firm. 'No. Tell me where Ben is.'

'Want Daddy!' Elodie wailed, before bursting into plaintive sobs.

'It's OK, darling,' I reassured her, all the while keeping my gaze fixed on Charlotte. 'Daddy's just having a little sleep.'

Charlotte gasped and her eyes widened with shock.

'And we're just going for a little drive,' I added, climbing into the passenger seat and slamming the door behind me. I pressed the tip of the knife into Charlotte's thigh, just firmly enough for her to understand that I was serious.

'Please,' she mouthed, looking anguished, rather than scared. 'Please don't do this.'

I increased the pressure of the knife a tiny bit more. 'Just drive.'

CHAPTER THIRTY-EIGHT

Charlotte could feel the beads of sweat on her forehead and her hands were suddenly slippery on the steering while. She knew it was vital that she tried not to show any fear, but it was impossible as she had never felt so scared in her life. It wasn't just the knife that was pressed with such delicate menace into her thigh, so much as the nightmarish thoughts that were racing through her mind about what Bella had done to Ben.

She knew she needed to call an ambulance and the police but couldn't think how to do it without Bella noticing. She decided that honesty was her only option. 'Can I at least call an ambulance?' she asked, trying to keep her voice level and her breathing steady.

Bella shot her a look of utter contempt. 'No. No need.'

Charlotte's heart momentarily leaped with hope. Maybe that meant that Ben was absolutely fine. Then again, she realized with a creeping horror, maybe she meant instead that it was too late.

'Where am I supposed to be going?' Charlotte stole a glance in Bella's direction, as she started to drive up the wide, dark road, as slowly and as carefully as possible. Elodie continued to cry piteously in the back seat and Charlotte's heart constricted at the confusion and pain in her young voice.

Bella fixed her with a cold stare. 'Just do what you're told and keep driving. And for Christ's sake, speed up,' she added, pressing the tip of the knife further into her thigh, causing Charlotte to gasp with pain.

Charlotte's eyes desperately scanned the road for other cars, but she couldn't think how to attract attention without Bella noticing. Maybe if she broke the speed limit, they might be lucky enough to encounter a police car who would pull them over. With that faint hope, she depressed the accelerator and increased her speed a little more.

'Stop bloody crying, Elodie!' Bella yelled suddenly, confirming Charlotte's suspicion that, despite her outward show of coolness, she was flustered and didn't have a plan. Charlotte didn't know whether to feel alarmed or reassured by this realization.

Elodie began to cry even harder at the harshness of her mother's words. Bella put her head back and rolled her eyes. 'For Christ's sake!' she muttered, before turning her gaze towards Charlotte and increasing the pressure of the knife a tiny bit further, stabbing agonizingly at her skin through her jeans. 'Right, I'm going to get into the back seat but don't even think about trying anything, or I will slit your throat.'

The strangely matter-of-fact tone of voice Bella used made her threat sound even more sinister than if she had shouted or snarled it and Charlotte's heart pounded with terror and tears of pain and fear filled her eyes. Was that what she had done to Ben? The only reassurance she could give herself was that the knife looked clean, although she was sure she could see traces of streaks of blood on Bella's hands.

Bella twisted her body until she was in a precarious crouching position, facing into the back seat, with one foot on the central console and the other on her seat. The knife was in her left hand, still pointed in Charlotte's direction, but less forcefully than before, as she also had to hold onto the backrests with both hands, in order to manoeuvre herself into the back of the car.

Up ahead, Charlotte could see a set of traffic lights on green but as the car approached at speed, the green light turned to amber and instinctively, Charlotte pressed the brake to slow down.

Immediately, Bella gripped the knife more firmly and thrust it dangerously close to Charlotte's cheek. 'Do *not* slow down!' she yelled, glancing over her shoulder at the lights. 'Go through!'

Charlotte's heart lurched with fear. 'But it's on red!' she screamed back, her foot hovering over the brake.

Bella jabbed the knife into Charlotte's cheek and she immediately felt the warmth of her own blood as it oozed down the side of her face. 'I said, keep fucking going!' Bella roared.

Charlotte whimpered with fear and said a mental prayer that there would be nothing coming from the other direction. She sped through the red light but clearly no one was listening to her prayers, as a white van smashed into them from the front, left-hand side and the car spun and spun and spun.

The world seemed to stand still as Bella flew backwards, almost as if in slow-motion, towards the windscreen, which shattered into a million pieces, as her beautiful head made contact, and then she kept on flying through the air. Until she was gone altogether.

PART FOUR

CHAPTER THIRTY-NINE

Three Years Later

'Happy birthday, Bertie!' Jo cried, placing a huge chocolate cake with three lit candles onto the wooden garden table in front of him.

Bertie's big blue eyes widened in delight and he grinned from ear to ear, as he knelt up on his chair to get closer to the cake. He brushed his blond hair out of his eyes and waited patiently while they all sang an enthusiastic but tuneless version of 'Happy Birthday', before leaning forward and puffing as hard as he could.

Only one of the candles was extinguished, so he tried again, but still the other two stayed alight.

'Shall I do it?' Elodie offered, sliding onto the chair and kneeling beside him.

Bertie looked up at her adoringly. 'Let's do it together!'

Everyone cheered and clapped as their joint puffing finally blew out the candles.

Jo cut into the cake and put a giant slice onto a paper plate in front of Bertie. 'First slice for the birthday boy!'

'Thank you,' said Bertie politely, waiting until Jo had looked away, before sliding the plate over to Elodie. 'You can have the first one,' he whispered conspiratorially.

Charlotte watched the interaction between the two of them and felt a squeeze of love. The bond they shared was so lovely to see, and having Bertie in her life had helped Elodie enormously after the difficulties of the past few years.

She was a sweet, clever little girl but there was a sadness within her that never seemed to be too far from the surface, which was hardly surprising. She had the same huge, dark eyes and full, bee-sting lips as her mother and it was already clear that she was going to inherit Bella's beauty. Whether she had also inherited the darker side of her character remained to be seen, but the signs were hopeful that she hadn't.

'Do you want some cake, Charlie?' Elodie broke through Charlotte's thoughts. 'You can have some of mine if you want.'

Charlotte walked over and dropped a kiss onto the top of Elodie's head. 'No thanks, sweetie. My tummy's big enough already!'

Elodie threw a sidelong glance at Bertie and they both giggled. Charlotte wagged her finger. 'Enough of the cheek, you two!' she teased. 'Now, who wants another drink?'

'Me!' shouted Bertie and Elodie in unison.

'Me!' shouted Matt, putting up his hand and pretending to bounce up and down in his seat as everyone laughed.

'You should be making Charlie one, not the other way round,' Freya chided him. She put her feet up onto the chair next to her and tilted her face towards the sun, dropping her sunglasses as she did so. 'But if you're making one, Charlie, I wouldn't say no?'

Charlotte laughed and followed Jo, who was heading back

into the kitchen. It was a relief to get out of the hot sun and into the cool, calm shade of the house. 'You sit down,' Jo told her bossily. 'I'll make the drinks.'

Charlotte thought about arguing but her body was protesting too loudly and she was happy to do as she was told.

'How are you feeling, darling?' Jo threw over her shoulder, as she bustled about, preparing a fresh round of drinks for everyone, while simultaneously slotting trays into the Aga and preparing different plates of salad.

Charlotte watched her in awe, feeling exhausted by her energy. It was good to see Jo looking so happy and in her element, compared to the husk of a person that she became during that awful, awful time. She would never be completely back to her old self – how could she be after what happened? – but she was certainly a million times better than before. 'I'm feeling . . .' Charlotte began, with a wry smile. 'Fat, sweaty and knackered!'

Jo stopped her bustling and turned to look at Charlotte. 'Well, I can honestly say that I've never seen you look more beautiful. And there's not too long to go now – hopefully!'

'No, thank God!' Charlotte agreed, cradling her enormous bump. She turned to look out over the terrace where everyone was still gathered, the adults chatting and the children laughing at some secret, shared joke. 'Emma next, I hope.'

'Yes.' Jo followed Charlotte's gaze to where Emma and her husband, Prash, were sitting. 'It would be lovely. Though I think they're still enjoying the novelty of being married and she's always known it might be more difficult because of her history. And her age, of course.'

Charlotte nodded. 'And what about you, Jo? How are you

bearing up? Days like today must be hard, when everyone's here, and yet . . .'

'. . . Not everyone's here,' Jo finished the sentence for her. She placed the drinks she had prepared onto a large wooden tray, before lifting her eyes to meet Charlotte's. 'I have good days and bad, but mainly good now.' She chose her words carefully. 'And days like today actually help enormously. Having a full house, like we used to.' Her eyes misted slightly as she dipped back into her memories, before snapping back into the moment with a smile. 'Children laughing and everyone having fun . . . it means the world.'

'I can imagine.'

'Peter would have loved it.' Her voice caught slightly and she cleared her throat. 'But, do you know what, Charlie? I think he'd be proud of me. For carrying on. Because I don't mind admitting that there were times when I didn't think I could.'

Charlotte nodded. 'I know. And you're right, he would be proud of you. As proud as we all are of the way you've coped,' she added.

Charlotte still had mixed feelings whenever she thought about Peter. She had loved him like a father and after her own dad died suddenly, she had grown even closer to him. But that was before she knew the truth about what he'd done. And now, even when she remembered the many good things about him, it was always tainted with the knowledge that he could have saved Ben from Bella, if he had just had the courage to admit his mistake and deal with it.

Jo would have forgiven him. Yes, she would have been hurt and angry, but she loved him too deeply to have let him go. She would probably even have accepted Elodie being part of

Peter's life if she had had to. The way she had welcomed the little girl into her home and her life over the past couple of years was proof of that.

Charlotte tried hard not to let the memories of that terrible night encroach on her brain, but it was impossible to banish the images that played like an old film on a loop.

More than the images, though, it was the guilt she felt at having agreed to take Elodie while Ben 'sorted things out' with Bella that haunted her. If she had refused, as every bit of her instinct told her to do; if she had insisted that Ben leave with her and Elodie, none of it would have happened.

By the time she reached him that night, she had known immediately that he wasn't in any fit state to be left. His car door was hanging open and Charlotte could see Elodie still sleeping peacefully in her car-seat.

'Right,' she told Ben, who was sitting on the front step, almost catatonic with shock, 'you're coming with me. Let's get you up.'

Ben allowed her to help him into a standing position and they were walking towards Charlotte's car, when he suddenly stopped and gripped Charlotte's arms urgently. 'No! I'm going to wait for her. She's on her way back. You take Elodie for a drive somewhere and come back for me in half an hour.'

'No, Ben, that's not a good idea. We'll all go to my place together tonight. You can speak to Bella tomorrow, when you're in a better frame of mind. I'll bring you back so you can get your car.'

'Please, Charlie. I just need to speak to her. To sort out a few things. Things I should have sorted out a long time ago.'

Charlotte had hesitated. Ben seemed to have recovered his composure slightly but she still didn't want to leave him.

'Please, Charlie,' he had begged her. 'Take Elodie. I don't want Bella being able to get to her.'

'Why don't you just come now? We can all go together.'

Ben's expression had hardened. 'No. I want to look her in the eye and tell her I know the truth. And I need some answers from her, Charlie. Please just do this for me.'

Charlotte hesitated again, before replying. 'OK.'

Looking back, it was that one small word that she regretted the most.

But if she had learned one lesson from everything that had happened, it was that no amount of wishing would change the past. It was only the future that you had some control over. The mistakes you made in the past were done. There was nothing you could do about them. But what you could do, was make sure you never repeated those mistakes in the future.

And although it was a cliché, time was a great healer. The pain didn't ever really leave you, but you did learn how to live with it. How to cope with it. Jo had been the greatest example of that.

'Are you coming back out?' Jo asked her now, carefully balancing the tray of drinks, as she headed towards the door.

Charlotte shook her head. 'Not yet. I think I might need to go and have a nap. I'm so tired all the time.'

'Good idea,' Jo said, before walking out onto the terrace.

Charlotte sighed happily. It had been an almost perfect day.

'What are you smiling at?' said a voice.

Charlotte turned to see Ben coming in from the garden, holding the toy computer console they had bought Bertie for his birthday. 'Oh, I was just thinking that this is almost the perfect day.'

Ben put the toy on the island and wrapped his arms around Charlotte, nuzzling his face into her neck and kissing her cheek, as always careful to avoid her scar. 'Only "almost"?' He looked up at her with his lovely brown eyes, now back to their twinkling best.

'Well, it's just that there'll always be one person missing from these occasions, won't there? Your dad. Whatever happened in the past, it will always be hard on your mum. She loved him so much.'

Ben stood up straight and stroked her bare arms contemplatively. It had taken him a long time and a lot of therapy, but he had long since forgiven Peter, reasoning that his dad had paid one hell of a price for his mistakes.

'Well, maybe there is one way we could honour his memory and make sure there's always a little part of him with us, and I think Mum would like it.'

Charlotte gazed up at Ben, thinking how much he looked like his dad. 'OK. What did you have in mind?'

Ben took a deep breath, looking nervous. 'We could call our son Peter . . . Although,' he added hastily, 'I would understand if you didn't want to.'

Charlotte thought for a minute. 'Even after everything that happened? You'd still do that?' Charlotte narrowed her eyes, trying to see into the deepest recesses of Ben's mind. They had taken the decision not to tell Jo the truth about Peter, not wanting to taint her memories and reasoning that what she didn't know, couldn't hurt her. But it had come at a price for Ben, who had struggled to carry the knowledge around, like a dead weight around his neck.

Ben smiled, but there was sadness in his expression. 'I think it would help me. It's my way of showing him that I forgave him. That I understand now that everything he did, he did out of love for me.'

Charlotte nodded, feeling like the luckiest woman in the world. She had come so close to losing everything and now she had it all. 'How can I deny you anything, after all that you've been through? OK, my darling husband, Peter it is.'

Ben smiled and Charlotte could see that the years of pain had all but vanished. 'You're perfect,' he said, stroking her face tenderly. 'The perfect girl for me.'

EPILOGUE

Jo hoisted herself off the loft-ladder and stood upright, dusting herself down as she did so. The loft was a vast, low-ceilinged space that spanned the footprint of the entire house. She had never come up here when Peter was alive. She said it gave her the creeps, with all the cobwebs and dusty corners, hiding goodness knows what kind of creepy-crawlies.

But with Peter gone, there was no choice. She needed to find some documents relating to the money that Peter had given Ben and Bella to buy a house, just before his death. Unsurprisingly, Ben had wanted to sell the house in Surrey and for reasons that Jo didn't quite understand, he was insistent that Peter's money should be repaid to Jo, despite her protestations that she didn't want it.

Ben and Elodie had moved in with Jo after Bella died in the car crash that night, so she figured that she could spend the money on them anyway, and make sure they wanted for nothing. If it made Ben feel better, then she was happy to go along with it. She had thought that once Ben and Charlotte got married and had baby Peter to complete their little family, they would want to move out into a place of their own. But neither of them wanted to.

They told Jo that they didn't want Elodie to have any more upheaval in her young life and now that she was so settled, they were more than content to stay living with Jo, for as long as she would have them. It took Jo less than a millisecond to agree. Having them living with her had saved her, in more ways than one.

She picked her way through numerous boxes, distracted by old photos, long-forgotten cards and the children's childhood certificates and trophies, smiling as her memories tumbled over one another. There was a photo of Emma on the swing in the garden of their first home, Rose Cottage, in Surrey, where they had been so happy, before moving to Suffolk. Family holidays on sun-kissed Greek islands and in the pouring rain on Cornish beaches were all caught in a freeze-frame of time on these now-yellowing cardboard squares. Peter smiled out at her, his sleepy brown eyes still having the power to make her feel weak, even from the distance of so many years. She would never stop missing him.

Finally, Jo found the box she was looking for and the bank documents she needed were right at the top. *It really was the last thing he did before he died*, she thought sadly, as she removed the documents and placed the box back on the floor, wondering why Peter had kept all this up in the loft, rather than in his office downstairs.

She stood up and sighed, thinking that the next time anyone would be up here would probably be after she was dead. She shuddered at the thought, imagining Charlotte and Ben clearing it all out, maybe when they were old themselves.

She was just about to turn around and make her way back to the loft hatch, when a white envelope that had been underneath the financial documents she had just removed caught her eye. It stood out because it was newer than the other documents in the box and therefore a brighter shade of white. On the front was written one word in Peter's handwriting: *Elodie*.

Jo frowned to herself, wondering why he would have hidden something that was meant for Elodie, up here? Maybe he had intended to give it to her, but never got the chance?

Jo lifted the flap and removed the folded piece of paper within. She gently unfolded it and read the handwritten note:

To my dear daughter
You will never read this letter but I needed to write it all the same.

I am so sorry for everything. If I could turn back time and change the past, I would. But the one thing I would never want to change is you. I'm sure your mother will have told you things about me and I will admit that some of them, to my shame, are true.

But, whatever she may have told you, I promise that from the moment you were born, I loved you. I know that you will grow up into a lovely young woman. I'm certain that you will be as beautiful as your mother – maybe even more so. I hope you will be a good person and that one day you will be able to find it in your heart to forgive me and understand that every single one of us is flawed and anything I did, I did out of a father's love for his child.

Love always,
Dad

Jo swallowed hard and carefully folded the letter back up, before replacing it in the envelope. She sank down onto the dusty floorboards, not caring any longer what creepy-crawlies might be hidden in the gaps between them.

She had known all along, of course. She had overheard Peter and Bella arguing, that first day when Ben brought Bella home to meet them. But she had made a decision there and then to forget what she had heard and do what she had done in the past, by wiping any memory of it from her brain, for Ben's sake.

To do anything differently – to act on what she knew – would mean the end of Ben's relationship with Peter and she couldn't risk that. So she had wiped the truth from her mind all those years ago and lived her life convinced that what they didn't know, wouldn't hurt them.

And it had been the right decision. Ben had loved Peter and Peter had loved Ben with a powerful and fierce love, which is why he had allowed Bella to blackmail him. He was protecting Ben. As he said in the letter, anything he did, he did out of love for his child.

Jo clambered to her feet and looked at the letter in her hand. She would take it downstairs and burn it, so that the next visitors to the loft never found it.

Yes, she decided, as she set light to the paper and watched it disappear into a small pile of ash in the fire grate. *What they didn't know wouldn't hurt them.*

ACKNOWLEDGEMENTS

I could not have written this book without the help of Nikki Shepherd, who read numerous early drafts, made many plot suggestions and provided endless encouragement (and bottles of wine!) to pull me through a very difficult year. Cheers to you, my lovely friend.

Huge thanks, as ever, to my fabulous agent at Curtis Brown, Sheila Crowley, who is always on hand with her wisdom, insight and tireless support. I am so lucky to have her in my corner.

I am also truly fortunate to be published by the inspirational Lisa Milton at HQ and to have the equally inspiring Kate Mills as my editor. Kate's steady guidance and brilliant ideas have steered me in the right direction and made me feel that I am in safe hands.

Love and gratitude are due to some very special friends: Jane Moore, Gary Farrow, Sarah Caplin, Robert Rinder, Leanne Clarke and Jacqui Moore. Thank you all.

Thank you to both the Warner and Duggan clans, especially my mum, Ann, who continues to be my biggest cheerleader.

And finally, thank you to the loves of my life, Alice, Paddy and Rob. You are everything.